Living in Shadows
The Complete Shadow Series

Walking in Shadows: Jilly
Hiding in Shadows: Savannah
The Hunter
Defender of Shadows

Anna Volk

DCL Publications, LLC
www.thedarkcastlelords.com

First Edition December 2018

DCL Publications
1033 Plymouth Dr.
Grafton, OH 44044

ISBN 978-1-7323742-5-6

Cover design by Lynn Hubbard

Cover Model: John Desalvo

PUBLISHED IN THE UNITED STATES OF AMERICA

Table of Contents

Walking in the Shadows:

Jilly

Chapter 1

"Sow and cub crossing Beaver Creek Road."

Jilly's marine band radio crackled as she drove down Winter Sports Road. "Damn it, Shenoa," she swore as she slammed her palm into the steering wheel and simultaneously jammed her foot on the gas pedal. Her little Ford Ranger fishtailed as she gained speed on the dusty gravel road.

Dylan's voice came across the airwaves, "Get the dogs here now. The trail is hot and Dan is running it alone."

"10-4, just turning off of G onto Beaver Creek Road," Jimmy replied. "Any sign of Jilly?"

"Not yet, but if I know that little hellion, she'll soon show up," Dylan answered.

"You bet your sweet ass I will," Jilly whispered. She looked toward the passenger seat; the wolf laying there showed no sign of interest in the events unfolding. "Don't sit there and act like you don't know what's happening. I could use your help," she pleaded. The wolf, uncaring, never raised her head from the cushion.

"Run, Leave There!"

Jilly slammed her truck into park and didn't bother to pull off to the side of the road knowing from experience the shoulder was soft and the truck could easily roll over. She sent out another telepathic message as she shifted on the run, settling the pouch around her neck. Muscles lengthened and elongated as her bones shifted and popped. Her wolf eyes searched for danger even as the smells of both human and dog drifted around filling her sensitive nostrils, the scent of danger was creeping closer.

Briars and branches grabbed her coat as she ran full out through the forest. In human form, her skin would be torn and bleeding. In wolf form, she was able to move swiftly beneath the rubble left from the tornado that tore through the woods one year ago.

The black bear and cub came into view at a run. "How many times must I tell you to stay away from the baits?" Jilly scolded as she shifted back into human form. "You endanger yourself and baby bear." She affectionately rubbed between the cub's ears.

"Baby is hungry," Shenoa answered, *"He wants to eat many times in the day. The food left in the hollow stumps is easy to find."*

"It's really good, Jilly, so sweet," the cub chimed in as he licked his paws, chocolate from the cookies still covered the end of his little black nose.

"Yes, it is easy to find and for good reason." She turned to little bear and squatted down to his level and then wiped the chocolate from his nose. "And yes, it is good to eat, but very bad for you." She tapped him playfully on the end of his nose and stood. "The hunters use this time to bait you in order to train their hunting dogs so that later during hunting season they can come back and hurt or kill you."

"I'm sorry, Jilly; I'll try to do better." Shenoa promised.

The little bear's look of regret along with Shenoa's promise tugged at Jilly's heart. She put out a hand and rubbed the sweet spot under the cub's ear reassuringly.

"I can only protect you if you stay away from the bait. Go now, the dogs will soon come. I will lead them away." The forest was dark and thick with blow downs from the tornado which had struck two years before, green leaves hung in clusters above and around them. Hiding from the men would be easy; the dogs were another matter entirely.

"How? You cannot be seen as you are with no covering and in wolf form they will kill you." Shenoa asked her voice showing her concern for the human whom had always shown her love and compassion.

"Do not worry I have clothing hidden throughout the forest. Hurry!" she encouraged.

The sun showed high in the sky. It would be at her back, if the men came in they would have to fight the blinding brightness shining in their eyes. She'd take every blessing available to her. No one must know her secret; it was not only herself she needed to protect.

"*Thank you, Jilly. Come Baby, we must leave this place quickly.*"

"*Mama, I'm not a baby,*" the cub whined as he followed Shenoa into the forest. They were soon out of sight and not a single sound could be heard.

The tracks could easily be hidden with the touch of a branch. But it was not the track that needed to be lost but the scent of the hunted.

Jilly grabbed the pouch from around her neck and smiled as she opened it and made a large circle back through the dense forest. The treats would lead the dogs in a wide circle allowing Shenoa and the cub time to escape.

"Dylan, they're coming back around, that sow must be leading the dogs in a circle and doubling back to protect her cub." Jimmy's voice called loudly over the radio.

The tracking box clicked as Dylan took a track on the dogs. "It was damn foolish of us to dump the dogs out on a sow and cub anyway, too dangerous for us as well as the dogs. Those old sows can be damn mean when it comes to protecting their young ones."

He folded the antenna on the track box and started the truck. "Come on, they're going to cross toward the end of the road." He slammed on the brakes around the first corner. "What the hell?"

"Hey Dylan?" Jimmy's voice came over the radio. "Isn't that …..?"

"Yeah," Dylan interrupted. "It's the hellion's truck," he called back. Setting the mike on his seat he stopped the truck on the wrong side of the road so that it faced the front of Jilly's ranger.

"Where do you suppose she is?" Jimmy asked. His truck now joined the other two.

"Damned if I know, but here come the dogs." Noses to the ground and barking excitedly Queenie, followed by Trego, Dan, Dixie, Diamond and Daisy charged out of the woods straight to Jilly's battered hunting truck. Queenie barked and jumped excitedly at the side.

Jilly stopped in the edge of the woods, not far from the front of Dylan's truck. She watched as Dylan and Jimmy started to gather the dogs. Dylan looked like a man that should be sitting behind a desk, not chasing hounds. His deep black hair waved back from his face, lying so thick and smooth you could tell that he'd been running his fingers through it; probably out of pure frustration, namely her. It was time to take the bull by the horns or, maybe in this case, dog by the tail.

"Hey guys, what's all the ruckus?" Jilly called as she came out of the woods on the same side of the road as the trucks.

Dylan looked around suspiciously. "What did you do?" No

way was she innocent, there was a reason Queenie and the other dogs had left the forest and come out on the road barking.

"I don't know what you're talking about," Jilly replied innocently. She watched as Dylan's blue eyes twinkled, knowing he held back his laughter by the way his dimples showed on his handsome face. "I was hiking on the Ice Age Trail, heard all the noise and turned around to see what was happening." She reached into the bed of the pickup and handed Queenie a doggy treat. "Hush, old girl, no need to get yourself so riled up."

"Yeah," he snorted, "You didn't do anything. Why did my best bear dog leave a hot bear track only to lead me and an entire pack of hunting dogs to your truck?"

Jilly smiled devilishly. "I've been hiking for hours and hours. Everyone knows that Queenie's a cold nose dog, she probably caught my scent. She loves me and of course my doggy treats. I'm sure that's the only reason she'd leave the trail."

Dylan reached over and fingered the brown leather pouch. "Sure, smart ass. What are you carrying doggy treats for?"

"My dogs of course, Sable is asleep in the cab." She cocked her head toward the front of the truck. She squatted down as Queenie rolled over for her favored belly rub.

Jimmy peered through the window to see the gray and white wolf gazing at him through the biggest, bluest eyes of any animal he'd ever seen. She looked so lost and forlorn.

"Jilly, how do you get away with keeping a wild animal for a pet? All wolves should be exterminated," he said with venom.

More wolves killed hunting dogs than bear or accidents. Once you've seen a dog mangled by a wolf pack you never forget it. Wolves are merciless, they kill without reason and hunting dogs don't stand a chance against a pack. No bear hunter tolerates the animal; many sport bumper stickers on the backs of their trucks that read "Wolves Are Government Sponsored Terrorists."

"Sable is a hybrid; I have papers to prove the legalities, thanks to so called concerned citizens of the community."

"She doesn't look happy. You should set her free," Jimmy stated.

"Sable was cruelly treated. She couldn't survive on her own. She needs to be near someone, that's why she always rides with me."

"Couldn't you leave her with your sister? Where is she anyway? I haven't seen her around in months." Jimmy tried to keep his curiosity low key; but Savannah had always intrigued him. "Is she working long hours somewhere in town?"

"Savannah's away Jimmy. Enough with the questions." Jilly turned her attentions to Dylan.

"Why did you drop down on a sow with a cub? A mother will do anything to protect her baby." She stepped closer to him. "It's not safe for you or the dogs. You should know better."

"Whoa, tiger." He held his hands up defensively. "You know I wouldn't knowingly drop down on a sow and cub, by the time I figured out what we had done, it was too late. I had a lone dog on the trail so I had to turn the others out to keep her moving so she wouldn't kill Dan." He smiled wickedly, "And, how did you know about the sow and cub if you didn't interfere with our run?"

"Female intuition, girls know everything," she said as she playfully hit him with the back of her hand on his chest.

Dylan grabbed her hand. "Jimmy, finish loading the dogs, will ya?"

"Sure thing, Buddy." Jimmy said as he whistled a tune and walked away.

"Have dinner and a movie with me, Jilly?" Dylan asked.

Jilly tried to pull her hand free. "You've got to be kidding. We argue about everything."

"Not true," Dylan argued as he gave her a wink. "We both like to field trial. It's only when it comes to hunting that we butt heads. You can't save them all, honey."

Jilly yanked her hand away and turned toward the woods. "I'm not trying to save them all, just a select few." She thought of Shenoa and her cub, what chance did she have of saving the small family? Animals were killed every day. Dylan was right, she couldn't save all of them, but she'd fight to her last breath for those she loved.

Dylan moved to stand behind her. "Come on, Jilly; give me a chance to prove I'm not the poacher you think I am."

Jilly sighed, tired of fighting for everything and everyone, tired of being alone. Sable lived with her but she seldom left her bedroom. It might be nice to have a conversation with someone else and Dylan was right they did share a lot of the same interests.

"Okay, dinner and a movie. I have to work at the bait shop until seven. I'll meet you at my place after I close." she conceded and climbed onto the bench seat of her truck, the slamming of the door echoed in the now quiet back road.

"Great, I'll see you then." Dylan looked to make sure her back was turned before fisting his hand and bringing his knee up "yes!" he mouthed while doing a little victory dance.

Jimmy watched the whole thing from the tailgate of his pickup and smiled before lifting another chip to his mouth.

"Later, Jilly." he waved as she pulled away.

Jilly winked as she threw a treat out the window which Jimmy caught one handed. "See that the old girl gets that, will ya?"

Jimmy laughed and saluted her with his pop can. "You're a trial, Jilly. You'll drive him nuts," he said to himself as she was already flying down the road with the dust trailing behind her. He tipped the can to his mouth and swallowed the last drops of the cola. All was good; Dylan needed someone special in his life and he'd always had feelings for Jilly. Things were about to get very interesting. He dusted the crumbs from his Levis and jumped off the tailgate of the old pick-up and rubbed his hands together. Let the fireworks begin.

Chapter 2

"Dinner was great, Dylan. Thanks for being so understanding about the movie," Jilly said as she glanced in the back seat of the truck. Sable opened one eyelid, puffed out an annoyed breath and went back to sleep. The wolf lay on the blue plush velour seat covers. She cringed; the wolf shed like crazy and was bound to leave her silver and black hair behind on the beautiful seats. "And for letting Sable go with us. We could have taken your old Nissan."

Dylan whipped his head around, "No Way, definitely not a date truck." The old yellow beater had a shortened box on it just big enough to hold a small dog box. He didn't trust it to get him through the forest let alone taking a woman he was crazy about out on the town. "I really don't mind her riding in the truck. She's not the first dog that's ridden in my truck, certainly won't be the last. Besides, you not wanting to leave her in the truck any longer gives me the excuse to get you alone for a private movie." he grinned.

"Don't get too excited big boy. You haven't seen my limited video selection." she warned.

Dylan had been a trooper when she made the suggestion of taking her truck so Sable could go too. He'd gone as far as offering his truck instead so the wolf could have the back seat to stretch out in. His truck wasn't an old beater like some of the guys drove for hauling the dogs. The 2006 4 Door Toyota Tundra was a sweet truck.

"It's not about the movie, Jilly. I've enjoyed myself. We really do have a lot in common. How many girls can you talk with about bears and dogs? The kind of stuff I'm interested in. You don't know how rare that is." He turned into her driveway. The house wasn't overly big, it looked more like a large cabin, with cedar siding and a big porch running along the full front of the house.

"What the hell….?" He cussed at the sight of the big black wolf standing boldly on Jilly's front deck.

Jilly opened the truck door and jumped out before he'd safely come to a stop.

"Get! Get out of here, Marcus. You're not welcome here!" she screamed as the black wolf trotted toward the tree line at the back of her property. "I catch you around here again and I'll fill your ass with buckshot. I mean exactly what I say, Marcus, don't ever doubt it!"

Dylan joined her at the corner of the house. "Calm down, Jilly. It's just an old wolf. He doesn't understand anything you're saying. You probably left some scraps on the porch is all."

Jilly shouted towards the woods where the black devil now stared back at her with yellow eyes. "Oh, he understands me alright. He better heed my warning because I meant every single word!" she spat.

"I have to say I'm surprised at your attitude towards the wolf. You're usually such a defender of the animals." Her apparent hatred for the wolf was almost personal. How could that be? Maybe the wolf had killed her cat.

"I only defend those who deserve it. Animals are like humans. There are some honorable and some that are not. That black devil is definitely not deserving of any respect. The world would be a much better place without him."

"Did he come sniffing around or threaten Sable?" Dylan asked. It had to have done something horrible to spur such hatred.

"Oh, god. Sable!" Jilly ran back to the truck, the front door was still open. Sable lay on the floor boards quivering in fear... "Come on sweetheart, he's gone." Jilly slowly opened the back door, the creaking of the hinges loud in the too quiet night. The wolf still didn't make a move to get out of the truck. "You can't stay in there forever, come into the house." She stepped back and Sable finally eased out of the back. The wolf didn't turn around as she sprinted to the house and through the doggy door.

Dylan stepped closer. "Your dog is spoiled rotten, Jilly." He didn't know how she trained hunting dogs if she gave them all the freedom she allowed the wolf/dog.

"Let it go, Dylan. It's not a good way to end our date and I've surprisingly been enjoying myself." She started walking to the house. "Come on in." She opened the door.

"Do you want something to eat or drink?" She didn't stop but headed immediately for the kitchen. The kitchen and living room were not divided so she could talk easily to him.

Dylan shut the front door and glanced around the open room. This was the first time he'd been invited to the house. It was nice, a large open living room with only a light colored floral couch and an old comfortable looking recliner. A TV sat in the far corner and a laptop lay open on the coffee table in front of the couch.

"No, nothing to eat, that steak filled me up. I could go for something to drink though."

Jilly opened the refrigerator door. "I don't have any beer. I can't stand the taste." She surveyed the contents of the fridge to see what she had to offer.

"Soda is fine." He picked up a paperback novel from the coffee table. The subtitle read Erotica. He smiled and raised his eyebrow; he never would have pictured Jilly reading sex books.

"I like your reading material darling, want to read me a story?"

"Stuff it. What'll you have, Diet Coke or Pepsi?" She held the cans up for him to make his choice. "Pepsi." Just the thought of diet pop made him cringe. "Mind if I find a movie?" He placed the book back onto the table and walked to the oak bookshelf sitting against the wall; most of the shelves were filled with paperback books, half of another shelf held diskettes, computer CD's and DVD's.

Jilly handed him his Pepsi, "I'm sorry I don't have any beer."

"Don't be, I don't drink the stuff anyway." He picked up a DVD, Steel Magnolias. No way. He quickly put it back on the shelf.

"I'm surprised. I thought all you guys drank beer." She set her Diet Coke on the stand and curled up on the end of the couch.

"Not me." He shook his head. "Oh, I raised hell in my younger days. But I'm ready to settle down and don't need the booze to have a good time." He picked out a new release, not even out of its wrapper. "Have you seen this yet?" He held up the DVD Million-Dollar Baby starring Clint Eastwood.

Jilly stood as Dylan walked towards her. "No, not yet. I bought it because I've heard such good things about it but I haven't had the time to watch anything." She'd actually bought the movie for Savannah. She was a huge Eastwood fan and she'd hoped it would draw her sister back into the world of the living.

"Stay put, I know how to operate a DVD player."

She flopped gratefully back onto the couch and made herself comfortable. He broke the protective seal and slid the DVD into the cradle. He sat on the other side of Jilly on the couch and looked at the bookshelf. "You've got a big library of computer games. I never would have taken you for a game player."

Jilly looked at the shelf and then Dylan. "I'm not a gamer. Those are E-BOOKS." She picked up a disc from the coffee table and handed it to him.

"I've never heard of an E-BOOK." He opened the case. The cd inside read Dark Hunger in sweeping script and had a picture of a half-naked man and woman on it. The word erotic sprang out at him again.

"E-BOOKS are books you can download off of the internet. You see a book you like and with the click of a button you can be reading the book. No waiting for it to appear in stores. There are a lot of terrific authors out there that don't get recognized because E-BOOKS aren't available through the big publishing houses. I love E-BOOKS; they take up a lot less space on my book shelves, which allows me more room to store more books." she grinned.

"I didn't know you liked to read and I never would have guessed you like to read about sex." He wiggled his eyebrows up and down. Her face turned such a pretty shade of pink.

Jilly's face felt hot with embarrassment. She took the disc and put it back on the table. "I've always loved to read. I just learned about E-BOOKS and really enjoy reading them. Not all of them or the books that I read are erotic," she defended.

Dylan twirled his fingers in her hair. "I didn't mean to embarrass you or make you angry. I just want to get to know you better and that includes all of your interests." A change of subject was in order, the evening was going downhill and he wanted to see her again. "It's amazing the new things computers can accomplish. It's another thing that we have in common. I love goofing around online." He leaned over to see what she had displayed on her computer.

Jilly quickly closed the lid on her laptop with her foot so Dylan wouldn't see the book she was currently reading. She'd die of embarrassment. "Me too, I've met so many wonderful people on the internet. I think of them as true friends."

Dylan smiled at her uneasiness, "Another sex book huh, Jill?" He turned sideways and opened his arms. "Let's start the movie. Scoot over here so we can cuddle."

"I'm not sleeping with you, Dylan," Jilly slid back on the cushions and turned, "dinner and a movie was all I agreed to. I'm not a one night stand."

"I'm not asking and would never treat you so lightly." He reached to pull her back to his front, "A little snuggling is all I'm after." He wrapped his hands around her waist and rested them on her stomach. She felt so small and delicate yet so right lying in his arms. All thoughts of watching Eastwood were forgotten. If he was going to keep his promise to her, conversation of some kind was in order. "Does that black wolf come around a lot?" He rested his chin on her shoulder.

Jilly went rigid in his arms. Had he asked her a question? The feel of his warm body so close distracted her. The firmness of his chest against her back and his hands resting so gently on her stomach made her feel safe.

"If he's bothering you, we can set traps or even poison to get rid of him."

Jilly shook her head, "Wolves are protected. It's illegal to harm them. Farmers aren't even allowed to protect themselves or their livestock." She tried to focus on the movie. Some girl just got knocked on her ass but she didn't know who or why. Dylan smelled like the outdoors. Musky, not sweet; his scent was intoxicating.

"No one would know and you have enough land here for a few traps set discreetly." He shrugged, "It's not your fault if a wolf is stupid enough to get himself caught." He nuzzled close, moving her hair with his face and placed a soft kiss on her neck.

Jilly relaxed, closed her eyes and leaned her head back against Dylan's chest... "Thanks, but I can handle the devil on my own. I don't want you to break any laws for me and I wouldn't want any innocent animal hurt."

Dylan traced the bare skin above Jilly's waistband with his index finger. "Your skin is so soft." He eased up under her blouse. It hurt to swallow, he was so nervous, but lord how he wanted, needed to touch her. "Jilly? I really want to kiss you right now." He waited breathlessly to see how she would react.

Her heart skipped a beat. She'd known Dylan for years. They'd gone to school together and were acquaintances but had never been what they would call friends. Now he wanted more. Did she dare hope for more from a man? Trust and acceptance were important and she couldn't afford to let someone close only to lose them. But, Dylan was known for his loyalty; he was so nice and she was really enjoying herself. It was past time for her to embrace life. She turned to face him, "A kiss, I guess that would be okay, but I'm not ready for anything more."

"A kiss is all I'm asking," he whispered and leaned into her, his hand on the back of her neck. His lips brushed softly over her mouth. She tasted sweet; he ran his tongue along her lips, nudging to gain entrance.

This was no simple kiss. Dylan didn't just use his lips; his tongue thrust into her mouth, exploring it in detail. He plunged deeply, gently, following a path only he knew. She turned more fully into his kiss, wanting to get closer. Straddling his leg she nibbled at his lips, lapping at his chin. His five o'clock shadow brushed roughly against her lips and the skin on her face. She didn't care, goose bumps rose on her flesh. Dylan's hand was now riding between her legs, softly petting her through the denim of her jeans. She was wet, it felt wonderful and she greedily wanted more. She rocked in time to the motion of his fingers. She moaned and moved harder against his hand trying to get closer.

She was so sweet; he slid his fingers in and out against the seam that rode between her material clad thighs. God he wished she had on a skirt, he wanted to plunge his fingers deep within her warmth, feel the wetness flow over his fingers. She was so close, her body was trembling and she was making wonderful little whimpering noises while pushing against his hand. If he didn't stop soon, it would be too late for both of them. His Johnson was so hard it was almost painful. "Jilly." He pushed gently against her shoulders, "Honey, we've got to stop." He kissed her lips, then her cheek. Just a little longer and he could bring them both the climax they so desperately wanted, needed.

Jilly groaned, trying to recapture Dylan's lips. She gripped the back of his head to pull him closer. She wanted to taste him again.

He put his hand over her lips. "We've got to stop." He gulped, trying to catch his breath. He ached with the need for release.

Jilly jumped back. She ran her hand through her hair. "I'm so sorry. I tell you to behave and I'm acting like a she dog in heat." She put her hand over her mouth, embarrassed beyond belief.

She was beautiful with her lips swollen from his kisses, whisker burns across her cheeks and chin. "Don't be embarrassed or sorry," He said reaching down to adjust his cock in his now too tight jeans. "Believe me. If I hadn't made you that promise, I'd have you pinned on your back right now. I want you so much, but I want to keep my word to you more." He scooted back on the couch to give them both some space. The need to touch her again was almost uncontrollable. He cleared his throat, "Are you going to the field trial in Hannibal tomorrow?"

Field trial? Who could think of dogs and field trials when she had just been so close to erupting in a mind blowing orgasm, without even getting naked? "Um, I hadn't planned on it." She stammered, smoothing her shaking hands down her thighs. "Cheyenne didn't do very well last week in Jump River." She turned on the couch and reached for her can of pop.

"She's young; it takes time for them to learn what they need to know." He picked up his can and gulped it down. He was hard and throbbing. Kissing Jilly, hell even talking with Jilly made him hot. "Come with me, even if you don't bring Cheyenne; I want you to spend the day with me."

She enjoyed spending time with Dylan and didn't have anything else planned. "Okay, but I'll have to take Sable." After seeing Marcus, Sable would be even more afraid to stay alone.

Dylan smiled. "That's okay; I'll have to take Jimmy," he teased.

Jilly laughed. "You are so bad. Are you calling your best

friend a dog?"

He loved to see her laugh. Her eyes glistened when she was happy. "Hey, if the shoe fits. Jimmy is my closest friend, but he's a hound dog and if I had a sister, I'd never bring him around."

"You really don't trust him? The two of you seem so close."

"I trust him with my life and all kidding aside, any girl would be lucky to get hooked up with him. Jimmy's one of the good guys."

"He's terribly good looking. I can see why the girls would like him." She picked at a loose string on the sofa cushion, still embarrassed by the way she'd acted.

Dylan sat up a little straighter on the couch. "Now wait a minute, if you're going to flirt with him, his ass will ride in the box."

Jilly shook her head and smiled, "I'm not interested in Jimmy. But, seriously I don't want to crowd you. I can meet you at the trial." The thread from the cushion came away. *For crying out loud get a hold of yourself you twit...*

"No way," Dylan grabbed her hand. "There will be plenty of room. I have space for six dogs and if Jimmy feels too crowded, he can drive himself. I got you to agree to a second date, let him find his own girl." he winked.

"Okay, if you're sure there's room, I'd love to go with you. I'll even take Cheyenne. Who knows, she may surprise me."

"Great." Dylan stood up and pulled Jilly to her feet, "On that note I'm going to head home before I do something crazy and you change your mind. Check in is at ten so I'll pick you up around nine o'clock."

Jilly followed him to the door. Her hand still linked with his. "I'll be ready."

"Night, Sweetheart." Dylan leaned over and kissed her softly and quickly on the lips. He opened the door and escaped to his truck. She was a temptation he'd never expected. He'd always found her attractive; add her quick wit and fiery temper…man he was in serious trouble. He grinned as he pulled away.

Chapter 3

"Good morning," Jilly called as she skipped down the steps.

Dylan watched her walk toward him across the lawn, her springy auburn hair bouncing with each step she took. "Hey, gorgeous." *Man, did she have to wear a skimpy little tank top with her jeans?* The black top made the red in her hair shine and the jeans clung snugly to her body as if painted on.

"Holy shit," Jimmy wolf whistled. "I didn't know Jilly was so stacked. She's usually in baggier clothes."

Dylan shoved him in the shoulder. "Watch it, buddy." Jimmy wasn't a problem but he'd be running interference with the other guys all day.

Jilly held up her pink nylon leash. "I'm just about ready. Let me run out back and get Cheyenne."

Jimmy met her half way. "I'll get her." He offered; taking the leash he walked around the front porch. Jilly's wolf dog stared at him from the open door. Something about that animal made him uneasy. She always seemed so sad.

"Sable!" Jilly called as she walked closer to Dylan. "I had a nice time last night. Thanks again for supper."

"So did I. You still owe me a movie," he whispered, moving closer, "I don't remember seeing any of the one you showed." He leaned in for a quick kiss. "It gives me an opening to come back and see if it lives up to the great reviews."

"We'll see." she grinned wickedly and then went to the truck bed when she heard Jimmy coming with Cheyenne. "Thanks Jimmy." She opened the top door of the silver dog box.

"No problem, but if the guys see me leading a dog with a pink collar and leash, I'll never hear the end of it." he grimaced. What was it with girls and pink? "Hunting dogs should not wear pink. Pink is for foofy lap dogs like Poodles or Pomeranians, not lean mean hunting machines."

"Ahh, there's a method to my madness. Owning a pink collar and leash, I know it won't walk away. No man would be caught dead holding a pink leash." She laughed as she leaned down to lift Cheyenne up into the box. "Your secret's safe with me."

Dylan slapped him on the back. "I'm not guaranteeing anything, pal. I've got her, Jilly, go ahead and get in the truck." He easily lifted Cheyenne in and locked the door securely with a snap. An excited dog could open the door with ease and jump out of the back of a moving vehicle.

"Thanks. Now I've just got to load Sable."

She opened the back door of the pick-up. "Come on, Sable, let's go." Sable wasn't talking or answering any calls. Truth to tell she was being a real pain in the ass.

The wolf dog slowly made her way down the path her head hanging low and a resigned look in her eyes. She hopped into the back seat. "I'll get in back," Jilly offered.

"No, I will," Jimmy stepped onto the sidebars and was met with a growl. "Maybe not." Jimmy slammed the back door closed. "Slide in, Jilly; looks like your wolf wants the back seat to herself."

Jilly slid across the seat her thigh rubbed up against Dylan's. "Sorry, I can get in back." She apologized and started to scoot out. Sable was in so much trouble when they got home.

Dylan grabbed her thigh, "Stay where you are. You're not crowding me, I like having you close." He kept his hand on her thigh. Automatic trucks were so much better than standards; if you only needed one hand to drive, the other was free to roam. "Anymore visits from that wolf?"

Jimmy hopped in and slammed the door. "What wolf?" He leaned around Jilly to ask. He hated wolves and the current laws protected them. They roamed free, killing with no consequences.

"It's nothing," Jilly answered quickly. Jimmy's hatred for the animals was well known. Wolves had killed a dog he'd bottle fed as a pup and he'd hated the animals since. She didn't want him wandering too close to her house. The pack didn't visit since they'd left it but other animals were frequent visitors. "I have animals of every kind strolling through the back woods." She laid her hand on Dylan's thigh and gave a squeeze of warning. "A wolf just happened to surprise us last night by being so close to the house."

"Watch yourself. They can be mean sons-of-bitches." He glanced at the hybrid in the backseat. "I'd watch that she wolf of yours if she comes in season. It might not be a bad idea to spay her; otherwise she could run wild with a pack."

The growls from the backseat let Jilly know that although Sable didn't act interested, she definitely paid attention to the conversations going on around her. "No worry there, Sable likes her creature comforts too much to live in the wild."

"I can agree with that," Dylan laughed, "last time I saw her she was sprawled on Savannah's bed, her head on the pillow, acting like she was human."

"You better break her of that habit fast. I can't see Savannah allowing a dog in her bed." Jimmy liked Savannah; she always seemed so delicate and unsure of herself, almost lost.

"You'd be surprised what my sister allows." Jilly quickly changed the subject, "Who did you bring? I didn't check the boxes." All the dogs had separate sides in the dog box with big circles cut out on the sides to allow them to stick their heads out for air.

Dylan pulled into the open field where the trial was being held and parked in the shade so Sable would not get over heated.

Already trucks were lined along the shade the trees provided and dodogs were staked out behind them. Plotts, Walkers, Blueticks and Black and Tans, all hunters had their favorite breed of hounds. "I brought Daisy and Trego," Dylan answered. "Daisy's running in first place; even though this trial isn't for points I don't want her to lose momentum."

Jimmy released his seat belt and stepped out onto the freshly mowed field. The smell of fresh cut hay rose up to greet him. "I only brought Skunk and Diamond." The two dogs were running poorly and if they didn't improve he'd have to make some tough choices.

"Will she be alright in there all day?" Jimmy asked. The dog should have been left at home. A Bear hunting trial was no place to bring a wolf dog. It was sure to cause trouble.

"She'll be fine," Jilly answered, "Lock the doors and crack the windows." The locked doors would keep any offended hunters from trying to get at the wolf. She turned to fasten the lock on Cheyenne's door.

"Hey, Jilly." Dylan reached into the front pocket of his jeans and drew her attention to the ridge of his zipper. It reminded her of last night and the hardness she had felt pushing against her. Her face heated. "Pay my entry, will you?" He placed a ten dollar bill in her hand. "I'll tie the dogs out."

She jerked her head up. "Sure, how about you Jimmy?" She held her hand out for his entry fee.

Jimmy already had his money in hand and gave it to her. "Thanks, I'll help Dylan and we'll be over that way soon." He was dying to ask Dylan about his date with Jilly. He'd tried earlier but Dylan had only said that he'd had a good time. He usually wasn't so close mouthed about the women he dated.

The registration table sat out in the open field. Jilly passed the line of trucks and men with dogs. She could feel their stares as she walked towards the blue tarp that offered shade for the ladies doing the paper work. Susan Grant sat behind the card table with a yellow legal pad to write down the registration of dogs and their owners. "Hi there, Jilly. I didn't see you drive in. How many are you registering?" She wrote down Cheyenne's name on the sheet marked females. It was amazing how you learned people's dog's names and could begin before they even started listing the dogs.

"I caught a ride with Dylan." She pointed at the paper, "I'll be registering for him and Jimmy too. Trego for males; Daisy, Diamond and Skunk for females. I'm sure you know who belongs to whom." She handed Susan twenty-five dollars.

Susan looked up with a surprised face. "You're kidding... you and Dylan in the same truck?" It was legendary around the trials how Jilly and Dylan argued. "You hate hunting. How can you be dating someone like Dylan?" He was an avid outdoorsman and hunted bear, bobcat, deer; you name it, he probably hunted it.

Jilly took a bidding number. "I don't hate hunters. I just

don't like illegal hunting. And I'm not dating Dylan." she argued. This was only their second date. She had no idea how Dylan felt and wasn't going to start rumors flying. Especially not here where everyone knew everyone. "Gas is expensive so we shared a ride." She turned to leave and could see Susan already whispering to Jay Connell. It wouldn't be long before everyone was talking. She sighed with frustration. Maybe she should have stayed home.

* * * *

"Dylan!"

Dylan placed the water dish on the ground in front of Daisy. He looked up as his name was called to see Brian Jessop walking his way. He wore the typical clothes of all the guys at the trial, a simple tee, jeans and a billed hat. No shorts for these boys; just wasn't done. Shorts and work boots just didn't mesh. "Hey Brian, how are you?" He held out his hand.

"Doing good," Brian returned the hand shake. "I heard you and Jilly rode together. Are you dating?"

"News sure does travel fast. She hasn't even made it back from registering the dogs." He poured more water in a dish for Trego. "Yeah we're dating. Something wrong with that?"

"No, not at all," Brian held up his hands in surrender. "She told Susan you were just saving gas."

He'd set her straight when her cute little backside came into view. "For the record, we're dating so be sure to tell the rest of these yahoos to back off; I don't share."

"Can do. You have balls, Dylan; I think the rest of the guys are too scared of the hellion to even attempt asking her out." He opened a can of chew and put a dip between his bottom lip and teeth.

Dylan grimaced. He never understood how guys could put what looked like worm shit in their mouth. "I better not hear anyone bad mouthing her."

"You know they wouldn't. Everyone respects Jilly even if they don't agree with her ideas on hunting." He nodded to the crowd, "There she is now."

The woman was too damn good looking. He watched as several guys turned to keep her in sight as she walked. They nudged each other playfully and nodded her way. Why hadn't he ever realized how the men flocked to her? "Talk to you later. Good luck on your run today." He slapped Brian on the back and walked to where Jilly stood talking to a group of five guys. "Hey honey, did you get us registered?" He wrapped his arms around her waist from behind and pressed himself tight against her back. There would be no doubt in anyone's mind that he'd just staked his claim.

"Uh, yeah," she stammered as Dylan placed a kiss below her right ear. "We're all set."

"Great." He grabbed her left hand, interlacing their fingers. "Let's go see what heats we're running in. See you guys later." He called back to the men still standing in the circle.

"What did you do that for?" Holy cow, he might as well have taken an ad out in the paper. "You realize that by now they've all decided we are sleeping together."

"Good. I didn't want them to think we were just being thrifty, saving on gas money," he grinned.

"You already heard that? They're faster than the internet." She rubbed her forehead with her free hand. Dylan still gripped her other. "I didn't know what to tell Susan when she asked. That woman needs to get a life, she's too damn nosey." Dylan stopped abruptly before they reached the crowd looking at the postings of the heats. She looked up at him with surprise.

"I'm not hiding anything. I told Brian the truth. I don't know how it happened, we've fought for years; maybe it was all part of a ritual." He took her other hand in his and faced her. "But, I'm hooked; as far as I'm concerned, we're an item."

"Are you sure? I get along okay with the guys at the trials. But the hunters really don't care for me. I don't want to alienate you from your friends."

"A," Dylan tapped her on the nose, "the guys might not agree with you, but they respect you. You've got back bone and they admire that." He leaned closer, "B, I don't give a damn whether they approve or not." He took her lips, his hand going to her hips to pull her in to feel the ridge of his hardening shaft. "C," he whispered, his nose pressed to hers, "does this feel like I care?" He rubbed himself against her.

"Hey, Rudolph, quit fooling around over there and get Daisy ready. You're in the first heat." Jimmy called from the posting site.

Dylan leaned his forehead against Jilly's to catch his breath. He'd only meant a quick kiss to reassure her of his feelings. It had spiraled out of control. His cock throbbed with the need to be inside of her. "I've got to go, wish me luck." He kissed her forehead and hurried to the truck.

"Good luck." She watched as he ran to the truck to get Daisy. Jimmy walked up to meet her.

"You've got that guy going in circles." Jimmy kissed her on the cheek.

"What was that for?" Jilly playfully wiped it off.

"That was for putting a smile on his face. Whatever you've done to him, keep doing it. I've never seen him so happy." He watched for Dylan to come back. No way did he want him to overhear this conversation.

"I haven't done anything."

Jimmy grasped his chest. "You mean the two of you didn't have mind blowing sex? Lord, what's he going to be like when he finally does get you in his bed?" He pulled her into a bear hug.

"Shut up, you ass!" Jilly laughed, shoving him away.

"Hey Pal, get your own girl," Dylan called. "Jilly don't hurt him, he's got to catch the dogs under the tree."

Jilly shook her head. "I'll catch up to the two of you later. I'm going to check out Cheyenne's competition." She knew Cheyenne didn't have a chance in hell of winning her heat, but Becca Moore was headed her way and she didn't want Dylan or Jimmy to hear any of the filth that was bound to spill from her venomous lips.

Becca turned and stopped directly in front of Jilly. Her voluptuous breasts spilled over the bright red halter top she wore. She rubbed her lips together which were covered in a matching red color. The lipstick made her lips look wet and kissable - just the look she was after. She flung her long curly hair back over her shoulders and put her hand on her waist thrusting her hip to the side to expose her long legs in the too short white shorts she wore. "You and the hunter are getting awfully cozy aren't you?"

Jilly walked around her. "What do you want, Becca?" She knew the answer. Becca was dressed like a slut. She was hunting for a man and by the way she licked her lips and kept looking around, about any man at the trials today would fit the bill.

"You know what I want. I want you to keep your sister away from Marcus. He and I will rule the pack as it was meant to be. He's strong and I'm stronger, the pack is weak but with our leadership we will no longer have to hide what we are."

Becca's outfit was having the desired effect. The men were openly staring at the two of them. Jilly lowered her voice so they wouldn't be heard. "You endanger all of us with such talk. No one can ever know what we are. I'm no longer pack and I don't care who the alpha pair is, but I will fight you if you expose us all to danger," Jilly promised.

"Don't make threats that you're in no position anymore to carry out. Keep your sister away from Marcus or I'll make sure that she does." Becca pointed her finger toward Jilly's chest.

Jilly swatted it away. "I don't have time to argue with you Becca and you have it wrong. You keep Marcus away from Savannah. We are no longer any of his concern." She watched as Becca stomped angrily away. Her Raven red curls bouncing with every step she took.

Brian ran toward her leading Cheyenne. "Jilly, grab Cheyenne and jump in the truck. They've already bid on her," Brian called, "I bought her for a buck both ways."

Jilly grabbed the leash and headed for the truck that would take all the dogs to the start line. "Thanks, Brian. See ya under the tree."

* * * *

Jilly squatted down to eye level to Cheyenne. "You know, girl, you're really starting to embarrass me." The only walker hound in her heat, you couldn't miss her white body as she turned and dashed back to the starting line. "You could at least have made an effort to follow the other dogs." she scolded.

Dylan watched Jilly leading her dog across the open field. The other dogs would soon come through the woods barking to the finish line at the tree. She squatted down and gently grabbed a hold of both the dog's ears, which made him smile. "See you guys in a few." He waved to Brian and the others as he walked toward Jilly. He didn't need to catch any dogs under the tree; Jilly's was the only dog they had in this heat. "Giving her hell?" he asked when he reached her.

Jilly shook her head. "Nah," she rubbed the top of Cheyenne's head. "She doesn't understand yet what she's supposed to do."

"You know, Jilly," Dylan adjusted his stride to match hers, "I've got a track at my place; you can bring her over any time. Let her run with the older dogs without all the excitement of the crowd." He could easily lay out a drag with bear scent.

"I might take you up on that." She definitely could use the extra training. "How'd Daisy do in her heat?" she questioned as she tied Cheyenne to the stake in the ground and gave her some water.

"She ran like the devil," he smiled proudly. He'd never had

such a runner. Daisy ran full bore, low to the ground and with full strides. It was a beautiful sight to see.

"Congratulations." She hadn't seen Daisy race, instead she'd gotten into the argument with Becca.

"How about a celebratory cheeseburger?" He linked their fingers and pulled her toward the food stand.

"Sounds good, I'm starving." She was glad she'd agreed to come. Cheyenne hadn't done well but Dylan was in the finals with Daisy. It would be exciting to watch him win.

They ordered their burgers and sat at the picnic table away from the crowd. "Was that Becca Moore I saw you talking to earlier?" Dylan took a bite and washed it down with the coke that was sitting on the table in front of him. "Looked like a pretty heated conversation."

Jilly finished her burger and got up from the table. There was no time to enjoy a leisurely lunch. The Finals would be starting soon. "Yeah, Becca and I have never been friends. She dislikes Savannah and is always trying to stir up problems." She picked up Dylan's empty pop can and threw the trash away.

Dylan tossed his napkin in the trash and walked toward the truck. He let Daisy out of the box to let her do her business. "I don't know much about the Moore's, they keep to themselves. I've never even met her parents. They live quite a distance back off the main road." He watched Daisy closely and when she was finished, he unsnapped her and headed to the circle with Jilly by his side.

"She's a loner, her parents are elderly and don't leave home much. Becca's always been a rival and I don't think that will change anytime soon. I've learned to tolerate her and try not to make waves." Daisy jumped and twirled with excitement, her bark loud and repetitive. Jilly patted her head when she jumped up against her.

"I'm sure it's nothing to worry about. She's always been extremely nice to me. It's probably nothing." Dylan gave her a peck on the lips and turned away.

"Oh, I'm sure she has," Jilly whispered. Becca was a real bitch and liked to spread herself around with the men. "Good Luck, I'll be waiting at the finish line." The start line was at least a quarter of a mile away so Jilly watched as Dylan loaded Daisy into the box of the pickup that would take all the dogs to the start line. She walked up to the tree where the finish line was stationed to watch the dogs come running over the line.

Jilly heard the crackle of the grass from footsteps approaching. She turned as Brian stopped beside her. "Jilly, there's some guy with long black hair monkeying around Dylan's truck. I was going to get either Dylan or Jimmy but they're both in the finals." He turned away. "I'll go see what he wants. That wolf of yours was making a terrible racket."

Jilly put her hand on his shoulder. "No Brian, I know him, I'll take care of it. There's no need to bother Dylan or Jimmy. You watch the final race; I'll be back before you know it." She hurried toward the truck. How in the hell had he known where to find them?

She heard Sable's mournful howl before she reached the truck. Marcus was yanking on the door to try to get it open. He stood up, his six foot plus frame towered over her by at least a foot. "Get the hell away from her, Marcus." she hissed as she stepped in front of the passenger door. "You have no right to be anywhere near us." She pushed at his chest.

Marcus pushed his long black hair from his eyes and secured it at his nape with a rubber band. "She's mine, Jilly. Let me take her and all will be well," Marcus pleaded. "I love her and would never intentionally hurt her."

"She was yours, you lost those rights," she snarled. "You don't love her, she was a possession. You flaunted the fact that you're alpha but you abused your title and now the pack is falling apart. You have no one to blame but yourself." No way would she let Marcus anywhere close to Sable. Her sister was so fragmented that she wouldn't speak let alone answer any telepathic messages. Any contact from Marcus could push her over the edge. "I'm telling you now, Marcus, get the hell out of here and leave us alone or I'll raise such an alarm that about fifty men will come running to my defense." She looked over his shoulder and could see Brian and some of the other men watching intently to see if she needed any help against the stranger.

Marcus glanced over his shoulder and saw the men. "You have won this time, Little Jilly, but I will reclaim what is mine." He slapped his hand against the fender of the truck turned and casually strolled through the field and disappeared into the tree line.

Jilly turned to the truck. Damn, the door was locked and she'd given Dylan back the key. "It's alright, Sable. He's gone." she soothed the she-wolf through the crack in the back window. "I'll be back soon and we'll go home." she promised.

She ran from the truck back to the tree. The dogs had reached the finish line and were all baying loudly by the time she got there.

"Jilly, what's this about someone bothering Sable?" Dylan asked. He'd wanted to go running to her rescue but Brian assured him they were keeping an eye on the problem. "You should have waited for me. Brian said you knew the guy." Just how well did she know him? Dylan kicked himself for not being the one protecting her.

"I'm fine. It was Sable's old owner, he wanted her back. I refused and he left." She shrugged her shoulders. It wasn't a total lie, only a stretch of the whole story. She hated keeping things from Dylan but he couldn't know, not yet.

"Okay, but be careful." He kissed her swiftly on the lips. "Let me collect my prize money and we can get out of here."

Chapter 4

The pitch black of night hazed with a thick fog. The deep scent of pine filled the air and mixed with the earthy tones of the forest. Amongst the giant pines and oaks a lone wolf sniffed the air and moved sure footedly. Jilly's wolf eyesight was keen in ways no humans could be in the unending darkness.

"Soon..." the voice whispered through her mind in warning. A vision of the bloodied heart left on her front steps caused her to shudder in revulsion and anger.

"I'm not afraid of you." she sent the message tumbling back. There was no doubt who issued the challenge.

"You will be." the menace in his voice promised retribution.

"Why are you doing this? We have done nothing for you to seek vengeance." Before leaving the pack she'd made sure to do everything according to pack law. Marcus could be ruthless; he would use any means necessary to draw them back to the pack.

"Oh but you have, Little Jilly. You deny me what is mine. I mated with Sable, by pack law she is mine." He would not accept

anything less than having his mate returned to him.

"Rape does not constitute mating." She ran deeper into the forest, the wolf's sleek body moving easily beneath the branches of the fallen trees. *"Pack law and by petitioning the elders, I have released my sister and me from your control."* It had not been easy to get the elders to release them from the pack. But once given, their word was kept.

"I will win, Little Jilly," he chanted. *"This is only the beginning."* His laughter trailed through the darkness.

The sweet smell of blood reached closer. The stillness of the forest gave warning of the death of an innocent. The little body lay broken and bloodied. She poked her nose gently at the mutilated corpse of the spotted fawn. He had not lost his life to feed the hungry. The pack only killed sick and injured. To protect themselves, they only hunted those that were dying. This baby had been killed to prove a point. This senseless slaughter showed clearly that Marcus followed no laws.

"I'm sorry, little one," she whispered and turned away. There was nothing more to be done. She ran as fast as her wolf legs would take her, no chances could be taken with Sable's safety. *"Sable."* She called as she ran across the open field. No one answered. Panic flared in her stomach, adrenalin pumped through her veins and surged through her muscles. She ran harder, the need to reach home strong in her heart. *"You must let me know that you*

are safe." She felt a familiar telepathic brush and let out the breath she'd been unknowingly holding in relief. *"Thank you."* It had not been words, just a sister's bond. It was enough.

The phone was ringing continuously as she raced up the front porch. She shifted before stepping on the landing. There was no slime or gel, no ugly contortion of muscles and bones. Changing from wolf to human was so natural that her body just flowed into her woman's body. She burst through the door and snatched the phone off the end table. "Hello?" she breathed heavily into the phone.

"Is this a bad time?" Dylan asked.

"Oh, no. I was running and sprinted the last mile." She twirled the phone cord around her finger.

"I haven't talked to you in a week or so and wondered if you wanted to come in the morning to run a drag?"

"That would be great." Still naked from the change; she snagged a towel off the back of the recliner to wrap herself in. "What time would you like me to stop by?"

"I was thinking around nine. It would give us the day to spend time together." He paused. "I've missed you."

"Me too," she whispered. The week had been terribly long; the bait shop had been extremely busy. "I had to work long hours this week; my help was out with the flu."

"I know. Jimmy caught it from his kid sister. The poor guy's been head in the toilet for two days." He chuckled, "He says he almost feels human today, said Carrie should be back to work by Monday."

"Yeah, I talked to her earlier, I feel bad for Jimmy. He must be miserable." The cool breeze hitting her bare skin made her teeth chatter.

"You sound cold. Please tell me you're not wearing one of those skimpy little spandex outfits. I don't think my heart could take it," he teased. The thought of Jilly in one of those body hugging items had his body hardening.

Jilly laughed. "Definitely not spandex, I'm not a spandex kind of girl."

"Sweatpants and a tee shirt? I can handle the thought of you in sweats." Her breasts bouncing as she ran along the hard packed gravel road; the firm muscles of her ass encased in well-worn cotton. Maybe he shouldn't picture it.

"Nope, not sweats either."

"A skimpy little tank top and shorts?" He swallowed the lump in his throat at the thought of her in the tight clothes. "Tell me you're not out running in just a sports bra and shorts."

"You're kidding right? I've got more sense than that." She might feed the dogs in her nighties, but even out here in the country you had to be careful alone, especially at night.

"Sorry, I know you do. My imagination is just running away with me. Please put me out of my misery."

Jilly smiled at the mournful sound of his voice. "Are you sure you want to know?"

"Please, the actuality can't be any worse than what I'm imagining."

"Um, actually I'm wearing a white towel. I was on my way to the shower after my run when the phone rang." she stammered.

"Geez," he groaned, "You're naked?" He could picture her cleavage pouring out of the top of a tightly wrapped towel. Her pale skin glistening in the soft glow of lamplight, the towel wouldn't fit securely, her naked flesh would play peek-a-boo as she tugged frantically to keep it closed. "You're killing me!"

"You asked." She pulled the towel higher on her chest. She could almost feel Dylan's interest burning through the phone line.

"I didn't expect you to be naked." He needed a shower - cold, frigid water. If he stood in it for an hour, he might bring his body back under control.

"Dylan, I'm really getting cold." The night air blowing through the open door caused goose bumps to form on her exposed skin.

He was a long ways from being cold. Sweat beaded his forehead; he readjusted his jeans to relieve the crimping of his cock. "Go take your shower, Jilly, I'll see you tomorrow." He could wait another day but not any longer. He needed to make love with her soon.

"I'll see you tomorrow," she whispered and hung up the phone. Sable stood at the edge of the living room as Jilly turned to face her. She stuck her wolf nose in the air and returned to her room. "Sable?" She sighed and followed her. Sable's decline was getting out of hand. The longer she stayed in wolf form hiding from everything and everyone, the harder it would be for her to return to human form.

Sable lay on her bed and faced the wall. "Sable, honey, you need to talk to me. I know you're hurting. I'm hurting, too." Jilly sat down on the bed and ran her hand through the wolf's fur. "I won't let Marcus or the pack near you ever again. You have to trust me." she pleaded. Sable never moved, never acknowledged her presence. Keeping the secret and caring for Sable were taking their toll on her emotionally. If just once Sable acted like she gave a damn about anyone but herself, it would relieve some of the pressure building inside her body. "Tomorrow I'm taking Cheyenne and going to Dylan's. You're going with me. I'm not leaving you here unprotected." She stood. "I love you Sable, but right now I don't like you very much." She wiped the tears from her face and headed for the shower.

Chapter 5

She was late. Dylan watched anxiously out the window, waiting for her Ford Ranger. He'd tossed and turned for hours after talking with Jilly on the phone the night before. Dust flew at the end of the road as her little red pick-up flew down the gravel drive. Dylan dropped the white curtain back into place and sighed in relief.

He opened the door and walked across the small porch. He waved with a big grin on his face as he reached the bottom of the second step.

Jilly stopped the red pick-up in the gravel driveway. "I'm sorry I'm late," she called out the open window. "I couldn't find Sable." She looked angrily at the wolf lying in the seat beside her. She was so mad at her sister right now that even if she started talking there'd be no answers from her. She'd looked for Sable for over an hour before she finally found her hiding in the closet.

Dylan walked across the yard and opened the truck door. "That's okay. You're here now and you look terrific." She wore gray sweat shorts with a black muscled tee. He couldn't help but notice how her nipples pebbled against the material. He gulped; she wasn't wearing a bra.

Jilly walked to the back of the truck, her sockless feet encased in her old scruffy tennis shoes. "Thanks, it's going to be a hot one today." She opened the tailgate and untied Cheyenne from the hook on the truck bed. "The internet weather said high 80's so I dressed accordingly."

Dylan took hold of Cheyenne's leash. "I'll tie her in the shade out back for now. I thought we'd take the four- wheeler and run a drag." He headed toward the big oak which shaded the house. A chain was permanently attached to the tree. "I've already got a cold bucket of water sitting there."

He quickly came back around the corner of the house. The white boards on the house would soon need paint but no other modernization. Inherited from his grandparents, Dylan wouldn't change the overall look of the old place. "Will Sable be okay here or do you want her to follow behind us?" The she-wolf usually did not stray far from Jilly's side but she hadn't even gotten out of the truck this morning.

Jilly walked back to the door of the truck and she let the window down. If Sable wanted out she could shift forms and open the door or jump out through the window. "She'll be fine." Sable was being so obstinate she really didn't care if she spent the day alone. There was no fear from Marcus today. He would have to stay close to the pack; he'd be tired from last night and probably laze the day away.

"Let her sulk, it will do her good to have some time alone." Marcus was not aware of any relationship with Dylan. Even if he were to search for them, he wouldn't think to look here.

The Polaris ATV sat by the shed across the drive from the beautiful old farmhouse. "Are we taking this one or the four wheel drive?" she asked

Dylan straddled the seat of the red and white machine. "We'll take this one. I already have drinks strapped to the carrier."

"Great." Jilly stepped over the seat and placed her hands on Dylan's hips as he sat in front of her. He turned the key and pushed the switch up; the engine roared to life.

The four-wheeler bounced across the rutted field. "Hold on." Dylan pulled her hands further around him and flattened them on his stomach. Her nipples pressed into his back through his worn tee shirt. He could feel her pebbled nipples pushing into his back. His mouth went dry and he licked his lips. *How am I going to make it through the day without making love with her? does she feel the same way? Am I the only one that feels this chemistry? Man, I am way out of my league with this woman.*

"Where are we going?" Jilly's chin banged against his shoulder. She yelled to be heard over the roar of the engine. The field was so rough she'd given up on holding herself away from his body, instead her breasts rubbed against his back and the inside of her thighs pushed against his hips. The vibration of the machine between her legs only added to all the pulses ready to explode in her body.

"There. The woods are free of briars and brambles." He stopped the 4 wheeler and climbed off.

Jilly looked around the open area. Trees stood tall and proud and the lush smell of pine drifted all around them "Looks like the tornado missed you." Many neighbors had not been so blessed when two years ago a tornado tore through the forest.

Dylan held out his hand and helped her from the quad. "Yeah, it was a real blessing. I got lucky." He turned and pointed off of the main trail. "The track winds through here and into a swamp. We'll start the drag here and end at the big tree at the edge of the field."

"I really appreciate all your help Dylan; I just don't have the time to lay out a run at my place. Luckily Carrie's back to work today. How's Jimmy by the way?" Carrie had laughed when asked the question; said green was definitely not his color.

"He's up and around but not ready for food yet." Dylan strapped the lead to the back of the four-wheeler and laid the hide on the ground. "Hand me the bottle in that pouch will ya?"

"Sure." Jilly leaned ahead to untie the string holding the pouch closed.

She was beautiful. Leaning forward, he had a perfect view of her bare breasts. The cold air from the shaded woods made her nipples pucker. He stared, there was no help for it. Her tiny tee was draping open allowing him to look his fill.

"Dylan. Dylan." she called only to notice where he was looking. Her breasts were practically falling out of her shirt. She stood up straight and grabbed the front with one hand and held out the bottle with the other. "Here's the scent."

"Don't cover up on my account, I was enjoying the view." he smiled teasingly. He opened the lid and poured the bear scent over the hide before reclosing the plastic cap. "Here you go." He handed the plastic bottle back to her. "We'll pull the drag through the woods here and from the swamp, it's not that far to the old tree."

Jilly returned the scent to the carrier on the rack. "Have your dogs run the same track?" she asked, readjusting her shirt as she climbed back onto the four wheeler. She wasn't going to be embarrassed. She'd sat straddle of his leg just days ago. He'd said he wanted a relationship; there was no reason to feel embarrassed.

Dylan made sure the rope was secure and walked back to the machine. "No, I try to run different drags; otherwise the dogs get wise to where the end is and take shortcuts. I've even seen dogs tree on a tree that was used in earlier runs instead of the new one so I like to mix it up." He swung his leg over the seat and started the engine.

Jilly slid onto the seat behind him but kept her body from rubbing against his. She put her chin on his shoulder with her arms around his waist. They took off in the direction he'd pointed to earlier. The ride through the swamp was rough, the bogs jostled her endlessly and she wished she'd worn a bra.

He could feel her breasts bouncing against his back, once in a while a groan of pain would escape her lips. He wanted to groan too but not for the same reason. The feel of her nipples rubbing invitingly against his thin tee was driving him insane with pleasure but from the sounds she was making, the rough terrain was making her very uncomfortable. He hadn't given any thought to the rough ride when he'd seen how she'd dressed. There was no way to put it delicately. "Jilly, I'm going to be blunt; bouncing around like that must hurt like hell. Press yourself tight against me, maybe it'll help."

She could feel the heat of embarrassment starting at her neck and working its way up her face. She'd thought she was far enough away from him that he wouldn't feel her bouncing. Obviously she was wrong and he was right, her boobs bouncing did hurt. She might not be well endowed, but it was still darn uncomfortable "I didn't know I'd be riding through a swamp or I would have worn something else." She pushed in tighter against his back and laced her fingers around his waist.

He turned around and winked over his shoulder. "Better?"

She nodded. Her chin hit his shoulder. "Much." The ground was uneven but holding her body tighter into his lessened the pain. The trail they were riding didn't look like it got much use. "I thought you would use your old drag?"

"No, I like to keep Daisy in practice. We'll let Cheyenne run with her and Apache. I'll throw Smoke in, too; lord knows he needs the training." He stopped the four-wheeler beneath a big oak tree. "I've already put a barrel with a hide up in the tree, just let me rub this scent along the bark on the trunk then we'll go get the dogs."

"Can I do anything to help? Want me to go get the dogs?" she asked, climbing off the machine. She pulled the clingy tee away from her skin, self-conscious about how exposed she felt.

He looked up from untying the knot in the rope. "Are you okay to ride back?"

"I'm fine, if you don't mind me plastered to you," she teased.

"I don't mind a bit, darlin', we'll both ride the quad back and load the dogs in my old hunting truck that way we won't have to make more than one trip." He rubbed the scent thickly along the bark of the tree. "That should attract the dogs." He recapped the bottle and stowed it on the back rack.

Once they ran a drag, Jilly was sure to find a reason to leave. He wanted to spend more time with her; all day, maybe even the night. "Are you in a hurry to run the dogs? Do you have other plans for the day?"

"No, why do you ask?"

"I figured maybe we'd ride the trails a bit before turning the dogs loose. If need be, we can drag the scent again to refresh it. Unless you'd rather not."

"Sounds like fun, I haven't ridden quad in a long while; the store takes up so much of my time that I don't do a lot of the things I use to enjoy."

"Great, grab hold of me and we'll make a day of it." *Yes, the two of us alone in a secluded wood, no friends, no dogs, no interruptions.* The day was definitely looking up.

The trails in the woods were shaded. Not much sunlight penetrated the leaves of the trees, branches hung low with the heavy weight so the air was much cooler than it was out in the open. Jilly shivered at the difference in temp. "I should have brought a long sleeve shirt." She rested her chin on his shoulder so he could easily hear her speak.

Dylan leaned his head back and kissed her. "I like what you're wearing just fine. Come on up in front of me. I'll warm you." He stopped on the trail and scooted back as Jilly swung her leg over the seat and stood with her weight on her left leg. She raised her right leg gingerly over his left leg and the seat to slide slowly down his body and fitted herself against his chest. "Are you sure you can drive with me in front of you?"

"Absolutely." He reached around her and pressed down on the thumb throttle. His left arm encircled her waist and his hand rested on her flat abdomen. "We're not trying to break any speed records, just enjoying a ride. I'll just drive slowly and we'll look at the sights."

"Sounds like fun." She tipped her head back the wind blew her hair from her face. She closed her eyes, the smell of pine rose up from beneath the needles scattered on the ground as the ATV traveled down the trail.

Her smile was gorgeous, she glowed. "Your eyes are so beautiful, almost violet when the sun kisses your face. I've never seen eyes so blue." He lowered his head to steal a sweet kiss. But one quick brush of lips was not enough. He nipped lightly and his tongue nudged softly to gain entrance. She tasted so sweet, like vanilla and coffee.

A pine bow brushed against the side of Jilly's head. She pulled away regretfully. "Uh, Dylan, shouldn't you watch where you're going?" Jilly teased.

"Oh shit." He ducked and turned the wheel to bring the quad back onto the trail. "You make me forget what I'm doing."

"I'm glad; you have a similar effect on me." She turned forward to hide her embarrassment. The relationship was still too new, she was afraid to believe that they could have a future together. The feelings that arose when Dylan was around were both exciting and scary.

She was pulling away; he felt it deep in his gut. What had happened to make her stiffen in front of him? "Jilly, what's wrong?" He slowed the machine to a stop and waited for her to turn back around to face him.

She shook her head. "Nothing; what makes you ask?" She didn't dare turn to look or he'd read her facial expression.

"Please look at me." He touched the side of her face with his finger to turn her towards him.

Her eyes were wary as she stared up at him. "What happened just now? We went from teasing to uncomfortable in a blink."

"I'm just not use to us; I'm not sure what you expect." she smiled and shrugged.

He returned her smile. "That's easy, darlin'. I don't expect anything from you. I want you to be comfortable with me. I would love to move forward and make love with you, but if it's not what you want, then it's not good for me either." He tapped the end of her nose.

"That's just it, Dylan; I've never felt so at ease with anyone else, it's kind of scary," she confessed.

"I'm glad that you're comfortable with me. Don't be afraid, Jill. I won't hurt you." He pecked her on the lips. "Trust me." He went in for another taste.

"I'm trying." She returned his kiss. "I believe honesty is

important in a relationship. But, there are things that I can't share with you."

"Don't." The need to lay claim to her lips with his was almost uncontrollable. He resisted the urge and instead gently kissed the corner of her mouth. "Whatever it is, it's not important. I've known you for years and there's nothing you could possible tell me that would change the way I feel about you."

"I wish I was free to tell you everything, I hope that the decision doesn't come back to haunt both of us."

"It won't. Enough worrying about something that's not going to happen anyway." He brushed the hair back behind her ear. "Let's ride." He pushed down on the throttle, purposely sending the quad flying through a puddle.

"Hey!" she laughed, wiping the water from her face.

"Hold on, darlin', that was just a little pot hole compared to the water standing up ahead." They moved slowly through the dense woods, the sun sending beams of light shining through the leaves.

"There's an open field not far from here that runs along the creek; I brought some food and thought we could stop for lunch."

"You're awfully sure of yourself, aren't you?" Jilly teased over her shoulder.

"No way!" Dylan snorted, "Never where you're concerned. Believe me, girl, you definitely keep me guessing, most times I don't know whether I'm coming or going."

"It's good to know that I'm not boring." she grinned, relishing the freedom and light hearted banter between the two of them. "Lunch sounds great."

Dylan pulled the four-wheeler to a stop. "Look there." He pointed to the sow and cub at the water's edge. The cub's ears barely showed over the tall grass that grew by the creek bank.

"What are you doing here?" Shenoa usually traveled across County G and didn't cross the busy highway with the baby.

"Baby likes to swim and there are less hunters and dogs in this area. We will go now. I sense your worry of the wolf Sable, I will watch over her this night and send you word should I sense danger. I owe you for all that you have done for me. Enjoy your human, Jilly."

Dylan rubbed her arm. "I was hoping she would be here today. I've seen her and the cub on occasion."

"She's beautiful. See the white patch on her hind leg? It's from a trap; the hair grew back white when it healed." She watched as the bear and cub scurried out of the water and disappeared into the forest.

"How do you know that?" Surely she had not gone near an injured bear.

Jilly stood up and slid off from in front of Dylan. "It's not important. Where's this picnic you promised me?"

Dylan swung his leg over the seat and hopped off. He

reached back and unstrapped the bungie cords holding the backpack in place. "Let's find the perfect spot." He grabbed hold of her hand and led her further into the trees that branched off the main path toward the sound of water.

The trees were not as thick here and the sun shone down brightly. A light breeze caused the wildflowers to weave back and forth as if waving in greeting. Violets and Lilies grew in abundance. The sweet smell of Lily of the Valley rose up with each step they took. Dylan stopped and set down the pack under a lone Lilac Bush. Its beautiful lavender blossoms added their scent to the mix.

He unzipped the duffle bag and removed two Ziploc containers and set them to the side. "Here, this spot is almost as beautiful as you." He stood and pulled her body tight into his, encircling her with his arms. "Are you hungry, Jill?" He whispered his hand caressed the side of her face, it was so smooth and soft. "I am. I'm so damn hungry for you, I'm like a starving man."

Jilly closed her eyes and leaned further into his body. She could feel his hardness as it pressed against her. "I want you, too." She reached up and laid her hand against the back of his neck. Her fingers delicately tangled in the hair at his nape.

Dylan shifted, his leg pressed between her thighs. "Kiss me, Dylan." Her weight rested on his leg. His head came down and finally the feel of his lips caressing hers. His tongue gently nudged, asking for access. She opened her mouth and they danced. He tasted like mint, his tongue darting in and out and around as it tangled with hers.

He pulled away, his breath ragged. "Hold on to me, darlin'." He put his foot behind her ankle and lifted. Gently, oh so gently, he lowered her to the ground. The grass felt soft like down. The weeds bent and molded around her body. Her hands traveled along his back, the muscles rippling with every caress. She traveled lower and cupped the firm cheeks of his jean-clad ass.

"Mmmm," she groaned.

He nibbled his way down to the soft spot below her ear. "You smell like lavender and your taste is like nothing I've ever known before." He licked a circle before drawing a small bit of skin between his teeth and sucking gently.

She ran her hands up his side under his tee. "I want to feel you." His skin was warm, smooth and tight. Her hands climbed higher as she pushed the shirt up still higher.

His nipples puckered beneath her fingertip. His breath caught and then he let it out with a guttural groan.

Dylan lifted his arms as Jilly pushed the shirt up and over his head. Her lips were swollen from his kisses and a small love bite glistened just under her left ear. He'd marked her and something primitive in him was happy to see the brand he'd left behind. "I don't want to rush. I plan to unveil you slowly and oh so sweetly." He bent to place a butterfly light kiss on her shoulder just shy of her top. His tongue ran wickedly along the neckline to dip into the cleavage that the shirt hinted at before playfully pulling back out and continuing along her collar bone.

"Dylan!" Her gasp of pleasure had him chuckling. His hand traveled slowly up over the soft cotton fabric to the mound that was so inviting. Her nipples at attention called out to him to lean in to tease. He laved the nipple beneath the fabric before turning and giving its twin the same.

The gentle breeze on her wet blouse caused Jilly's nipples to tighten. Dylan gently bit the extended flesh and laughed as Jilly bucked beneath him.

"I want more." She lifted her hips against his hardness. Rubbing, teasing, she wanted him with a desperation she'd never felt before.

He reached beside him and fumbled with the containers he'd brought. "You'll get more, Jill. I promise." He brought a strawberry to her lips and gently rubbed it back and forth first on the top then the bottom. "Let me see." He licked gently at her lips following the same path the berry had just left. "Mmm." He reached down and pulled her shirt up and over her head.

Dylan leaned slightly away. "What?" She raised her head to see what he was doing. *Why is he stopping?*

The whip cream was thick and so sweet as it coated her lips. She licked without thought. "No way, darlin'. I want this honor."

He was driving her mad. He laved her lips, the whip cream all but gone as a new trail appeared between her breasts and around her nipple. It was cold but not a bone chilling cold. He followed the trail back and around the opposite nipple. "Open up." He dipped his index finger into the bowl for a big dollop of whipping cream. He carried it to her open mouth.

He was driving her mad and she decided this was the perfect opportunity to return the favor. She sucked gently, rolling her tongue around and around the digit. Licking and sucking it clean of the delicacy he offered. She closed her eyes in ecstasy.

He moaned as she mimicked the motion of sex. He was so turned on just having his finger in the warm recess of her mouth. His jeans were so tight they were painful. Jilly's moans gave testament that she was just as hot as he.

"Not yet, sweetheart." He laved and sucked his way down the trail of whipped cream, down through the valley of her beautiful breasts and up over the mounds to encircle first one rose colored areole and then the other. He licked and nibbled as his hands traveled down so slowly over her flat stomach. Her shorts rode low on her hips and he nudged them down. He skimmed the shorts down with his booted feet and pushed them around and off of her ankles.

She was beautiful, her skin as unblemished as a baby's. No tan lines marred her body. The hair on her mound the same color as that which covered her head. He ran his fingers through the soft thatch of curls. She arched into his touch.

"Wait for me, darlin'." He rolled off of her and started to hastily untie his work boots. The laces knotted and it took him precious time to loosen them. He toed off first one and then the other and shucked his jeans and boxers in record time. He reached into his back pocket and removed the foil packet and placed it next to Jilly's bare hip.

Jilly stared at his gorgeous body. His pecs were well muscled, not like a body builder but no fat rode on his toned body. "I want you, Dylan." She reached simultaneously for the foil wrapped rubber and his swollen member. Smooth and warm, it throbbed in her hand. "Don't make me wait any longer." She tugged gently and tore the foil with her teeth. One handed she rolled the rubber on to his penis and guided it where she needed him so desperately.

Dylan sank deep. Pure ecstasy. He didn't move. Her wet heat surrounded his sex, causing him to let out a groan. She felt right, so perfectly wonderful wrapped around him tightly.

Jilly gasped and closed her eyes in bliss. Dylan's forehead rested against hers, his hips tight against her. He filled her completely. "God, Dylan. If you move, I'll explode." The feelings were so intense, there would be no long, slow thrusts. There couldn't be this first time. It was all consuming.

Dylan lifted his hips slowly. "I have to move, Jill. I'm sorry but I can't stay still." He thrust deeply back into her.

She moaned and arched against him. "Don't apologize, Dylan. I need you to move." She thrust against him again. The pressure building and building with each thrust. Harder and faster he pushed into her until at last she screamed Dylan's name with her release.

Dylan felt her body clasping his tightly. He came as she called out is name with her climax. Exhausted he dropped his head to rest in the crook of her neck. "You've done me in, Jill."

Her hand worked up his sweat covered back. She ran her fingers through the damp hair at the nape of his neck. "Same here," she was breathless. His weight rested heavily against her but she didn't want to let him go yet. He still rested inside of her.

He kissed her softly on the neck and rolled to her side. "Stay the night?" He pulled her back to his front to tuck her securely against him.

"Yes," she sighed and nestled into his body.

Chapter 6

The sheets were crisp against her bare legs and the down comforter was so warm and soft against her bare skin. Jilly sighed in bliss, her eyes still closed as she wiggled further under the covers.

Wait... was that the aroma of coffee drifting to her? She peeked through half closed eyes.

"Good morning, beautiful." Dylan held a white coffee mug in front of her. He wore a pair of royal blue boxers with a big smiley face over the pee hole.

"Nice shorts," she grinned.

"Thanks, darlin' and as you can see, I'm very "Happy" to have you here this morning. Coffee?" He handed her the cup and scooted onto the bed beside her. The white cotton sheets crinkled as he slid across and leaned in for a quick kiss.

She met him halfway, breathing in the scent of old spice. "Thanks." The kiss was quick as Dylan pulled away.

"Jilly." Dylan took a sip of his steaming coffee. "I went out to check on your wolf. She was on the porch so I was going to give her some dog food but as soon as I opened the door, she scampered out and is laying under your truck."

"Sable, are you okay?" Last night Sable had still been in the truck when they'd returned to the house and no coaxing had convinced her to enter Dylan's house.

"I'm fine...no thanks to you. I spent the night on a cold porch floor." the reply came back.

"That was your choice and you can have things differently anytime you choose to come back and face everyone." Savannah had been in hiding long enough. It was time she came out to face the world and people who cared about her.

"She'll be fine, Dylan. Thanks for thinking of her." The coffee was delicious, strong just the way she liked it.

He set his cup on the night stand beside the bed. "It was nice waking up with your warm body snuggled in beside me." He took her cup and sat it beside his.

The cool air of morning hit Jilly's naked skin as Dylan lifted the down comforter and crawled in bed beside her. "Brrr. It's cold."

Dylan leaned over her. His left arm moved across her body to envelope her. "I'll keep you warm." His head dipped and she rose up to meet him. His lips were warm and he tasted of sweet creamed coffee. Her tongue darted inside to explore his flavor more deeply, then pushed against his shoulder and brought her right leg up and over his midsection to straddle him. She was hungry, not for food, but sex; hard, hot burning sex. One day, one night with Dylan was not enough to satisfy.

"Jill," Dylan mumbled between each of her bone melting kisses. Man he was so hard and aching. He wanted nothing more than to peel his shorts away and bury himself deep into the warmth of her body. He sucked deeply on her tongue unable to deny himself the pleasure of hearing her moan. "Jill," He called again, not aware that he shortened her name when loving her. "It's six o'clock." He nibbled along her jaw bone as she sucked the lobe of his ear into her mouth. "Six o'clock, Monday morning." He continued to nibble along her neck.

"What?!?" Jilly shrieked and rolled off of him onto her left side.

Dylan grinned. "As much as I would love to continue this…" Car lights shone through the bedroom window illuminating the opposite sky blue wall. The slam of a car door confirmed his suspicion. "We have about 5, 4, 3,…."

"Hey Dylan, Come on Buddy. We gotta go," Jimmy called out loudly. The house door slammed shut even as his voice and footsteps announced his arrival to the bedroom door with a big grin on his face. "Hi there, Jilly. Did you kids have a sleep over and not invite me?"

Jilly squealed and yanked the comforter up over her head.

Dylan turned and saw Jimmy at the open door. He pulled his

pillow from behind his back and threw it at him. "Get out of here, you ass! I'll be right there."

Jimmy caught the pillow and waggled his eyebrows up and down. "Time's a ticking, pal." He tapped the top of the Rolex on his arm and threw the pillow on the bed before turning and shutting the door behind him.

Dylan pried the comforter from Jilly's fingers and kissed her on the end of the nose when she became visible. "As I was saying before we were so rudely interrupted, Jimmy will be here any second and I have to get to work."

"Shoot." Jilly wrinkled her nose. "I forgot it was Monday. I have to go, too. Carrie started school so I have to open the bait store." She scooted up higher in the bed.

Dylan pulled the covers back and placed his feet on the hard wood floor. The old braided rug was rough against his bare feet. He reached for his jeans lying over the wooden chair which stood near the door. "I'll go keep Jimmy company while you dress or the letch will be back in here trying to get a peek." He tucked himself carefully into the tight jeans and zipped them slowly up, the snap loud in the quiet room. He grabbed the navy blue shirt off the floor. "See you in a few minutes." He opened the door and shut it behind him.

Jilly flopped back onto the bed. "Oh My God! *Good thing Dylan had some control or Jimmy would have gotten an eyeful when he walked in.* How embarrassing!

Jimmy laughed somewhere further in the house. She threw back the covers. The cold air hit her naked flesh and goose bumps formed on her arms. She grabbed her shorts off the floor and slipped her legs into them and her tennies lying on the floor beside the bed. Her summer blouse would in no way be warm enough with the morning chill so she grabbed a maroon hooded sweatshirt off the clothes basket that lay in the corner. The familiar smell of Downy reached her nose telling her the shirt was clean. She picked her pink undies up off the end of the bed and stuck them in the front pouch of the shirt.

The master bath adjoined the bedroom. The room was decorated simply with cream colored walls, a claw footed tub sat against one wall with a shower in the corner. The single sink perched on a pedestal beside the white toilet. After going through her morning rituals Jilly used her finger to brush her teeth and rinsed with the green scope mouthwash that sat on the back of the toilet stool. She couldn't avoid the men in the kitchen any longer. She flushed the toilet and walked through the door. The still closed bedroom door did not make a sound as she opened it and stepped out into the living room. A leather sofa sat just to the left of the bedroom door. She could hear the men's voices coming from the kitchen and walked across the carpeted floor to the archway that led to the room.

"Sorry it took so long. I'll just go out back and get Cheyenne so you guys can head off to work." Her face blazed with heat. She couldn't bear to look at Jimmy. Her embarrassment over the grinning idiot catching her in bed with Dylan still made her want to hide under the blankets.

Dylan handed her the cup of coffee he held in his hand. "We've got time yet and I'll drop Cheyenne off later this afternoon. No sense in you stumbling around in the dark. She'll be fine."

Jilly took the white cup. The coffee wasn't steaming which told her he'd poured it soon after coming into the kitchen. "If you're sure, that would be great. I have to go home and change." She pulled at the Wisconsin Bear Hunter sweat shirt. "I borrowed a shirt. Hope you don't mind?" The hood covered the love bite on the side of her neck.

"Keep it." Dylan stared at her longingly. The hood didn't cover the hickey he knew she was trying so desperately to keep hidden from Jimmy who over her shoulder was rubbing the side of his neck and wiggling his eyebrows up and down with a big stupid grin on his face.

"I'll be in the truck. See ya later. Oh and Jilly, better fix that muffler." He tossed back good naturedly as he opened the door and walked out.

Jilly shook her head. "You're right. He's a menace."

Dylan crooked his finger. "Come here you." He wrapped his arms around her waist. "I really do have to get going. But I wish like hell we hadn't been interrupted this morning. Things were just getting interesting." He kissed her lips causing the coffee from her cup to slosh over onto the floor.

"Dylan, my coffee is spilling all over."

The horn honked outside and he took a step back. "Damn, we've gotta get going." He grabbed her hand. "I'll walk you to your truck."

He let go of her hand and flipped the light switch beside the door off and opened the door. He placed his hand against Jilly's back and led her across the porch. Garbage cans aligned both sides of the doorway. The porch had no door and was open to the elements.

Jilly walked down the two steps and across the flat dirt packed ground then stopped. Yellow eyes glowed beneath her truck. Sable peered out at them, her eyes menacing in the dark of night. Jilly pursed her lips and shook her head at the she-wolf.

She opened the door wide and indicated with a wave of her hand for the dog to get in. Sable scrambled from beneath and jumped in the passenger seat. Jilly placed her hand on the top of the door with her body turned toward Dylan. "I had a good time, Dylan." He stood close to her, his body pressed tight against her.

"Come on guys, I'm too young to be witnessing this," Jimmy called from the Red Ford F150 parked in the drive.

Dylan kissed her swiftly. "I'll call you later. My menace is calling." He waved as he ran toward the truck and opened the passenger door. The truck roared to life and there was a grinding of gears. Gravel flew from beneath the tires as the vehicle took off down the drive, a cloud of dust following in its wake.

Jilly got in her truck, shut the door and turned the key. "Oh Savannah, What am I doing?" She looked at the wolf but wasn't surprised to see her sleeping on the seat as though she didn't have a care in the world.

Chapter 7

"It's what I love about Sundays. Cat nappin on the porch swing, you curled up next to me, grab a tackle box and a cane pole, only one place to go, steal a kiss as the sun fades, It's what I love about Sundays."

Jilly turned the truck radio up as she sang along to Daryl Worley. Sable swayed to the music as she stared out the passenger window next to her.

The radio crackled to life. "The dogs have a bear treed just off of G."

Jilly looked quickly over to Sable who now lay with her head hanging off of the seat, her eyes squeezed tightly shut.

"Damn it, can't they take a Sunday off?" She swore as she stepped harder on the gas pedal. She recognized the voice on the marine band and she was sure that Sable had too. It was why she now lay docile in the seat.

"You can't hide forever, life is too short." she said softly.

"Jilly, help me! Jilly! Help!" The telepathic message came

through broken. She could feel and hear the fear.

"No, No, No!" she screamed aloud as fear and anger shot through her chest. She sent a message back. *"I'm coming, what's happened?"*

"We were not eating from the trees with holes. Tango, funny isn't it? I finally named him. Baby is real proud of his new name."

Jilly quickly interrupted. *"Shenoa, I need to know what's happening."*

"Tango wanted to play. We were on our way to the water when the trucks passed over the bridge. They knew exactly where we would be and released the dogs." Shenoa's confusion was evident in her voice. Jilly understood exactly how they had known the bears' whereabouts. That Rat Bastard Marcus sold out the mother bear and her innocent baby. *"I told little Tango to run and I led the dogs away,"* Shenoa continued.

"Hold on! I'm on my way." Jilly promised as she sped along the highway, still five miles from the general area of the stressful call. She stepped down harder on the gas pedal; the steering wheel began to shimmy as she reached dangerous speeds. Her urgency to reach Shenoa her only priority.

"Please hurry, Jilly, something's different. They usually let me down from the tree by now. They're pointing something at me."

"Oh god, Oh god, I'm sorry." she repeated the thoughts through her mind, carefully keeping any of them from running over

to her scared friend. They would not be letting her friend down from the tree, not this time. Training season was over and it was now kill season.

"Close your eyes think happy thoughts," she ordered soothingly. *"I'll be there as soon as I can."* Already, she knew that she would not make it in time.

The tears rolled silently down her cheeks as she swerved off the road, the bumper of the truck slamming into an embankment. Her head hit the side of the door casing making her dizzy. She ignored the pain and jumped out of the truck and ran. She pulled the hem of her sundress up between her legs so that she could run faster. The long grass grabbed at her legs and tangled with her ankles, burrs scraped her shins and broke the skin open but she didn't pay any mind. The only thing she focused on was getting to Shenoa in time. Her heart pumped wildly in her chest; Jilly vainly hoped the hunters would hold off just a moment longer so she would get there before they pulled the trigger.

The first blast of the twelve gauge shotgun split the silence before she reached the woods. Black birds flew from the woods calling out their eerie warning too late.

Saplings and berry briars scratched and tore the skin on her bare legs as she ran. Blood trickled down her pale skin, she never noticed the pain. A different pain ate at her heart as another shot rang out. Dogs howled and barked excitedly.

Jilly stopped. All the air whooshed out of her lungs. A huge vacuum surrounded her and she couldn't breathe. Her muscles burned with exertion and she contemplated just dropping where she stood and never getting up again. But her friend needed her.

Move! her inner soul demanded. With new determination, adrenaline surged through her body. Throwing off the sensation of drowning, she drew on her inner strength took a deep breath and ran. She broke into the clearing surrounding the location she knew the bear to be and stopped. She walked slowly toward the dogs and the man standing there with a triumphant look on his face.

Jilly knew the sight that would greet her at the bottom of the tree. Still she was not prepared and dropped to her knees beside the beautiful black body. A deep red river of blood lay pooled on the leaves beside her. A massive hole in her right shoulder and another in her chest still leaked with the last drops of life.

Sobs shook her body; she could taste the bile rising in the back of her throat. Her rage was uncontrollable.

"You bastard!" she screamed as she jumped up and hit Marcus square in the chest. She swung again to slap his face. But he grabbed her arm. "You knew that it was Shenoa and her cub. You led the dogs and hunters right to them."

Marcus laughed; his yellow-green eyes glowed. "You are so right, Little Jilly, and unless you give me what I want, more of the ones you care for will be hurt."

Jilly glanced behind Marcus's shoulder to the tree line where the other hunters were talking amongst themselves, curiously watching the drama unfolding. They looked to the ground as if ashamed. They should be, every sportsman, hunter knew it was illegal to hunt a sow and her cub. What was the point of prosecution? The damage had been done and Shenoa had paid it.

She tugged at her arm but Marcus would not release her, instead he drew her fist to his chest and held firmly. "Give me what is mine."

"You stay away from her," Jilly whispered venomously.

"I don't think so. I'm Alpha and she and you are my pack. I will do as I please when it comes to my members," he stated.

Jilly thrust her chin out stubbornly. "You gave up your rights to me and mine when you attacked and raped Savannah. I petitioned the elders of the pack and won. We no longer belong," she argued.

"Ah yes, the princesses," he hissed derogatively. "Whatever you ask, the elders agree. You talk tough for a woman all alone. The nights are long with no protector," he threatened.

Jilly struggled again to escape his grasp.

"What the hell is going on here? Let go of her now!" Dylan ordered.

He'd heard the call come across the radio and was not surprised to see Jilly's truck parked in the ditch. The surprise was seeing Jilly being man handled by Marcus Cooper. The man was a viper. He fed on the fear of others.

Marcus again jerked on Jilly's arm. "Don't make things any worse. Give me what I want," he demanded.

"Apparently you're not hearing me, Cooper. Turn her loose!" he growled. No one had the right to treat Jilly so roughly.

"This isn't your concern, Rudolph," Marcus returned, "This is between me and Jilly."

Jilly pulled on her arm, when that didn't work she drew back her leg and gave Marcus a good hard kick in the balls. Marcus gave a whoosh of pain as all the breath left him. He released Jilly and crumpled to his knees. "I'm done talking and there's nothing between us now and there never will be," she snarled and turned away.

Dylan cringed and only just kept from protecting his own family jewels. "Honey, remind me to never piss you off." He moved to draw her into his arms and saw the blood. She was covered in it, her legs and arms were scraped raw. The delicate floral dress she wore was torn and she had bruises rapidly forming around her wrist.

"Stay right here," he said gently as he coaxed her to sit on a log, "I'll be right back."

He walked over to where Marcus had regained his feet but was still bent over with his hands on his smashed testicles. Dylan brought his fist back and swung it at the wheezing man. He caught him in the chin knocking him to the moss covered ground. He knelt down on one knee moving close so that he wouldn't be overheard. "I heard you threaten Jilly. For the record, she's not alone She'll never be alone again. She's mine."

Marcus rubbed his chin. "Is that right?" he snarled. "We'll see how long you stay when you find out what a bitch she really is and I mean that literally," he laughed.

Dylan stood and wiped the moss and wet leaves from the denim of his jeans. "Stay away from her, Marcus," he said and turned back to the log he'd left Jilly sitting on. She wasn't there but was sitting next to the still body of a black bear.

Softly she pet Shenoa's head. The tears rolled quietly down her cheeks. "Tango is a beautiful name. You've done yourself proud. I will find Little Tango and make sure that he is safe. I promise." She sniffed and wiped her arm over her wet cheeks.

Dylan dropped down on one knee beside Jilly. He placed his arm around her shoulders. "Come on, honey, let's get out of here."

Jilly shook her head, still looking at her dead friend. "I can't leave. She has a cub out there. I have to find him."

Dylan rose to his feet and grabbed her hand to help her stand. He used his fingers to brush her hair back from her face and his thumbs to wipe the trail of tears from her cheeks.

"You're a mess darling. You can't help him in the shape you're in. Let me take you home and get you taken care of," he pleaded.

Jilly looked around hoping for a sign of Tango, only now was she feeling the stinging from the scratches on her legs. "Okay, but I can drive myself, there's no point in you leaving your truck on the highway." The world tilted and darkened as she swayed from exhaustion both physical and emotional.

"Easy." Dylan grabbed her around the waist to steady her. "I won't have to leave my truck; Jimmy is with me. Sable seemed upset so he stayed by the trucks."

Jilly wrapped her arm around Dylan's waist. "Thanks. I'm not feeling so hot right now; the ride home sounds great."

They exited the woods to find Jimmy anxiously pacing. "What in the Sam hell is going on? Jilly's wolf was whining and howling so much that she gave me goose bumps."

Dylan shook his head and nodded it down toward Jilly trying to tell Jimmy without talking to shut up. Of course he didn't take the hint. He took one look at Jilly and what he saw caused a whole other round of questions.

"Jilly, my God! Are you alright?"

Dylan held up his free hand. "She'll be fine. Take my truck Jimmy, I'll call you later."

"Should I call an ambulance or something?"

"No, I'll take care of her myself. I swear I'll get a hold of you later and explain everything."

"Alright," Jimmy finally agreed. "I do a good thing and stay in the truck with a wolf having an anxiety attack and what thanks do I get? None! Next time I play the hero and run into the woods." He grumbled as he put Dylan's truck in gear and did a U-turn onto the highway.

Dylan opened the driver's door and helped Jilly inside. "Sit next to me, sweetheart. I think both Sable and I need to have you close."

Jilly laid her head on Dylan's shoulder as he backed the truck out of the ditch. Idly she rubbed Sable's head where it lay in her lap. "I couldn't save her," she whispered brokenly.

Dylan started the truck, threw it into gear and took off down the highway. He laid his hand on Jilly's thigh. "I'm sorry. I can't say I understand, but I know she meant something to you." He squeezed tenderly and left his hand on her leg as he drove them home.

"I was lost in the woods," Jilly began, "I couldn't have been much over seven or eight years old. We were hiking; mom and dad were on the path in front of me."

Dylan didn't interrupt her whispered tale as he pulled into her driveway and parked. The engine gave a little sputter as he turned the key off in the ignition. Sable licked Jilly's hand before turning and jumping out of the open window. She glanced back once before going through the doggy door. Dylan knew from experience that she would go to Savannah's room.

"I saw a baby raccoon. He was so small. This was the first

hike mom and dad had let me go on. Savannah was so jealous that she was not allowed to come with us." She smiled wistfully remembering how proud she was to be able to go exploring. Her big adventure had turned to tragedy.

"I never saw my parents again. I remember it being so cold and dark. Hunters found me two days later. They didn't know how I had survived alone in the wild for two days." She looked Dylan in the eye. "I wasn't alone; Shenoa found me, fed me and kept me warm at night. She protected me from the black bear that killed my parents. It was the same black bear that the hunters' had shot and injured days before. We've been friends ever since. I let her down today."

Dylan pulled her close and rubbed her back. Jilly laid her head on his chest, accepting his comfort. "I watched her through the years. The cub she had with her is her first to live. I have to find him, I owe her."

"I'll help you any way that I can, but first I'm taking care of you." He opened the door and stepped out onto the hard packed ground.

Jilly slid over to get out only to be swung up in Dylan's arms. "Dylan!" she shrieked, "I can walk."

He kissed her on the lips to keep her from arguing.

Jilly laid her hand alongside of his neck and returned his kiss.

"Let me take care of you," he whispered as he carried her through the house. He kicked the bedroom door shut on his way to the master bath. Gently he set her on the edge of the garden tub. Warm water ran as he poured rose scented oil into the flow.

Jilly watched as Dylan reached for the buttons on her sundress.

"You scared me today." He unbuttoned the first button and kissed the end of her nose. "I don't know what I would have done if Cooper had hurt you any worse. I wanted to break the bastard's arm." He continued to the next button and kissed her lips. "Please be careful around him," he pleaded kissing her neck. The last button slipped free and he pealed her dress back to reveal her bare shoulders.

Goose bumps formed on her arms from his kisses and caused her to shiver. "I'm not afraid of Marcus." There was no reason to be. Marcus wouldn't hurt he;, it was the people she cared for that she had to worry about.

"Hush," he said as he reached for the front enclosure of her lacey bra. Dylan nuzzled his way down her arm, his lips brushing softly against her soft skin to the bend of her arm where he laid a tender kiss. "I'm not finished giving you hell," he lectured while bending to kiss just above her belly button. She gasped at the sensation of his lips running softly, caressingly across her navel. The snap finally gave on her bra and he pulled the cups back allowing him to see her full breasts. Gently he kissed first one and then the other. They puckered under the assault of his lips and tongue. "You are so brave and so beautiful." He rose up to once again kiss her on the mouth.

Jilly opened her lips to allow his caressing tongue entrance.

"No, not yet." Dylan scooted back to snag the top of her matching panties. "Lift up." When she complied with his order he easily pealed the flimsy lingerie down and threw them to the floor.

"What about you?" Jilly reached for the snap of his washed out jeans.

"This is for you, not me. I want this for you." Dylan toed off his shoes and leaned across Jilly to shut off the water. Bubbles gathered at the top of the tub and the soft sweet scent of roses from the oil drifter through the bathroom.

Jilly nuzzled the opening of Dylan's silk shirt. "You smell so good." She licked a trail up his chest to the hollow of his neck. "You taste good, too." She grabbed the hem and lifted the shirt over his head as he stood to get away from her eager hands. All that remained were his jeans.

"You keep talking and looking at me like that and I'll never get you into this tub." The sight of her sitting there gloriously naked had his penis pushing painfully against the zipper of his jeans. All his good intentions flew out the window. He slowly lowered the zipper to relieve the pressure and his hard, aching cock sprang free.

"You're not wearing any underwear," Jilly gasped. "Good god, Dylan, how many Sundays have you been sitting next to me in church without underwear?"

Dylan chuckled. No way would he reveal that the only reason he wasn't wearing underwear was because he hadn't done laundry and didn't have any clean. "I love to keep you guessing, sweetheart." Slowly, never taking his eyes from Jilly he placed his fingers in the waist band of his jeans and lowered them to the floor, with a flick of his foot they landed with the pile of clothes they'd collected.

"Now, where were we?" he asked as he bent towards her.

"Right about here," Jilly whispered; pointing to her lips. He softly kissed her, sweeping lazy circles with his tongue through her mouth, reacquainting himself with her sweet taste and pulling away to murmur against her lips. "I remember now." He nibbled gently down her jaw line to her neck and placed a small kiss before suckling the skin between his teeth to mark her. "So beautiful." His left leg pushed between Jilly's as he stepped into the tub with his right.

"Hang on to me, sweetheart." He rolled them in and with Jilly straddling him he easily slipped into her welcoming heat.

"You fit me just right," Jilly murmured. Her forehead pressed against his as she slowly lifted herself to readjust.

"Careful, Hon, or it'll be over before we get started," Dylan warned. His hands gripped her hips holding her steady.

"I want to feel you," Jilly pleaded, "I need to feel your strength filling me."

"Not yet. I want to enjoy you." Dylan slipped his hands up over Jilly's ribcage to rest on the underside of her breasts. Jilly's nipples glistened hard and erect, begging to be inside of his mouth.

"Dylan, please." She pulled gently on the back of his head guiding his mouth to where she wanted him to be.

"It'd be my pleasure." He opened his mouth, licking around her dark areola and over the tip of her pointed nipple.

Jilly groaned as pleasure shot through her body. Her back arched and she unconsciously pushed herself more fully into his mouth. He nibbled his way into the valley between the two mounds to lavish the same treatment onto her other breast. Her body was on fire, Jilly moved slowly, rocking on his shaft, the gentle sounds of the water lapping between and around them only added to the pleasure. The rose scent floated around and above them and still she rocked, the momentum building as Dylan continued to suckle.

He pulled away enough to whisper against her flesh, "You feel so good. The taste of you drives me wild." Dylan continued his assault on her breasts, bracing his feet on the length of the tub to keep them above water as Jilly continued to rock above him. Just watching her take her pleasure was beautiful. "Come for me, sweet Jilly. I want to feel you fall apart in my arms," he whispered as he raised himself up to meet her gentle thrusts. Her hoarse cry filled the air as her climax overtook her will to hold on. His will power where Jilly was concerned was nonexistent and the feel of her milking him had him crying out with her. He folded his arms around her limp body. "Let's get you dried off and in bed. Wrap your legs around me." he ordered. Holding onto the side of the tub, he levered them out onto the floor.

"Let me walk, you're going to slip." Jilly started to drop her legs from his waist.

"Stay where you are," Dylan ordered. He was still embedded deep inside of her and wasn't ready to lose their connection. He snagged the towel from the rack and headed into the bedroom rubbing her back with it as he went. "I'm not ready to let go of you yet." He laid her on the bed and came down over the top of her, kissing her gently. "Let's just rest here; I need to keep you close."

"I'm fine. Marcus is an ass but he'd never really hurt me," Jilly argued.

"Couldn't prove it my me, you've got bruises on your wrist. I won't forgive or forget as easily as you." Dylan rubbed softly at the bruises that encircled her wrist. He rolled to the side and pulled her snuggly against him, pulling the light blanket up to engulf them in a cocoon. "I'm here for you, whatever you need." He listened as her breath became still and she drifted to sleep. Mourning her friend and sheer exhaustion had finally claimed her.

* * * *

Jilly sat on the couch with her knees drawn up and her feet flat on the cushions. She rested her forehead on her bent knees. Tears wet her cheeks and sobs shook her body. Not wanting to wake Dylan she'd come to the living room. Dylan's silk shirt offered comfort and covered her nakedness.

"I'm sorry about Shenoa. I know how special she was to you."

Jilly held her breath. *"Savannah?"* she answered the familiar telepathic wave.

"Yes, I mean no," she stammered.

Jilly turned her head to see the gray wolf sitting in front of Savannah's bedroom door.

"It has been months since you've talked with me without me begging you for a response. I am so happy to have you back."

"Don't, Jilly. I'm not back," she argued.

"But, Savannah, you're talking."

"Yes, a little, I'm not ready to face anyone yet, not even you. Besides you have Dylan now." Savannah/Sable paced angrily in the hall.

"You don't approve?" Jilly questioned. She needed Savannah's support now more than ever.

Sable walked closer, sniffing at Jilly's legs. *"His scent covers you. The smell of sex clings to you. I cannot bear the thought of man or wolf touching me."*

"You'll change your mind." Jilly reached out to the wolf.

"Don't touch me, Jilly. I want to be left alone." She turned and went back to the bedroom.

Savannah, Shenoa and now maybe even baby Tango were lost to her. Uncontrollable sobs racked her. Tears trailed down her cheeks. What could she do to help Savannah recover from her attack? Could she find and keep Shenoa's cub safe?

Warm familiar arms encircled her. She was enveloped in the calm scent that was Dylan. "Come back to bed, sweetheart." He scooped her up in his arms. "I need to hold you some more."

Jilly wrapped her arms around his neck and placed a kiss on his bare chest. "You must think I'm the biggest baby. I've cried more in the last twelve hours than in the last twelve years."

"I think you're about due for some tears." He placed his index finger below her chin. "But, the next time you need a good cry; don't hide from me. I'm here for you." He kissed her lips. "Okay?" He suckled at their fullness His hands began roaming up her leg. "Now," he whispered wickedly, "who's not wearing underwear?"

Jilly surrendered to his kisses. He had answered her calls for help, but would he still be here if or when he learned the truth? She was just needy enough right now to give herself up to all that he offered.

Chapter 8

"Ouch, shit!" Jimmy muttered as he tripped over a log. "Tell me again why we're wandering through the brush in eighty degree heat, when we could be sitting at the pub sipping a cold one." he grumbled and used the tail of his tee to wipe the sweat out of his eyes.

"You saw Jilly. She was a complete wreck after they shot that sow. I've never seen anyone so upset." Dylan walked around a fallen tree. "I told her I'd take a look this afternoon and see if I saw any signs of the cub that belonged to the dead bear."

"So just lie and tell her you didn't find anything," Jimmy winked over his shoulder. Not watching where he was going he found himself doing a belly flop over a fallen tree limb.

Dylan shook his head. "Way to go, Grace." He reached down to help Jimmy up. "And no I'm not lying to her; this is important; besides lying is no way to start a relationship."

"Relationship? Whoa, this sounds serious." Jimmy rubbed his stomach.

"It is serious; I want her like I've never wanted another woman. As far as I'm concerned she's it for me. Just wish I was a little more sure of her feelings."

"Think long and hard before getting yourself too involved buddy. I think Jilly comes with a lot of baggage." Jimmy looked around at all of the fallen trees. Trucks had begun to clear away the remains of the tornado but there was still a hell of a mess. "I don't think we're going to find him today."

Dylan smiled. "There's nothing about her that would change the way I feel; I'll take her baggage and all," he vowed. "You're probably right about finding the cub though and after your swan dive anything within a five mile radius is long gone. I'll set a couple of barrel traps out and see what I come up with. Maybe I'll get lucky and the chocolates will be hard for him to resist."

"Sounds good to me." Jimmy turned and stumbled back through the briars, picking his path carefully Dylan followed just as cautiously. "What's on the agenda for the rest of the afternoon?"

"I'm headed for the bait shop. Jilly's closing tonight and I have a surprise for her." He patted the pocket of his jeans to make sure the gift was still safe.

"Okay." Jimmy stepped out of the forest onto the gravel road. His Ford pick-up sat about one hundred yards down the road. The ground was dry; dust flew under his booted feet as he walked toward the vehicle. "I'll see you there. Carrie's car wouldn't start this morning so I dropped her off and told her I'd pick her up this afternoon."

* * * *

Dylan jumped onto the counter by the cash register. "Hey there, kid." He chucked Carrie good naturedly in the chin. His knees stuck out the holes in his jeans and his old tee had a hole close to his abdomen. Jilly watched from where she refilled the cooler with cans of pop that sat in cases on the floor. Dylan was such a flirt and judging by the pink of Carrie's cheek the young girl had a slight crush on him. Dylan of course didn't have a clue as he ruffled her head like you would a kid sister. Jimmy stood just to the left of the door reading a hunting magazine from the rack. Heaven forbid he be caught buying reading material.

The bell over the door jingled and Jilly swung her head around to see who the new customer was. Becca sauntered through the door, her curly hair swaying with each step she took. A murderously red bikini top barely covered the thrust of her breasts coupled with very short cut off blue jeans. Jilly could tell by the way her stiletto heels clicked as she walked on the cement floor and the determined set of her shoulders she was a woman on a mission and wouldn't stop until she reached her goal which happened to be right between Dylan's legs.

"Hey there, Hunter." Her voice screamed sex. So did her actions. Her long red fingernails started at the base of Dylan's throat and scraped down over his pecs. "MMMMMMMMM," she purred swinging her angry gaze at Jilly. "Princess, the hunter would have made an excellent alpha, don't you think?" She licked her kiss me red lips. "Oh, that's right you didn't want the job, so you don't get the alpha either." Her outrageous laugh rang throughout the small store. She leaned forward her nose just brushing the sensitive skin along Dylan's neck. "He smells of outdoors, pine, musk, and a strong sensual scent all his own. Are you interested in a little fun, Hunter?" she whispered huskily.

Jilly took a step forward. The she bitch needed to be put in her place. The bell over the door rang again. "Becca!" Marcus's voice bellowed with authority. He walked tall and proud into the store. His cowboy boots snapped on the hard floor. His faded jeans hugged his frame tightly. Muscles bulged beneath the white tee he wore. "You were told not to interfere here." He pushed his long black hair back from his face. "Did you think I wouldn't find out about the mischief you were causing? Pay attention, Becca, because I won't tell you again. Stay away from Jilly and Savannah."

Becca turned and walked slowly, seductively to where Marcus stood in the center of the store. "But, Marcus," she whined, "I only wanted...."

"Stop," Marcus held up his hand, "I don't want to hear your

excuses. Leave and don't come back."

She turned and looked from Jilly to Dylan and down to where Sable now cowered under the stool sitting in the nook by the counter. "I have rights and I won't be denied what is rightfully mine." She whipped around and stomped out of the store, the door slamming hard behind her.

Marcus bowed his head. "I apologize for Becca's action. She won't bother you again. You have my word." He looked toward Sable and took a small step. The wolf whined and curled herself into a tighter ball. Marcus hesitated and shook his head. For a moment he slumped, mixed emotions crossed his face, then he took a deep breath and squared his shoulders. "I'm truly sorry." He turned and walked proudly out the door.

"Man, is he cute," Carrie uttered, her hand on her chest. "Isn't he the guy that protects the wolves north of here?"

Jimmy stepped forward. "Don't even think it, young lady."

"He's way too old for you," Dylan and Jilly said simultaneously.

Carrie laughed. "Cool it you guys. I just said the guy was hot. Don't have a cow." She put her hands on her hips. "I'm not a baby."

Jimmy watched the door. "What was that all about?"

Dylan shook his head. "I have no idea but, girls, I want to personally apologize for all mankind if that's the way you feel after a man gives you the once over." He shook his body and brushed his hands down the front of his shirt. "I feel unclean."

Jilly walked over and gave his face a slight pat, lightly tweaking his dimple. "Relax, big boy. It's me she was trying to get a rise out of, although you are pretty darn cute." she winked.

"Thanks, darlin'." He gave her a quick peck on the lips. "I have something for you," he whispered and reached into the front pocket of his jeans. "Turn around." He gently pushed on her shoulder to turn her back to his front. He lifted her hair as he slipped the chain around her neck and fastened the clasp in back. "I know it can't replace your friend, but I thought it would be a nice memory of her."

Jilly fingered the small charm and turned to face Dylan. "Thank you so much, Dylan." Tears slipped down her cheeks and she swallowed the lump in her throat. The replica was of a mother bear with a small cub sitting beside her. "I'll treasure it." She reached up and wrapped her arms around his neck, her tears falling on the bare skin of his neck.

Dylan gently rubbed her back. "And I'll treasure you darlin'."

Chapter 9

The pain was excruciating. The vicious teeth of a trap bit into her left hind leg. Tendons lay exposed through the broken skin and raw meat of the leg. She licked delicately at the open wound. A true wolf would have eaten her leg off by now to free herself. All she could do was wait. Shifting was out of the question, there was no way to concentrate with searing pain burning from ankle to hip. She had to get free, Tango needed her protection. Without guidance he would fall to the same fate as Shenoa. She struggled in vain, but stabbing agony tore through her body. The trap would not release and no one knew to come looking in the woods this time of night. Her howl of frustration carried throughout the night.

Dylan stopped at the eerie cry, it was a cry of pain, and somewhere an animal was hurt. Jilly's truck was parked along the road and he could only assume she too was answering the animal's cry for help.

He pulled his truck up behind hers and shut off the engine. "Jilly, can you hear me?" He called into his hand held radio but no reply was forth coming. He'd chew her cute little ass out when he found her for wandering into the forest alone with no radio. Bears and wolves prowled at night. Wolves virtually gutted and skinned hounds and he could only imagine what they would do to a lone woman Jilly's size.

The thought just about stopped his heart. He opened his door, picked up his flashlight and stepped out onto the gravel road. The cry came again. He turned on the light and stepped down into the ditch. He shined the light out in front of him. It only stretched a small beam about ten feet in front of him before being swallowed by the dark.

"Jilly!" he hollered as he broke into a run. Tree limbs ripped at his clothing and tore the skin on his face and arms. He didn't recognize or acknowledge the pain, concern for Jilly his only thought. The woods were deadly quiet, no night creatures stirred. Even the air was quiet. He stumbled over fallen logs and broken off saplings.

A soft growl almost a whine about a hundred yards in front of him sounded almost desperate. He broke into a run. He tripped and fell, his flashlight landed a few feet in front of him and went out.

"Shit, Dylan break a leg or your neck and you won't be any good to anyone." he mumbled. He felt for the flashlight and his fingertips came away sticky. He banged the flashlight on his leg and shined the beam of light; his worst fears confirmed when blood dripped from his hand.

What the hell had he tripped over? A whimper came from the darkness beyond. He turned slowly, shining the beam of light behind him. A wolf and him with no gun. A lump formed in his throat. His heart pounded so hard he swore it would burst from his chest. He was so scared his mouth was dry. He looked around for a sturdy club; it wasn't the most humane way to take care of the animal, but his and, more importantly, Jilly's safety came first. He chose a sturdy branch about seven inches in diameter. "I'm sorry. Wish I could make this quicker, but the woman I love is wandering around here somewhere."

The wolf whimpered. Her big eyes looked so sad, almost as if wanting to cry. But that was ridiculous; animals didn't have feelings. She couldn't even understand what he was saying to her.

"Oh Dylan, not you! Why not anyone but you? I love you, will always love you and I forgive you for killing me. How I wish things had turned out differently." Jilly wished desperately that Dylan could understand what she was trying to tell him; knowing that when she died she would automatically shift back to her human form. Dylan would be devastated. She would do anything to save him from that hurt. Of all the people that could have found her in the trap, why did it have to be the man that she loved?

She rolled to her back, stretching as far as the trap would

allow, bending her head back.

Dylan shifted the light, wanting to make the kill quick, no need to let her suffer unnecessarily. What was the crazy devil doing? Trying to roll over? She acted as though she was trying to beg him to let her go. It was, of course, not going to happen. He could not consciously let her live knowing that the next time he or his friends hunted, their dogs could fall victim to this killer and her pack.

Something glinted on the wolf's neck. Was she tangled in barbed wire? If so, it would be a blessing to end the suffering. No, it almost looked like a diamond shining back at him.

He bent for a closer look, warily keeping his eye on the wolf… one quick snap of her jaws and her teeth would sink deep. A bear charm gleamed back at him, mocking him.

How was that possible? He'd given the charm to Jilly, it was one of a kind, specially made for her after the death of the bear sow. He stepped back swiftly and fell flat on his ass.

"Jilly?" he whispered. "No! What am I saying? You couldn't be."

"Yes, it's me. I'm so so sorry." she whimpered again and rolled back and forth on the ground, the trap pulling painfully on her leg. She didn't even feel the pain anymore. She only wanted to save Dylan from finding out the truth like this yet knew there was no other alternative.

He crawled slowly forward. "Easy girl, let me see." It was

unbelievable to him what he was about to do. There had to be some explanation. Yet he knew there could not be, Jilly would never have given the charm to an animal and there were no others like it. Therefore, as unbelievable as it seemed, the wolf in the trap was somehow the woman who most nights he cuddled in his arms. The trap was snapped onto her back leg. When he reached back to examine the damage, the wolf lapped at his hand with her rough tongue.

"I'm so sorry," he whispered. The tears fell swiftly down his face, the hurt, anger and confusion all rolling through his body. He wasn't ashamed of the tears, they were allowed after such devastation. He pushed against the opposite sides of the trap and released her leg.

Jilly curled into a ball. Although still hurting, it was not as excruciating as the teeth of the trap biting into her flesh. Ever so slowly she stretched her body; the blood flowed through her veins starting at the pads of her wolf feet and moving slowly up into the fingertips of the naked woman that now lay on the forest floor.

Dylan sprang back from the creature that was slowly metamorphosing from an animal to the beautiful woman that he had planned to spend the rest of his life loving. He watched as she slowly rolled and sat up on her bare ass, the wound on her ankle was not visible.

"How is this possible?" He cautiously reached out to touch

her, his hand encircled her narrow wrist. He stood swiftly and pulled her to her feet. She was so beautiful standing there in all her naked beauty.

"Let me go, Dylan. I don't have time to explain now. I have to find the cub," she cried, jerking her arm to loosen his grip.

He quickly released her. "Jilly, I need to understand." His heart was breaking; he could feel it, the pain ripping through his chest. Who was this woman he loved? What was she? Did they even have a future? Did he even want one? He dropped to his knees in the damp leaves on the forest floor and held his hands up pleadingly.

Jilly knelt cautiously in front of him, sensing his fear of the unknown, feeling the same pain of loss she was feeling. "I'm sorry," she said gripping his hands, "I'll try to explain everything to you later. I've got to find Tango."

He pulled his hands away. He couldn't touch her, not yet, not now, maybe never again. "Explain…how can you explain? What are you?" his voice broke. Tears flooded his eyes, all his hopes and dreams falling in puddles to the forest floor.

"The cub, that god damned bear! My life, our life is falling apart and all you can think of is an animal. Oh wait," His laugh was bitter. "That's right, you're two of a kind, both animals. Do you want to hear the kicker, Jilly?" He held up his hands when she started to walk toward him. "I came out her tonight to surprise you. Boy did that back fire. I got the surprise instead. Yours is in the back of my truck. Your precious bear cub is snug and warm in a pet carrier. Take him and get out of my sight." He turned and walked away. He headed deep into the forest, away from any reminders of what may have been.

"Dylan, please come back!" Jilly stood in the dark and watched as he disappeared into the thick underbrush. He was hurt, but so was she. Apparently he didn't love her enough. She turned and headed to the road...the cub needed her.

Chapter 10

"Dylan." Jilly ran across the clearing to meet him. "Thank you so much for meeting me here." She waved her arm in the air encircling the dark forest. No crickets chirped; it was eerily silent. "I'm sorry. I know you hate me and I'm the last person you want to see but I need help and you're the one person I trust."

"Hate?" God, if she only knew. He shook his head. "Baby, I could never hate you. Don't you know how much I love you? You're my life."

She shook her head. "You ran. You left me. It's been over a month since I've seen or heard anything from you." The tears seeped from her eyes and she deftly wiped them away with the back of her hands. "I called and you wouldn't answer. You never returned my phone calls. Until tonight. What's happened that you're finally willing to speak to me?"

"Let's just say I've finally got my head out of my ass. You'll never know how sorry I am that I ran. I'm not ashamed to admit I was scared. Hell, I'm still scared but I can't live without you. I understand things better now. Wolf or no wolf, I need you in my life."

"I really can't talk about this now." She gathered supplies, wildly throwing flashlights, food and clothing that were scattered haphazardly at her feet into the duffle bag resting on the forest floor. "I have to track Marcus and I need your help."

"Marcus, what's he got to do with this?"

"He took Sable and I have to get her back." Jilly cried jumping to her feet and twirling wildly in a circle trying to get her bearings.

"I just left Marcus at the bar. He was with Jimmy having a beer." Dylan continued, "There's no way he could have done what you're suggesting. I've been with him for the past couple of hours."

"He must have snuck out when you weren't paying attention because he took Sable not more than an hour or so ago."

"I'm telling you, he's still at the bar with Jimmy. We were all playing pool."

"Oh my god!" Jilly slumped down on a blown down pine. "If not Marcus, then who? I was so sure," she whispered. Tears slid down her cheeks, confusion clouding her mind.

"Why would Marcus steal your dog? It doesn't make sense." He backed up a couple steps as the pieces to the puzzle fell into place. "Sable's not just a hybrid wolf dog is she?" he asked the question already knowing the answer.

"She's Savannah," Jilly confessed. "What I tell you, Dylan, can never be known beyond the two of us. I'm entrusting you with more than just my life. Can I trust you to keep my secret?"

"I can't begin to understand what's happening, Jilly, but I love you. I'd give my life for you. Whether our relationship survives the truth, no one else will learn any of it," he promised.

"Marcus is the Alpha of the wolf pack in the forest. He wanted Sable/Savannah for his mate. She refused him and he brutally raped her to force her into accepting the role." Chills formed on her arms, the thin tee shirt no protection against the night air and the shock still rocking her body.

"Here, put this on." Dylan removed his jean jacket and placed it over her shoulders. He wanted to touch her so badly, to wrap her in his arms and tell her everything would be okay, but couldn't because he honestly couldn't say how he felt or would feel when he heard the whole story.

"Thanks." She pulled the edges of the jacket together and rolled her shoulders in protectively. "After the attack, I petitioned the elders. My parents were at one time the alpha pair and as their offspring, Savannah and I were princesses of the pack and had certain rights. The elders granted my request and Savannah and I left the pack. Marcus has been trying to force Savannah to return."

"How can that be? I haven't seen Savannah in months. You told Jimmy she was away; I assumed she was visiting friends or family out of state."

"She never left. Savannah shifted to her wolf form shortly after the attack becoming Sable. I haven't seen Savannah since. She has only communicated to me telepathically and then only a few times."

Dylan scratched his head; shifting wolves, talking telepathically...he felt like he just stepped into a movie scene or some paranormal book. "Telepathy, that's where you talk through your mind right? So try to contact her now and find out who has her." He sounded sarcastic and knew it but damn how much could a guy take in one night?

"I've tried; she's shut me out or is unable to answer me. I've got to find Marcus he has to know something." She got slowly to her feet, defeat weighing heavy on her shoulders. "I promised her that he would never hurt her again. I failed."

"You didn't fail. No way could you have planned for this but I can just about guarantee that Marcus had nothing to do with Savannah's disappearance. I've spent the last hour sitting at a table listening to him praise both you and Savannah. Savannah would never be happy without you. The man is in love with her and he wouldn't risk alienating you by kidnapping her."

Dylan reached for the cell phone strapped to the belt at his waist, "I'll call Jimmy and have him bring Marcus." He walked further in to the clearing to get better reception.

Jilly watched anxiously as Dylan placed the call. After a minute he pulled the phone away from his ear punched a button and put it back in the holster on his belt. She grabbed Dylan's arm when he walked back close enough for her to reach. "Are they coming?"

Dylan nodded, "They'll be here in about fifteen minutes." He slowly pulled her in tight to his body and closed his eyes. How he'd missed the feel of her body pressed close to his, the smell of lilac and musky outdoors that was uniquely Jilly. "I love you, Jill," he whispered and kissed her below the ear, "Whatever happens I won't run again."

"I love you too, Dylan. I'm so sorry that I wasn't honest with you. It wasn't just my secret to tell." She stepped back and tipped her head up to look at him. "But, I'd like to tell you everything now."

Dylan placed his finger over her lips. "You've told me most of it right?" He waited for her to nod. "All I need to know is how this will affect us and any family we may have."

Jilly smiled beneath his finger and reached up to encircle his wrist. She kissed his finger and removed it from her lips. "I can promise you that we will end my line with me. The only way to carry out the line and have babies who will be shifters is for the shifters to mate as their animals would mate. You and I, my love, will have only human babies. I shift only when I want, not by the full moon, not certain times of the month. It's my choice to shift and if you never want me to change, I will promise you to never, ever leave my human body." She felt torn by the promise but Dylan's love and acceptance were more important than her hurt feelings.

Dylan closed his eyes. The relief of knowing he would not have puppies as kids lifted a huge brick from his chest and allowed him to breathe. "I don't have a problem with you shifting, Jill. It's part of who and what you are. But I have to be completely honest when I say I'm glad that our kids will not have to live with the burden of hiding who and what they would be. We have plenty of space here and whenever you feel the need to run freely, I want you to feel safe and secure enough to do so."

"Thank you." She turned her head to the side. "They're coming." She winked playfully, "I also have excellent hearing."

Dylan laughed aloud. For the first time in weeks he felt joy. Jilly was back where she belonged. Now he just had to help find his future sister-in-law and everything would be right with their world.

* * * *

"I told you it couldn't be anything too bad. I can hear Dylan laughing. Ouch! Damn it, Marcus, slow down," Jimmy hollered as a berry briar slapped him across the face. "How in the hell can you see where you're going? You have eyes like an owl!"

Jilly ran forward as the two men came into sight. "Where is

she, you son of a bitch?" She let her fist fly and socked Marcus below the right eye. His head snapped back but he stood tall.

Dylan caught her around the waist as she pulled her arm back to let him have it again. "Jilly, calm down. I told you he doesn't know."

Jilly struggled against his hold. Her feet dangled above the ground. "He knows! He has her or knows who has her. Turn me loose, Dylan. I have to find her!"

Marcus rubbed his cheek. He made no move but waited patiently for Jilly to calm enough to hear him over her curses. "What am I now accused of? I have been at the bar with your two friends all night."

Jimmy finally regained his breath. "That's right, Jilly. We've been playing pool. What's happened?"

Dylan set Jilly on her feet and pulled her tightly against him. Her back was snuggled to his front and he wrapped his arms around her both for comfort and to make sure she didn't attack Marcus again. "Savannah is missing and Jilly thinks that Marcus had something to do with her disappearance." Dylan carefully watched Marcus; the man's face lost all color and he looked ready to fall down.

Marcus stumbled forward. "Tell me." He was shaken. Never did he expect to be accused of such an atrocity. His Savannah was missing. *There must be a mistake.*

"I was away from the house and Sable," she looked quickly as Jimmy and corrected herself, "Savannah called out to me. It was faint but definitely her." She knew the tale was sketchy but Jimmy didn't know the truth. She couldn't let it be known that the call came to her telepathically.

Marcus paced as he replayed the events of the last couple of months. The fear and the hatred he'd witnessed on Sable/Savannah's face. The decision of the pack leaders to release Jilly and Savannah from the pack and thus him. Sorrow tore through him, all the time wasted on hatred and vengeance. He turned to Jilly. "I vow to you that I do not have your sister, but I do have an idea who does and if I'm right, there is only one place where she could be."

"The Haven," Jilly whispered and broke from Dylan's arms to run for the trucks. As a wolf she could have run the distance in a shorter period of time but Dylan and Jimmy would never make it and if things didn't go as planned, she wanted Dylan with her. "We have to hurry." She didn't look back but the brush cracking behind her let her know who followed.

"I will meet you there." Marcus ran in the opposite direction his two feet swiftly changing into four as he leaped over logs and under blow downs. The black wolf threw his head back as he ran and let out an ear splitting howl of warning. Revenge would be his as was pack law.

Chapter 11

"They're going to execute her," Jilly rushed forward. Sable stood alone in the center of a snarling pack of wolves. Her body shook with fear.

"Wait." Marcus stepped out from the shadows.

"Where in the hell did you come from?" Jimmy looked around but saw nothing but more shadows and trees.

Marcus shook his head. "It's not important. Listen."

"You will die," Becca's voice rang with hatred from where she stood on a rock ledge. The wolves continued to circle the lone she-wolf awaiting the order to finish the punishment Becca had initiated.

"I will be the Alpha-Bitch and to do this I must rid the pack of you; only then can I take my rightful place as ruler at Marcus's side," she continued her speech.

"You overstep your bounds, Becca," Marcus called as he stepped from the tree line. "You cannot step in and order the pack."

"Stay back," Dylan grabbed Jilly's arm as she moved to

follow Marcus.

"She has to be stopped. They'll kill Sable if for no other reason than the challenge. Listen to them." The wolves howled and yipped excitedly. "She has them craving the kill; the taste for blood is riding them."

"Trust Marcus to handle the pack. From what you told me, you no longer have any control. Involving yourself now could make matters worse," he pleaded.

"I'll wait but if things get rough, I have to save my sister," she whispered.

"What's happening? How can Marcus and Becca be this close to the wolves?" Jimmy asked and was ignored.

Becca stepped toward Marcus and sneered. "I over step nothing, I only wish to join with you as your mate. You will never accept me until this she bitch is dead!"

"No!" Jilly screamed

"Kill them!" Becca shouted; just now noticing Dylan, Jimmy and Jilly standing in the shadows. "They are not pack and endanger life as we know it." Surely the pack would kill the humans to protect their secret.

"Stay back, you bastards," Dylan stepped in front of Jilly to protect her as the pack turned as a unit and started forward to obey Becca's order. He'd die before letting any of them get hold of her.

The pack divided snarling and howling. "We're in deep shit

guys and gals," Jimmy looked around for a way out of the mess as the wolves eased closer. Drool ran from their jaws as they growled, their teeth bared.

"What are you waiting for? Kill them! I am Alpha and I gave you an order!" Becca shouted.

"Dylan, take Jimmy and go," Jilly pleaded. She was scared. But anger and the determination to save Savannah won out. She could only hope that Dylan would have the good sense to take Jimmy and get the hell out of here.

"Don't even ask, because it's not going to happen." He argued.

"Uh guys, a little help here?" Jimmy walked backwards as the wolves circled to push him into the dense forest.

"I have to fight, Dylan. There's no other way." Jilly took the picture of the wolf into her head, rejoicing the soul of the wolf as it reared towards the surface. She kept her mind centered on the wolf, blocking out all other sounds as her wolf overtook her human body.

"If you fight, we fight together." Dylan stood to the side and watched as the woman he loved slowly, gracefully became a wolf.

"I'll take care of the She-Bitch myself." Becca's body bent forward as fur rippled along her arms. Graceful hands became large paws on the cool, damp rock face; her back arched and the clothes fell from her back as the woman became wolf. She stepped slowly, majestically one step at a time off the stone ledge; her purpose clear, her howl of victory echoing in the night.

"Enough!" Marcus roared, His body shifted quickly and without flare into that of a large black wolf. *"You will not touch her!"* He leaped gracefully through the air as he watched the small wolf he'd loved for years leap through the air to knock Jimmy from the killing bite of the wolf pack.

"You will never be Alpha. I warned you not to harm Sable." Marcus's big body slammed hard into Becca's auburn body. The she-wolf would not stop; he had hoped she would get over her jealousy but it was not to be. *"As Alpha, I find you guilty of treachery and endangerment of our pack. I hereby sentence you to death."* His voice rang strong and clear as he sent out his telepathic message to all of the pack. His teeth sank deep into Becca's throat. The only sound in the now silent clearing was the gurgling death rattle as she gasped for breath while her blood pooled on the ground. The leaves and pine needles absorbed the puddle as steam rose from the warmth of life lost. The coppery scent filled the air and enticed the other wolves to tear at the flesh when Marcus tossed her lifeless body to the ground.

"Back Off," Jilly threatened the small wolf she stood over. *"Your Alpha has spoken."* She rose from all fours onto her feet, shifting with ease.

"Here." Dylan removed his denim shirt and handed it to her. Nakedness obviously didn't bother these people and he was sure they'd seen Jilly without clothes many times but it wasn't something he wanted to think about.

"Thanks." She slipped her arms into the shirt and quickly buttoned it. "Where's Savannah?"

"She's over by Jimmy." He stepped back. The small wolf lay with her head across Jimmy's chest. She snarled as the black wolf walked toward her across the clearing. The wolf stopped and sat on his haunches his head cocked questioningly to the side before lowering it in defeat.

"Marcus, don't," Jilly began. He looked so sad as if his dreams had just ended. The wolf got slowly got to his feet and turned to the caves along the water way.

Dylan bent to feel for a pulse in Jimmy's neck but jerked his hand back as Sable growled. "Damn it, wolf, we just saved your ungrateful hide. You could be a little more sociable," he grumbled.

Marcus walked back into the clearing wearing only a pair of washed out denims. His bare feet not making a sound as he approached the wolf and man lying on the leaf covered ground. He knelt on one knee and bowed his head. "I offer my most humble of apologies, little Sable. Please believe that I never purposely meant to hurt you. In my heart, I believed you to be my mate and my love for you blinded me from the way in which we were raised. I now understand that we were never meant to be and I see that you have chosen another." He reached up to smooth a hand gently across the side of the wolf's head. "Know that should you ever want for anything, little sister, all you have to do is ask."

"Oh, damn." Jimmy groaned and closed his eyes as the trees twirled around him. The back of his head felt like he's been bashed with a pool cue.

"Jimmy, are you alright?" Dylan knelt on the opposite side of the wolf. He eased his hand under Jimmy's shoulders and helped him to sit up.

"I think so, what happened?" he asked.

"You don't remember?" Dylan looked over his shoulder at Jilly and across the way to Marcus; both were dressed in a lot less than what they'd been wearing a few hours ago.

"I thought I saw Jilly and Marcus change into wolves," he rubbed the back of his head. "I must have hit my head harder than I thought." He shook his head gingerly. He felt like he was in a dream, nothing made sense and his head hurt like hell. "The wolves were close and Jilly's dog was fighting her way through the pack and just before they reached me she jumped and hit me square in the chest." He looked down at the wolf dog; her head now lay on his lap. "I guess she saved my life." He reached to pet the top of her head but changed his mind; too often he'd made advances to the wolf dog only to be growled and snapped at.

"Yeah, she did save your worthless hide. But, Jilly and Marcus becoming wolves... we better have you checked out buddy." Dylan joked. Could it possibly be that simple? Jimmy's confusion in the whole nightmare could keep the secrets that everyone had fought so valiantly to protect.

* * * *

"Marcus?" Jilly called quietly as Dylan dealt with Jimmy. "Could I talk with you for a minute?"

"Jilly, I really just want to be alone. My humiliation should be more than enough even for you." He turned to leave.

"Wait." She grabbed his bicep and stepped in front of him keeping her voice purposely low. "I know that you lost much tonight. Your words to my sister touched my heart," she laid her hand over her chest. "For all that you lost, I'd also like to think you gained." she continued softly.

"What have I gained? I killed tonight; even now the pack is finishing off the remains of one of our own." He looked at the wolves grouped around the bloodied body. Their growls as they engorged themselves on Becca's wolf body sickened him. "I found her guilty. It is pack law that she be destroyed, yet I am saddened by the outcome." He turned back to her. "I practically groveled to the only woman that I have ever loved for nothing, she chose a human. Tell me, Jilly, what have I gained?" he questioned.

"I would like to think," Jilly grabbed his left hand and placed it in hers, "that you have gained a friend." She shook his hand. "Thank you for helping me tonight. I'm sorry for your loss and for doubting you."

He returned her hand shake and gave it a squeeze. "You are welcome. I will be leaving here for a time. The pack is a mess and it's in part to my neglect. We will return when I deem we are a family again." He looked at Sable who was gently licking Jimmy's hand. "She has chosen and I must come to terms with that. Goodbye, Princess." He kissed her cheek and disappeared into the forest.

"Until we meet again," she whispered.

Epilogue

The full moon shined brightly through the sheer curtains moving gently from the light breeze blowing through the open window.

Jilly lay with her head cradled on Dylan's shoulder. "Did I ever thank you for capturing Tango?"

His hand idly stroked her bare hip. "I heard that you relocated the cub. Have you seen him?"

She shook her head. Her hair glided across his shoulder. "Not up close. I decided a clean break would be best. He's across Highway 64 where it's illegal to use dogs. I explained to him to stay away from the hollowed logs with treats. I'll have to believe that he'll survive. He's Shenoa's legacy."

Dylan rubbed his chin idly on top of her head. "A lot has happened in the last month. Do you think Savannah will ever change from her wolf body?"

Jilly shrugged her shoulder. Her hand lay low on Dylan's stomach. "I sure hope so. She surprised me tonight when she reached out to help Jimmy. Maybe she'll eventually come back. I really think Marcus is sorry for what happened. In his mind he truly felt that he was following pack law. In time, I hope that Savannah will realize that and come to forgive him and maybe trust men again."

Dylan rose up on his elbow. "I have an idea. Let's leave Sable with Jimmy while we take a honeymoon." He grinned mischievously, "Maybe our families will bond while we're gone."

Jilly smiled. "Why, Dylan Rudolph! Are you asking me to marry you?"

"You bet, darlin'. I'm gonna love you forever, two-legged or four. No more walking in shadows." He bent down and kissed her on the lips. The full moon slowly drifted in the sky and the room was consumed in darkness and the whispered words of love and laughter.

Hiding in Shadows

Savannah

Chapter 1

Run. Faster. Sable leaped through the air. Her fur covered legs moving as fast as the wolf body would carry her. She yipped in fright, his breath warm against the back of her neck. Muscles ached from overuse but she knew what would happen if he caught her. Pain. She'd felt it before—his big body enclosing hers, taking, claiming—never again would she be caught unaware. He was getting closer, closer. He brushed against her leg, then up along the side of her body and finally his hand rested against her shoulder. She would not go docilely. She would fight for her freedom or die trying. Death was preferable to what she had learned loving was.

"Ouch! Turn lose you she-bitch!" Jimmy held his hand still as the wolf dog clamped her teeth around his wrist. The hybrid was yipping with her legs twitching as if chasing a rabbit. At first he'd thought it funny, but the wolf seemed to become upset as if in pain and so he grabbed her shoulder to wake her only to get an arm full of teeth for his trouble.

The wolf growled low in her throat but released his wrist.

Jimmy rubbed his arm; no skin was broken but red marks remained to remind him that he was dealing with a wild animal. "I don't know how I get myself talked into these messes. I could be out playing pool or better yet sitting in my own house with my feet up relaxing. Instead, I'm babysitting your fuzzy ass."

Sable stared intently at Jimmy. She had been dreaming about Marcus and had never meant to hurt Jimmy; she was beginning to like him. Gently, she licked the wound she had inflicted.

"Don't try to butter up to me now; just because your owner spoils you rotten, you're not getting the same treatment from me. For half a cent I'd lock you in the kennels and go home but I know Jilly and Dylan will be calling from their honeymoon to check up on your pampered ass." He laid his head on the brown sofa and let the wolf console him. Truth be told, she held a special place in his heart. Her blue eyes always looked so sad, almost haunted, and made him feel the need to protect and comfort. And for a man that absolutely hated wolves, this was no small admission.

Jimmy absent mindedly stroked the she-wolf's head. "She'll be home soon girl." His words were whispered softly as his eyes drifted closed. He listened to the deep breaths of the she-wolf; it was calming. He wasn't sleeping well on Jilly's too small couch but couldn't bring himself to crawl into Jilly's bed knowing what she and Dylan had certainly done in said bed. It just didn't sit right with him. He had tried to sleep in Savannah's bed but the she-wolf had been stretched out on it and any attempt to get close had her baring her teeth and snarling and so he was relegated to the couch. Soon his breaths seemed to match hers as too-many-nights-spent-sleeping-in–an-unfamiliar-bed exhaustion finally claimed him.

Savannah slipped quietly from the couch. One foot at a time, her sleek wolf's body stretched to full length with her hind end higher as her back arched. Bones cracked from being in this shape for such a long period of time. What she wouldn't give to shed this body and take human form. But no, it was safer to be Sable; the wolf was brave and could shut out the ugliness of the world. Her padded feet made no sound as she headed for the doggy door. The night was calling to her.

* * * *

Jimmy's dreams took him back to the night months ago when Jilly's she wolf had been stolen by some ex-girlfriend of her previous owner. That night and the things that happened were confusing and he didn't understand why his dreams always returned.

They were deep in the forest. *"They're going to execute her,"* Jilly ran forward to where her she-wolf Sable stood alone in the center of a snarling pack of wolves.

Jimmy reached in his dreams. "Stop ..." Jilly would be tore apart by the vicious animals.

"Wait." Marcus stepped out from the shadows.

Jimmy jumped. His body twitched in his restless sleep.

"Where the hell did you come from?" He looked around wildly but saw nothing but more shadows and trees. His eyes moved rapidly beneath his closed lids. He knew what was coming but was powerless to stop it as the dream was always the same.

The crazy bitch that use to date Marcus was speaking. "You will all die!"

What in the hell was she talking about? No one was going to die.

"I will be the Alpha-Bitch and take my rightful place at Marcus's side." She raised her fist in the air.

Someone really needed to call the men with the white coats this broad was totally whacked. Dylan grabbed Jilly's arm and was whispering rapidly to her but Jimmy couldn't hear what they were saying.

Jimmy's body jerked. He didn't want to see anymore. He had to wake from the nightmare. Why did he keep having this weird dream?

Marcus stomped across the clearing. Jimmy could hear the dried leaves and snapping of twigs just as clearly as if he was once again standing in the dark witnessing the carnage that was about to take place.

"You overstep your bounds, Becca," Marcus called.

"I overstep nothing! I will join with you as your mate. You will never accept me until this she-bitch is dead!"

Mate? Who the hell talks like that? And how can Marcus and Becca be so close to the wolves that surrounded Jilly's pet? Surely they realized just how dangerous the situation was.

"No!" Jilly screamed.

"Stay back, you bastards!" Dylan stepped in front of Jilly to protect her from the wolves.

The pack divided snarling and howling. "We're in deep shit, guys and gals," Jimmy looked around for a way out of the mess as the wolves eased closer. Drool ran from their jaws as they growled, their teeth bared. He could see Dylan and Jilly arguing but could not hear what they were saying. Dylan was probably begging Jilly to get the hell out of Dodge, which sounded like a pretty good plan to him.

"Uh guys... a little help here." He back pedaled as the wolves circled to push him into the dense forest. He looked to Marcus for help— the last time he had seen him, he was arguing with Becca.

"Enough!"

He heard Marcus roar and turned to look. Holy Mother of God! As Marcus leaped through the air, his face elongated and his arms and legs thinned out as his body became encased in black hair. When he landed, he stood on four legs as a big black wolf.

"Are you seeing this shit?" He turned to Dylan in time to see Jilly's clothing fall to the forest floor and she too was a wolf. His

head swung back to Marcus as he heard a piercing, gut wrenching scream of agony.

This was new. Never before had he heard such a sound. The hair on the back of his neck stood on end. He wanted to wake up; no way did he want to see what was causing that terror.

Marcus's big body of the black wolf slammed hard into what could only be Becca as now yet another wolf stood where the woman had only moments before been. Teeth sank deep into the smaller wolf's throat. The only sound in the now silent clearing was the gurgling death rattle as she gasped for breath.

Jimmy could only stand there staring, forgotten were the wolves that were slowly making their way to him. Only seconds had passed; it had seemed longer while watching the drama unfold before him. Growling reminded him that his life was also in danger. Growls, teeth chomping, getting closer and suddenly pain exploded in his chest as Jilly's wolf attacked him and knocked him to the ground. His head hit the dirt and his ears began to ring. Ringing ears...that too was new. Why wouldn't it stop? He jerked trying to get away. His eyes opened. It was not his ears ringing. It was the sound of his cell phone.

"Hello," he said groggily, sleep still weighing him down. There would be time later to search through each and every event of his dream. He had a feeling it wasn't a nightmare that was haunting him, but that he had truly seen his friends turn into wolves.

"Oh, hey Jill. How's Cancun?" How was he supposed to act around Jilly now that he had these doubts? Should he come right out and ask her? Oh, hey Jill, let me ask you… are you really a dog? He'd end up with a black eye. Jilly was tough and didn't take shit from anyone. Not to mention that her husband and my best friend would kick the holy hell out of me for insulting her. No, it was better to wait and search through the memories because he was almost sure now that is what they were rather than dreams.

"Is that right? And how about Dylan? Are you bringing him home with you or did you come to your senses and are going to leave his sorry ass down there?" He laughed as she began to go into detail of Dylan swimming with the dolphins.

"Bet that was a sight with his lily white chicken legs. Jeez, the sun had to glare off those suckers!"

"Sable? Oh she's right…." He looked beside him on the couch. Sable was gone. Oh shit, where the hell had she gone?

"What? Sorry, yeah she's doing great. You know, Jilly, I'm probably not really the best person to be watching your wolf. You know I'm not all that fond of them." And now I've lost her. Christ how long has she been gone? I couldn't have been sleeping that long.

"How about you give me Savannah's number and I'll give her a call and maybe she'd come home and watch out for your pet while you're gone." He got up from the couch and walked over to the window and looked out on the porch in hopes that the wolf-dog was lying on the deck. Of course, no such luck.

"Unreachable huh? No, I know you trust me Jill and it's no bother I just thought maybe Savannah would be a better person to take care of things here and at the store." He walked through the house to check Savannah's bed; Sable spent a lot of time spread out on the feather comforter. The bed was unfortunately empty.

"The store's fine. I talked to Carrie earlier she said it's been relatively quiet so not to worry. I'll go over tomorrow and check things out myself. Look Jill, I gotta go. You guys have a great time and I'll see you in a week." He flipped his phone closed ending the call and walked back to the couch. He dropped down and ran his hands through his hair. Then put his head in his hands, elbows on knees. He wasn't overly worried, wolves like to roam at night. She would return when she was ready. This was the first time she'd left his side since he began staying here, but he would wait. She'd return when ready.

Chapter 2

Savannah/Sable stood on the steps and put her nose in the air, always on the alert for danger. It was getting harder and harder to tell the difference from Savannah the woman and Sable the wolf. She battled daily to find herself but in the wolf body she was safe.

"Come," the wolf whispered to her. *"It is safe. Let's hunt."*

Sable hesitated and turned her head to look back toward the doorway of the cabin. She hadn't left Jimmy since the time in the woods. The wolves could still come for him. Marcus had promised he would be safe, but she trusted no one except her beloved sister Jilly.

"Come," the wolf insisted, pushing her will. The strength of the wolf was growing, overtaking the will of the woman. *"You love being in wolf form, do not become weak. I can smell that you care for him. Do not! We saved him, protected him from the pack. You're will overrode mine, but the male cannot be trusted. You know what they can do to your body, to our body. Come, let's run."*

And there it was, the fear that kept her captive to her

wolf…she was terrified of interacting as a human. She turned away from the cabin and the human male sleeping on the couch and loped down the steps. She turned the corner at the end of the house and was at a full run by the time she hit the open field out back.

The air was brisk but pleasant; her senses on alert. Pine intermingled with the sweet scent of the forest as she edged closer to the wood line. In the distance, the barking of hounds announced hunters. Coon season had opened weeks ago but she was unafraid as no hunting was allowed on this land.

The wolf slowed as they edged deeper into the woods. *"Deer. I want to feel the thrill of the chase and the triumph of leaping upon its massive body; sinking my teeth into its jugular, the ecstasy as its warm coppery blood runs across my tongue and down my throat."*

"No," Savannah answered. *"The doe already most likely carries young. I will not kill babes."* Due to the cold weather, the bucks have been in rut for weeks and many deer were probably already impregnated. There was no way she would kill a mother and baby. She loved to watch the fawns in the spring as they jumped and played in the meadow. It was pure joy to watch them nursing on their mothers with short little tails wagging so happily.

"You are too squeamish. It is in our nature to kill." Sable replied. *"We must eat; neither of us will survive if you continue as we have eating only berries or rodents. We are and will always be*

hunters."

"Alright, I will concede we will hunt, but not deer. A nice plump rabbit will give you the race you so crave."

The wolf was not happy but settled in to be on alert for fresh game.

An owl hooted also looking for sustenance. The night was alive with sights, sounds and wonderful smells. The brush cracked as something stumbled in the dark, much too large to be that of a rabbit. The wolf stopped, nose scenting the air. Blood—rich, fresh. Her adrenaline pumped; the need to give chase struggling with Savannah's plea for caution. They crouched low, prowling an inch at a time, stopping to listen. A soft grunting, a heavy sigh, the leaves crunching as something hit the ground.

The wolf circled knowing what she would see when she peered through the heavy brush. She could smell the deer as it lay on the ground, an arrow protruding from its belly. Blood pooled on the pine needles beneath the large buck. Puffs of white formed from the nostrils as the great stag struggled for each breath.

"He's injured, an easy kill. I want to chase my game." The wolf was a fierce huntress and missed the excitement of the hunt.

"You wanted fresh meat; this is the best of both worlds He is dying. We can end his suffering." Savannah had no taste for killing but knew that the wolf was right, they needed to eat. Jilly always provided her with the same food that she ate, sitting the plate in the

bedroom so Savannah had only to gobble down the food. But Jimmy would only fill a dog dish full of Diamond dog food which both Savannah and Sable refused to eat. Even now her mouth watered in anticipation of the sweet meal that waited.

Coyotes yipped excitedly. The smell of the fresh blood bringing them closer. They didn't care that something else had caused the injury, they would eat whatever was available.

"We must decide; the scavengers will soon be upon us." Savannah pushed her will into the wolf. Sable accepted that she must concede this time. She crept though the bush, her eyes and nose scenting for danger.

The buck thrashed on the ground, trying without success to regain his feet. He could smell the predator. He bleated in fear. It was the adrenaline rush the wolf needed. With a burst of speed, she leaped across the remaining space and landed with a howl of victory onto the buck's back, her canines sinking deep into the jugular of the large animal.

The buck twisted and jerked trying desperately to break free, but even at full strength he would not have stood a chance against the massive wolf who even now was ripping and tearing at his neck.

Sable glorified in the fight of such a prize. *"Feel the strength of him. Even in death, his strength pours into us."* Rich blood flowed through her body, feeding her organs, muscles and tendons too long denied the protein it craved.

Savannah tried to fight the joy rippling through her body but the wolf was so high on the fresh kill that its will took over. She too relished in the taste of the warm blood, its coppery taste like a drug to an addict as the wolf gulped, eagerly letting herself go. She bit greedily into the tender under belly of the deer and gorged herself on the juicy treats available. It took no time at all for the wolf to devour the deer when the coyote's arrived all that would be left was scraps.

The wolf, satisfied that at last they were truly living as they were meant to, rolled in what was left of the bloody carcass.

Chapter 3

Jimmy still sat on the couch thinking about the dream when he heard the slap of the doggy door. He turned to look at her. "So you're ba...." He jumped to his feet. "What have you done? You murdering she-bitch." Here he was thinking to comfort her, sure that she was missing Jilly, but one look confirmed that while he had been sitting here worrying about her, she had been out killing. Her muzzle and fur were covered in blood.

Sable stopped and shrank back, her ass tight against the wall. She had been high from the recent kill but was now on alert for danger. She growled and bared her teeth, the hair on her back rising.

Jimmy stood perfectly still. Clearly he had frightened or royally pissed the wolf off, but it had been such a shock to see her covered in blood. He knew of course that she was a wolf hybrid but never suspected that she would hunt as the wild packs did; surely Jilly didn't allow such atrocities. As a matter of fact, Jilly seemed to spoil her with the same meals she ate. A practice he had not been following. She was a dog therefore she got fed the same food he fed the hounds.

"Easy girl," he spoke quietly. "I'm not going to hurt you."

The wolf's ears laid back tight against her head. Her teeth covered in blood were clear to see as she snarled and growled at him.

"Okay girl, I'll admit you are scaring the hell out of me. I'm dually impressed." He slowly sank back down onto the couch never taking his eyes from the beast "I'm just going to sit down here and let you do your thing. Maybe you want to go to Savannah's room. You like that, don't you girl?"

Still drunk on the high of the blood Savannah wasn't paying attention to what was happening around her. She was well sated, comfortable and willing to let her wolf see them safely home where she would sleep soundly on a full belly in her nice comfortable feather tick bed. Unease ticked at her. Something wasn't right; Sable was defensive, set to attack in a killing rage. What was happening? Where was the danger? She peered out from deep within the wolf's body. They were safe in their home. Nothing could hurt them here. She smelled fear, but it wasn't her fear. She looked at Jimmy sitting with his hands raised, white faced, sweaty, eyes enlarged. He was afraid of her.

"Back Off!" Savannah warned the wolf when she saw they were safe in their home. *"You will not attack him."*

"He threatens us!" Sable growled low in her throat.

"No, we are scaring the hell out of him. We are covered in blood. Back down." Savannah was strong once again, her body replenished. She pushed the wolf to the back, ashamed now that she had let her take over. The wolf was unpredictable and it was her duty to stay in charge. She had learned her lesson. Jimmy could have been killed. There was no excuse for allowing the wolf to take over.

Savannah whined and bowed her head. She slinked slowly to the bedroom and leapt gracefully up onto the white coverlet circled three times and lay down.

"Shiiiit, that was close." Jimmy let out the breath he'd been holding. "Damn," his palms were sweaty. Never had he been so scared. Now that the crisis had passed he wondered what the wolf had just killed. "Christ, I hope it wasn't one of Jilly's hounds." He hadn't heard any commotion from outside but wolves were sneaky bastards. He jumped from the couch and grabbed the flashlight off the end table by the front door. Grasping the knob on the door he yanked it open and ran out into the night. The hounds were tied in the rear of the house he shined the flashlight on each dog house and counted the yellow eyes that glowed back at him. He sighed in relief when he counted five pairs of eyes. Jilly's hounds were all safe which left the question what *had* her wolf-dog killed?

He walked slowly back to the house, opened the door and as an afterthought, he slid the plastic panel over the dog door so that

Sable could not leave the house without him opening the door. "At least I won't have to worry that you're out ravaging some farmer's cattle." he grumbled as he walked back to Savannah's bedroom. Sure enough the wolf lay sleeping on her side. He grimaced as he noticed the blood stains she was leaving on the white bedspread. "I suppose I'll have to give your fuzzy ass a bath tomorrow."

Savannah not yet asleep raised her head. *"Over my dead body."* she thought but the glare she gave would have sent fear through his body had he still been standing in the doorway.

Jimmy walked to the kitchen. He needed coffee in a big way. It had taken him a couple days to get use to the Keurig coffee pot which sat on the counter, a wedding gift Dylan and Jilly had received. He took a K-Cup Black Magic, placed it in the holder closed the lid and waited the five seconds it took to brew the black liquid. He took his cup and retraced his steps back to the couch to think more about his dream. Never before had he dreamt of the wolves tearing Becca apart. Dylan and Jilly had told him Becca moved on when Marcus left town. Would his best friend lie? And if so why?

He picked up his phone and flipped it open he couldn't call Dylan but maybe Marcus could answer some questions. He started to punch in the number. "Oh yeah, dick head, what are you gonna say? *Oh hey, Marcus. Remember a while back when we were rescuing Jilly's dog from a pack of wolves? Did you by chance turn into the big bad wolf and eat your ex girlfriend?* Shit." He closed the phone in frustration and threw it on the stand.

Savannah lay in the bed for hours listening to Jimmy move around in the kitchen and living room. The lights turned out and still she waited. Gentle snores soon reached her wolf's sensitive hearing. She smiled he was asleep, it was time. The wolf eased off the bed one padded foot at a time she made not a sound. Quietly she padded down the short hall her nails didn't click on the hardwood floors. Jimmy lay on the couch, one arm thrown across his forehead; the other dangling, almost touching the floor. Savannah felt a rush of excitement and fear as her decision was made. She turned and padded back to the bedroom.

No way was she going to suffer the humiliation of Jimmy giving her a bath and she knew with his stubborn determination that was exactly what would happen when tomorrow came around. Once inside her room, she stretched her wolf's body envisioning her long sable hair, pale skin, blue eyes. Her bones and tendons began to pop. It was painful and she gasped for breath; she had stayed in the wolf's body too long, At last she lay naked, free of blood, on the cool floor. Not very graceful, Jilly could shift on the run, but this was the price she paid for hiding so long. She eased up on her hands and knees and pushed up onto her feet. Her back muscles protested not being used to this position. She flexed her fingers and shook her arms and legs. The full length mirror on the wall caught her reflection.

"Oh man, Savannah, you look wicked." she whispered. Her body was too thin, her hip bones protruded, her hair was a wild mane flying around her face and ending at the middle of her back. She brushed her hands through it trying to tame the tangles. A pink satin robe hung on the back of the door. She walked on shaky legs over and took it off the hook and slipped it over her bare body. She hugged it tight to her and inhaled the smell of the detergent Jilly always used. It felt wonderful to be wrapped in its comfort.

"You should come back to me." Sable whispered. "I keep you safe."

"No, I have hidden behind you long enough; it is time for me to take over. But, my friend, we are one in the same and I still rely on you, but know this, even while in the wolf's body, I will now be in control. I thank you for taking over when I was broken and could not function, but your duty is now done and I must become strong enough to come back to the living." She glanced out the window, the pink glow of the sun rising told her that Jimmy would soon be waking but she wanted just a little more time in her body.

A picture on her dresser captured her gaze and she walked unsteadily over and picked it up. It was a picture of Jilly and Dylan on their wedding day. They looked so happy and Jilly had been so beautiful. "Oh sis…I really messed up." she whispered. "I should have been brave enough to stand up and be part of your wedding, please forgive me." Jilly had begged her to be a witness at her wedding to Dylan but she had not been ready. "I'm ready now though and can't wait to see you." She kissed her fingertip and pressed it against her sister's cheek smiling back at her from the photo.

The creak of a floor board alerted her that time had run out. Quickly she shifted back into wolf form, the pink house coat falling gracefully to the floor she leaped and landed on the bed.

Light was filtering in through the big bay window. Jimmy stretched, damn he was stiff. He swung his legs over the edge of the couch and sat up. It was morning, time to get the she-wolf and give her a bath. She probably had to go out as the dog door was still tightly closed. He got to his feet and walked down the short hall to Savannah's closed door. "That's strange. I don't remember closing the door." He twisted the knob and pushed it open. The she wolf raised her head and looked at him with her big blue eyes. He glanced around the room and noticed something pink lying on the floor. He walked over and picked it up it was some slinky sexy bit of a robe so fine that the material snagged on his callous-covered hands. "It's not bad enough you ruin Savannah's bed with blood stains, now you have to shred her clothes too? Where'd you get this anyway?" He looked about and saw the hook on the back of the door. That explained how the door was shut; the mutt must have jumped against it when she was tugging on the robe.

The wolf stared at him, her eyes haunted. How could he stay mad at her? She always looked so sad and in need of rescuing. "Come on girl let's get you cleaned up."

Sable stood up on the bed and stretched, her beautiful coat shiny and blood free.

He shook his head. "I don't know how you managed it, fur face. You must have been cleaning yourself all night, but I'm relieved because I wasn't looking forward to wrestling your fat ass around in the bath tub."

Savannah growled within the wolf's body... *"Oh no, he did not just say that I had a fat ass."* She jumped off the bed and haughtily walked passed Jimmy where he leaned against the door case.

Jimmy chuckled; he'd swear the wolf had understood every word he said. She looked so regal as she walked by. He followed her down the hall to where she sat at the front door. "Okay girl, I'll let you out. But let's not have a repeat performance of last night or I swear your pampered ass will spend the rest of the time we're together fastened on a leash. I guess I'm just lucky you didn't crap on the floor when you locked yourself in the bedroom."

Savannah had never been so insulted and she had a wicked thought. Instead of going out the door he held open, she squatted and relieved herself on his bare foot.

"Son of a Bitch!" Jimmy sore as he looked down at the

yellow puddle he now stood in.

Savannah gave a yip and ran out the door. She hadn't felt so alive in months! She giggled to herself as she ran across the open meadow. A good thing Jimmy couldn't read her mind as he would surely know that she was laughing at him.

Chapter 4

"Come on mutt." Jimmy opened the door of the bait shop. He still couldn't believe she had the audacity to pee on him.

Sable growled at him but held her head high as she loped through the door. She stepped behind the counter and sat down patiently beside Carrie.

Carrie reached down and patted her on the head. "Hey there, girl. I've missed you." She grabbed a piece of jerky out of the container. "Here you go"

Jimmy looked over the counter to see the wolf dog now curled on the fancy dog bed happily chewing on the treat. He glanced at the jerky container and shook his head. "At $25/lb don't you think a dog treat or raw hide bone would work just as well? That wolf eats better than I do."

Carrie looked at her brother and raised a delicate eyebrow. "Hi to you too bro. What's got your undies in a bunch?" She glanced from Jimmy's angry face to the wolf dog. "Jilly always gives her the jerky. You know, Jim, if you hate Sable so much, I'd be glad to take care of her."

"No way," Jimmy shook his head. "After what I saw last night there's no way I would trust her with you. She's dangerous."

Carrie laughed as Sable lifted her head and licked her fingertips. "Yeah right she's a real killer."

"I'm serious Carrie. She went out last night and when she came back she was covered in blood." He didn't tell her about the standoff he and the wolf had in the living room of Jilly's house. He wouldn't admit to his kid sister that he had almost wet himself over a damn dog.

"She was probably hungry. Are you following the instructions Jilly left?"

"Yeah right," Jimmy scuffed. "There's no way I'm cooking for two just to feed her like a queen. She gets the same food as the other animals."

Carrie reached across the desk and whapped hi beside the head. "Jimmy you ass, she won't eat that food. Haven't you noticed her dish is still full?" She squatted down next to Sable. "Poor girl, you were starving, weren't you?" She put her nose against the wolf's and looked into her sad eyes. "Don't worry sweetie, I'll fix you up. How about a burger?"

Jimmy watched his sister and the wolf. Could it be that simple? "If she's hungry enough, she'll eat the dog food." He hunched his shoulders, a little embarrassed that his kid sister was giving him hell.

Carrie got to her feet and reached into the cooler. "No she won't. She never has, never will. She eats what Jilly eats."

Could it be that simple? Did Jilly keep her wolf so well fed to curb her natural inclination to hunt? Was it his fault that she had gone out last night and killed? He was a piss poor care giver.

"Earth to Jimmy." Carrie nudged him in the shoulder."

"What?" he looked at her.

"I asked if you wanted a burger too." She held one up to him.

"Nah," he shook his head. "I'm not hungry." He walked around the front counter and squatted down next to the wolf. He felt guilty for the way he had been treating her so put his hand gently on her side. She was not responsible for the death of his dog years ago. "I'm sorry girl, I'll do better."

Savannah lifted her head and laid it on his knee.

Carrie watched her brother interact with the wolf. Jilly was right, Jimmy and Savannah would be good for each other. She of course knew all about Savannah and Jilly, someone had to be involved to keep the girls safe. That's why she had expected Savannah to stay with her and had in fact been a little hurt while Jilly was away. But Jilly had been adamant that Sable/Savannah stay with Jimmy and now she understood why. "Here you go, Hun," she handed Sable the burger which had been cooling on the counter. "Careful, it's still a little warm."

Savannah grasped the burger in her teeth she rose to her feet and headed to the back of the store.

"Where the heck is she going?" Jimmy shot to his feet and started after her.

Carrie reached out and grabbed his arm. "Just a minute." She crooked her finger at him and tilted her head. "Come here," she whispered. Quietly she walked to the end of an aisle.

Jimmy peered over his sister's slender shoulder. Sable sat as if human in the big brown recliner. Her burger lay on the arm of the chair and she was gazing intently out the huge windows that took up the whole back wall of the store. "What's she doing?"

Carrie turned. "She's just chilling, Jim. She'll spend hours sitting there watching while Jill works."

"Watching what?

"Be patient…jeez!" She pointed back to the window; a large flock of Canadian geese were just landing on the not yet frozen pond, their giant wings extended to the side flapping to slow themselves down, their webbed feet dropping like landing gear on an airplane as they hit the water.

"Look there." Three does came out of the woods to drink and then headed to the cobs of corn nailed to a wooden fence.

"Jill should know better than to bait the deer, she's going to get fined."

Carrie laughed. "She's not stupid, the ranger already stopped and talked to her. She told him and I quote," she put her fingers up like rabbit ears and bent them, "Now Bob, I know and you know that feeding the deer is illegal. That corn is for the squirrels." Carrie continued to giggle.

Jimmy smiled as he watched her. She even put her hands on her hips as Jilly tended to do.

"She even grabbed that poor man by the arm and drug him out by that tree. Can you see what that sign says?" Carrie asked.

"No."

"It says, 'Squirrels only'."

Jimmy began to chuckle, he knew what was coming.

Carrie nodded her head. "Yep, you guessed it. She said I'm sorry but the deer that come here must be illiterate. They look at the sign and eat my corn anyway."

Jimmy laughed loudly and struck his palm against his jean clad leg. "She's a fire cracker, isn't she? Dylan's going to have to stay on his toes."

"She's good for him and he loves her" She bumped his shoulder and headed back to the front of the store. "What about you? What are you going to do now that your best bud is an old married man?"

"He's married not dead, Carrie, and Jilly is cool. We're good." He looked at his sister; she'd worked in Jilly's store for a couple of years... maybe she could help him. "Hey Carrie, what do you know about Marcus Cooper?"

Surprised Carrie's whole body stiffened. *Oh brother if you only knew what I know about Marcus.* She stopped in her tracks to calm her racing heart. What did he want with Marcus? She drew in a deep breath to collect herself and turned around. Now to throw her big brother for a loop. She put her index finger on her chin and started tapping. "Marcus? Hmmm Marcus?" her eyes got big and her lips posed in an "o" expression. "Do you mean mister tall, dark and dangerous?" She gasped in excitement her eyes overly bright and waited for the reaction.

"Eww? God! Cut it out! That's just gross!" Jimmy shivered in horror.

"What?" she asked innocently.

"My kid sister should not be looking that way about any man."

"What way?" she raised her eyebrow.

"Like you just took a huge spoonful of a turtle Sunday you love so much with all that gooey chocolate and caramel garbage."

"I bet he does taste mighty fine." she whispered with just a hint of suggestiveness in her voice.

"He's way too old for you."

"You do realize big brother," she walked over and put her finger in the center of his chest, "that I will be leaving for college when Dylan and Jilly get back?"

"Well yeah but just because you're rushing off to school doesn't mean you need to be thinking about guys and especially not that guy."

"I thought you liked Marcus. The two of you use to go shoot pool and hang out."

"He's alright for me to hang with but not someone I want my sister to get hooked up with."

She raised her shoulders in a shrug. "It's a moot point. From what I heard, he left town, moved somewhere to take care of some wolves." She turned away and began to clean up the mess from the burgers.

"Why are you being so evasive?" She was acting weird and he wanted answers.

"I'm not, I'm working here." She used the rag to wash down the counter and the inside of the microwave. Jilly had told her things in strict confidence. She didn't want to break that trust.

"You haven't answered any questions?" Jimmy was frustrated, usually Carrie loved to gossip but for some reason she was not talking."

She looked at him. "You haven't asked any questions." She turned as the bell above the door rang. Never had she been so relieved to see a customer. "Got to go. See ya later."

Chapter 5

"Rise and shine, Princess, I have to go to work." Jimmy poked his head in the bedroom. "Breakfast is served." He couldn't believe he actually make a skillet big enough for two just to feed the she-wolf but hey, if it kept her from hunting, he was all for it.

"Here you go girl." He set the food on the floor using a plate instead of the dog dish. "Eat up and then outside you go."

Savannah sniffed the egg cheese mixture and took a delicate bite. It actually tasted wonderful. Jimmy had really changed since his talk with Carrie. He had been more caring, almost gentle. She gobbled the food because just after waking up, the need to go out and pee was more important than enjoying the food.

Jimmy slurped his coffee; he really needed it intravenously. "Jeez, I can't wait to move back home and get a decent night's sleep." He downed the coffee and put the cup under the spout and readied another k-cup. He didn't have time to drink it, but would take it to go.

The doggy door opened and closed as Sable came back in.

She walked over and licked Jimmy's fingers. His heart softened a little more. He squatted down and scratched between her ears. "What is it about you that gets to me? You have the most beautiful, soulful eyes."

Savannah melted, *he thinks I'm beautiful.*

Jimmy got to his feet and walked over to lock the dog door. "Okay fur face, I know Jilly usually takes you with her. But I have to work and you can't go so you're in for the day. Don't crap on the floor." He grabbed his keys, coffee and work bag off the counter and opened the door. "Behave yourself." He gave her a piercing look and closed the door.

Savannah heard the truck start and the gravel crunch as the vehicle left the driveway. She visualized herself standing in the kitchen and with little pain this time she shifted. She stretched her arms above her head and bent from side to side loosening her cramped muscles. "Fur face, don't crap on the floor." she mumbled and walked to the window. No sign of him. "You were off to such a good start, boyo, but those last remarks sealed your fate for today." Her heart had skipped a beat when he talked about her eyes, but then he just had to turn around and tell her not to crap on the floor. "Oooh, you are such an infuriating man!"

She stomped down the hallway, her bare feet slapping against the wood tapped out her anger. Something back and white on the floor in the bathroom caught her eye. "Oh this is perfect." She bent down and carefully picked up a pair of Al Pacino boxers by the waist band. "Tell me to stay out of trouble. You'll learn to pick up after yourself and not leave a mess." She got a pair of scissors out of the medicine cabinet and cut holes in the crotch of the underwear than dipped them in water.

"That'll teach you." She smiled as she carried them into her bedroom and laid them in the middle of her bed.

"Now, Savannah my girl, time to get dressed and go exploring." She walked to her closet and pulled out a brown floral skirt, then grabbed her salmon colored cashmere sweater. The clothes against her skin were unfamiliar yet it felt wonderful to once again be human. She slipped her feet into brown moccasin slippers and darted out the door. "Oh man I could really go for some coffee." Did she dare? Jimmy would be gone for hours yet; she'd watched how he operated the coffee machine and used a Styrofoam cup so that he wouldn't discover the used cup. Seeing the full garbage can she had another impish idea. "Don't crap on the floor indeed." She shook the garbage can upside down and spread the garbage throughout the kitchen and laid the can on its side. She'd be back long before Jimmy returned and be lying on the bed innocently with his underwear...

"Okay girl, buck up." she muttered to herself and opened the front door and stepped outside as a human for the first time in months. "Oh," she shielded her eyes against the sun's glare. She'd forgotten how bright it was to her human eyes. As a wolf the brightness didn't bother and lucky for her, even now the wolf regulated the temperature somewhat. She would still need a coat if it was real cold, but on days like today with the sun so nice, she was quite comfortable in the cool, crisp air.

The grass was no longer green as it was in late October and it had already dropped below freezing. But oh how beautiful the trees were with their changing colors. Fall was one of her favorite times of year with all the vibrant colors. By November it would no longer be as pretty as the leaves would fall from the trees heralding the arrival of winter.

"Hey guys," she greeted the hounds, stopping to give each of them a pat and scratch behind the ears. "I've missed you." As a wolf she couldn't go near the dogs as its instincts would have taken over and killed the pets. She would not have been strong enough to keep the emotions at bay. "I'll come see you again," she said as Cheyenne rolled over to have her belly rubbed. "I promise, but right now I need to explore while I still have my nerve."

She edged around the dog houses and into the forest. The walking trail that led through the woods would be a nice easy walk for her first time out. Squirrels stopped their search of nuts and chattered, warning of an intruder. She laughed at their antics as their fluffy tails waved in the breeze. "Aren't you the big brave guardians of the forest? I mean no harm, I'm just walking through." She was not worried about getting lost as she and Jilly had walked the trail many times when they picked apples. "I wonder if..," she took off running, her hair flying behind her and her tinkling laughter sending the grouse flying up in front of and around her. Pure joy radiated from her as she stopped. There it was and, oh my, there were still some apples. She bent down and picked one up from the ground and polished it on her sweater. She was almost giddy and could hardly wait to sink her teeth into it. The first bite was fantastic, she closed her eyes in pure bliss, the juice running down her chin as she swallowed that magnificent bite. She wiped at the juice and looked around; the area had not changed much although there were a few downed trees probably due to a storm. Something black lay at the roots of one of the trees and she tiptoed over to have a look already guessing what it was. Sure enough, curled up in a ball lay a small black bear most likely a yearling who's mama had chased it off. Cubs stayed with their mothers for a little over a year but when the second year came, the sows chased their yearling off so that they could mate. Last year at this time, he was safe and happy curled up with his mother and now he was all alone and had decided to den at the foot of the tree which was a very common occurrence. It was a misconception that many had that bears hibernated in caves and never woke all winter. Bears did in fact hibernate, but often got up periodically to relieve themselves. They were not overly active but if she startled it, the bear would in fact awaken. She turned and slowly, quietly walked away. Her apple finished, she threw the core beneath the trees, hoping the seeds would take root and in years to come, more trees would thrive in this special sanctuary.

A small creek trickled nearby and she headed for it, the sound almost musical. The forest brought her such peace. For months she had been so frightened, in shock after the attack by Marcus. She knew now that he really had meant no harm; that he did in fact believe that she was meant to be his mate and so had acted accordingly, which by pack law had been his right. She felt sorry for him carrying the worry and defense of the pack on his shoulders. She wished him the best, but did not know how she would react if she were to ever see him again; was even unsure how she would react if any man touched her. She was beginning to care for Jimmy. As the wolf, it was easier to allow him to touch her. As a woman, those feelings would be completely different. He was so funny, even caring with Dylan and Jilly but he didn't share those same feelings with her, of course to give him credit he didn't really know Savannah the woman only Sable the she-wolf. And that was a major problem, his feelings towards wolves. Jimmy hated them with a passion. How would he react when he found out that she could in fact turn into one of his most hated enemies? There was no way to keep it a secret if she became involved with him. Dylan had come to accept Jilly and her wolf but it had taken time and he didn't share Jimmy's hatred.

The spring-fed creek flowed freely and was crystal clear. She knelt down, cupped her hands scooping the water and drank thirstily. The brush cracked across the way and she looked up to see a doe standing on the opposite bank. Savannah didn't move and barely breathed as the deer came down the slope and lapped at the water. The doe drank her fill then twirled around and leaped up the bank, her white flag of a tail saluting as she ran. Never would she change the life that she led; where else on earth could she enjoy the wildlife and the many joys she got to see and experience daily?

* * * *

Jimmy turned into the driveway; he couldn't believe he'd forgotten his wallet. Hopefully there would be enough time to grab some lunch before hurrying back to work. He jumped out of the truck and left the engine idling. He'd just run in, grab his wallet and run back out. He turned the knob and opened the house door. "Holy Shit!" There was garbage everywhere. "Sable!" He bellowed as he went to Savannah's room. "You spiteful…. Where are you?" There was nothing on the bed except some black gob. He walked over and picked it up. "Well son of a bitch; she even ate my underwear, they're still wet from where the little bitch chewed them. Bad dog, come here right now!" He so didn't have time for this shit. He raced down the hall to the living room. "That's just great!" He'd left the front door open and she must have bolted. "Unfuckin believable." He went through the door and slammed it shut; if he didn't see her he'd have to leave her out and hope she came back on her own. He couldn't afford to be late for work. "Sable!" He called once again.

Savannah was in the clearing when she heard Jimmy's voice. "Oh no, what's he doing home so soon?" Her first instinct was to turn and run. She ran fast into the edge of the trees before shifting. Still high from her wonderful morning, she bounded merrily through the tall weeds of the meadow to greet Jimmy and share her joy.

Jimmy could have sworn he saw a glimpse of orange out by the trees but when he blinked, all he saw was the she-devil running straight at him and she wasn't stopping.

"Ooof!" She hit him square in the chest and knocked him flat on his ass. He lay flat out on the ground. He wanted to bang his head in frustration. "What in the hell's gotten in to you? You mangy mutt!"

Savannah was so excited she pounced on his chest and licked his face and neck. She was happy to hear him laugh. Not once all day had she felt frightened or depressed.

"Cut it out." He chuckled and pushed against her trying to avoid the doggy slobber.

What was that he had in his hand? *Oh Oh, his boxers.* Savannah, in her play, had forgotten about the mess she made in the house. She sat back on her haunches.

Jimmy, free from the weight of the wolf, was finally able to sit up. He wiped his face with the damp boxers which only pissed him off. He threw them to the ground as he got to his feet. "Get in the truck; obviously you cannot be trusted alone in the house, which is probably why Jilly took you everywhere." He started walking back to the truck. "Come on," he slapped his pant leg. "I'll drop you at the bait store with Carrie."

Savannah loped along beside him she felt a tad guilty over the mess she'd made but her temper had gotten the best of her. She licked his hand before jumping up onto the seat of the truck.

"Kissing on me isn't going to change my mood, wolf." He hopped in the truck, slammed the door and reversed out of the driveway.

Carrie looked up as the bell above the door chimed. "Hey guys." she looked at the clock on the wall surprised to see her brother and Savannah. "Shouldn't you be at work?"

"Yeah, listen Carrie; can you watch her while I go back to work? I left her alone for four hours and she destroyed the house and ate my favorite pair of boxers."

Carrie put her hand over mouth and tried without success to muffle her giggles. "What?"

Jimmy shook his head. "Never mind. Can you watch her or not? Otherwise she'll have to stay in my truck and if she eats my upholstery I'm going to have a wolf hide hanging on my wall."

Savannah growled.

Carrie moved between them and put her hand on Savannah's head. "Of course she can stay here, I'd love the company. She's welcome anytime."

"Okay thanks I gotta go. I'm gonna be late."

"Ah Jimmy, What were you doing home so early anyway?"

"Oh, damnit!" he grabbed his back pocket. "I forgot my wallet but it doesn't matter now. I don't have time to eat anyway."

Carrie ran behind the counter. "Hold on," she threw something in a bag, grabbed a soda from the cooler. "I just heated the burger for myself so it's still warm, there's a bag of chips and a soda. Get going; we'll see you after work."

"Thanks sis," Jimmy leaned down and kissed her cheek. The bell rang as he headed for his truck.

"Oh girl, what were...?" The bell rang as someone came in and Carrie turned away.

Savannah walked to the bathroom. She needed some girl time. Once there she closed the door and shifted. "Now what am I going to do? I'm bare assed naked." Way to think things through.

Carrie looked down the aisle expecting to see Savannah sitting in her chair and was surprised but not alarmed when she didn't see her.

"I need some minnows."

"Okay," She walked over to the reservoir and dipped water

into a minnow bucket. "How many do you need?"

"Two dozen should be fine."

Carrie scooped out a generous amount of the small fish and carried them to the front counter. "Will that be all?"

"Yep, that'll do it?"

"That'll be four dollars." She accepted the money and gave him his change. "Thanks Blake and good luck fishing."

"Thanks, Carrie. Catch you next time."

Savannah waited until she heard the bell on the door and Carrie wishing the customer farewell before she called.

"Carrie."

"Ahh!" Carrie screamed in surprise and whirled around. She had not seen anyone else come in the store. A little nervous, she cautiously walked to the back of the store. "Hello, may I help you?"

"Carrie, it's me, in the ladies room."

"Well I'll be, you scared the spit out of me. Come on out here."

"Umm, you wouldn't happen to have any extra clothes around here would you?' Savannah opened the door a little wider.

"Of course, Sweetie. They're not fancy, just jogging pants and a tee. I was going to go running after work but let me run get them." She ran out to her car so excited that she was shaking. Could Savannah finally be ready to face the world? Hallelujah! She grabbed her backpack out of the car and ran back inside. "Here you go, hon. Don't think my shoes will fit you though."

"That's okay; I don't mind being bare foot. Thanks, Carrie." She took the black jogging pants and gray tee and closed the door. Wearing pants felt foreign to her she preferred skirts and the tee was a little tight across the chest but it was much better than the alternative. She opened the door and stepped out.

Carrie wrapped her arms around Savannah. "Oh, Sweetie, I'm so happy to see you! Wait until Jilly finds out your back."

Savannah returned the embrace then stepped back. "No, you can't tell her... not yet."

"But why? She'll be thrilled."

"I'm still broken, Carrie. I'm trying to get better but it's going to take time. Let's not call her. If she knew, she'd coming racing home. She coddled me and took care of me long enough; she deserves to be happy. Let her enjoy her honeymoon."

"Okay, but promise me you won't go into hiding again."

Savannah didn't answer but headed to her favorite chair. She sat down and curled her feet underneath her.

Carrie followed and sat down directly across from her on the end table. She reached out and grasped Savannah's hands. "Savannah? Promise me."

~~~Savannah shook her head. "I can't do that. Not yet anyway. You know, I went out for the first time today." She smiled. "I had such fun, not once did I feel scared or threatened. But still,

I'm not whole."

"Sweetie, you're not broken. With what you went through, you have every right to feel as you do. You were terribly wronged by someone you trusted and had faith in. You should have pressed charges against that bastard and had him strung up by his balls."

Savannah laughed and squeezed Carrie's hand. "Oh how I've missed you. It's alright, I forgive Marcus."

"But..." Carrie started to protest.

"I forgive him. I know no one would understand and many would be in outrage saying I let him get away with rape. But things are different within the pack. Marcus believes in the old ways and the laws dictated that he had every right to claim me."

"It's not right." Carrie argued. "Jilly told me how you had petitioned the pack, he should have honored your word."

"Maybe, but Marcus has redeemed himself to me. He helped in my rescue and because of me, the whole pack is scattered and at risk. He carries a huge burden on his shoulders. I feel sorry for him. His life will always be controlled by what he feels is his responsibility to them."

"He sure is a handsome devil, I give him that." Carrie smiled.

"Be very careful, Carrie. Yes he is handsome... handsome and dangerous." Savannah cautioned.

"But you just said you forgave him."

"Yes and I do, but Marcus is a champion of the underdog. The wolves are fighting a battle, they are now legally hunted. Marcus will die defending them."

"He's gone you know?"

Savannah nodded. "And that's probably a good thing because, although I forgive him, I'm not sure how I will react if I see him again."

"You're a lot stronger than you give yourself credit for. At any rate, he left right after the whole Becca disaster so no worries." Carrie cocked her head questioningly. "I never did get that whole story." She was shamelessly searching for information.

"And you never will." Carrie knew and accepted the fact that she and Jilly shifted into wolf form. They had needed someone they could trust in case anything had ever happened to one or both of them. Carrie was invaluable and had proven herself time and again, but she did not know the harsher side of being a member of the pack.

Carrie nodded. "Fair enough. So tell me what made today the day and you have got to tell me about destroying the house. What's up with that?"

Savannah sighed and leaned back in the chair. "The wolf was getting too strong and taking over. It's my fault, I was so weak and out of touch for so long that I just didn't care, but the other night her need to kill was so empowering and I felt her power and enjoyed it.

That's never happened before and what was once my safe haven went against everything I believe in. It was time to take my life back."

"And the house?" Carrie asked.

Savannah chuckled embarrassed over the whole incident. "I'll tell you all about it. But do you think maybe you can close up early and take me home?"

"Sure hon. Are you okay?" Carrie jumped to her feet.

Savannah rose from the chair. "I'm fine honest, I just feel bad for the mess I made and would like to go clean it up so your brother won't have to deal with it when he gets home."

Carrie was disappointed. "So you really are staying in your wolf form?"

"Yes, for now, but I'd like to send some of my things with you and maybe I can come here while Jimmy's at work? We can work on me becoming more me again."

"Absolutely! Let me get the lights and we'll lock this puppy up." Carrie hugged her and started going through the routine of closing up shop. She couldn't wait to hear the whole story about what had happened that morning. Jimmy's nose had been bent out of shape, not much rattled her big brother. She grinned; things were going to get mighty interesting.

Chapter 6

Carrie turned the knob and walked into Jilly's house. She whistled in appreciation. "Sweetie, you really outdid yourself."

Savannah stepped in behind her. "Oh wow, I'd forgotten what a mess I made." She giggled and covered her mouth. "Let me go change out of your clothes so I don't get them all stinky. I won't be long."

"No problem, I'll just run out to the shed and get a scoop shovel." Carrie laughed.

"It's not that bad." Savannah's tinkling laughter floated down the hall.

The laughter alone made cleaning up the mess worthwhile. Jilly once said that she didn't know if Savannah would ever come out of hiding; she'd tried sympathy, pleading and bullying her, but nothing had worked. Obviously, she was working it out on her own. Carrie went to the closet and got the broom and dust pan. She overturned the dumped garbage can and began sweeping.

Savannah came out of the bedroom carrying a back pack?

"Here you go Carrie, thanks for the use of the clothes. I'd offer to wash them but don't want Jimmy to get suspicious." She noticed the garbage was picked up. "You didn't have to do that, I made the mess I should have cleaned it up."

Carrie took the bag. "No biggie, it only took a sec, now tell me what possessed you to tear into the garbage and did you really chew up my brother's underwear?"

Savannah laughed aloud. "No, of course not" she giggled. "But I sure made him think I did." She walked over to the freezer and took some steaks out. "You'll stay for supper?"

"Sure, it could be entertaining." she smirked. "So why did you do it?" Carrie was curious. Savannah had been very timid since the attack which made Carrie wonder why she was now so mischievous. "Weren't you afraid that Jimmy would spank the wolf for its destructive behavior?"

Savannah swung around. "No, never. Carrie, you should be ashamed of yourself. Jimmy would never be mean."

Carrie grinned. Oh how the mighty had fallen. "I know that, I just wasn't sure if you knew it. You care for my big brother." she teased.

"It's too soon for that," Savannah denied as she busied herself with putting the steaks in the microwave on defrost. "But I do trust him."

Carrie pulled out a kitchen chair and sat down. "Given the

way he feels about wolves, I would think you would feel the opposite."

Savannah too sat down in a chair across the table from Carrie. "Maybe and there lies the problem; if Jimmy ever finds out what I am, he would never let himself care for me."

Carrie sat up straighter in her chair. "You have a plan." She leaned forward excitedly. "Tell me."

"I want him to get to know me as the person, but as the wolf too. Maybe he can then accept that we are one in the same."

Carrie looked around at the now cleaned house. "Well, I would say the wolf in you better work on your people skills."

Savannah sighed. "I know but your brother can be infuriating sometimes with his greater than thou attitude."

"Oh honey, you're not telling me anything new. So what did big brother do this morning that set you off?" She'd been dying of curiosity and she wasn't stopping until she found out what had truly happened that morning.

"Really, he's been better since you set him straight the other day. He's finally been feeding me real food instead of that god awful dog food he was trying to make me eat. Eeew!" She made a terrible face.

"I'm sorry about that. If I would have known sooner, I would have stepped in." Carrie apologized. "I just assumed he was following the explicit list that Jilly left. So he was doing okay, what happened this morning?"

"He came in the bedroom and woke me at an ungodly early hour insisting that I eat, shit and behave myself." Savannah huffed."

"What?" Carrie was horrified.

"Well not in those exact words, but with no coffee, it's the way I took it. Then he proceeded to lock me in because I couldn't be trusted out in the world without him to keep me on a short leash, and I quote."

"I see," Carrie tried to control her grin. "It's a wonder you didn't tear him limb from limb instead of just his poor boxers." They both laughed.

"Now about this plan of yours, you definitely have to watch your temper. It's going to take a lot to get him to change his mind about wolves. He's hated them for a lot of years."

Savannah sighed. "I know and I don't have much time. Dylan and Jilly will be home in two weeks."

Carrie shook her head. "No, I don't think so; she called last night and asked if I minded if they extended their vacation. Seems the two of them are having a ball on their honeymoon and want to stay an extra two weeks so in reality you have about a month to win over my brother."

Savannah was nervous. "I don't know if I'll know what to do with him when the time comes."

"Oh trust me, you gain Jimmy's trust, loyalty and love and

he'll take care of the rest."

Savannah got up and removed the steaks from the microwave. She had preheated the oven so stuck the steaks in on broil. She washed off the potatoes and stuck them in the microwave. "Do you want a vegetable to go with the steaks? I think I saw a bag of lettuce in the fridge." She opened the refrigerator and saw a can of Diet Coke. "Oh my gosh!" she grabbed it and popped the top. The popping fizz on her tongue was wonderful, the taste decadent. She gulped the whole can."

Carrie got up. "I'll get the lettuce." she laughed as she swept past Savannah. "Good huh?" She eyed the now empty can.

"Oh, you have no idea! I'd forgotten the things I've missed, Diet Coke being on the top of that list. I wonder if your brother will notice the missing can. Maybe I shouldn't have."

"Don't worry about it; enjoy yourself. He'll just assume that I helped myself." She grabbed the bag of lettuce, French and ranch dressing plus cottage cheese and set them on the table. "Let's see what else." She went back and grabbed butter, sour cream and shredded cheese. "That should do it."

"You forgot steak sauce," Savannah looked at the table full of food looked like they were feeding Cox's army.

"No I didn't, but he will want ketchup." Carrie opened the fridge and located the bottle of Heinz ketchup. "Jimmy hates steak sauce but the man does love his ketchup."

Savannah cocked her head. "He's coming." She reached over and hugged Carrie, "I've had so much fun today. Thank you."

Carrie returned the hug. "You're welcome, now scoot."

Savannah dropped the empty coke can in the trash and darted down the hall.

"Hey Carrie," Jimmy came in and shut the door behind him. "Why did you want to meet here? I could have stopped on my way home and picked her up." He looked around at the spotless kitchen and the table set for supper. "And you certainly didn't have to clean up the mess and fix supper."

Carrie waved him off. "It was slow at the shop, so no problem and I'm going to eat with you so it killed two birds with one stone."

"Well Thanks; I wasn't looking forward to cleaning the house. Where is the demon dog?"

Carrie pointed down the hall. "Back in Savannah's room. Be nice; she probably misses Jilly." Carrie followed him down the hall.

The wolf raised her head when they entered the room.

"What's this?" Jimmy reached down and picked up a green sage skirt and cream colored sweater.

"Oh I left those there." Carrie came forward and grabbed them out of his hand.

"I don't remember ever seeing you wear a skirt and sweater."

"I was trying on some of Savannah's clothes; I'll just hang

them back up." She put the sweater and skirt on the same hanger and hung them in the closet.

"You shouldn't be messing with Savannah's things, Carrie." Jimmy was uncomfortable even touching her things without her aware of it.

Carrie laughed. "Relax, Savannah and I are friends. She wouldn't mind a bit, just like she could freely go through my closet. It's a girl thing, big brother." She patted his chest. "Come on, supper is ready."

"Come on, Sweetie," she called to the wolf. "Let's eat."

Savannah followed the two out into the kitchen glad that Carrie had followed Jimmy to her room. She would have to be more careful when she shifted to hide the clothes.

Carrie grabbed the extra plate on the table and placed a steak on it. She took a knife and cut the T-bone into small pieces. The bone she took off the plate and put it in a plastic bag. "Here you go, Sweetie," she set the plate on the floor for the wolf. She hated to see Savannah eating off the floor. As if reading her mind Savannah licked her hand before digging into the juicy dinner.

"Here you go, Carrie," Jimmy carried their plates filled with the steaks and baked potatoes to the table. "Eat up while it's still hot." He cut into his steak and dipped it in ketchup. It practically melted in his mouth. "Oh man, that's good. Thanks again, Carrie. This was really nice."

"You're welcome and it is nice, you and I don't spend enough time together. I'm going to miss you when I leave."

"I'll miss you too, kiddo, we'll have to spend more time together before you head out. Plus, we can talk on the phone and before you know it you'll be home for the holidays." He took another bite of his steak. He waved his fork in the air, "What do you know about Savannah?"

Carrie stopped in the process of cutting her steak and put down her knife. She glanced at Savannah who also stopped eating and was looking back at her. "What do you mean? You know Savannah as well as I do."

"Yeah, I know. But don't you find it weird that she just up and disappeared. Jilly refuses to talk about it. I mean she didn't even come to her sister's wedding. Don't you find that strange?"

Carrie looked over at Savannah whose head now hung in shame. "Savannah went through something really terrible. She was hurt badly and needed time to heal."

"What do you mean by that? Was it a car accident or what?" Surely he would have heard had that been the case.

"No, she was in a bad relationship and I'm not able to tell you any more than that." She picked up her fork and started to smash her baked potato hoping that her brother would let the subject drop.

"I still think it's weird that she hasn't been home and that no one has heard from her."

"I don't know where you got that idea. I talked to Savannah today and given what she told me, I'm sure we'll be seeing her fairly soon." She looked at Savannah; the wolf was now on her feet ready to flee.

"You did? Well why didn't you say so? Did you call Jilly? Last I knew Jilly thought she was unreachable." He reached to grab his phone intending to call Jilly right away."

Carrie grabbed the phone from his hand. "No, she asked me not to call and I'm going to honor her request." She put his phone on the table. "And so are you."

Jimmy reached for his phone. "Did she give you a reason?"

"Yes, she said Jilly deserved to be happy and she didn't want her bothered; there would be time for them to catch up when she returned."

Jimmy took his hand off his phone and nodded. "But she was okay, right? She didn't need anything? Because all she would have to do is call. I'd be there."

Carrie reached across the table and gave his hand a squeeze, never had she been so proud of her big brother. "She's good."

Savannah had tears in her eyes. She walked over and laid her head on Jimmy's lap.

He looked down as he felt a brush on his pant leg. "What's the matter girl?" He reached down and massaged behind her ears.

"That's strange; she's never done that before. She's usually very standoffish and spends most of her time alone in Savannah's room."

"She likes you. You do know that she has nothing to do with what happened years ago. I understand why you feel the way you do about the wolves."

Jimmy stopped her. "You didn't see what I did, Carrie; you can never understand. When I got back to where I heard Jaeger screaming in pain, all that was left of him was his tracking collar and my name collar. They had picked his bones clean." He continued to rub the wolf's head. But, you're right. She's not one of them. She's a hybrid and has always been around humans. I'm trying to work through it." He smiled, "I'm a work in progress."

"A diamond in the rough." She got to her feet and started to clear the dishes.

"Leave them. I'll clean up; you've done enough." He patted Sable one last time. "Watch out, pooch." He got to his feet and took the dish from Carrie's hand. "Thanks for all your help today. I really appreciate it. I don't know what I would have done with Sable."

"You're welcome and about Sable, I was thinking why don't you just drop her off on your way to work? She can spend the day with me." She picked up the ketchup and cottage cheese.

Jimmy took them away from her and carried them to the fridge. "Are you sure? I don't want to put you out."

"Absolutely, she's used to being there, she's comfortable and you won't have a repeat performance of today."

"That sounds great. Now you better get going so you'll be home before dark."

"Okay." She kissed his cheek and grabbed her back pack from the chair by the door. "See ya tomorrow."

Jimmy followed her to the door. "Drive safe and watch for deer."

She waved to let him know she had heard him and hopped into her little Geo Tracker.

Jimmy shook his head as he watched her pull out of the driveway. He swished she'd get rid of that little POS vehicle but she loved it and even fondly named it Bertha. He closed the door. "Well wolf, we've had a good night. Let's clean up this kitchen and then we'll see what's on the boob tube. He loaded the dishwasher, added the soap and turned it on. He turned around and was surprised to see Sable sitting on the couch as if waiting for him.

He sat on the opposite end of the couch and picked up the remote. "What'll it be girl? Should we find a movie?" He began flipping through the satellite channels. There wasn't much to choose from so finally settled on an old favorite. "GI Jane, always good when you can watch somebody blow shit up." He kicked his shoes off and put his feet up on the coffee table.

Savannah sat completely still staring intently at the TV. She watched as Demi Moore shaved her own head and how she fought beside the man and eventually gained their respect. It was peaceful sitting here listening to Jimmy snore. She smiled to herself; the poor guy hadn't even made it to see Moore's character reach seal training camp before his eyes had closed. He really wasn't sleeping well on the couch. She didn't understand why he wouldn't sleep in Jilly's bed and the one time he'd tried to crawl in hers she'd growled and chased him out of the room. Of course, in her defense, he had tried to make her leave her own bed which was her sanctuary.

She got down off the couch. He didn't move; he really was exhausted. Gently she nudged his hand where it hung over the arm of the couch. She repeated the nudge and added a whine continuing until he began to move.

"What is it girl? Do you have to go out?" He put his feet on the floor and rubbed his hands over his face.

Savannah whined again.

"Okay, give me a sec, I'm not awake yet." He got to his feet and went to the door. No wonder she was whining to go out, he had forgotten to lift the slider on the dog door. He opened the door, "Come on girl, you can go out now."

Savannah waited in the edge of the hall and whined.

"Come on," when she wouldn't go out the house door he reached down and slid out the slider for the doggy door.

Savannah walked to him and whined again than turned and started down the hall.

"Crazy dog, wake me up and then you go to bed." Jimmy shut off the lights, closed and locked the doors. The credits were rolling on the movie so evidently he'd been sleeping for a couple hours. He clicked the remote off.

Savannah came back up the hall and whined again. Man, what was it going to take to get the man to follow her? She came the rest of the way, opened her mouth and latched on to his hand and whined. She again turned and walked down the hall.

"You want me to come with you girl?" Jimmy finally got the hint.

Uh duh! Savannah was frustrated, try to do something nice for someone and what do you have to do paint them a picture? She yipped and went to the doorway and turned back to be sure he was finally understanding.

The glow from the moon shining through the window at the end of the house offered just enough light for Jimmy to see where he was going. "What do you want, wolf?"

Savannah yipped softly just inside the doorway and leaped onto the bed.

Jimmy reached in and turned the light switch on which operated the lamp that sat on the stand beside the bed. The wolf lay on the far side of the bed stretched out on her side much like a person with her head nestled in the pillow. Strangely enough usually when she lay on the bed she lay sprawled sideways as if protecting the bed. Now she almost looked like she was giving him permission to share the bed.

"Are you missing Jilly, girl?" Cautiously he approached the bed and carefully sat down. She didn't growl so he reached out to touch her. She nuzzled his hand and whined. "She'll be home soon." He scooted further onto the bed and swung his legs up on the spread. Man this bed was so comfortable. The feather tick seemed to wrap right around his aching muscles.

Savannah scooted closer to him.

Jimmy froze as the wolf crawled across the bed. He wasn't scared, more worried because she had made it clear on more than one occasion that he wasn't welcome in this room.

She scooted still closer until at last she was able to lay her head across his midsection.

Jimmy was shocked, but raised his right arm slowly and laid his and along her neck. He heard her sigh as if in pleasure. "We'll be alright girl." He reached over and shut off the lamp sending the room into darkness.

Savannah lay still barely daring to draw a breath. She'd done it, she'd found the courage to crawl across the bed and now she lay in a man's arms and didn't feel terrified. She was so happy she could jump up and dance a jig. But she was so comfortable and content that she too closed her eyes and went to sleep.

Chapter 7

It was daylight. Jimmy tried to move but something heavy was holding him down. He looked and, sure enough, Sable was still stretched across his stomach. He raised his left arm and glanced at his watch. "Holy Hell, 8 o'clock!" He pushed at the wolf and jumped out of bed. "Come on girl, get a move on! No time for breakfast this morning." He ran out of the bedroom and into the bathroom, slamming the door behind him. He never slept until 8, not even on his days off. He jumped into a cold shower to wake himself up.

Savannah stretched on the bed and sighed she heard the shower running; what she wouldn't give for a shower but by the sounds of it, she was even going have to wait until they got to the bait shop before she could eat. Luckily Jilly had a shower there also. She climbed out of bed and went out the doggy door.

Jimmy took the shortest shower possible. "Sable, let's go." He was jumping on one leg trying to put his socks on and calling for Sable. He hoped like hell she didn't get in her head to take off this morning. He put his truck keys in his mouth, grabbed his boots and wallet and yanked open the door. Sable sat on the porch. "Good girl," he mumbled around his keys. He headed for his truck and yanked open the door. Sable still sat on the porch. "Come on, I'm going to be late."

Oh my gosh, he is gorgeous. He stood there in the sunlight with water droplets glistening off of his bare chest. She sighed; the man had forgotten his shirt.

"Come on, wolf! I don't have time for your games."

Savannah gave a woof and ran into the house. She dug through Jimmy's duffle bag that lay on the floor and gripped a blue tee in her teeth before dashing back out the door.

"God damn it!" Jimmy swore as the wolf ran back into the house. He threw his wallet and boots in the truck and started after her. They met on the step, the wolf with his shirt in her mouth. "Well, crap! Jeez, it was going to be a rotten day. Thanks, pooch." He patted her on the head and grabbed the shirt. "Let's get rolling." She raced him to the truck.

Carrie was waiting outside when they arrived.

Jimmy stopped the truck and hopped out still in his stocking feet. "I'm late. Thanks. See you tonight."

Savannah jumped out behind him and went and sat down next to Carrie.

"We'll be fine, have a good day." Carrie waved and watched

as he took off out of the graveled parking lot. Throwing stones and dust in his hurry to make it to work on time.

"Alright girl, should we go in and you can tell me what you all were doing that you were late?"

Savannah gave her a killer look, spun around, nose in the air and walked haughtily to the door.

Carrie ran ahead and opened the door for her, she was looking forward to spending the day with Savannah and had worried that Jimmy had changed his mind when they hadn't arrived.

Savannah went into the bathroom and shut the door. She saw her back pack sitting on a shelf and quickly shifted. It was second nature now and didn't hurt at all. She reached in and turned the handles to turn the shower on; steam soon filled the small bathroom. She stepped in and sighed as the warm water cascaded over her naked body. Suave shampoo sat on the shelf and she poured a generous amount into her hand and rubbed it into her long mane of hair. She massaged her scalp almost viciously and it felt wonderful. She rinsed and was tempted to wash it again but decided against it and used the raspberry scented body wash to cleanse the rest of her body.

Carrie was waiting with a cup of coffee when she stepped out of the bathroom ten minutes later. Her hair was still wet but was freshly combed and she felt wonderful. "Oh, bless you." She took a healthy gulp of the coffee and rolled the sweet flavor around on her tongue. The rich, sweet taste of the vanilla creamer Carrie had added was just right. "This is fantastic. I needed this."

"I figured as much," she raised her hand from the top of Savannah's head down to her moccasin encased feet. "You look fantastic, that color is perfect for you."

"Thanks," the olive green free flowing ankle length dress was one of her favorites. "Do you have time to sit with me or are you busy?"

Carrie chuckled. "You tell me, you're the closest thing to a boss I have right now."

"Well then, I say you deserve a break. Do we still get fresh sweet rolls delivered?"

"Yep, as a matter of fact they arrived while you were in the shower. Still like the custard filled ones?" she asked as she headed toward the front counter.

"Oh, most definitely." Savannah followed.

"Go grab a seat I'll grab my coffee and the rolls and join you."

"Are you kidding? I need a refill too and I want to help." It felt good to be participating. "I see we upgraded" She pointed to the Keurig that sat on the counter where the old Bunn coffee pot use to sit.

"Yeah, most people like a variety of tastes in their coffee we were throwing away more coffee than we were selling so economically this works out better." Carrie selected an English Toffee brew for herself and inserted it into the machine. In no time at all, its rich aroma filled the room.

"That smells divine." Savannah stepped forward to see all the different selections. She always used French Vanilla Creamer as well as Splenda in her coffee but was willing to try different flavors to go with them.

"Are you wanting leaded or unleaded?" Carrie asked.

"Oh, definitely leaded."

"I suggest Donut Shoppe; it's got a strong, bold yet smooth flavor."

"Sounds good to me."

They got their coffees and donuts and headed back to the big windows.

Carrie couldn't wait any longer. "So how did it go last night? What did you guys do?"

"It was good. Jimmy washed dishes and then we watched a movie or should I say I watched a movie. Jimmy fell asleep."

"Oh busted!" She laughed and slapped her hand on her thigh. "The big bad boy bombed out."

"He hasn't been sleeping well." Savannah defended. "I don't know why he's been trying to sleep on the couch instead of Jilly's bed. It makes no sense to me, but he absolutely doesn't go into her room."

"Oh that's easy," Carrie replied. "He doesn't want to lay where Dylan and Jilly have had sex."

"What?" Savannah choked on her coffee.

Carrie nodded. "Oh I know my brother and something like that would drive him nuts. That's Dylan and Jilly's personal space and there is no way he would violate it."

"Well, that's sweet in a weird kind of way." Savannah was thoughtful and gazed out the window. A bobcat was stalking a rabbit that was taking advantage of the corn lying on the ground that the squirrels had wasted in their haste to eat.

"What I don't understand is why he didn't sleep in your bed? After all he thinks you're a wolf."

Savannah glanced at her. "Because, until last night, anytime he approached my bed I growled and snarled at him until he left my room."

Carrie scooted forward, quickly to catch on to what Savannah wasn't saying. "And what was different about last night?"

Savannah nibbled on her bottom lip. She leaned forward and set her coffee cup on the table. She looked at Carrie. "Last night was absolutely wonderful."

Carrie gasped. "You didn't? I mean you came here in wolf form." She was confused and felt kind of sick.

"Oh jeez, of course not! That's would be bestiality. I'm a wolf for crying out loud and that even grosses me out! Get your mind out of the gutter." She pushed against Carrie's shoulder. "We slept, but god Carrie I've never felt so complete and utterly content." She wiped tears from her eyes. "He actually put his arm around me and I slept all night with my head lying on his chest."

"Oh, sweetie," Carrie gripped her hand, "that's wonderful."

"You just can't know what a relief that is to me. I was worried that I wouldn't be able to let a man touch me."

"I hate to put a damper on your excitement, hon." Savannah was so happy she really hated to bring it up, but she was her friend and better they discuss the possible problems and work them out than to have someone get hurt. Jimmy was her brother and she had to protect his heart.

"What? Is Jimmy seeing someone?" That would be horrible. Why hadn't Carrie said something yesterday when they'd discussed her plan?

"No of course not. You said you felt safe and were able to lay in his arms without fear. Was that you or was that your wolf?"

Savannah sighed in relief. She understood Carrie's concern. "It was me or us, Carrie. We're one and the same."

"I don't understand, you yourself told me how she was taking over."

"Yes, that part of me is more dominant and I sometimes tend to think of it as a separate entity, but there is no me without the wolf and vise versa." She held her hands out palms up. "I'm the total package good and bad. I've just decided to claim the part of me that is more human."

Carrie smiled. "And I am so glad that you did."

Savannah shared a small smile with her friend and squeezed her hands tightly. "It was a very near thing; I was very close to choosing the animal part of me. I felt such self-pity for so long that I was almost too late to make the choice."

"I had no idea that you could have been trapped in wolf form" Carrie was both shocked and relieved.

"The longer we stay in our animal form the more difficult it is for us to return. Our animals are powerful and they have a survival instinct, they will do whatever it takes to insure that survival. I'm honored to call you my friend. Jilly and I are so very blessed to have you in our lives. You know more than anyone else about us and our shifting abilities except maybe now Dylan." Jilly had most certainly shared every aspect of their lives with Dylan before committing to their marriage. "But there's a lot that you don't know and would probably find revolting."

Carrie shook her head. "I'm the one that is honored. You girls have trusted me with a secret that could destroy you and many others. There is nothing that you could do or say that would make me love you less." She got to her feet and picked up their empty mugs. "And for the record, if things work out for you and my brother, you'll both be the luckiest people in the world."

Savannah got up and hugged her. "Thank you so much. Now put me to work. I need to start earning my keep. I've been idle long enough."

"Are you sure about that? I mean, Savannah, you're actually my boss. You own part of the shop."

"No, I'm not, I'm your friend. Jilly is your boss. I've contributed nothing to this place. Jilly was kind enough to include me but I haven't earned the right to claim any ownership. Give me something, anything to do."

"Okay, the minnow tanks need to be cleaned. I noticed some floaters when I came in this morning." She looked at Savannah slyly and winked.

"Consider it done." Savannah headed to small room situated off the main floor of the bait shop."

"Savannah, wait." Carrie called and chased after her. "I was just kidding. You watch the counter and I'll take care of the minnow tanks."

"Nope, I'm no better than anyone else and you know what? I'm looking forward to getting my hands dirty. You just go on and do what you need to do; I'm having fun. Don't worry, really I'm good." She grabbed up the small net and began to pick out the dead minnow that were floating on the top of the water.

Carrie shook her head and went up front. "Stubborn." Man, if Jilly found out that she had her sister skimming smelly fish, she'd have a fit. Then again, she probably wouldn't say anything. Jilly wasn't afraid to get her hands dirty either and didn't ask anything of her employee that she herself wouldn't do. As a matter of fact, Jilly many times took on the nastiest jobs so someone else didn't have to deal with them. She couldn't ask for better employers or friends.

* * * *

Jimmy walked into the shop. "Hey, Carrie," but there was no one at the front desk. He heard laughter coming from the back. Carrie must have had some friend drop by it; sounded like they were having a good time. He'd just grab Sable and get out of her hair. She'd been great about taking care of the wolf dog but she deserved to have some fun. Carrie worked hard and would soon be going to school; all of her time would then be divided between working to afford her tuition and studying to keep up with her classes.

"Hey Sable, come on girl you ready to go home." he called and stopped dead in his tracks.

Savannah was startled at the sound of Jimmy's voice and jumped up from the chair. She and Carrie had been having such fun that they complete lost track of time and now she was caught.

Carrie looked at Savannah's panicked face. "Hey Jimmy. How was your day?"

"Ah, fine," he walked to the girls. "Savannah it's great to see you." He wrapped his arms around her. "I heard you were hurt. Are you okay?"

"Jimmy!" Carrie scolded.

"It's alright," Savannah whispered to her and returned Jimmy's hug. She closed her eyes and leaned her head on his shoulder, enjoying his strength for just a few minutes. "I'm good Jimmy and you?"

He released her and stepped back. "I'm good. Sit, sit... you should be resting." He grabbed her arm and eased her back into the chair.

She smiled. "I'm fine, really. No injuries, at least not physically." She shrugged her shoulders. "It's been a rough couple of months but I'm doing much better."

She was absolutely beautiful. Her long red-brown hair rested mid back and curled loosely around her face. And her eyes, she had always had the most mesmerizing blue eyes of any woman he had ever known. "I'm glad to hear that. I'm sure Jilly will be thrilled to have you back."

"I hear that you're taking care of Jilly's wolf. How's that going?" She looked over his shoulder to see Carrie raise her eyebrow.

Jimmy nodded, "Yeah, but now that you're back, you'll be wanting to stay at the house I'm sure so I'll head back to my place."

"No," Savannah was shaking her head rapidly. "I won't."

Jimmy was startled by her reaction.

Carrie could see her becoming upset and stepped forward. "What she means is that she has some things she has to take care of before she can commit to such a big responsibility." She moved her head slightly to Jimmy.

He could see Carrie glaring daggers at him. Damn women were hard to understand but apparently she wanted him to shut the hell up and agree with whatever they were saying. "Okaay. Where is Sable anyway?"

Carrie pointed out the big window. "She was right there just a bit a go I'm sure she hasn't gone far." It wasn't a total lie; Savannah had gone out earlier and refilled the feeders with corn.

"Shoot. I hope she didn't wander off too far. I need to stop by my place and feed the dogs and Jilly's haven't been done yet either. I stopped at Dylan's before I got here. I wish they would have moved the dogs to one place or the other before they left."

"Don't worry about yours, I'll take care of them when I get home."

"That'd be great sis. This running three different households is starting to get old. Savannah, are you sure that I'm not keeping you from your home?"

"I'm positive, Jimmy, but thank you for asking."

"Okay I'm going to go out and call for her," he opened the door and walked toward the pond. It really was nice out here. Jilly had it fixed up with different feeders for each of the animals. "Sable!" He called.

"Holy cow! That was a shock!" Savannah had her hand on her chest.

Carrie laughed. "You should have seen the look on your face. You looked like a deer caught in headlights."

Savannah joined in her laughter. "Well, did you see his face? I don't know who was more surprised, him or us." She watched Jimmy walk across the grounds. "I better get going. Thanks for today I had such fun. I'll see you tomorrow."

"You're welcome." Carrie too looked out the window. "Hurry up; he's coming."

"Oh shoot! He didn't look for very long.

"That's my brother. He's very impatient. Hurry."

"Cripes!" Savannah took off running for the front door. She shifted on the run.

Carrie giggled as she ran behind her and scooped up the dress and moccasins. Savannah shifted so effortlessly now. She opened the door just as Jimmy came around the corner of the building.

Sable ran up to him and put her paws on his chest to lick his face.

"Hey there girl, you ready to go home?" He patted her and pushed her off of him. "I'm just going to run in and tell Savannah goodbye."

"You can't." Carrie backed against the door with her hands behind her back so that he couldn't see what she held there. "She left while you were out looking for Sable."

"Well damn, I wasn't gone that long. I hurried to get back so I could talk to her a little longer." He was disappointed; he'd always had a thing for Savannah but always felt she was out of his league.

"She said that she had some things to take care of. I'm sure you'll see her soon."

Jimmy nodded. "Yeah, you're probably right. I'm just glad that she's home where she belongs. I feel bad that she felt like she had to leave her home when she had problems."

"You have a good night bro and I'll see you two tomorrow."

He opened his truck door, "thanks you too."

Chapter 8

Blood curdling screams. Marcus leaping in the air and landing on his feet as a big black wolf. Jilly running, shifting shape into the body of a sleek gray and white wolf, her clothes lay scattered on the forest floor behind her. More screams as wolves attacked and ripped the flesh from Becca.

Jimmy gasped for breath and sat up in bed. He shivered, his body chilled from the sweat covering him. The nightmares were coming more frequently.

Savannah whined and cocked her head to the side. Jimmy's restless sleep had woke her. She wondered what dreams were disturbing his slumber.

"I'm sorry girl." He patted her head. "Do wolves dream? Do you have nightmares about the night we rescued you?"

So that was it. He was reliving the night at the Haven. The night Becca had planned to murder her in the hope that Marcus's would than claim Becca as his mate. She rolled her eyes sympathetically at him and nudged his arm. She nudged him again and whined.

Jimmy raised his arm and put it across her back. He had to find answers. The dream was so vivid but always basically the same only a few more details revealed each time. "Go back to sleep, wolf. I should be good for the rest of the short night. God willing, I won't dream anymore."

Savannah lay quietly until she heard his breathing change become deeper. She knew he had dozed off. She slid out from under his arm and got out of the bed. She shifted and stood over him and watched as he changed position, his arm sprawled out to his side. "Oh, Jimmy! I'm so sorry." she whispered. She didn't know that he had witnessed the carnage that had taken place that night. She had run across the clearing when the wolf pack split and knocked him to the ground. He had been knocked unconscious and when he awoke, didn't remember anything. Obviously it was all coming back to him now. She picked up the throw on the end of the bed and wrapped it around her naked body before crawling back in beside him. She knew she was taking a terrible chance but she needed to be close to him. She snuggled in tight against his body and laid her head on his shoulder. She kissed his cheek and waited. She wouldn't sleep, could not afford to be caught in this form. But just for this brief time, she wanted to feel like a woman protecting her man even if only from his dreams.

* * * *

"He has nightmares."

"What are you talking about?" They were sitting in the back having their morning coffee and sweet rolls. Carrie got up to refill their cups but stopped and turned around at Savannah's words.

"Jimmy he has nightmares every single night" And each night after he drifted back to sleep she crawled in bed and lay beside him. It was getting harder and harder to keep her secret from him. She was not sleeping now either and worried that some night she would drift off and he would wake before she had shifted back to wolf form.

Carrie came back and sat their empty mugs on the table. "Do you know what's causing the nightmares?"

Savannah nodded. "He saw something that night. You know, when they rescued me." She twisted her hands together. "I didn't know, neither did Jilly or Dylan but he's remembering now."

"Was Marcus involved? I wonder if that's why he was asking about him."

Savannah shot to her feet. "Oh God, he's asking about Marcus?" She started to pace. "He's going to figure it out, Carrie. I'm running out of time. He's going to put two and two together and come up with my four furry feet." She dropped in the chair and put her hands over her face.

"Calm down, you don't know that. You're jumping to conclusions."

"No I'm not, your brother's not stupid and if he saw what I think he did, he's going to figure out what I am."

She looked so devastated. "Then we're going to have to up your game plan. It's time for Savannah and Jimmy to go out on a date."

"How are we going to manage that? I can't be in two places at one time."

"You just leave that up to me." She patted Savannah's hand. "Come on. You get to clean the bathrooms today."

Savannah laughed. "I think you're enjoying the boss thing just a little too much. Lead on, old wise one."

He heard them laughing as soon as he walked through the door and smiled. Savannah had been to the store a couple different times when he had stopped by to pick up Sable but had disappeared soon after his arrival. He was determined today that he would get to spend more time with her.

"There you are," Carrie turned at the sound of the bell. "I was just volunteering you."

"Carrie, no really..." Savannah argued just as they'd rehearsed.

"Volunteered me for what?" He was curious when he saw the blush on Savannah's cheeks. Again he was struck dumb by her beauty.

"Savannah wants to go see that new Thor movie. She was going to drive to Medford by herself but I told her you'd be more than happy to take her."

Jimmy could have kissed his sister. "Of course I will. Did you want to go tonight? We could even grab some dinner first, if you would like?"

"Jimmy you really don't have to. I don't want you to feel obligated." Savannah really was embarrassed. They were tricking him and putting him in a position where he couldn't say no.

"I don't feel obligated. It's Friday night. I don't have to work tomorrow and truth be known, I'm getting sick of sitting home all the time with only a wolf for company." *Sorry Sable but she's a hell of a lot more attractive than your furry ass.*

Savannah didn't know if she should be insulted or grateful. "Well, if you're sure, then I'd be happy to have dinner and a movie." She smiled.

"Great, let me go home and get Sable settled. That'll give me a chance to do the chores and grab a quick shower and change my clothes. Where should I pick you u?" He looked around anxiously for Sable. He was in a hurry to get going before Savannah changed her mind.

"Why don't you leave Sable with me? I'll watch her the whole night and drop her by in the morning?"

"Carrie are you sure? I mean she'll be fine for a couple hours at the house. She's gotten much better." He would miss the wolf; he'd gotten used to having her warm body curled up next to him at night. He didn't know what he was going to do when Dylan and Jilly returned and he had to give her up. Maybe he'd get a dog of his own.

"Absolutely! That way Savannah can just go with you now. She probably wants a change of clothes too and that's where her closet is." She was a genius; she knew she'd just sealed the deal. Jimmy was practically drooling with the thought of spending time with Savannah. She wished she hadn't made the promise to Savannah to not tell Jilly—as far as Jilly knew, Savannah was still in wolf form. Being best friends with both sisters was sometimes extremely challenging but it sure as hell wasn't boring.

"Well, yeah, put that way it makes perfect sense." He turned to Savannah. "Is that okay with you?"

"That would be great. Carrie's right; my wardrobe is kind of limited. I'd love the chance to dig through my closet. Plus, I miss the dogs and will enjoy seeing them."

"Alright then, let me just explain to Sable." He looked up sheepishly at the two girls. "I know you probably think that's stupid, but I don't want her to think I just left her. I really think she understand me."

Savannah shook her head. "Not stupid at all. I think it's

sweet and you're right. I'm sure she understands every word that you speak."

"She's out running around someplace; go ahead she'll be fine. We're good buddies. I promise I'll bring her around in the morning." Carrie didn't think her brother was going to have a problem with the whole Sable/Savannah dilemma... he seemed to think highly of both.

"You know, Jimmy, we don't have to go to the movies. I'm just happy to connect with you again." They were in the truck on their way to the house.

"I don't mind really. Although, to be honest, I have no idea what this Thor movie is about." He turned on to Short Road. They would be at the house in a matter of minutes.

Savannah laughed. "Me neither."

He stopped the truck and shifted it into park before turning to look at her. "You're kidding? Then why did Carrie say you wanted to see it?"

"Your sister is a good friend. She thinks it's time for me to start dating again and unfortunately for you you're the poor sucker she picked." She plucked nervously at her sweater.

Jimmy reached over and covered her hands. "It's not unfortunate at all. I'm sorry you've had a rough time of it. I hope you know that you could have come to me and I would have done all that I could to help you."

Savannah looked at him. She had tears in her eyes but didn't try to hide them. "I couldn't. I was too hurt and embarrassed."

"If not me, surely you could have gone to Jilly. You should not have had to leave your home." He ran his thumb back and forth across her hand in a caress trying to soother her. He hated seeing her tears.

"The pain was too close. I needed to heal and find myself.

"And have you healed?" He held his breath waiting for answer.

She shook her head. "Not totally. It's going to take time and patience," she smiled. "But I am on the mend."

He nodded and smiled back. "That's good," he turned the truck off and opened the door. "And Savannah?"

She stopped with one foot out the door and turned to him. "Yes?"

"Just so you know, I'm a very patient man." He waited, not moving.

"I'm counting on that Jimmy." she whispered as she got out and shut the door.

He was grinning like an idiot. She had just given him the green light. "Yes, it's about damn time!" he whispered. He'd been waiting forever for this woman to notice him and would do whatever it took to win her heart because she had owned his for years.

Savannah stopped half way up the steps to the house.

"Jimmy?" She turned. He was just rounding the hood of the truck. "Do you have your heart set on going out?"

"No, why? Is there something else you want to do? My plans for tonight were just a frozen pizza and a movie."

"I can do better than that. I'd love to just stay here and cook us dinner. That is, if you don't mind." She was rushing things, but time was running out she didn't have a choice. She cared for Jimmy, but had to be sure of his feelings. Her heart couldn't take being broken and, mentally, she didn't know if she would survive having him turn her away.

"A night alone with a beautiful woman? I would be crazy to turn that down. Sounds great to me." He wouldn't have to share her attention with a hunky god at the movie theatre or a crowd of people in a restaurant.

"Great! Any preferences on supper?" She hoped he didn't want anything to extravagant; she was a little rusty in her culinary skills.

"Honey, you could feed me big bologna sandwiches and as long as I had you sitting across the table from me, I would be a happy man."

"Oh, Jimmy, where have you been all my life?" he was going to make her cry. No one had ever spoken such sweet words to her before.

"Right here darling," *Just waiting for you to notice me.* And he prayed to god that his dreams of a life with her would finally be fulfilled.

"Okay, I'll start some supper while you do the chores."

* * * *

"This is really good." Jimmy scooped another fork full of the creamy noodles with peas into his mouth. He grabbed another slice of bread and smothered it with butter.

"It's just tuna casserole. There really wasn't time to take anything out to thaw." She set her fork down, she was too nervous to eat. "Jimmy, why didn't you ever ask me out? I mean we've been friends for years. We went to school together. Do you not find me attractive?" She put her hands over her face, what the heck was she doing. "Forget I said anything. God, I'm so embarrassed."

He just about choked on his bread which was now stuck to the roof of his mouth. He reached for the glass of milk sitting in front of him and took a healthy drink. *Wow, when this girl decided to get her gumption back she jumped right in with both feet.* "Truth is, Savannah, you intimidate the hell out of me."

"What?" She dropped her hands. "Why?"

"Look at you. You're the most beautiful woman I've ever seen. Even when we were kids you were like this porcelain doll that I was too afraid to touch. You just seemed destined for bigger and better things." He pulled at the neck of his flannel shirt. "Look at me; I'm just a good old country boy. I'll never be anything else and I'm not ashamed of that. I love where I live and what I do. But, I'm a logger. In a month I'll be ass deep in snow and won't be able to work again until spring. I can never offer any more than what I have right now."

She was insulted and hurt. "Did I ever give you the impression that I thought I was better than you?" She didn't know if she wanted to scream or cry. He thought she was an uppity bitch.

"No, of course not, I'm saying it all wrong. Never were you mean or stuck up, I'm just saying to me, I felt like... Oh hell, Savannah, I look into your beautiful blue eyes and I just get lost, it's always been that way. I'm surprised you didn't notice how I followed you around. I've been pestering Jilly for months for any news about you."

"For the record, Jimmy, I would have said yes, had you asked." She fiddled with her utensils on the table, twirling them around so she didn't look at him.

"What about now Savannah? At the risk of sounding corny, if I asked now would you be my girl?"

"I'm different now than I was years ago, I come with a lot of baggage. Are you sure you want to get involved? I'm telling you, Jimmy, I have a lot of intimacy problems. I don't know if..."

"Whoa," he held up his hand. H could tell she was really

uncomfortable with whatever she was going to say. He wanted her with a burning passion but he had heard the rumors of her attack and put the pieces together and knew without her saying anything that she had been abused sexually. He winked at her hoping to lighten the mood. "What kind of a guy do you think I am? I'm talking about holding hands on long walks, sweet kisses in the moonlight or lying together on the couch spooning and cuddling. Anything more can wait until you're ready."

She got up and walked around the table and put her hand on his shoulder. "You deserve so much more than what I can give you right now."

He pulled her down onto his lap. "You let me worry about what I deserve. I've waited years for you, girl, and not for sex. If I wanted sex, I could go anywhere and get it. I want you. I don't care how much baggage comes with you. We'll work through it. I want friendship and companionship. We have that and we'll build from there."

Savannah cupped his face in her hands and leaned her forehead against his. "Are you sure? You've got to be completely sure. Don't break my heart, Jimmy. It's still in pieces and I don't know if I can put it back together again."

"Darlin', I'll keep your heart safe, you have my word. Just trust me." He leaned forward and gave her a soft kiss on the lips. He didn't deepen it, there was no need. This one sweet, butterfly soft kiss meant more to him than any deep tongue tangling kiss he had ever given or received in his life.

The kiss happened so fast she didn't have time to be frightened. It was nice, soft, not hard and bruising. "I do trust you, but your words will be tested and I only pray that you remember what you promised when the time comes."

He tilted his head back and stared into her eyes. She was worried. What could be so awful that she was sure he would run? He already knew about the attack on her, surely she knew that he wouldn't hold that against her. "Do you want to talk about it? Maybe if you get it all out there now, you won't have to worry."

"No, it's too soon. I want to enjoy the time we have together getting to know one another again. I don't want to take the chance of it all going up in smoke before we've had a chance." She laid her head on his shoulder and wrapped her arms around his neck.

He returned her hug with his arms around her waist. She felt good in his arms and he closed his eyes and just savored the feel of her body against his.

Chapter 9

Jimmy drove the truck smoothly. One hand on the wheel the other caressing the wolf's head as she peered over the seat and rested it on his shoulder.

"You guys seem to be getting along better." Carrie smiled from where she sat on the passenger seat.

Savannah gave him a lick from the bottom of his jaw line up to his hair line between his eye and ear.

He chuckled. "Yeah, things are great."

"And how are things going with Savannah? You guys are spending a lot of time together." She glanced back at the wolf and saw her do an eye roll and snuggle her face up against Jimmy's neck.

"Things are going great there too. By the way, thanks for bringing Sable home the other morning. It must have been early."

Carrie was surprised because she hadn't dropped Sable off. "Why do you say that?"

"Well, because I dropped Savannah at the bait shop after

dinner and it was too late to come get Sable, I didn't want to wake you. But when I woke Saturday morning, she was snuggled up tight against me." He reached up and scratched between the wolf's ears. "You like sleeping tight up against me, don't you girl? I don't know how Jilly and Dylan are going to feel about that. It was probably a bad habit to start." He chuckled. He could imagine Dylan's reaction if the wolf wanted to sleep in the same bed as him and his new bride.

"Oh yeah, I got up early Saturday morning and decided to go for a run so we parked at the shop and I just dropped her off. The lights were out but I watched her go through the doggy door before I finished my run."

"I wish you wouldn't do that."

"What?"

"Run in the dark, it's not safe." The girl had no common sense.

Carrie laughed. "Jimmy I'm not afraid of the dark. There's nothing there in the dark that's not there in the daylight. Besides, it's so peaceful running at night. I enjoy it."

"Well, I don't like it. Make sure you carry your cell phone. What if you fell and broke a leg or something? And don't be running at night when you go off to school. There are scarier things in the cities than running into a bear out here on the roads."

"Yes, dad," she laughed. "Where are we going?" She was

tired of the lecture and they had been driving for hours. "I hope I'm dressed okay. You didn't even give a hint as to where we were going. I was shocked when you called. You never ask me to go anywhere. You're usually off doing manly things with Dylan."

"You're fine. It's a surprise. I wish Savannah could have come with us but she said she had plans today." He grinned. He couldn't wait to see the look on Carrie's face. "I wanted to spend time with you before you leave."

Carrie reached over and put her hand on his arm. "Thanks, that means a lot."

He glanced at her but then quickly looked back at the road. He was unfamiliar with the area and didn't want them to end up in an accident. "I'm proud of you, sis. I only wish mom and dad were still around to see you going off to college. They would be proud too."

She choked back tears and nodded. "Me too, I miss them, especially in times like now. Mom would be so excited, bustling around to make sure everything was just right."

"And dad telling her to settle down." He laughed. He slowed the truck and turned on an unnamed dirt road. He stopped at a gate with a high fence and rolled down the window to push the button. "It's me," he said into the intercom. The gates slid open and he drove through. The deep ruts and holes made driving at a fast speed impossible. "Shit." He swore as he hit a deep rut that rocked the truck.

"Ah, Jimmy? It's nice spending time with you, but if you brought me out here to look for new hunting grounds, I'm really not going to be happy with you There are a ton of things I could be doing. I haven't even started packing yet." It was a pretty drive; the trees were growing over the road which wasn't much more than a cow path. Heavy with brightly colored leaves, the branches scraped the top of the truck.

"Just wait. Jeez you're impatient!" Why in the world would someone want to live way back in this godforsaken hole? Although with the huge job he'd undertaken, it was probably the best possible place. They rounded a corner and a small cabin came into view. Jimmy smiled and stopped the truck.

"Sweet Mary Mother of God." Carrie whispered. He was more handsome than she remembered. His long black hair fell well below his shoulders. Shoulders and a chest that stretched the tee he wore way beyond the stretching point. And man oh man, nobody should look that good in worn jeans with holes in the thighs. Coupled with his cowboy boots he was every girl's fantasy of a bad boy. She looked at Savannah and then at Jimmy horrified for herself and for Savannah. "What have you done?

Jimmy couldn't understand her reaction. "Surprise! What's the matter with you? I thought you'd get a kick out of seeing Marcus. Aren't you the one that called him Tall Dark and

Dangerous?"

She looked at Savannah who was now cowering in the back seat. "Look at me! I asked you if I was dressed okay."

"You are. He looked at her blue jeans and sweat shirt." He was totally confused. His sister looked pissed and the wolf looked scared shitless. "What's wrong with you two?"

"Oh, man, you don't have a clue." She yanked the rubber band out of her ponytail and fluffed up her hair. "No woman wants to meet a man who looks like that," she pointed to where Marcus stood in the yard, "looking like this." She pointed to herself. "It's bad enough I'm wearing a beat up sweatshirt and jeans but Christ, I don't even have a face on." That'll teach her for not carrying a purse. Most women would have mascara or lip gloss in their purses but oh no not her...she hated carrying the damn things.

Jimmy shook his head. He would never understand how a woman's mind worked. "You look fine. Let's go he's probably wondering what the hell is going on." He opened the truck and got out. "Come on, Sable." The wolf didn't move but cowered in the back seat. "It's alright girl come on out." he coaxed. She growled low in her throat and backed further into the seat. "Fine stay in there." He slammed the door shut, a little pissed. He'd planned this day thinking to have a good time with Carrie and letting the wolf run in a different environment and this was how they paid him. He wished he would have left both their asses at home.

Carrie turned around in her seat. "I'm so sorry, Savannah. I didn't have a clue that this is where he was bringing us." She wasn't sure if the wolf even heard her, she looked like she was in shock. "I'm going to get out now and maybe I can divert their attention. You don't have to get out, you just stay in the truck. If Jimmy gives me any grief, as much as I love my brother, I'll knock him on his ass." Although, to be fair, he didn't have a clue so really couldn't be blamed, but dang it she was surprised too. "Okay girl, here goes. Just stay here and don't worry, I'll take care of it." She opened the truck door and got out.

"Hey Jimmy, how are you?" Marcus held out his hand.

"I'm good." Jimmy returned the hand shake. "You know my sister, Carrie."

Marcus nodded. "Hey there, sprout." He nodded his head at the young woman that had always been so nice to him at the bait shop even when he knew she had been warned against him. He'd taken to calling her sprout just to get a rise out of her.

"I've told you before my name is Carrie." Tall Dark and Handsome, but yet oh so infuriating. He knew that she hated being called Sprout but did it anyway.

"Where's Sable? Couldn't you get her to come out either?" Jimmy started back to the truck.

"Leave her alone, Jimmy. She doesn't want to get out." Carrie grabbed his arm.

Marcus looked between the siblings. "Maybe I can help." He knew of course that Savannah was in the truck. He could smell her. *"Little one?"* He sent the question telepathically but got no response.

"No," Carrie stepped between Marcus and the truck as he made a move to go to Savannah.

"Carrie! What the hell's gotten into you? Let the man pass."

They stood face to face. Marcus with his back to the other man "Please, let me try." he whispered. Carrie was one of the few people that knew about him and Savannah. Jilly had talked openly in front of the girl. He had to give the Sprout credit, she stood her ground, not afraid of the big bad wolf. "I won't hurt her. You have my word."

"You better not, wolf, or I'll be hanging your ass on my dorm wall." she threatened as she stepped to the side.

Marcus grinned. Yep, she was full of piss and vinegar. He liked her. *"Savannah, little one, I'm coming to the truck."* He opened the door. My God, she was shivering uncontrollably and backed tightly into the corner of the back seat.

"I'm frightened of you. Marcus. Even though I know you won't hurt me, I cannot shake this uncontrollable fear." The fear was overpowering. She forgave him; why could she not overcome the fear?

"Oh little one," he fell to his knees beside the open back

door of the pickup. *"Please believe that I truly thought I was doing right by you and the pack. I want only what is best for everyone. The pack is so scattered I'm afraid that I have failed on all counts."*

Savannah looked at the tears trailing down Marcus's cheeks. He didn't even try to hide his sorrow. *"I know that, truly I do, and I forgive you. I know you're not a monster. We were friends for many years and I understand what you are trying to achieve but, Marcus, you cannot shoulder this alone and I am not the woman to help you carry this burden."*

Marcus turned and got to his feet at the sound of gravel crunching beneath booted feet. He hurriedly wiped the tears from his cheeks. *"I know that now and I think that you have chosen."*

"Any luck? I don't know what's gotten in to her. We've been getting along great. Well after the first week anyway. That was a nightmare." Jimmy said as he approached the truck and peered in at the wolf.

Marcus looked from Jimmy to the wolf. "Why what happened the first week?" He was curios as Jimmy's face had turned red.

"She was a giant pain in my ass is what happened. She pissed on me, ripped up garbage and chewed up my underwear and that was just the first two days."

Marcus roared with laughter. *"Little sister, what have you been up to?"*

Savannah huffed indignantly and rose to her feet. *"He said I had a fat ass."* She pushed her way through both men and leaped to the ground. She walked over to Jimmy and sat next to his feet.

He reached down and touched the top of her head. "Since then we've gotten along really well and she spends her nights curled up next to me in bed. Except for the nights that Savannah and I have dates, then she spends the night at Carrie's."

Marcus stopped. "You've seen Savannah?" Thank God, he had worried that she would stay in wolf form too long. The longer in the form, the more powerful the wolf became and he was worried that in her fragile condition, she would not be able to find her way.

"Yeah, she got back a week ago, I was hoping she'd come with us today but she had other plans."

"You've chosen well, Savannah. He's a good man. Trust him."

"I do trust him but I don't know how to tell him about me. He's had this blind hatred for all wolves for years. I couldn't stand being rejected."

"Carrie and Dylan both know and have accepted us for what we are. Trust in your man enough to let him know the truth." Marcus turned to Jimmy a big grin on his face still tickled over the mischief Savannah had created. "Man, let me clue you in on a she-wolf. Never, and I do mean never, piss them off because though they do not hold a grudge, they will get even."

"You know, I think you're right. I believe that she understands me. I never would have believed it, but each time I said or did something mean to her she would retaliate in one way or another." He ruffled behind her ears as she leaned into his jean clad leg.

Marcus nodded. "She's very intelligent. Now tell me, what brings you way down here? You said on the phone you needed my help with something."

"Carrie, why don't you take Sable and go for a walk? I need to talk to Marcus."

"Stay close to the cabin. The pack is close by and they won't take kindly to strangers in their territory." Marcus wasn't happy with the pack's attitude. They wanted to run wild and right now at the sanctuary he had a mix of true wild wolves and hybrids like himself. They were unpredictable.

Savannah knew right away what was on Jimmy's mind. She had to warn Marcus. *"He has dreams about what took place at the Haven that night."*

Marcus never changed is facial expression he didn't want to give anything away. *"Does he know?"*

"About me, no, but he saw you and Jilly change. He also saw what the pack did to Becca. He's not sure anymore if it was a dream or reality."

Marcus gave the equivalent of a nod. *"I'll take care of it."*

"I have great feelings for this man, Marcus. I don't want to lie to him."

"I'll only answer any questions he asks directly and only about me."

"Thank you."

Carrie was pissed. She could tell Marcus and Savannah were talking telepathically she'd seen Savannah and Jilly often enough to know when it was happening. Their bodies grew still not even muscles twitching. She wanted to know what Jimmy was up to and instead he was sending her off into the woods. She didn't care if she made a good impression or not. She was sick and tired of being told what to do. "You bring me three hours away from home and then send me off into the unknown. If you didn't want me in on your conversation, why in the hell didn't you leave me at home?"

"Would you please just stop arguing with me? We'll only be a minute." He didn't understand why his sister was being so uncooperative, but she was pushing all his buttons.

"Fine. But if we get eaten, I'm gonna come back and haunt your ass." She stomped off and heard Sable's soft padded feet following. She rounded the end of the little cabin and saw how beautiful it was in the back yard. The maple trees were in full color; the leaves had not yet fallen this far south and the fall colors were at their peak. She sat down on the steps and Savannah joined her. "You know, he's going to ask Marcus about that night right?" Savannah laid her head in Carrie's lap. Carrie covered her head with her hand. "What do you think Marcus will tell him? Damn Savannah I wished you could shift, this is a one sided conversation and I could really use your input."

Savannah whined. She agreed; she wanted to shift so she could shift and rant and rave and pace worriedly. She couldn't very well shift and have Jimmy come around the corner and see her standing there stark naked; it wasn't as if she or Carrie had brought along extra clothing. And if she did shift and Jimmy saw her as Savannah, how would she explain how she had gotten there or why she was there? No, all she could do was wait patiently to see what the outcome of Jimmy and Marcus's discussion would be.

Marcus walked over and leaned up against the hood of Jimmy's truck. He crossed his arms and waited.

Jimmy looked behind him to make sure Carrie and the wolf was out of sight. He kicked at a rock that was sticking up in the driveway. "It's nice here Marcus, quiet, secluded."

"Cut to the chase, Jimmy. When you called, you said you needed to talk to me about something. What is it?" He never left his position by the truck. If Jimmy wanted any information, he was going to have to come right out and ask. There was no way in hell he was going to volunteer it.

"I don't know where to start and it's going to sound crazy as hell." Jimmy began. He ran his hands through his hair. "It sounds crazy to me but I just…I don't know, it seems real."

"What are you talking about?"

"Remember the night we played pool and got the call about Jilly's pet?"

Marcus nodded. "I remember we went and rescued her and while we were there you slipped and hit your head and were knocked unconscious."

"I'm having dreams, dreams that I can't explain about that night."

"Head injuries can be tricky that way. You more than likely had a concussion. We probably should have taken you to a hospital but you seemed fine." Good idea to make him think his brains were scrambled from a head injury.

"That's just it; I don't think I had a head injury. I got knocked down yes, from Sable, she saved me from a pack of wolves. At least, I think she did." He paced back and forth in front of Marcus. He sounded like an idiot; the guy was going to think he was nuts. "I saw you and Jilly and wolves and Becca."

"Well, yeah…Jilly and I were there as was Dylan. Remember, we all went there to get Sable?" Marcus was careful with his words. He didn't want to lie outright to the man but wasn't going to offer any extra information.

"They ate Becca; there was blood and screaming." He looked at Marcus for answers. "Why aren't you answering me?"

"You have yet to ask me any questions." Marcus didn't realize just how telling his words were.

"Oh my God! I've heard those exact words from my sister not two weeks ago about you." He stepped closer. "She knows doesn't she?"

Marcus stood up straight and uncrossed his arms. "Your sister is a very intelligent woman."

"You're not going to tell me anything, are you?" He was disappointed but not surprised.

"You too are intelligent, Jim, and I'm sure you've already reached some conclusion on your dreams. Go with your gut feelings. Now, how about a tour of my compound?" He walked to the rear of the house and didn't wait to see if the other man followed.

It was a wasted trip. He didn't know any more now than what he had before. He just wanted to get home and see Savannah. "Come on, Carrie. Let's head for home." He called as he reached the rear of the house.

Carrie got up from the steps. "Now? Marcus was going to show us around the sanctuary." She could tell Jimmy was upset and wanted to go home. But now that she had Marcus's attention, she wanted to keep it a bit longer. She used her trump card. "I'd really like to see the set up, it's what I'm going to be studying. Having a little insight on the whole aspect will help me to get my degree in Zoology." It wasn't a lie; she really was interested and not just in the wolves protected in the sanctuary but also the big bad wolf standing so defiantly beside her.

Jimmy glanced at his watch. If Carrie really thought that looking around at this set up would help her in school, he didn't want to disappoint her. It was two o'clock. If they left here by three or so they would still make it home before seven. He could then call Savannah and maybe spend a couple of hours together. "We can check it out if you're really that interested."

Marcus was surprised. He had no idea that Carrie was going on to school let alone going into the field of Zoology. "You are going on to school? I had no idea. I'm proud of you, Sprout."

Carrie flipped her hair over her shoulder. There he went with the Sprout comment again. Of course dressed like a frumpy school girl what did she expect? She so wanted to kick her brother's ass for not letting her know they were coming here today. "Yes, I leave for the University of Wisconsin in Madison at the end of the month. I'll be studying Zoology and Animal Biology."

"That's fantastic. Is there a certain area that interests you?" He led them down a path through the woods that led to the enclosures.

"Absolutely. I'm studying wolves." She raised her brow in challenge.

He tripped over his own feet. The little vixen had done that on purpose. "These enclosures house our new arrivals. Right now I have a bitch with four young pups."

"Why do you keep them separated?" Jimmy walked up and peered into the cage but could not see anything."

"I have eighty acres here on the compound. As you could see when you arrived, it is all fenced in for the protection of people, livestock and the wolves. The new arrivals are separated until the others accept them."

"And if they don't?" Carrie watched as a she wolf poked her nose out of a den dug into the ground. A little white wolf cub was trying to escape under her chin. She grabbed it in her teeth and placed it back in the hole.

"I'm hopeful that they will; if not one pack, then another. With eighty acres, I'm able to have more than one dominant pack. They tend to stay in their own territory. But if for some reason someone is not accepted, then I of course will care for them in the enclosure."

"That's sad. They deserve to run free."

"I couldn't agree more but now with new law making wolf hunting legal, the wolves are in even more danger than before. I can protect them here and they have as much freedom as I can safely allow."

Savannah tipped her head. Something smelled off, she scented …She turned her head and looked up at Marcus. *"I smell hybrid."*

"Yes, there are a few of our pack here. Not all but I am hopeful that eventually they will all return here. I can protect them within these fences. If they choose to live outside my boundaries, I cannot keep them safe. The pack had divided after the fight at the Haven. Those loyal to Becca had decided to go on their own. He hoped and prayed that they changed their minds and came back to the family.

"You can't save them all, Marcus. They have to learn to fit into the world."

"It's my duty to protect them. I failed them once and I won't make that mistake again."

Savannah knew it was useless to argue with him. He was and would always be a defender.

"What do you feed them?" Jimmy wondered if he treated the wolves as pets. He didn't see any dog dishes and couldn't imagine how dangerous it would be to approach the hungry wolves.

"I don't... well I guess I do, but not personally. I keep the acreage stocked with wildlife." He could tell from Jimmy's confused look that he didn't understand. "I buy small herds at a time of red deer or occasionally rabbits I steer clear of any domestic animals. The wolves hunt for their meals the same as they would in the wild. This is a sanctuary they are not pets and therefore I don't treat them as such."

Carrie was impressed. "You're doing a wonderful thing here.

It's a lifelong commitment."

"Thank you, I'd love to show you more but with the time restrictions, I'm afraid that taking a four wheeler out and scouting for a pack is out of the question."

"Yeah, I'm sorry man but we really should get going." He looked at his watch. Time was slipping away and he was more than ready to head home and spend some time with Savannah. "Thanks a lot for showing us around." He held out his hand.

"You're welcome to come back anytime." Marcus returned the hand shake. They proceeded to walk back toward the truck. He ruffled Carrie's hair. "Good Luck at school, Sprout. I'm sure you'll do great."

"Savannah, little sister, trust in your man. You've picked an honorable one and once he comes to accept who and what you are, he'll never betray you."

"I will Thank you." She jumped into the truck when Jimmy opened the back door and sat patiently in the seat.

"The gate has a sensor and will open when the eye recognizes a vehicle. Drive Safe." He waved as Jimmy started the truck and turned it around.

Chapter 10

The sound of laughter reached him when he walked through the door. He could smell the rich aroma of coffee and knew they were having a good old fashion coffee clutch. Nothing was going to stop him from spending time with Savannah. He had tried all weekend to reach her on the phone and only got her voice mail. His boots tapped on the hard wood floor as he made a bee line for the big windows at the back of the store. He knew that's where they would be sitting as it was their favorite spot.

"Come walk with me." He held out his hand.

Savannah jumped to her feet and linked her fingers with his. She had not heard him come in and was surprised at his abrupt appearance and not even a hello. She and Carrie had been laughing so hard it was no wonder she didn't hear the bell.

"Well, aren't you just a ray of sunshine? What has your undies in a bunch?" Carrie didn't bother getting up. Jimmy was acting like an ass and she wasn't going to go out of her way to be nice. He'd been pissy since leaving Marcus's on Saturday and she was tired of dealing with his shit.

"Shut up, Carrie, and watch Sable."

"You know I'm not your personal baby sitter." If he wanted to be an ass so could she. Of course there was no Sable to watch, but he didn't know that.

He stopped. "I'm sorry. Can you please watch Sable?"

"Fine." She huffed.

"Thanks." He grabbed a black throw off the back of the couch and wrapped it around Savannah's shoulders. "You never have a coat. It's cold out." He opened the back door and they walked out.

Savannah pulled throw closed at her neck. She squeezed Jimmy's hand as they walked across the back yard toward the pond. "What's wrong? You seem upset and were rude to Carrie. That's not like you."

"I know, I apologized but I missed you. I tried calling all weekend and couldn't get a hold of you. I guess I kind of panicked and thought maybe you had left town." Deep down he knew that was the truth he hadn't admitted to himself until now. There was always that fear that she would leave.

"I'm not going anywhere. I'm home to stay. My cell phone was turned off and I didn't realize it until this morning. I'm sorry if you were worried." Truth be told, she just wasn't use to the dang cell phone; she hadn't used one for so long that now she just didn't think about having one. So had not checked her messages and since she had spent the whole weekend as a wolf curled up beside Jimmy, she had been more than content and had not shifted until reaching the store this morning. Living the double life between wolf and woman was becoming more and more difficult.

"My insecurity is not your fault. You don't owe me anything."

"Jimmy, we made a commitment to each other and I meant it. If you can handle me and my baggage, I'm all yours. I should have checked my phone. I had no idea that you would be worried."

Jimmy stopped and pulled her into his arms. "I don't want to own you, Savannah. You're a grown woman and have a life of your own. I over reacted. I wanted to spend time with you and couldn't so I was acting like an ass." He leaned his forehead against hers. "I missed you," he whispered and brushed his lips against hers.

Savannah let go of the throw and wrapped her arm around his neck. She returned the sweet kiss. His breath tasted of mint and she shyly ran her tongue along his mouth.

Jimmy opened for her probing tongue. He was surprised at her boldness. Savannah never took their love play any further than gentle kisses. He knew that she was gun shy and he was willing to wait until she was ready. He groaned and let her take the lead.

She tightened her arm around his neck and turned her head to kiss softly along his lips, jaw line, then gently nuzzled at his throat.

He smelled so good, musky and like the outdoors. She had never liked the strong cologne many men wore, she much preferred Jimmy's subtle smell. She shivered and held him tighter. "I missed you too."

He knew that she had gone as far as she was able and kissed her cheek. "Let's walk." He released her and continued to walk still holding their laced hands. "So what did you do all weekend?"

She sighed and walked softly beside him. She loved every moment they were together. She wished she had the nerve to take their love making further but she couldn't overcome that fear. She hoped and prayed that soon she would be able to share all aspects of herself with the man she had come to love. "I had a fantastic weekend, nice and peaceful. I spent it snuggled up on the couch watching movies and just vegging out."

He was disappointed. It sounded like she had a wonderful time and she hadn't missed him at all. "That's what I did too, me and the wolf."

"Jilly will be home in a day or two and then you won't have to take care of her any longer."

"It's funny, when Jilly first asked me to take care of the wolf I absolutely hated the very idea of having to spend any time in the company of the killer."

"And now?" Savannah asked softly.

"Now, I'm going to miss her like crazy. I don't want to give her back."

"Oh Jimmy, she loves you too." She was ecstatic he had come to love the wolf. Now if only she knew how he would feel when he realized that she and the wolf were one in the same. It would be absolutely devastating if he was horrified over the very idea of her being a shifter. It was not something she could change and she wouldn't even if she could. She loved having the freedom to shift and run free through the forest, the wind and the branches of bushes pulling at her fur coat. Colors and scents were so much more vibrant through the senses of the wolf.

"Damn mutt," he said fondly. "She has a funny way of showing it; she spends half the time with Carrie staring out that big window." They had reached the edge of the woods that separated the bait store from Jilly's house. "Are you coming home with me?" He held his breath and waited; he knew what he as asking and if she was not ready to take such a giant step, then he would turn around and take her back to the shop.

Savannah hesitated, not sure if she could go through with it but she had to try. Jilly and Dylan were returning soon and then everything would be out in the open. She only had days or hours until the secret came out. She wanted to be the one to explain, but first she wanted to spend the night making love to the man who had captured her heart. "Yes, but what about your truck?"

He reached in his pocket and flipped open his phone.

"Carrie, can you lock up my truck and take care of the wolf? Savannah is spending the night here. I'll come by and collect them in the morning. Thanks." He closed the phone and put it back in his pocket. "All set." He let go of her hand as the walking trail through the woods wasn't wide enough for them to walk side by side. "It's going to be darker when we get in the woods. Are you going to be able to see alright? Maybe we should have brought the truck."

Savannah laughed. "Have you forgotten? I grew up here. I'm not afraid to walk in the woods at night besides it's not that far and we'll be out in the open before we know it." Already she could hear the hounds barking in the back yard. Their keen hearing had alerted them that someone or something new was in the trees. She heard the brush cracking and the scrunching of the dead leaves. "Look," she pointed as a fisher ran up a tree, its long nails clicking as it climbed higher into the tall pine.

"I'm surprised to see it this close to the house." The animals usually stayed in the dense forest to avoid any contact with humans.

"They're use to the sound of the hounds. I love to watch them; they're so unique looking and magnificent hunters. I once saw one take on a porcupine and win."

"You're kidding! I didn't know that." He looked at the animal with new respect. Porcupines were truly hated by hunters because if a dog and a porcupine got into a fight, the poor dog came out on the losing end full of quills and then it was a real pain to pull all of the quills from the dog. Some have even been known to die from infection.

She grinned. "I grew up in the country. I know lots of animal related things, but ask me to do anything with a computer and I don't have a clue."

"Fine by me." He kissed the end of her nose. "I love that we have so much in common. Carrie starts talking about Facebook, Twitter and Skype it's like she's talking some alien language. I'm completely lost." Computers had never interested him he had no use for them with his job and his free time was spent either out doors or vegging out in front of the TV. "Are you ready or do you want to watch him a little longer?"

"No, we can go. It's really starting to get dark and we won't be able to see him much longer." The trail was well worn, since Jilly tended to walk back and forth to work instead of driving, so the walk was easy even in the fading light. She could see the setting sun shining through the tree line and knew that it wouldn't be long before they reached the back yard.

Jimmy stepped out into the tall weeds that stood in the meadow. He waited for Savannah and once again laced his fingers with hers as they walked across the open field. Two deer knelt down on their knees and proceeded to bed down about one hundred yards from where they walked. The doe raised their heads and looked but apparently didn't feel threatened as they didn't get up.

"I love it here. Where else can you see nature as it was truly meant to be seen? I would wizzle up and blow away in a city." The hounds spotted them and were now barking and jumping excitedly on the ends of their chains. "I could live without all the barking though." she joked.

Jimmy laughed. "Barking dogs go hand and hand with hunting. I don't mind it." He was so used to the sound of dogs barking that he didn't pay attention unless the barks turned aggressive. Dogs had unique barks for how they were feeling and unless the pitch changed, he knew they were just barking to bark.

"Have they been fed?" Savannah asked as they got closer the dogs.

"Yep, all taken care of. They'll quiet down once we're in for the night."

"If I haven't said it before, thank you for taking care of things while Dylan and Jilly have been away." The tall weeds ended as they reached the yard. This late in the year the grass was no longer a dark green but an ugly brown because of the frost.

"You don't have to thank me, I'd do anything for Dylan and Jilly... and you." He turned to her. "You know that right? I'd do anything to make you happy."

"I know that, and I feel the same. But there are things about me that you still don't know and I'm so afraid that it will change the way you feel about me." It was past time that she told him the truth.

The longer she waited, the harder and more likely it was that he would find out from someone else and the results would be devastating.

"You are so wrong, sweetheart. We grew up together; I know that you've been through something horrible that no woman should have to deal with and if I could find the bastard that treated you so callously, I would beat the holy hell out of him. But there is absolutely nothing that will change the way I feel about you." He tightened his hands around hers. "Believe in me, in us."

"I pray that you remember those words, because I do love you, Jimmy, and I hope that love is enough to pull us through."

Jimmy stumbled as he cleared the top step with his hand on the door knob. "Do you mean it?" He held his breath; she had said the words he'd longed to hear spill from her beautiful lips.

She nodded, "With all my heart."

He pulled her into the house and kicked the door closed with his foot. "Thank you, God! It seems I've been waiting a life time to hear those words from you." He kissed her with such force, his hands on each side of her head.

Savannah returned his heated kisses, her hands gripping his sides. She was not afraid and loved the taste of him. He started backing down the hall. She knew where he was leading and didn't try to stop him.

As he backed down the hall, he continued kissing her; his

tongue probed her mouth and encircled and entangled in a dance with her tongue. He suckled softly. His body bumped into the wall and he continued on, passing the open door of the bathroom. "I love you" he whispered between heated kisses. He grabbed the bottom of her sweater and pulled it over her head. "Trust me." He pulled her floral skirt down from her hips and let it pool around her feet. She was breathtakingly beautiful. He clasped her hand and led her to the edge of the bed. She sat down and he brushed kisses across her knuckles and nibbled his way up to her wrist. "You are the most beautiful woman I have ever seen." Her long hair fell in cascades of loose curls around her face and shoulders, brushing the tops of her rose tipped breasts.

Savannah gulped nervously as she watched Jimmy slowly unbutton his flannel shirt and peel it from his shoulders. He grabbed the bottom of his tee and pulled it over his head. He was built like a body builder; long hours of working in the woods had paid off. His muscles rippled across his chest and the man had a six pack that just didn't quit. She reached out hesitantly and ran her index finger down the groove of muscles over his navel and lower. "I don't know if I can do this, I don't want to disappoint you."

"Shh," he pressed his finger over her lips. "There are no expectations here. Do I want to make love to you? Absolutely, but love is not about sex. I just want to be with you, lay with you skin to skin and feel you in my arms." He toed off his boots and unbuttoned the button on his jeans and slowly lowered the zipper.

Savannah shuddered and pulled her hand back.

The fear on her face stopped Jimmy from lowering his jeans. "You're comfortable with me holding you and touching you?"

She nodded never taking her eyes from the ridge in his unzipped pants.

"Savannah, look at me, please. You like my kisses and caresses?"

She looked up at him with tears in her eyes. She was so ashamed; he didn't deserve the fear that she felt.

"I love when you hold me."

He held out his hand and she grasped it. He pulled her to her feet and pulled back the bedspread. "Trust me." He kissed her lips swiftly. "Scoot in."

Savannah crawled across the cool sheets and lay on the opposite side of the bed. Being a shifter she was comfortable in her nakedness and so made no move to hide her body from Jimmy's hungry gaze. "What are you…?"

"Hush," he said and crawled in beside her, jeans and all. He yanked the covers over them and pulled her into the circle of his arms. "How's this? Not scared?"

"No," she shook her head and moved closer, laying her head on his shoulder. "I'm not afraid of you, Jimmy. I love the feel of you holding me. It's the whole act of making love, the intimacy of it.

I've only known force and violence. I'm not sure that I will like making love."

"Trust me, sweetheart," He kissed the top of her head. "When the time is right, you will be ready and I'll make sure that we both enjoy every moment of it."

"But it's so not fair for you. You deserve to be with someone whole."

"You let me decide what's fair. Love making is supposed to be pleasurable to both of us and if you can feel no pleasure, then it is not pleasurable to me."

She sighed and put her hand on his chest. She inhaled his scent deep within her lungs and ran her fingers through the whirls of hair on his chest. This may very well be the first and last time she lay in his arms and she was going to savor every single moment.

Jimmy smiled and ran his finger up and down her naked spine. He felt her quivers of pleasure. She may not feel comfortable making love but she definitely enjoyed being in his arms and in his bed. "We'll be fine, sweetheart." Time and patience would heal her wounds and he had an unlimited supply of both. It wasn't about sex, he could get that anywhere. He had offers and quick rolls in the hay before, but those were meaningless. This, just lying here with her cradled in his arms, had more meaning than the countless one night stands he'd had in the past.

She hoped what he said was true. She laid there and listened as his breaths slowed and the caresses on his back stopped and his hand settled on her hip. Never had she been so content, but it was unfair of her to expect him to wait for what most women could and would offer whenever he wanted it. Hours passed as she savored their time together and as the sun began to rise and show pink sky through the lace curtains, she crawled from beneath his arm. She bent and picked his flannel shirt up from the floor and slipped it on. "I love you." she whispered and padded out the door.

He heard the front door open and shut and sat up in bed. He woke up the moment she left his bed but had figured she was just going to the bathroom. Now he slipped on his boots and grabbed his jean jacket off the couch on the way to the door. The damn woman wasn't wearing anything but his flannel shirt. He expected to see her sitting on the front deck but was surprised to see her nowhere in sight. He jumped off the platform and rounded the end of the house. The sun was high enough that he could see clearly without a flashlight. She was just entering the edge of the woods on the far side of the meadow. He would have to hurry if he was going to catch up to her and took off at a jog. Halfway through the meadow and focused only on the tree line ahead of him, something tangled around his feet and he did a crappy flop and landed on his belly in the dirt. "What the hell?" There was an orange sweater and a skirt tangled on the toe of his boot. He vaguely remembered seeing something orange out in the field weeks ago.

Savannah walked aimlessly with no thought where she was going. Today was the day that she had to tell Jimmy the truth. She had no idea how to go about it; maybe she could ask Jilly how she had explained it to Dylan. The woods were peaceful, the ground covered in color from the leaves that had fallen from the trees. She didn't make a sound as she walked quickly down the well-traveled trail. She was stronger now, but could feel the wolf's impatience to run. It would be hours yet before she had to return to the house and maybe in the body of the wolf she could find the answers she needed. Carefully she unbuttoned the flannel shirt and removed it; she hung it on a low hanging tree branch so she could come back for it later. Visions of her wolf formed in her mind, she stretched her hands above her body and arched her back to lean forward, her muscles rippled as tendons reformed and the blood rushed through her veins. She landed on four feet and knew right away she was no longer alone.

"Oh my God..." Jimmy couldn't believe his eyes. He stumbled back and fell against a tree. At first he couldn't understand why Savannah had been undressing her skin had glowed and then rippling fur had appeared over her entire body. He recognized the animal standing in front of him right away. It was a friend and companion he had grown to love and trust. It should have dawned on him with the memories that he had of Jilly that, of course, her sister would have the same abilities. But he had been so wrapped up falling in love that he had subconsciously not wanted to know the truth. "I don't fucking believe it! You all lied to me."

Savannah gasped and quickly shifted back into human form. She grabbed hold of a tree, as changing so quickly made her weak. "Jimmy, let me..." she grabbed the shirt off the limb and pulled it around her naked form. "Let me explain." She started to walk to him.

"Stay away from me." He held his hand out to stop her from approaching him. "You've all been lying to me. Dylan, Jilly, Marcus, you, even my own sister. For months you've all kept secrets from me. Poor stupid Jimmy! You let me believe that I was having nightmares when all along it was the truth, wasn't it?"

She didn't answer soon enough to suit him.

"Answer me, God damn it! You owe me that much!" The pain of their betrayal was ripping him apart.

"Yes, it all happened." She cried tears falling down her cheeks. It was too late; he was furious and so hurt. She had ruined her chances at a happily ever after.

"You all must have had a good laugh."

She started to walk to him again. "It wasn't like that. I didn't know how to tell you."

"Stop! Don't come any closer. You've been sleeping with me for weeks cuddled up tight to me night after night. Maybe not as you are now, but as a wolf. Are you telling me in all that time you couldn't find the time to explain something so important to us? I told you I love you, for Christ's sake. How could you betray me?"

"I was shattered, it wasn't until I spent time with you as a wolf that I started to become alive again. I fell in love with you. But I knew how much you hated wolves, so I wanted you to meet me in both forms and learn that we are one in the same. I wanted you to love me for what I truly am."

"Well you got your wish. It's just too bad you had to make a fool of me in the process. You know, all the signs were there, I was just too damn wrapped up in falling at your feet to pay attention. He threw the clothes on the ground between them. "I saw you weeks ago, the day I came home early for my wallet. You were in the meadow that day weren't you and I surprised you by coming home?"

"Yes," she whispered. "It was the first time I had shifted since the attack. I should have told you then but I was still so frightened."

"No, don't..." he didn't want to hear her excuses. "All the times that we were together, my sister helped with the deception by offering to keep Sable. She betrayed me just as much as you did."

"We weren't betraying you. I love you. Please, try to understand." she pleaded, crying in earnest. Her sobs were making it hard for her to speak.

"You have a funny way of showing it. There's no need for

me to play the slave taking care of the house, dogs, and the poor wolf. What a fucking sap. You all played me and I fell for it hook, line and sinker. Now that the charade is over, I can get the hell out of here and on with my life." He turned and ran.

"Jimmy!" she screamed in agony.

He didn't turn around. He ran, tree branches ripped across his cheek leaving a long scratch down his face. He didn't stop as he hit the meadow. Tears blinded him as they poured from his eyes and down his face, burning the scratch on his face. But that pain was nothing compared to the pain of the knife that had been stabbed through his back by everyone he cared about that went straight through and pierced his heart. He wiped his face with the back of his arm. The jean coat only added to the abrasion. He didn't care. His only thought to get to his truck and get the hell away from the hurt. It was only when he got to the front yard that he remembered his truck wasn't there. He had left it at the bait shop last night. Last night when he had thought his world couldn't get any better, he had the woman he loved curled up in his arms. Now his life was shattered. His truck wasn't there but Jilly's ford ranger sat parked in the driveway. He yanked open the door and jumped in; she always kept the key above the visor. He got it and shoved it into the ignition. The engine roared to life, he shifted it into gear and threw gravel as he roared out of the driveway. The drive to his home took longer than usual, his vision blurred from his tears. His guts twisted and he thought he might be sick. He swallowed the bile and turned into his drive. One light shined through the kitchen window. It was just his luck that Carrie was already awake.

Carrie turned at the sound of the door opening and closing. She set her coffee mug on the counter when she saw her brother's tear stained face and blood shot eyes. He looked absolutely devastated. "Oh, Jimmy." She enfolded her big brother in her arms. "She finally told you."

"You shouldn't have kept it from me. You're my family."

Carrie held him as sobs rocked his body. "I'm so so sorry," she whispered. "It wasn't my secret to tell." Time passed and she continued to hold him until the shuddering of his body let up.

He pushed away from her and wiped his face with his shaking hands. "What am I going to do? I feel like such a fool yet how am I going to live without her in my life?"

Carrie put her hands on her hips. "I love you with all my heart, Jimmy, but you are such a jackass! Why would you have to live without her?"

"How can you ask that? She's a wolf; she can change her body and become an animal. I don't even understand how she can do that." He paced back in forth in the living room running his hands through his tousled hair.

"She's the same woman you fell in love with. Have you asked her what it means? Did you talk to her? She must have explained things when she told you."

He shook his head. "She didn't tell me, I saw. She was walking in the woods so nakedly beautiful and all of the sudden her body changed and before my eyes, she molded into Sable."

Carrie smiled. "It's a remarkable sight, isn't it?"

He cocked his head. "How long have you known?"

She shrugged. "Years; it seems like I've always known. They're the same women *you've* always known, they just have special gifts that make them extraordinary."

He nodded. "And Marcus? He fits into this puzzle of her past somewhere too doesn't he?"

"It's not my place to talk about that. It's something you'll have to talk over with Savannah, but make sure you're ready to listen and accept. I love you, Jimmy, but don't you break that girl's heart." She kissed his cheek picked up her coffee mug and walked into her bedroom and closed the door.

Chapter 11

Savannah sat on the corner of the couch, her arms wrapped around her bent legs, resting her chin on her knees. She rocked her body and stared straight ahead. Time passed but she never moved. Her wolf cried, wanting to protect her, enfold her into another world. She was stronger now and fought the urge to give in. The pain was excruciating, it was so tempting to give in and run to not feel.

She heard the front door open and thought maybe Jimmy had returned. She heard giggling and hushed whispers and knew she was wrong.

"I think we have the house to ourselves. Even my truck is gone which is totally weird." Jilly whispered.

"Fine by me, we can crawl back into bed and spend a couple hours breaking in your bed as Mr. and Mrs. Rudolph."

"I do like the way you think, Mr. Rudolph." she sighed and returned his kiss. She grabbed his hand and stopped in her tracks when she saw her sister sitting on the couch. She looked devastated, worse than the days following her attack. She released her Dylan's hand and ran to the couch.

"Savannah, sweetheart… what is it?" Jilly wrapped her arms around her sister. Her body was freezing. "Dylan grab me that blanket."

Dylan reached for the throw on the recliner and handed it to his wife. "Is everything okay? I didn't realize she was back. Where's Jimmy?"

At the mention of Jimmy's name Savannah let out a gut wrenching keening sound. "I've ruined everything. It's all my fault, all my fault, I ruined it." she cried repeating herself again and again as she rocked harder.

Jilly held on tight to her sister. "Hush, hon. You're not making any sense." She placed her hand on the back of Savannah's head and pushed it to her shoulder. "Take a deep breath and calm down." Savannah was so overcome that she was taking great gulps of air. "Everything is going to be okay. Take your time and when you're ready, tell me what happened."

"Jimmy." she rasped. Her voice broken from her tears and terrible screams.

"What about Jimmy? Where is he? Is he hurt?" Dylan stepped forward concerned. Jimmy was his best friend. If he was injured, he wanted to go to him. "Damn it, Savannah, snap out of it! Is Jimmy hurt?"

Jilly reached up and placed her hand on Dylan's arm. She could feel Savannah shaking her head no. "Dylan, wait."

"No, he's fine. At least I think he is. He left." She sniffled and raised her head.

"What happened? I'm so surprised to see you." The last time Jilly had seen her sister she had been in the form of a wolf. To see her now as a woman was such a shock but to see her in this condition was frightening.

She wiped her face with her hand and accepted the tissue Jilly handed her. "At first, things were bad after you left. But, gradually, I became to trust Jimmy more and more and I really liked him." She glanced at her sister and her brother-in-law. "He even started to like the wolf," she gave a smile. "Despite the bad stuff the wolf did."

Jilly returned her smile. "And someday I'm going to want to hear that story but why don't you tell me what happened that has upset you."

"The wolf was getting stronger and I knew it was time for me to take back my life."

Jilly hugged her. "That couldn't have been easy. I'm so proud of you. Why didn't you call me? I would have helped

Savannah reached out and grabbing her sister's hand and her brother-in-law's hand, she joined the two together. "You sacrificed enough for me. You two deserved to have this special time together without all of my drama. It was past time for me to stand on my own."

Dylan squeezed her hand. "Thank you for that but you are family and if and when you need help, there are no boundaries. You call and we will do all we can to be there."

"You have a good man, Jilly."

Jilly smiled at Dylan. "I know, but you're straying from the story. What happened?"

"Things were going so well."

Jilly interrupted. "You mean between Jimmy and Sable?"

"Yes, but also between me... see, that's what I mean. It's so confusing. There is no Sable there's just me, just Savannah, but how was I supposed to explain that to him?"

"So you've been playing the double role?" At last Jilly understood.

"Yes, I was trying to figure out a way to tell him. We spent the night together. It was beautiful but I wanted to tell him everything and didn't know how. I went for a walk and ended up in the woods. I was going to go for a run and didn't know he had followed me."

"He saw you shift?" Jilly guessed. She glanced at Dylan and saw him wince. He remembered what it had been like when he had first figured out what Jilly was capable of doing.

"Yes, you should have seen his face. He was horrified." She

got slowly to her feet and let the blanket drop to the floor.

Dylan arched an eyebrow and looked at his wife. He recognized the shirt that was the only clothing covering Savannah's body. "I'm sure he was shocked."

"No, it was more than that. He felt betrayed. Not just by me but by you and Carrie."

"What do you mean?" Dylan stepped closer to Jilly and pulled her to her feet enveloping her in his arms.

"He's been remembering that night at the Haven and he feels like we treated him like a fool, like he couldn't be trusted with our secret."

"That's bullshit! I trust him with my life."

Savannah nodded. "I wanted to talk to you guys before I spoke to him to see how Jilly explained our shifting so that maybe he could come to accept it more easily."

Dylan laughed sarcastically. "There is no easy way to explain your unique way of life. I accepted it because I love Jilly and cannot imagine my life without her in it."

It was hopeless. The look of horror and hurt on Jimmy's face proved that he would never accept a life in which she was a shifter. "I'm going to leave."

Jilly gasped in pain. "Savannah, no," she reached out to grab her sister. She had just gotten her back and was not going to let her go without a fight.

"The hell you are!" Jimmy stepped through the door. He had been standing there since just after Dylan and Jilly arrived. He'd listened to the three of them talk. It had helped him to understand that they hadn't betrayed him.

"Buddy, maybe you bett..."

"Stay out of it, Dylan." Jimmy interrupted his best friend. "This is between me and her." He approached Savannah. "You're not going anywhere. You've hidden long enough. You're stronger than that!"

"I'm not!" she argued. "I have to leave. I saw the look on your face when you saw me."

He laughed, it wasn't funny but it was either laugh or cry and he'd by God shed enough tears today. "What did you expect? I just had the woman of my dreams get out of my bed naked. I followed her not knowing what to expect, but it sure as hell wasn't seeing her change into the same wolf that's been spending weeks in my bed."

Dylan chuckled and put his face against the side of Jilly's head and whispered in her ear. "Honey, I do believe we have a lot to catch up on. Maybe we should leave these two alone."

Jimmy turned. "No, stay. There have been enough damn secrets. We're a family and by God we are not keeping any more!"

Dylan held his hands up in surrender before settling himself and his new bride on the edge of the couch.

Jimmy walked up to Savannah and grabbed a hold of her

shoulders. "I told you to trust me. To trust in us. How can you even think about leaving?"

"I tried to explain but you didn't even want me near you." It was heaven having him touch her. "You left me!"

"I was shocked and hurt. I needed time to process it. I love you." He finally gave in to the urge and pulled her into his arms and kissed her like he'd been aching to do since he stepped foot inside the door.

Savannah sank into his arms and returned his kisses. She felt such relief and joy. "Does this mean that you can accept my life?"

"Sweetheart, I can't even begin to understand what your shifting will mean to us but I just spoke to my little sister who, by the way, is wise beyond her years and she pointed out to me that you have always been you. Nothing has changed." He kissed her again. "And she's absolutely right. I've been crazy about you for years and the fact that I just found out that you become furry on a whim doesn't change that fact."

She stepped back. "It's not a whim; I don't have to shift. If I have to choose between that part of myself and loving you, I'll choose you."

Jimmy heard Jilly's surprised gasp.

"I love you. I'd never ask you to give up that part of yourself." He went down on one knee. "Say you'll spend the rest of your life making me the happiest, luckiest man alive."

"Oh, Jimmy," tears collected in her eyes and rolled softly down her cheeks. Never did she expect to hear those words. "But what if I can never..."

"It doesn't matter. It's for better or for worse and forever." There were no guarantees and as long as he had her in his life, the rest would come with time.

"Yes," she whispered.

He whooped for joy and picked her up to spin her around.

"Congratulations!" Dylan came up and pounded him on the back and kissed Savannah on the cheek.

"Dylan?" Jimmy asked as the sisters continued to hug and laugh and cry.

"Yeah?"

"Do you have a gun here?" It was time to take care of some long overdue business.

Savannah had heard Jimmy ask for a gun and was afraid she knew exactly why he wanted it. "Why do you need a gun?"

He pierced her with a dangerous look. "I have the need to have a big black wolf pelt hanging on our wall." He walked up to her. "It was Marcus wasn't it?"

"It was but..."

"There are no buts. I promised you that when and if I found out who it was, I would beat the Holy Hell out of him. I've changed my mind. He's a dead man!" Savannah grabbed his arm and planted her feet as he pulled her across the floor.

"I've forgiven him and you have to do the same." she pleaded.

"Like hell I do."

She tried again. "Marcus made his amends. You told me it would take time to understand about my shifter life. Well, this is one of those times that I need you to listen and follow my lead. He's paid the price."

Jimmy stopped and turned to her. "Are you sure?"

"Do you love me?" She asked with a small grin.

He was surprised by her turn of topic and should have known that she was up to mischief. "With all my heart."

She let go of his arm and crossed her arms across her chest. "And we are going to be married and live in your house?"

He smiled. She stood their challenging him in front of his best friend and her sister in nothing but his flannel shirt. If she raised her arms any higher, his good friend was going to see just what she wasn't wearing underneath that shirt. "Absolutely."

"Well, I ask you…do you want us to have to look at his fuzzy black ass every day for the rest of our lives?"

"Hell NO!" he laughed and scooped her up in his arms. "I do love you, my she-wolf." he whispered as he captured her lips in a crushing kiss.

"And I you." She returned.

The End

The Hunter

Chapter 1

The sun shone bright; the heat beating on her fur covered back. Joy radiated through her body as she raced across the open meadow. Heavy breathing alerted her to the closeness of the other. She looked over her shoulder and was not surprised to see how near the big male was to her. She put on the brakes, tucked her head and somersaulted. Extending her legs and paws, she encased the big male in her hold, taking him with her she came to a stop straddle his massive body. They were both human and very naked. "Got ya." she giggled in delight, bending down and capturing his lip with hers.

Michael wrapped his arms tenderly around Cassandra's body and rolled them so his body now shielded hers from any prying eyes. "Who's got who?" he cocked his brow.

Cassandra pushed his long sun kissed hair back from his eyes. "We have each other." She whispered raising her shoulders from the cushioned ground. She again tasted his lush lips. He was divine; she could happily spend her days kissing the man.

"I love you Cassandra." Michael nuzzled her neck. She

smelled sweet; vibrant like lilacs. Never before had he uttered those words to a woman other than his mother.

Cassandra smiled. "I love you too." She tipped her head as he nipped at her neck before lapping it tenderly with his tongue.

He pushed himself up and rested his weight on his hands as he gazed into her beautiful green eyes. "I want to spend the rest of our lives waking up together, snuggling curled around each other every night. And more than anything, I want to make lots and lots of beautiful babies with you. Marry me?" He waited breathlessly for her to answer. He hadn't meant to ask her today and didn't even have the ring with him. But she looked so beautiful lying naked amongst the wild flowers, her golden hair entwined with the petals, that he couldn't help himself. "I'm sorry sweetheart, I botched this I don't even have your ring."

She placed her fingers over his lips. Tears fell gently, rolling unashamedly down her cheeks. "A ring is not important. I don't need a ring to know that you love me." She pulled his head down to meet hers. Her fingers entangled in his shoulder length air. The kiss was soft, sweet and tender. His whiskers were rough against her smooth cheeks as she rubbed her face alongside his, much like a cat rubs along a human's leg claiming ownership.

He wanted to make love with her so badly that the ache in his hardened erection was almost painful. The need to be inside of her bordering on unbearable. But he didn't want to pressure her with his love making. Marriage was something he didn't take lightly and he wanted her, needed her to feel the same undeniable need to become one.

"You know that I love you with all of my heart." she gazed into his eyes, her hands on both of his cheeks.

"I know, he nodded. "I feel a 'but' coming here." Oh my God, if she said no, he would be shattered. Never did he have a doubt about her feeling. He never imagined that she would say no to his proposal. He swallowed the lump forming in his throat.

"Not about us." she shook her head. "I would marry you in a heartbeat. But," she smiled tenderly, "what about your mom? You've still had no word on her whereabouts?"

Michael sighed in relief. "Mom took dad's death hard. She needed time and space away from the memories they shared here. I've allowed her to grieve long enough. I want her here for our wedding and that's why I hired a private investigator to locate her."

"You didn't tell me." She felt a little hurt that he hadn't shared that important information with her.

"I didn't want to be presumptuous. Truth is, I want her to share in our happiness. I wanted my asking you to become my wife to be special and not have you thinking I was doing it to help mom overcome her grief."

"I would never think that. Your mom is an amazing woman. I love her. She was always so kind to me after my parents' death."

"She loves you too. Uh, sweetheart? You're killing me here! Are you going to answer me? Will you make me the happiest man on this earth? Will you be my love for now and always?" Time stood still. It seemed like hours passed but in fact, he knew it was only seconds.

"Yes."

He gasped a huge breath of air, only now realizing he had been holding his breath.

"I would like nothing better than to be your wife." She squealed with delight and peppered little kisses across his face, neck and chest.

"Thank you, Lord." he whispered and collapsed on her chest. His lips and tongue nuzzled along her neck and found the sweet spot just below her ear. She shivered and he knew that all talk would now cease to exist. Her nipples pebbled against his chest and he lifted up to slide his hands up over the mounds to roll the pink buds between his fingers.

Cassandra reached down and wrapped her hand around Michael's erection. She squeezed tightly and smiled as she heard his gasp of pleasure. They did not need any foreplay as both were more than ready to become one. She guided him to her moist entrance and arched her hips as he slowly pushed his way into the honeyed warmth.

"You feel so damn good." he whispered as he slowly pulled

out before once again slowly sinking into the hilt, his hips pressed tightly against her. The slow, gently dance elicited moans of pleasure from them both.

Cassandra ran her hands up and over Michael's hip and across the cheeks of his ass where she palmed them, gently pressing her nails into his flesh. He groaned and pushed harder and faster. She smiled mischievously as he began to lose control.

"Stop!" he moaned. "I'm trying to make this last."

"I don't want to make it last, I want to soar." She raised up and nipped his shoulder while again sinking her nails into his cheeks.

He came undone, pumping furiously into her welcoming body.

Cassandra kept pace with him and could feel her release coming. The warmth spread through her body and she gasped as pleasure seemed to shoot from her toes. She knew there was no need to wait on Michael as she could feel him growing thicker and slicker within her. She let out one final moan and arched up just as Michael groaned deeply and sank upon her. She smiled, totally satisfied, and wrapped her arms around his sweat covered body.

"You are amazing." Michaels kissed her full lips and rolled off of her. Pulling her close, he spooned their bodies together, not yet ready to let her go.

"It was beautiful." She kissed his arm where it lay beneath

her breast.

He kissed her shoulder. "I can't wait to tell everyone. Let's stop by my place first so I can give you your ring. I've been holding it for you for months."

"Not so fast, boyo." she chuckled. "Did you forget that we're naked?"

He pinched her ass. "No, I didn't forget, smartass. We'll have to shift and run back as cats. I'm sure I have something of yours at the house you can throw on."

"Okay, let's do this." She rolled over onto her hands and knees. Her breasts dangled down toward the ground, her bare ass in the air.

Michael groaned. "God, you're killing me sweet heart!" He had made it to his knees, but the feast she put before him was undeniable. He grabbed her from behind and palmed her delectable breasts in his hand.

"Cassandra! Cassandra! Are you out here?"

"Oh Shit!" Cassandra jerked her head up.

"Ouch! Damn It!" Michael grabbed his chin.

Cassandra rubbed the back of her head and winced. "Oh, dang! Sorry, Hon. It's Amelia. Get down." She pushed his head below the line of wild flowers as she popped up on her knees and peered over the blooms.

"Crap, she's coming this way. Stay down. I don't want her

seeing your junk."

"Well, Cassandra Ann! Are you jealous?" Michael chuckled and started to rise to his knees.

"Just stay down." She pushed his head back down and had to stop and admire the picture he now made with his very sexy ass pointing up.

"Uh, Cassandra?

"Huh?"

"Amelia?"

"What?"

"Amelia headed this way… naked."

"Oh yeah right." She popped her head back up above the flowers. "Hey Amelia!" She tried to keep her voice steady but Michael's chuckles plus his roaming hands were distracting.

"Hi, Cassandra. Uhmm… Jody said he saw you running this way." She avoided her eyes because she could plainly see that Cassandra was naked.

"Did you need something?"

Amelia shook her head. "No, but Justin needs to see you right away. I ran back to your place and picked up some clothes for you after Jody told me you were in your cat form. I hope that's okay."

"Sure, fine. But how did you know where to find me?" She didn't like the fact that someone had been in her home, but being caught butt naked was even more humiliating. From now on, she would be locking her door to keep unwanted guests out of her sanctuary.

"Everyone knows you like to run in the meadow, so when Jody said you were headed this way. I just figured it out."

"Oh, well, good thinking. You can just leave my clothes there and I'll get them. Tell Justin I'll be there soon."

"Okay. Uh, do you want me to wait?"

"No. Thanks for the clothes though, I'll be along shortly" Cassandra plopped down on her naked ass sitting Indian style.

Michael grinned. She looked so perplexed. "Are you all right sweetheart?"

"Yeah. I wonder what Justin wants to see me about." Michael's brother was an ass and being in his company made her very uneasy.

"It's probably just something to do with the books. You know how anal he is when it involves money." He reached for her hand and kissed her palm. "I'll shift and run home to grab some clothes and meet you there. We can tell him our news."

Cassandra tightened her hand in his. She didn't think Justin would be overjoyed to hear of their upcoming marriage. "No, give me an hour or two, if he wants to go over the accounts it could take a while."

"I can't wait to tell him, maybe now he'll get over his

obsession of you."

"What!" Cassandra gasped.

Michael smiled. "You didn't think I noticed the way my brother looks at you? I love you. I notice everything that involves you."

"You know how I feel about Justin."

"Yeah, you can't stand him. That's what makes this all the sweeter. It'll knock him off his high horse."

"Michael," she reached out and grabbed his other hand. "Justin is dangerous. Please don't provoke him." She was now worried. Michael wanted to believe that his brother was just overly ambitious and wanting what was best for the shifters. She knew better. Justin was evil personified. She would never trust him with her life or her love. Michael was the single most important person in her life and she would do whatever it took to protect him.

"I'll see you there later." She leaned forward and gave him a quick kiss before jumping to her feet and running to grab her clothes.

Chapter 2

Cassandra knocked on door to Justin's two story house. He'd had it built high upon a hill looking over everyone else's smaller ranch style houses. Secretly she thought he had done it on purpose so he could feel as if he was a king looking down on his kingdom. She knocked again and turned the knob. "Justin!" She called as she walked through the door, being the accountant she had an office in the basement of the house so didn't really need to announce herself, but today was her day off so she felt she should give him his privacy.

"Come in my dear."

"You wanted to see me?' She followed his voice into the family room.

"Yes, I've made a decision and have decided that it's time that you become aware of your duties to the family."

"Duties? I don't understand. I'm the accountant and keep all the books related to the various businesses. My time is pretty much taken. I'm not sure I can take on any other duties." She didn't have enough hours in the day as it was and now he wanted her to tackle something else?

"Oh, not to worry, you'll have the time to do this. I'll make sure of it." he grinned and scratched his groin.

Cassandra turned away. Justin had a disgusting habit of touching himself in public and it made her stomach turn. The sooner she heard what he had to say the sooner she could get the hell away from him. "What is it you wish me to do?"

"Oh, I don't wish anything, Puss. I'm demanding it. You will marry me Cassandra." He sat back in his chair built on a platform...the better to look down on his followers.

"Are you crazy? I won't. I barely tolerate you. Why would you ask me to marry you?" Just the thought of being close to Justin made her skin crawl. The man was pure evil.

"Oh, you misunderstand Cassandra. I'm not asking. I'm demanding." He never took his eyes from his prey. She would be his. He didn't care if it was willingly or by force; in the end, the outcome would be the same.

"You can't demand that I marry you. This isn't a cult. People are free to come and go as we wish. We live here because it's beautiful and we are free to roam in either form. It's a beautiful sanctuary, not a dictatorship." The man was clearly mad. What was she going to do?

"You may think you're free, but make no mistake, I say who

comes and who goes. Don't cross me, Cassandra. You will not like the results." She was so beautiful in her anger, she made his cock harden. He had to have her.

"You should love the person you're going to marry Justin. I'm not in love with you. You should find someone that will meet all your needs." Surely she could reason with the crazed man.

"You're beautiful. You should be honored that I chose you to rule by my side.

Cassandra shook her head. "Being beautiful is no reason to marry someone." She looked to the left. Amelia sat in an oversized chair, curled in a ball playing on her cell phone. "If beauty is your sole requirement, why not marry Amelia? She adores you."

The young girl with deep brown eyes lowered her cell phone and looked up shyly. Her silky, brown hair fell, shielding her face from view, but she could see Justin staring at her.

Amelia's heart fluttered excitedly. Justin was so handsome, to have him showing her the tiniest bit of attention made her heart soar.

Justin laughed. "She's afraid of her own shadow. She wouldn't last through the wedding night." He stood and walked down the steps. "She is a beauty, I'll give her that." He reached out and lifted her chin with his index finger.

Amelia gazed up at him adoringly. She smiled tentatively. Always timid, the self-proclaimed leader of their group made her extremely nervous.

"What do you think, Puss? Could you handle this lion? He reached down and grabbed her hand placing it on his enlarged erection.

"Knock it off Justin!" Cassandra took a step toward the couple. "You've proven your point."

Justin released Amelia's hand and raised his own. In the blink of an eye, fur covered it and sharp claws replaced his fingers. "That is where you are wrong, Sweet Cassandra." He extended his paw to the front of Amelia's white blouse. "I am just beginning to make you see that only you can satisfy my beast."

"We are not beasts! There is no reason to act as if we are." she argued.

"If not beasts, then what, pray tell, are we?" he flexed his claws.

"We are people. Humans with extraordinary gifts." She watched Justin carefully. He was evil, but given his present mood, he could be even more reckless and dangerous. The hair prickled on the back of her neck and goose bumps formed along her arms when she saw the merriment in his golden eyes and the sadistic smile on his face. He was enjoying himself.

"Humans are weak pathetic people. They soil our race!" he spat the words as if they left a foul taste in his mouth.

"How can you say that? Michael is ..."

"Do not wax poetry about your darling Michael!" he flicked the first button on Amelia's blouse.

The young girl gasped and jerked in surprise.

"Justin!" Cassandra took a quick step to intervene.

"Stay where you are." He flicked another button. "You will not interfere."

Cassandra bit her lip and fisted her palms so hard that her nails bit into her palms. Anger radiated through her body. Sweet shy Amelia had tears of humiliation pouring down her face.

The last string to the buttons severed, Justin sliced through the front of the young girl's bra exposing her bare breasts. "So tell me again, Kitty, can you handle being my play thing?"

"Enough!" Cassandra slammed he hands against his shoulder, pushing him away from the young girl who now trembled violently and sobbed uncontrollably. "You are an evil bastard!" She knelt down and pulled the gaping blouse closed. She enfolded Amelia in her arms and whispered to her. "Go. Go now." She helped her to her shaky legs and pointed her to the door with a gently push to get her moving.

Amelia needed no other nudging. Still sobbing, she ran, never looking back.

Cassandra whirled around. Her temper out of control, uncaring of any repercussions. She only saw red. "You uncaring, selfish son of a bitch!"

Justin stood before her, his arms crossed, a satisfied smile on his lips. "Now, dear Cassandra, I have proven my point."

"You've done nothing except shatter the feelings of a young girl."

"I've proven that she is weak. Her mixed blood makes her so. She's nice to look at and I may consider giving her a good fuck, but there is no way I would ever consider mating with her and producing more of her kind. That is why I will never allow you and your precious Michael to mate." He smiled as he saw the shock on her face. "Oh, I know all about your so called feelings for one another. People talk and I have loyal followers."

"Mate? Listen to yourself. We are not animals. We do not mate."

"Are we not?" He lifted his hand and fur once again rippled across his skin.

"No." She marveled at how effortlessly he could shift just one part of his body. It was unnatural. "I'm human. I embrace the cat. I love the fact that I can shift, but I am first and foremost human."

"You are a purebred. Your fire and fearlessness only add to my determination to have you." He slowly advanced on her. "Together we can rule our people and weed out the weak half breeds that my father allowed to contaminate our line."

"No, Justin. You may think that you rule the people." She

jabbed him in the chest with her index finger. Her anger grew as he chuckled as if amused by her antics. "But no one rules me. If and when I marry, and make no mistake, it will be marry not mate." Again she poked him in the chest. She stood toe to toe with the stupid man, her anger not allowing her to be afraid. "It will be to the man of my choosing, the man that I love. Human or pureblood, they are all the same in my mind."

He grabbed her hand and held it against his chest. "Cassandra, my lovely, I do so enjoy your zest. There will never be a dull moment with you by my side. Our kittens will be marvelous." He bent his head and raised her hand to his lips, caressing them with his tongue.

Cassandra grimaced in disgust. "Release me!" Yanking her hand away, she wiped the back of it on her jean clad leg. "It'll be a cold day in hell before I let you touch me." She whirled around and headed toward the door, but his next words stopped her cold.

"It had better be a cold day before you let that weak ass half breed touch you too. I don't want you coming to my bed already carrying his mutant offspring."

Cassandra turned and faced him. "You can't dictate whom someone falls in love with."

"You are such an innocent. Who said anything about love? I'm telling you that if you dare to spread your legs to my half-breed brother, there will be life changing consequences."

"You can't kill your brother. There are laws and we follow the same laws as 'the humans' you despise." she reminded him, making quotation marks with her fingers.

Justin chuckled. "Oh, Cassandra. I'm not going to kill him, that would be too easy. I have something much more painful in mind."

She was afraid to ask. The man was truly demented, but she had to know what he had panned in his devious mind. "What could be more painful than death?" Her beloved Michael was in danger. They had made beautiful love together many times. Thank god Justin had yet to find out just how far the relationship had evolved.

He smiled gleefully, excited to tell her his plans for the bastard. "If I find out that he's soiled you with his weak seed, I'll tranquilize him in cat form and personally neuter him. Let's see how attractive he is to you when he can't get it up anymore. The pain and humiliation alone will kill the sorry bastard."

"You wouldn't dare!" She was horrified. Bile rose in her throat, the acidity almost choking her.

"Try me. And my dear, don't even think about speaking with him on this matter. He must believe that our mating is your choice."

"Never! You'll never be my choice." she vowed and walked out the door.

"Follow her. I don't want her out of your sight." He called to the two men who were standing in the shadows.

Chapter 3

She walked slowly until she got around the corner of the house and then took off on a dead run. Tears streamed down her cheeks. *"I have to leave."* She whispered to herself. Michael's safety and well-being were in her hands. There was no way in hell that she would ever let Justin get his slimy hands on her. The thought of him touching her in any way made her want to vomit. There was no other option.

Sobs racked her body. *"Pull yourself together Cassandra Ann."* She talked to herself to calm the cat. She could feel the feline trying to rise to protect her from an unknown danger. It didn't take long to reach her little log house. God she was going to miss this place. Decorated all in hard wood, she felt safe and close to nature when she was tucked away inside. She didn't stop to soak in the bright colors of her grandmother's homemade quilt that lay over the back of her couch or her mother's painting hanging over her stone fireplace, but ran straight to her bedroom.

The king size bed, where only weeks ago her and Michael

had spent the entire day making love, seemed now to mock her. She grabbed a duffle bag out of the closet and set it in the old rocking chair by the window. She couldn't bear to look at the bed. Undies, bras, socks, blue jeans and t-shirts she threw in the bag in abandonment not bothering to fold them. Her cell phone lay upon the dresser and she dialed the familiar number. There was only one person she could think to call. "Savannah, I need help."

"Whatever you need, Hon." The warm voice on the other end gave her hope. "Do you need to meet in our secret spot?"

"No, I'll come to you. It may take some time. I'm going to have to be very careful not to lead them to your family."

"Cassandra, you're scaring me. Let me send Jimmy and Dylan." Savannah begged.

"Absolutely not! It's not safe for any of us. Please, Savannah, let me do this my way." She pleaded with her childhood friend. If her husband and brother-in-law came, things could turn deadly. No way would she put Savannah's family at risk.

"Tell me what's going on."

"I can't; there's no time. I have to move quickly. Can you agree to my terms?"

"Okay, we'll do it your way. But if I don't hear from you in a week, I'm sending in the Calvary."

"That's plenty of time. I'll keep in touch, but promise you won't do anything rash for at least a week." There was silence on the other end of the phone. She could almost see Savannah chewing on her bottom lip. She was very protective and this would kill her to wait. "Promise me or I'll go somewhere else."

"Oh alright, I promise, but you better be safe, Cassandra Ann, or I'm going to be one pissed off wolf!"

"I love you, Savannah. See you soon." She hung up before Savannah could argue anymore. She tucked her phone in her back pocket and grabbed her keys off of the dresser. Her car was parked in the parking garage with all the others. A quick dash down the trail and she would be on her way. She grabbed her duffle and opened the front door.

"What the hell?" The two men standing at the door startled her. They stood as if on guard, one on each side of the door.

"Are you going somewhere?" Edmund asked.

"I'm going out." Savannah slipped the duffle off her shoulder and set it behind the door out of sight.

"We'll go with you. Where are you going?" Rory took a step away from the logged wall.

Surely Justin wasn't having her followed. She thought leaving would be easy and avoiding the search party after would be more difficult. Now, she would have to think quickly. "I don't need you to go with me. I've been walking these paths for years. Besides, you know it's safe. Why the sudden interest in my comings and goings?"

"We have our orders, Cassandra. If you go out, we go with you." Edward didn't care for Justin but had seen firsthand what a mean son of a bitch he could be. If he wanted them to watch Cassandra, he'd be sure to not let her out of his sight.

Cassandra wanted to stomp her foot in anger. "This is ridiculous! I'm free to come and go at will." Neither of the two men were overly bright, but they were indeed brawny. She'd have to think of a different means of escape.

"Not tonight. Tonight if you go, we go. That's the way it is. So what's it going to be, are we going out or staying in?"

"Forget it, I changed my mind!" She slammed the door in their faces. "Shit! Shit! Shit!" There was no way she would make it to the parking garage undetected. She couldn't shift and make a run for it either; the big males would be on her before she got to the border. "Yes," she smiled as a brilliant idea occurred to her. She ran back to the bedroom and rummaged through the lock box on the closet floor. Carefully she picked up the small vial before going to her stereo and turning it up. Toby Keith was blaring away about Red Solo Cups as she carefully lifted the window and pulled the screen inside. She listened carefully for any sound from the front of the cabin. Slowly, she eased one leg and then the other out the window, scooted her ass through and stepped onto the thick grass below. The cover unscrewed easily from the container and the initial smell caused her eyes to water. Two or three drops on the bottom of each tennis shoe and along each jean clad leg. She began the walk along the outside wall to the back of the house. More drops were placed at the corner of the step at the back deck. The smell was enough to make her wretch but she didn't dare. Not yet satisfied that her scent would be covered, she doused her feet in the remaining liquid before taking off on a dead run through the woods. She didn't stick to the trail since she knew the woods intimately. Jumping over downed logs and around underbrush, she hoped to be miles away before they noticed her gone.

"Why must she play that blasted music so loud? Edward hollered, his hands over his ears to drown out the noise. One of the benefits of being a shifter was their acute hearing and the loud music was hurting his sensitive ears.

"She's pissed that's why." Rory had sisters he knew better than to piss them off because revenge was a bitch. Cassandra was not one to take this insult lying down. He was surprised that she had given in so easily.

"Oh ,Christ! Do you smell that? God damn skunk and it must be close too." Edward put his arm over his nose to try to stop the odor. The smell was so strong he could taste it. "Man it's got to be right here next to us." His voice was nasally as he tried not to breathe in the rancid smell.

It was like a light bulb lit in Rory's mind. "You don't suppose…?" He took off around the corner of the house.

"Where are you going? You want to get sprayed too, you idiot?" Edward called. No way was he facing a skunk.

"It's not a skunk you dumb ass, she's tricked us!" Rory called as he got to the open bedroom window. The smell was stronger here and his eyes began to water. His stomach lurched and he knew he was going to puke. He crumbled to his knees and began to heave. The little bitch was smart. Devious too.

"Oh shit! Justin is going to kill us when he finds out we let her get away." Edwards nasally voice hitched and he doubled over and lost his dinner. "There's no way I can track her. All I can smell and taste is skunk. What kind of woman keeps skunk scent in her house?"

"A smart one." Rory gasped. Cassandra was known for her tracking skills. It would not be easy to find her if she didn't want to be found. They had to go tell Justin the news but getting themselves up out of their own vomit was going to take some time. He was so sick right now, all he wanted to do was curl up in the fetal position and let the sickness pass.

Cassandra ran until she reached the falls, her eyes watering from the smell of herself, but she didn't dare stop. She swam across the cold river was cold, the water tugging at her clothes, weighing her down. It took precious minutes to fight the current to get to the other side. Once there, she removed her clothes and shifted. Her phone, like her car, would have to be left behind. Her cat slid down the embankment into the river and she let the swiftly moving water carry her downstream. Her heart was breaking as she left her home and her beloved behind. *"I love you, Michael. Forgive me."*

Chapter 4

Sunlight filtered through the leaves of the trees, splashing bright light on the mostly shaded path. The sanctuary consisted of mainly footpaths. The council had voted years ago not to disturb the rustic peaceful area. Everyone had vehicles, of course, but they were all housed in the big parking garage with the paved driveway that led to the main road.

Michael hurried along the footpath. He couldn't wait to slip the diamond on Cassandra's left hand. He patted his jean pocket to reassure himself that it was still there.

"Cassandra," he called as he opened the front door. "Are you finished with work for the day?"

"Ah, Michael…what perfect timing. I was about to send for you."

Michael looked around anxiously. "Where's Cassandra? I thought she was here."

"I have no idea where she has gone, but you're going to find her."

"What do you mean? I was supposed to meet her here, we have some exciting news to share." What the hell was going on? Justin was acting strange and where was Cassandra?

"She's been here and gone. I'm afraid little Cassandra did not care for her new duties and she has now run off in a snit. I need you to locate, capture and return her to me."

Cassandra had left without saying anything to him. Surely Justin was mistaken. Michael knew she loved her home and, more importantly, loved him. She would never leave. "Justin, what the hell are you talking about? What new duties? Cassandra is one of the hardest working people I know. She would never shirk her duties.

Justin nodded. "So true, Cassandra is very ambitious and is a regular firecracker."

"This makes no sense to me. Cassandra loves the sanctuary and would take on any duty if it benefited the good of the people living within our circle." There was more at work here than Justin was admitting. Something terrible had happened in this room before his arrival.

"I'm so glad that you feel that way brother." Justin held out his hand. "Congratulate me. I have found my mate."

"Mate? I don't understand. What does that have to do with Cassandra?" he ignored the outstretched hand. He had a very uneasy feeling.

Justin was practically jumping out of his skin in excitement. He couldn't wait to see the look of horror on his brother's face when he told him the news. "Well, you see brother," he sneered, "Cassandra is going to be my chosen mate. In her surprise at the glorious turn of events, I'm afraid she has bolted."

"The hell you say!" Michael exploded. "Over my dead body!" He charged for Justin, his hands extended for his exposed throat.

"No, brother. Not your dead body but your sainted mother's." Justin never moved to avoid the hands coming toward him. He knew that his next words would stop his aggressor before he reached his goal.

Michael froze, his hands dropped to his side. "What do you know about my mother?" Justin had never cared for Michael's mother. He assumed it was just jealousy because of her taking the place of Justin's own mother, but maybe there was more to it.

Justin took out a jack knife and began cleaning under his finger nails, one by one. Taking his time to let Michael stew over his announcement. "Your mother is a weak fool. And the only reason she did not meet the same unfortunate accident as our dearly departed father is because I needed her to torment you."

"What are you talking about? Dad should have known better than to run beyond our perimeter. It could have been a hunter, trapper, some scared town person, but no one knows what really happened."

Justin laughed loudly. "Oh, you are so naive! Dad did know better and as much as he preached it into everyone's heads to stay in the boundaries, none of you fools questioned it when his body was found so close to town.

Michael clutched the back of the chair closest to him. He felt weak as if he might pass out. Words escaped him.

This was absolutely priceless. Michael's utter horror was more than he could have wished for. "Our father was weak. He diluted our pure blood by marrying your mother...a human. He allowed others the same freedom."

"Are you mad?" My God, the ramifications of the sickness spilling from Justin's lips.

"Not at all. The pollution was spreading beyond control. Dad would not see reason. He was blinded by lust. I tried to make him understand. We shifted and went running like we often did." He smiled and cocked his brow. "Daddy dearest was getting slow in his old age. He mistakenly thought we were playing as cats often do."

"Stop, Justin. Do you know what you are confessing?" This had to be some kind of sick joke.

Justin walked across the hard wood floor, his cowboy boots stomping with each step. "I'm not confessing. I'm telling you that if you do not go and bring that bitch back, your mother is dead."

Michael's mind was in turmoil. He could not hand Cassandra

over to this mad man, yet if he didn't agree to Justin's demented scheme, his mother's life was in danger. Stalling was all he could do until he came up with a plan. "How do you know that she's left the sanctuary? She could just be out running." He knew in his heart that she was gone. Justin had to have threatened her somehow to make her leave with no word.

"Come." Justin motioned with his finger and walked to the door leading to the kitchen. There, lying on the floor, were Edward and Rory with their throats slit. "These two blundering idiots failed in their task to see that Cassandra not escape."

"My God Justin, you can't go around killing people! We are not animals!" The men's lifeless eyes stared up at him. Blood pooled on the floor around their bodies. The smell of death hung in the air. He'd know them since childhood, knew their families. The sanctuary had suddenly turned into a dark, evil place.

"I'll do as I wish; our blood will once again be pure. Cassandra is strong enough to lead by my side. I want her. Do not disappoint me brother or you too shall meet the same fate as these two fools, but not before you witness the painful death of your mother."

He had no choice. "Cassandra is excellent at avoiding detection." They'd played cat and mouse many times. "She won't be easy to find and I can think of nowhere to begin the search." As far as he knew Cassandra had never been away from Sanctuary. She had even taken her college courses for accounting online, not wanting to leave home.

Justin smiled triumphantly. "Oh, tracking her will not be a problem." He threw a hand held devise.

Michael automatically caught it. "What's this?" It fit snugly in his hand.

"It's a GPS. Turn it on."

Michael held the button in and watched as the screen lit up.

"See the blue dot? That's your quarry. Go bring her back to me."

"How is this possible? You inserted a foreign object into her body. When? How?" Michael was outraged. "The swine flu vaccination, that's how you inserted it! You were adamant that we all receive it." He ran his index finger along the ridge in his left bicep. "You injected all of us with trackers." The bastard knew the whereabouts of everyone at any given time. All these years they thought they lived freely, safely and all along they'd been puppets on a mad man's string.

"Very good, you're not as stupid as I thought. Leave now, Michael, and good hunting." Justin dismissed him and walked up the platform to sit on his self-made throne. His plans were in place. Michael would bring Cassandra back if only to save his mother. He would marry the girl of his dreams and torment the thorn in his side until he got tired of the game. Killing him would wait until

Cassandra was swollen to bursting, carrying his pure offspring.

* * * *

Michael glanced at the GPS. Cassandra was following the river. He had to find her and together they could figure a way out of this mess. It was beginning to get dark as he started down the foot path, the faint odor of skunk still hung in the air. His girl was smart. He chuckled imagining her putting the scent on her clothes. She had guts, no doubt about it.

"This is Michael." He answered.

"Michael, this is Edmund Blake. I have news about your mother."

"You've found her?"

"I'm afraid the news is not good."

Oh God, he had already killed her. Michael sat down on a big bench along the path, his elbows on his knees, and waited for Edmund to give him the news.

"She's in a medical facility. I don't know the details as I'm not family. I can tell you that the patients at this home do not survive long. I'm sorry I could not find out any other information."

"She's safe though? No one is holding her against her will? Give me the address." He put his phone on speaker and brought up the note app and jotted down the address. He knew the area, it was a good distance away." The son of a bitch had been bluffing. He didn't have his mother.

"Why yes, she's as well as can be expected given her illness. It did take a bit to find her as she's using the alias Abigail McKay.

"I need you to stay there and make sure that no one gets in to see her until I get there. I have something here that I have to take care of before I can head there." His mother was safe for the time being, but he had to get to Cassandra before Justin sent someone else.

"I'm afraid I can't do that. My job is finished. I'm a private investigator, not a body guard. I'm not good in a fight."

Michael sighed. He could see the weasely little man and knew that Marcus would wipe him out in one swing. "I understand Thank you so much for doing a remarkable job. I really hadn't expected to hear something this quickly."

"You're very welcome and if there's ever anything else I can help you with, please do not hesitate to call. Have a good evening." The line went dead.

Michael knew that his mother was safe for the time being, he was in no hurry. Now he had to make sure that Justin could not track him. The man obviously didn't know where his mother was and he wanted to keep it that way. He dialed his phone. "Jordan, grab a couple of guys you know you can trust and meet me at the river."

Chapter 5

The facility was small not at all what he had expected. It had taken him five hours to get here and he was exhausted. Dim lights welcomed him through the windows and the door as he mounted the cement steps. He tapped lightly on the door as a woman in a nurse uniform walked down the hall. It was late and he didn't want to disturb those that may be sleeping.

"Can I help you?"she asked as she opened the door. "I'm afraid visiting hours are over."

"I'm sorry to come calling so late, but I've just been notified that my mother is a patient here. I've driven for hours and wondered if I might be allowed to see her?" He hadn't thought of the time and it wouldn't have made a difference, he had to know that she was okay.

"And what is your mother's name?" She smiled. There really was no policy against allowing family members in at any hours. It was just unusual in a small town to have such late night guests. The town practically rolled up its sidewalks by nine in the evening.

"Abigail. Abigail Hu.." he caught himself in time remembering what Edmund had said. "Abigail McKay." His mother was using her maiden name. She must have suspected that Justin would look for her. She was right to be cautious.

"Oh, I'm so sorry Mr. McKay. Your mother is not doing at all well. Please, please come on in. I'll take you right back to her room." she gushed as she ushered him through the door.

Michael didn't contradict the nurse on his surname, it wasn't important. Besides, if she knew that their last names didn't match, she might change her mind about allowing him entrance.

The place looked like a home on the outside but definitely smelled like a medical facility on the inside. Disinfectants had such distinctive odors. He heard moaning in many of the rooms and beeps from various monitors.

"Right this way." She opened the door at the end of the hall and peeked in. "Abigail, you have a visitor." She talked softly and turned on the bed side lamp. The bulb shined a soft light, casting the room in shadows as to not hurt the eyes.

The air in the room was stagnant and very warm, as if the person inside was always cold. "Hi mom." he called softly as he entered. He stopped. It was the wrong room, the nurse was mistaken, the frail skeletal woman lying in the hospital bed was not his beautiful vibrant mother.

"Michael?" The voice was raspy as if in pain and short of

breath.

"Yeah mom, it's me." He swallowed the tears. His chest hurt and his eyes watered. He approached the bed, never noticing when the nurse left shutting the door quietly behind her.

"Look at you, you're beautiful." She coughed as if speaking robbed her of what little air she could draw into her struggling lungs.

He clasped the delicate hand she held out to him. "So are you." He spoke quietly there was something about sick people and hospitals that made a person want to whisper. Her once full head of bright auburn curls was gone, replaced by a bald head. Her beautiful green eyes were now sunken and lifeless.

"You always were a sweet talker, even as a child."

He leaned down and kissed her forehead. "You'll always be beautiful to me. I've missed you."

"Come, sit and tell me what you've been up to." Abigail patted the bed beside her.

Michael moved to pull the chair up beside the railing of the inclined bed.

"No, sit here." She again patted the bed, there wasn't much time and she'd missed her boy so badly she wanted to keep him close for as long as possible.

He lowered the rail and perched on the mattress. Her body barely took up any room. She was wasting away.

"Tell me everything. I'm sure I've missed lots. Are you

happy?" Her heart monitor increased as if the question was very important.

"I'm good. I'm getting married." He smiled the first genuine smile since entering the gloomy room.

"Oh Michael! I'm so happy." She clasped her hands together and raised them to her mouth. "That is wonderful news. Do I know her?"

"Well..." Michael began.

"Wait, don't tell me. It's Cassandra isn't it? Well of course it is. Who else could it be?"

She looked so excited. He tapped the end of her nose. "Now how would you know that?"

"Oh pish." She waved her hand. "You and that girl have always been thick as thieves. I wasn't blind I could see the way you looked at her. I knew someday she would be my daughter."

"We want you to be at our wedding. We'll get you home and you'll soon be back on your feet. Then we'll have our wedding." Again the monitor changed tempo. "Mom, this isn't a rehabilitation center is it?"

"No Michael, I won't be leaving here. It's a hospice, I'm dying."

He shook his head, he'd just found her surely there was something they could do.

She lifted her left hand it shook badly but she laid it to rest against his bristly cheek. I've missed you, handsome, and there is nothing more I would like than to see you wed that girl of yours, but I'm at peace. And I'm dying on my terms, not at the whim of a mad man. I beat the bastard."

"Justin." It dawned on Michael why his mother had left with no word. "You knew what happened to dad."

She nodded, silent tears slid down her pale face. "Yes, I knew I also knew that if I stayed, he would eventually use me to hurt you and so I made the hardest decision of my life. I left everything and everyone I loved behind to keep that threat from you."

He already had but Michael didn't tell her that. She deserved to die thinking that she had done what every mother promises. Keeping her kids safe I'll be damned if he would let her know that her sacrifice had been for nothing.

He could see her eyelids drooping. She was so weak and exhausted. "Why don't you rest mom? I'll be here when you wake up."

"I'm going to be resting soon enough. Where is Cassandra? Did she make the trip with you?"

"No," he squeezed her hand. "She had some business to take care of but I promise I'll bring her for a visit soon. Rest now." He sighed as she closed her eyes.

"Just a few moments. Don't let me sleep long. I don't want to miss any time with you." Her breathing was shallow, short gentle pants as if she couldn't draw a full steady breath.

He got up from the chair and walked to the window. He hoped Cassandra was safe. She had to have a haven in mind but for the life of him he didn't know where she was headed. He couldn't leave his mom's side. She didn't have much time left and he would be here with her until the end.

* * * *

"Robert? Robert?"

The sun was just rising, its pinkish glow shining on the horizon when Michael heard his mother calling for his father. He stood up and gripped her hand. "No, mom, it's Michael."

"What? Oh Michael, you're still here." she smiled.

Michael turned as the door opened. An elderly man with black rimmed glasses came in the room with a chart. Michael assumed he was his mother's doctor but ignored him for the time being. "Were you dreaming mom? You were calling for dad." It was eerie hearing his dad's name on her lips after so many years.

"Well, I must have been. I could have sworn I heard your dad calling to me." she yawned.

"It's early mom. Go back to sleep." He needed coffee. Surely there was a cafeteria somewhere in the building. His eyes were scratchy from too little sleep. He had been awake most of the night listening to her uneven breathing. Sometimes he swore she stopped breathing altogether.

"You'll be here when I wake?" she asked, her voice already fading as she drifted back into a fitful sleep.

"I'm not going anywhere." he promised.

"I hope you're prepared son, it won't be long now."

Michael looked at the man standing beside the bed. "I know., She's gone downhill just in the last few hours."

"I'm Dr. Kincaid." he held out his hand.

Michael took it in a firm grip. "Thanks for taking such good care of her."

The doctor nodded. "I'm sorry that we can't do more." He turned to the table. "Here." He handed Michael a cup. "The nurse sent this in for you. She peaked in earlier and saw you were sleeping in the chair. She thought you might need this."

Michael accepted the cup. "Please thank her for me." He took a sip of the dark liquid.

"If you need anything just let us know." The door made no sound as the doctor walked out.

* * * *

"Look at that squirrel sitting so pretty up there." Abigail pointed at the wall across the room. "Isn't he the cutest little thing with his tail twitching?"

"Yeah mom he's a cute little bugger." Michael agreed. The doctor had been wrong. The hallucinations had started three days ago. Her arms were now covered in long scratches where she had tried to dig the imaginary spiders off that were crawling in her skin.

"Rob…" She gurgled.

Michael took the rag and wiped the thick slime that gathered in her mouth. Her lungs were filling with fluid and she was slowly choking to death.

"Oh Michael, I'm so sorry you have to do this. I'm such a nasty mess. No mother wants her child to see her in such a condition." she apologized, lucid for the time being.

"You always took good care of me mom. Now it's my turn." He used a clean damp cloth and ran it along her forehead and down her neck.

"Oh God, it hurts." she moaned and arched her back. Pain racked her body, the pain pills no longer having any affect.

"I know mom, try to rest." He prayed that she would sleep, her lucid periods were few and far between, most times she had no idea who he was. It broke his heart. He prayed that it would soon be over and she would at last be at peace.

"I love you, Michael."

"I love you too mom, forever and always." He stood and bent over to kiss her forehead.

"Robert, I'm right here. I'm coming." she called to the man she had always loved. Her breath hitched.

Michael sat up straighter in his chair and leaned forward waiting for her to take another breath, one second and then two. She breathed again. She opened her eyes and looked straight into his and smiled a big beautiful smile. She drew another deep breath and then drew no more.

"Say hi to dad." Michael whispered. He laid his forehead on his clasped hands on the bed beside his mother's body and sobbed. His body shook as he let his grief over take him.

Chapter 6

The current was stronger than she thought. The big cat struggled to keep her head above water. The river carried her for miles downstream. Logs and tree branches grabbed at her body leaving long bloody slashes in her hide. The water stung the open lacerations. The cat snarled. She hated water. *"Calm down, we'll soon be able to reach land. Don't resist, let the current carry you."* Cassandra spoke to her cat trying to reassure her that they would be okay. She could sense the feline wanting to shift to get away from the pain from the cuts but Cassandra knew in human form she would most definitely drown. She used up precious energy controlling her other self.

Finally, the rapid rush began to slow and the depth became more shallow. The cat scrambled and got her footing on the rocky surface. Exhausted, she pulled herself up the embankment and collapsed on the ground. Her heart pounded and her breathing was irregular. She had to rest for a few precious moments. Time was of the essence, Justin would have been notified by now and he would be coming for her.

* * * *

The sleek body moved carefully through the tall grass. Branches from the closely grown sumac bushes pulled, tangling in the fur covered body.

She tried to move quietly but the branches were unmovable as she struggled through them. Even crouching low and crawling through did not keep the thorns on the branches from entangling in her coat.

She had been walking for days. Exhaustion and hunger were growing stronger with each step the worn out cat took. Discipline would only last so long and then Cassandra would lose control and the cat's personality would take over.

The rapid thumping of a heart and two pulled them off course as a doe with a new born fawn lay beneath a tree not fifteen yards from her. *No, stick to the plan! He will find us. Keep going, we must find a safe haven.* Cassandra was harsh with the cat. No way was she going back. Justin's demands that she mate with him and bring the breathen closer, make them stronger was delusional. We live in the 21st century. No longer were we governed by the rules of generations ago. Females were free to live the lives they wished. Justin had become unstable and so far no one had stood against him.

The cat growled in irritation, she turned her head and sank low on her belly prowling toward the frightened doe. Cassandra was losing control of that part of her that was human. Fear and desperation had her screaming, pleading with the cat. *"No! Keep moving we have to find some place to hide."*

The cat retreated for the time being and once more Cassandra was in control. She turned and slowly resumed the painful trek through the briars. The stream offered protection, the water masked our scent. Again the cat hesitated not wanting to get wet, remembering the current of the river. *"We must go into the water, it will aid us in our escape from those who even now hunt us. We need all the help we can get. Please, for me."*

The water was frigid; this early in the year the sun had yet to warm it. Ever so slowly she eased her body into the stream. The bottom was rocky and she walked down for several hundred yards. The route would have been easier had she just simply crossed, but she hoped to lose those pursuing her by taking this longer trek. Small fish banged against furred legs as they swam with the current of the water while the cat walked against it. She stopped and listened, small rodents ran in the grass and the usual nocturnal animals roamed unafraid. Cassandra sighed in relief all was well. If her enemies were near the night would have warned her by being deathly still. Carefully she put one foot in front of the other and pulled her body up over the embankment. *"No don't shake."* she warned the cat who wanted to shake the water from her body. *"It will spread our scent. We can't risk it."* The cat growled in irritation but let the water run from her body, stinging her eyes and dripping down her nose.

The logging road was a blessing. They would never expect her to take such an easy course. Her body couldn't continue at this pace. She'd been on the move for almost a week sleeping only when absolutely necessary. Savannah wouldn't wait much longer before calling in the cavalry, namely her husband and brother in law. She had to reach the house before that happened. Savannah was a wolf and wolf and cougar didn't normally mix well. She felt terrible running to the small pack and of course wouldn't stay long as she had no wish to put her in danger; the only saving grace was that no one knew of their friendship. They had met years ago as cubs. Knowing that it was taboo, they had never let others know of the deep friendship and even after Savannah moved away, they kept in touch secretly. Savannah was and always would be her greatest friend.

The cat moved along the logging road for an hour before turning off and once again traveling through the forest. This time the walking was easier as the trees were larger and no longer grabbed at her fur covered body.

* * * *

"What the hell?" Dylan turned from the big window of the bait shop. A favored spot, everyone loved to sit on the furniture and watch the wild life through the big patio windows. "Jimmy there's a damn cougar walking through the yard."

"The hell you say." Jimmy let go of his wife. "I'll grab my gun. Christ, I haven't seen one of them in years. We sure don't want one of those buggers hanging around."

"Wait!" Savannah ran to the window. The big cat moved slowly, her majestic body floating through the meadow. Her head down as if exhausted. She stumbled but kept on walking as if not knowing her actual destination.

"I'm gonna need help. Come on." She grabbed a blanket off the back of the couch and ran for the door.

"Savannah, what in the sam hell do you think you're doing? That's a cougar out there, a killer!" Jimmy yelled at his wife but followed her faithfully out the door. "Dylan grab the gun, crazy ass woman is gonna get herself killed."

"You won't need it, that's my best friend out there." She ran down the patio steps and raced across the meadow. She could hear the stomping of feet behind her and knew her husband and brother in law were following.

"Cassandra!" She called when she got within fifty feet of the big cat.

The cat snarled and swiped its paws.

"Damn it, Savannah, get back!" Jimmy warned.

"Cassandra sweetie it's me," Savannah stopped and talked softly. "You made it, you're safe now."

Cassandra fought within the cat. She could hear someone calling her name. She was starving and so exhausted. Endless miles and days of walking, running and worrying had taken their toll, her mind felt shattered.

Savannah knelt on the ground the blanket laid beside her. "Come on Cassandra, come back to me."

Safe. Savannah. We made it. Safety. She repeated it over and over to the cat. She had to fight the instinct to tear anything apart that threatened them. She looked up and saw the beautiful sable haired woman kneeling in the meadow and recognized her immediately. She dropped to her belly and pulled herself across the ground.

"Will you look at that?" Dylan couldn't believe his eyes as the big cat crawled right up to Savannah and laid her head in her lap.

"You're alright now. You did a good job of protecting my friend. We've got her now, rest." She pet the big lion's head and crooned softly to her.

The big cat let out along puff of air and closed her eyes.

Savannah felt the bones moving beneath her hands. Fur then skin lay beneath her palms. Long hair and then short along the body lying across her lap. The fact that the shift was taking so long attested to how bad a shape her friend was in. "Boys, either close your eyes or turn your back." she called to Jimmy and Dylan while never taking her eyes off the struggling transformation taking place.

"Woman, I'm not turning my back on that thing!" Jimmy argued.

"Do it now!" she yelled back. "I'm not in any danger, but I don't want her to be embarrassed by you two galoots staring at her naked either.

"What?"

Dylan grabbed Jimmy by the shoulder and turned him around. "There's more going on here than we know bud."

The cat gave a long shudder, her back arched and the fur disappeared. Savannah's hands lay entangled in Cassandra's long hair. She grabbed the blanket from the ground and wrapped her friend's naked body in it. Cassandra never moved; her body had gone as far as it was able. "Jimmy."

"Right here, hon."

She looked over her shoulder to see her husband standing there with a look of wonder on his face. She smiled and shook her head.

"You didn't really think that I would keep my back turned did you?" The woman lying upon his wife was beautiful but much too pale.

"You'll have to carry her." Savannah scooted back as Jimmy squatted down and lifted Cassandra into his arms.

"It's Cassandra, isn't it?" Jilly held the door open for them all, then went into Dylan's arms.

Savannah ran ahead and moved the pillows to the end of the couch adjusting the blanket as Jimmy gently lay Cassandra on the soft cushions. "How did you know about Cassandra?" Their friendship had been a secret.

"I've always known." Jilly lifted her shoulders.

"You never said anything." She pushed the hair back from Cassandra's forehead and checked for a fever.

"She's fine love. Just exhausted." Jimmy pulled her back against his body and wrapped his arms around her kissing the side of her neck.

"How come you've never mentioned her?"

"She's a cougar." Jilly answered.

"She's my dearest friend." Savannah defended.

"And that's why I never mentioned it." Jilly replied. "I figured if you wanted me to know, that you'd tell me. I'm glad you had someone. If she's your friend, then she's ours too and we'll protect her from whatever scared her so badly that she arrived on our doorstep in that condition."

"Absolutely." Dylan and Jimmy agreed simultaneously.

Chapter 7

"I'm going to have to leave. I've been here too long already. Sooner or later, he will find me." Cassandra wiped down the table that had just been vacated by two young boys who had devoured burgers and fries after a long day of fishing out on the lake.

Savannah took the rag from her and threw it to Jimmy. "Will you stop thinking you have to work to earn your keep? You're welcome here for as long as you want to stay. As for that bastard, let him come." She snarled, her wolf rising to the surface.

Jimmy tossed the rag into the sink. "Savannah's right. You're welcome to stay for as long as you like. Nobody will get close to you here. We'll see to it."

"What's this about leaving?" Dylan joined the discussion. His hands linked with Jilly's.

Cassandra smiled. "I swear you are all like newlyweds, all this touchy feely stuff going on. But seriously, you guys have been great. I care about you all too much to put you in any danger and believe me there will be trouble. You don't understand what he's like."

"We've dealt with bullies before." Jimmy pulled Savannah closer, remembering the attack on her, but she had survived. They all had and they were a tight knit family which he now considered Cassandra a part of.

The bell above the door rang and they all looked up to see who had entered.

Michael stepped into the small bait shop. It was a nice, family owned business. Cassandra had been in this same location for the past two weeks according to the GPS. She must have found a safe haven so he took the extra days and laid his mother to rest. Now it was time to reclaim his love. He looked around and saw two couples surrounding Cassandra. He took a deep breath. Her familiar scent had the hair rising on the back of his neck. His boot heels echoed on the hard wood floor as he ate up the distance between them.

"My my my..." Savannah murmered. "Who is that tall drink of water?"

Cassandra gasped. "It's Hunter. Michael Hunter."

"Cassie Ann, you have been holding out on me! Will you look at that body? The man sure knows how to fill out a pair of jeans! And his arms... oofda! I bet he's even carrying a six pack under that shirt."

"Uh, Savannah? I'm standing right here." Jimmy grumbled.

Savannah never looked at him but patted his chest with her palm. "Yeah, I know honey. The Michael?" she arched her brow.

Cassandra could only nod as she watched him approach, looking into beautiful brown eyes she thought she would never see again.

"Oh, Cassie Ann. You ran from my arms into the ranks of a pack of wolves?"

Jimmy and Dylan stepped forward to protect the women. Savannah was faster she leaped at Michael and hit him full force with her hands in the square of his chest. "Back off, kitty!"

The blow never moved him, but he stopped and held up his hands in surrender.

"It's fine, Savannah." Cassandra placed her hand on Savannah's shoulder. "What are you doing here, Michael?" She stepped forward. He looked so tired, so handsome. She'd missed him. "You can't be here." It was breaking her heart seeing him, knowing that she had to let him go to keep him safe.

"Justin sent me." The shock on her face confirmed to him that Justin had somehow threatened him. His brother used torture and fear to manipulate those he deemed beneath him.

She took a step back, her hand going to her mouth. "How did you find me? I was so careful to hide my tracks." No one knew of Savannah's connection to her. "I was sure I would have more time."

Michael grimaced. "I'm sorry, sweetheart, but I've known

where you are every moment that you've been gone."

"Impossible!"

He held up the hand held device and pulled up the map. "By the looks of it, you had quite an adventure on your way here."

"What is that?" It looked like a small walkie talkie you could carry in your pocket.

"It's a GPS. It seems that Justin had us all injected with small tracking devices." He turned to the side and showed the small incision on his left shoulder. He and Jordan had removed the tracker from each other and the rest of the group before he left the sanctuary. By now they would have all been removed from the rest of the people living there. No longer would Justin be able to track and manipulate the people.

"Son of a bitch!" Jimmy muttered. "That is one twisted bastard."

"Excuse me." Cassandra turned and headed for the bathroom.

Michael nodded at Jimmy's words but never took his eyes from Cassandra's retreating back.

"She wants to leave." Savannah spoke. "Says it's not safe."

"She's right." Michael looked around the small store.

"I know someone. Somewhere you can take her. He'll keep you safe."

"No way." he shook his head. "I don't need someone to help

me keep my fiancé safe."

"Look, cat, that girl is my best friend. If you let anything happen to her because of your enlarged ego, I'll hunt your fuzzy ass down!" Her skin prickled, she could feel her wolf moving within wanting to defend her.

"Savannah calm down." Jimmy tried to grab her but she was quick to avoid his grasp.

"No! You guys and your macho bullshit! I won't gamble with Cassandra's well-being just to keep the kitty happy. I don't know shit about him, but that girl means the world to me."

"She's lucky to have you."

Michael stared at the closed door. What the hell was she doing in there?

* * * *

Cassandra felt around her arms, breasts and legs; she felt no bumps or ridges. Wait...there on her inner thigh, a small ridge. She had no idea when or how it had been placed inside her body. Knowing Justin's love for tranquilizers, he had to at some point tranqed her and installed the small device and in his twisted mind placed it in an intimate spot. The how and when were not important; she had to remove it. She dug through the cabinet drawer, no knives but there was a pair of scissors. She jabbed deep. The pain was excruciating she felt the tip hit the tiny device and maneuvered under it.

"Oh my God!" she whispered. She couldn't pass out. The hole wasn't big enough to extract the foreign body. She see sawed around the edge to make the incision bigger. Blood oozed from the wound making it hard to see. With her free hand she spread the now gaping hole open and again used the tip of the scissors to extract the unit. "Come on." She bit her bottom lip to keep from screaming in agony. Finally, she saw a corner sticking out of the crevice. She grabbed it with her fingers and pulled; it was tiny, maybe quarter inch in diameter. With a sigh of relief, she threw it in the toilet and flushed. Exhausted and weak from pain, she allowed herself to sink to the floor.

Michael knew something was wrong. She'd been gone too long. "Excuse me." He started in the direction she had taken.

"Just a minute, cat! I'm not done yet." Savannah called after him. The stubborn man never looked back.

"You were sending him to Marcus weren't you?" Jimmy strolled up and wrapped his arm around her.

She leaned into him and nodded. "Can you think of another bad ass that could protect them? Marcus might be a lot of things, but he's a protector. He wouldn't let anything happen to her."

"I have a hard time forgiving the man for what he did to you, but you're right. He's a mean SOB and would die protecting the underdog."

The door was partially open. "Cassandra, are you okay?" Michael pushed softly on the door. "Oh Jesus!" She lay on the floor, her jeans around her knees, blood spilling from a wound near her hip. "I need help in here!" He dropped to his knees beside her and cradled her head in his lap. "Oh Cass, what have you done?" He brushed the hair from her forehead and kissed her softly.

Savannah, Jimmy, Dylan and Jilly all stood at the door. "I'll get the suture kit." Jilly knelt at the cabinet and pulled out the first aid kit. "She'll need stitches but under these conditions I don't think we want to risk questions at a hospital. I can do it."

Jimmy, Dylan and Savannah knelt around her body to help hold her.

Michael nodded. "I think she hit the femoral artery." He grabbed a towel off the rack and blotted the blood.

Jilly looked at the wound. "No, it's bleeding quite heavily, but it's not the artery. If she shifts, she'll heal faster."

"No." Cassandra shook her head. "I can't."

Michael knew she must be in terrible pain if she couldn't shift. "What were you thinking, Cass?" he whispered, his palms caressed her cheek and she leaned into his warmth, feeling his love radiating through them.

"I couldn't let him find me."

"Oh, but I already have."

Michael looked up to see Justin standing in the open doorway.

"I got tired of waiting for my bride, brother. First, you remove your tracking device and go off the grid and now I find you here. It seems you have been a naughty kitty. I'm afraid your mother is as good as dead." he threatened.

Michael growled. His big body leaped over top of all five people on the floor. "My mother *is* dead, you dirty son of a bitch!" His fist connected with Justin's jaw, his body followed through taking the man to the floor. "She's dead! I was with her through the end and now Cassie is lying in a pool of blood." He hit him again. "Your days of manipulating..." He hit him again. "...terrorizing..." Again he slammed his fist into Justin's face. "...and treating people like you are the lord and master are over." He struck again and again, seeing red, just wanting it to end.

"Michael. Michael stop." Cassandra called.

Her soft voice reached him when no other could have.

"He's not worth it."

Michael crawled off his bloodied brother and made his way back to Cassandra.

"I suggest you get your sorry ass out of here." Dylan pumped the gun, the sound of the shell going into the chamber alerting Justin that he did indeed mean business. He rolled to his feet.

"Justin, I suggest you find somewhere else to live. You are

no longer welcome at home." By now Jordan and the rest of the guys had spread the word about the killings and the tracking devices. They wanted to live in peace but would fight for their freedom. Justin would no longer dictate their lives. Dylan followed the man out and locked the door behind him.

"What do you think of Cass's cat now?" Jimmy asked Savannah.

Savannah smiled and looked at her friend cuddled against the big man as Jilly sewed up the hole in her hip. "I think she's got a bad ass kitty of her own and I'm so happy for her."

Epilogue

6 months later

"I can't believe we're doing this?" Michael grumbled.

Savannah knocked on the door. "If you want to back out, we can." She would be hurt, but Michael was more important than her feelings.

"Hell no! I'm not backing out. I can't wait for tomorrow."

"Savannah's my best friend. I want her to be there."

"I know, darling. I'll always be grateful to your friends for keeping you safe, it just goes against my nature to share a meal with wolves." he chuckled.

The door opened. "Happy Thanksgiving!" Savannah chimed. "Come in."

"It's cold up here in your north woods, Savannah, and the snow, my goodness!" Cassandra stepped into the toasty warm home.

Savannah chuckled. "I know, but it's wonderful for business. The snow brings the snowmobilers and the cold has them stopping in for warm drinks and food."

"I'm so excited to see you! We have so much to be thankful

for this year. Family," she smiled as Jimmy was joined by Dylan and Jilly, "old friends and new."

"Yes." Savannah smiled slyly and unzipped the huge parka. Michael helped ease it from her shoulders. "We have much to be thankful for." She put her hand over her extended belly and Michael placed his upon it.

"Oh, my gosh! Cassie Ann, you do have a way with keeping secrets! That's why you wouldn't shift, isn't it?"

Cassie nodded. "I wasn't certain but didn't want to take the chance of hurting the baby."

"Congratulations!" Jimmy extended his hand to Michael and kissed Cassandra on the cheek.

"What a wonderful surprise!" Jilly joined the fray of hugs and kisses.

Savannah squealed in delight. "I'm so happy for you! How are things at home?'

"They're great." Cassandra replied. "It's so peaceful there, you must come and visit us. How about Christmas?" she pleaded.

Savannah arched her brow in question at Jimmy, at his nod she agreed. "We'd love too. No problems with the brother from hell?" she asked.

"Nope, no one has seen hide nor hair of him." Michael caressed Cassandra's belly, smiling as her baby kicked his palm. "Although, I did see your man slinking around a couple times."

Marcus had reported back the same news. No sign of Justin, for now anyway, but a man as twisted as him was sure to turn up somewhere. "He's not my man, but he is good in a fight. I'm glad things are good. We have much to be thankful for this year. Come on let's eat. Today, we celebrate Thanksgiving with our new family; tomorrow, we celebrate your wedding. We're honored that you chose to have your wedding here. Happy Thanksgiving!"

"Happy Thanksgiving to our first of many together." Cassandra leaned up on her tiptoes entwining her arms around her soon to be husband's neck and gave him a sweet kiss. "I love you forever and always."

"Happy Thanksgiving, Cass." he returned her kiss.

Defender of Shadows

Chapter 1

After six long years at school she was finally going home with her degree in hand. Her cell phone rang the notes of "Bad Boy" by Tim McGraw. She knew it was Jimmy calling. "Hey bro, so am I an Aunt?" Jimmy had been devastated not to be able to make her graduation yet elated because his wife Savannah had gone into labor just hours before they were due to leave for the ceremony. "That's wonderful! A baby girl! I'm on my way. I can't wait to see everyone! Don't be upset. I'm so happy for you and Savannah." Their courtship had not been easy but they were so happy now and after five years of marriage they finally had a little one to share their love with. "I should be there in about four hours. And I have awesome news...I was offered a job at the university." She lifted her shoulder to hold her phone in place as she pulled the lever to dim her lights as she met an oncoming car.

The deer came out of nowhere. She slammed on her breaks. "Oh shit!" The big buck hit the bumper of her little Geo Tracker and rolled up over the hood, busting out her windshield. "Oh my god!"

she screamed as something sharp cut her cheek. She cranked the steering wheel, a reflex action and the tiny SUV careened down through the ditch. The car bounced and tilted. "God, please help me!" It was like everything was in slow motion; she saw the trees in front of her, the shadows dancing eerily around her little car. The SUV bucked as it tore over rocks, limbs scraped the side of the car. She held on fiercely to the steering wheel, but still her body rocked against the door and center console. There was a terrible crunch as the vehicle crashed into a massive tree. Someone was screaming, it had to be her, but all she saw was a bright light that seemed to be moving closer to her. She tried to turn her head but pain exploded and then she saw nothing.

* * * *

"Come on, Carrie. Wake up." A warm hand pressed against her forehead. "Why won't she wake up?"

"Jimmy, sweetheart, she's suffered a terrible trauma. The rest is good for her. It will allow her body to heal."

"We should have been there, Savannah." He sat down by the hospital bed and picked up his sister's hand. She lay as still as death. Her skin was so pale. A big bandage covered the left side of her face and her left leg was in a cast from thigh to ankle and hung in traction.

"It wouldn't have mattered if we had gone or not... she still would have driven home. Who knew that our daughter would arrive on the very day that Carrie graduated?" Savannah herself had just gotten dismissed from the hospital. She refused to stay put when her family needed her. She stood at the back of his chair and wrapped her arms around Jimmy's neck.

He grasped her hand and kissed her knuckles. "I'm sorry, Darlin', I didn't mean it like that. I love you and Samantha and would not change her birth for the world. He looked over at the car seat where their new born daughter lay sleeping. "I'm just so damn scared."

"I know you are, sweetie, but she's going to be fine"

"Thanks to whomever it was that stopped. He was able give me directions to exactly where the wreck was. The doctor told me that if he hadn't wrapped her leg, she would have bled out." The man hadn't given his name and the paramedics said that there was no one at the scene when they arrived.

"I wonder why he left the scene? Surely he knew that we would want to thank him."

"I don't know, darlin'," Jimmy ran his hands through his hair. "I can't help but think his voice sounded familiar."

* * * *

Carrie could hear them talking. She tried to open her eyes but was not able to. She felt as if her arms and legs had weights lying across them.

"She's going to have a terrible scar on her face, even with the surgery. The doc said that there was no more they could do." The cut ran from her left eye down her cheek to her jaw line. "And her leg...the doctor said that she would need extensive physical therapy but even then would walk with a limp for the rest of her life. She loved to run and now that option is gone."

"Yes, sweetie, but she is alive."

"No thanks to that damn cracker jack car she was driving! She's going to be pissed when she finds out it's totaled but now I'll make sure she gets something that will be built to protect her." The little tin can of a car had been bent right around her body. They had to use the Jaws of Life to remove her from the wreckage. "It's a miracle to me that someone was able to shimmy through the wreckage and wrap her leg."

"Jimmy, the deer came through her windshield. A different vehicle probably wouldn't have made a difference."

"Carrie, can you hear me? Open your eyes; you're scaring the holy hell out of me." He stared hard at her face, waiting impatiently for any sign that she was waking up.

Again Carrie tried to open her eyes, but she was so groggy. They must be giving her sedatives because her whole body felt heavy.

"It's been three days, she should be waking up."

"She's fine. They've done brain scans, cat scans and blood work. You name it, they've done it. Everything has come back normal."

The door to her hospital room opened and Dylan Rudolph walked in. "Ah, Jimmy? This package just arrived for Carrie."

Jimmy stood up and eyed the package. "What is it?"

"I'm not sure but it has holes poked in the sides." Dylan handed the box to Jimmy.

Jimmy took it. "Who's it from?"

Dylan shrugged his shoulders. "The nurse said someone just delivered it and the card just reads 'Get Well Soon'."

"That's weird." He took out his pocket knife and carefully cut through the shipping tape. He heard shuffling in the box. "What the hell?" He opened the flap and inside was a little fur ball with legs.

"Oh, what a cutie!" Savannah gasped and picked the small puppy out of the box.

"Look there's a note." Dylan grabbed the folded paper and read the message. "Congratulations Sprout. I'm proud of you."

"Son of A Bitch!" Jimmy looked at his wife. "It's from him isn't it?"

"How did he know?" Savannah asked.

"It was him on the phone. I knew that voice sounded familiar!"

Dylan looked back and forth between the couple "What the hell are you two talking about? You know who stopped and helped Carrie?"

Jimmy nodded. "It was Marcus Cooper."

Savannah carried the little Shih Tzu puppy over to Carrie's hospital bed. She placed it alongside of Carrie's neck.

"Savannah, what are you doing? Get rid of that thing before she wakes up! My sister is not keeping any gifts from that man."

"Look, Jimmy." She backed away from the bed and looped her finger in Jimmy's belt loop. She leaned her body into his and whispered. "Look at her face."

The small brown and black puppy snuggled against Carrie's uninjured cheek, its little pink tongue darted out to lick Carrie's pale skin.

Jimmy watched as a small smile flitted across his baby sister's face. Tears fell silently; the first signs of life had just appeared. His breath hitched as he tried to keep himself from bawling like a baby in relief.

Dylan stood at the foot of the bed. Jilly had told him about the whole dirty mess with Marcus. He was glad she was home with the baby but she'd be pissed that she had missed out on the surprise. "Why is Marcus sending your little sister gifts?" He better have answers when he repeated tonight's happenings to his wife or there would be hell to pay and he did not want an angry she-wolf wife on his hands.

Jimmy shook his head. "Who knows but what I do know is that the man saved my sister's life." He angled his head to the bed with the small woman and puppy, the smile was still on her face. "And for that act alone, I owe him and can forgive him anything." He glanced at Savannah and she nodded her head in approval.

Savannah smiled and squeezed her husband tight. She knew how much it cost him to say that he forgave Marcus, something she'd done years ago. "I'm proud of you, Sweetheart." she whispered and brushed a kiss across his cheek.

"What are we going to do?" He looked at Carrie; her recovery and rehab were going to be long and painful.

"We're going to take it one day at a time. She's a fighter."

* * * *

He stood in the dark shadows of the large parking lot. The rain fell and he squinted up at the dim lights in the second floor window of the hospital. Water ran down the back of his neck and he pulled his coat collar up and around it before shoving his hands in the front pockets of his jeans. It wasn't luck that he had come up on the accident. He had been following Carrie home to deliver the puppy as a graduation present. He'd been surprised and yet delighted to receive her invitation to her graduation ceremony. She'd been in contact with him over the years via email. She always used the excuse of her studies and research of the wolves for contacting him. He let her. The loneliness sometimes ate at him and her emails were often the highlight of his day.

He'd kept his distance these long years knowing how Jimmy would rather skin him as look at him. He missed the friendship that they had begun but understood his feelings.

When he'd received the invitation, he'd been honored. He'd stood in the back, not wanting to intrude on the family's special time, but had been shocked to see Carrie leave on her own with no sign of Jimmy or Savannah. The accident had been horrifying to watch. The big buck popped out of the road ditch into the little car's path. There had been no time to stop. The collision was unavoidable. He stopped his own vehicle and ran to where the Geo had crashed into a tree. Carrie was unconscious and bleeding profusely. He took off his white tee and wrapped her leg tightly. Her phone lay on the seat and he could hear someone screaming Carrie's name. He recognized Jimmy's voice and without identifying himself, gave exact directions to the scene of the accident and told him to call for an ambulance. He stayed by her side until the EMS arrived and then quickly left the scene. He could not be involved with these people again. It would hurt too much when he had to again return to isolation.

He saw Jimmy come to the window of Carrie's hospital room and stare down at him. They now knew he was close and also had probably come to the conclusion that it had been him who had helped. Jimmy placed his hand against the window glass as if thanking him. Marcus nodded and turned to walk to his truck. Carrie was safe and he could now return to his lonely life and the endless fight to try to save the wolves.

Chapter 2

15 Months Later

"He's a mean son of a bitch." Glen whispered. "They say he's a demon."

"What are they going to do?" Justin asked.

"They don't know; apparently some guy ran a sanctuary to protect them. He was protecting the wolves in an eighty acre enclosure. He's now disappeared. The rumor is that the wolves got him, probably the alpha, a big black bastard."

She hadn't really been paying attention to their gossip until she heard the word sanctuary. When they mentioned "a big black bastard," she knew instantly that Marcus was in trouble. She was one of the privileged few that knew that the man running the sanctuary and the black wolf were one in the same. She quietly shuffled closer to hear more without alerting the two men.

"I heard they want someone to go in the field." Justin looked at the map of the area. "Right now they have armed guards around the clock keeping people out. Apparently there have been threats from hunters wanting to go in and slaughter the pack and animal activists want them protected. They want someone from the lab to go observe the activities and document the wolves' behavior."

"They'd have to be crazy." Glen circled the area on the map. "It's in the middle of nowhere. Who would be stupid enough to want to live out there?"

"No one I know. It's a suicide mission. I don't know why they don't just call open season on all their furry asses and get it over with." Justin held his arms up as if holding a rifle.

"It's more than likely what they will do if they don't find some poor sap that will take on the duty.

"No!"

The two men looked across the room.

"What?" Justin wasn't even aware Carrie was in the room.

"They can't kill the wolves! I'll do it. I'll go to the preserve." Carrie turned to the two men. She limped to where they stood, Sprout followed at her feet.

"Are you crazy, Carrie?" Glen gaped at her. "You're the assistant in the lab. Next in line to run it. Why would you want to go to this god forsaken place?"

Carrie took the map and looked at the circled area. "I never wanted to be stuck in a lab. My dream has always been field work." Marcus was in trouble. There was no choice; she had to go. There was no way in hell she was letting them talk her out of it. She would protect Marcus and what was left of his dream.

"But, Carrie… you're giving up on your career. You've worked hard to get to this position. You could be running things. In another year you could be giving seminars and raising funds for our research." Justin tried desperately to get her to change her mind.

Carrie pulled her shoulder length hair over the scar that ran down her left cheek. "I never wanted this. I'm not comfortable speaking in public. I would serve everyone better in the field."

"What's going on here? To what field are we talking?"

Carrie turned to see Dr. Lucas Clark standing in the doorway. His glasses, as always, were cocked on his face, white medical tape held the broken bow in place.

"Carrie has this wild idea to go into that den of killers. You've got to talk her out of it, Doc." Justin liked and respected Carrie, but damn she was just a little thing. She was like a bird with an injured wing. Someone had to talk sense into her.

* * * *

Lucas Clark recognized the determined stubborn look on his assistant's face. *Oh hell.* Not much frazzled him but just the thought of Carrie going alone into the untamed sanctuary gave him chills. "A word, Carrie." He motioned for her to follow him into his office.

Carrie smiled as she followed Dr. Clark into his inner

sanctum and closed the door. She'd shocked him; his eyes had looked like a deer when caught in headlights. That, along with his too long, shaggy black hair now standing straight up because he had run both hands through it on the short journey to the back room, showed just how distraught he was.

"Carrie, you're not seriously considering this venture? You have such promise and you know I had hopes of one day turning the research lab over to you." He had to talk her out of this outrageous plan. The wolves had over run the preserve. It was only a matter of time before some judge somewhere signed on a dotted line and sharp shooters were deployed to wipe out the pack. The animal activists could only hold off the inevitable results for so long. Marcus Cooper had run the sanctuary quite successfully but something had gone dreadfully wrong and he had now disappeared.

"Please sit down and let's talk about this."

She walked over and took a seat in the leather bound chair. The legs wobbled as she sat. It was a castoff that should have been thrown in the dumpster long ago but Doc didn't think about comfort or fashion. The room was sparse, cold and uninviting. "I am not only considering it, I've made up my mind. Justin and Glen said that unless someone goes in and manages things, the wolves will be put down. You know how passionate I am about protecting them."

He paced. Again he ran his fingers through his hair. "I'm aware of how dedicated you are; it's why I hand-picked you for this position."

"And I appreciate the opportunity you've given me." She tried not to smile but with his hair sticking up straight, his grays showed and he looked like Einstein. "But, you know my first love has always been to work in the field. I want hands on experience and to see personally the success of all of our hard work."

He took his glasses from his face and began cleaning the lenses on his untucked shirt. It was a nervous habit and he was stalling for time. "I know my dear," he continued to clean, careful not to knock the broken bow off. "But, after your accident, I did think that you had given up on that idea."

Carrie sprang to her feet. "Never! My accident should have nothing to do with working in the field. I'm perfectly capable of handling any situation I may be placed in."

Clearly he'd blundered. He held up his hand and replaced his glasses. "I didn't mean to offend you, my dear, and in no way was I insinuating that you were impaired. On the contrary, I think you would be the exact fit. You and Cooper, before he met his unfortunate demise, shared the same unending passion for the protection and well-being of the wolves."

"Thank you." Carrie held out her hand.

There was nothing to be done. She had clearly made up her mind and quite frankly no one else wanted to take on the task. He clasped her hand between both of his. "You will be missed."

"I'll miss you too." She patted his hands. "Thank you for everything." She turned and headed for the door. Excited to get started on her new adventure, she couldn't wait to get to the sanctuary. Marcus was in trouble and she needed to help him. *Where the hell was his pack?*

"Carrie?"

She turned, the tone in his voice giving her pause. "Did you need something finished up before I leave Doc?"

"No, not at all. Glen and Justin can handle things. Not as well as you, of course, but they'll earn their keep. No, I just wondered if your brother was aware of your decision."

She shook her head. "Of course not, I just now found out about the trouble down south." There was no way in hell she was telling Jimmy about her intentions. At least not until it was too late for him to do anything about it.

"You are going to tell him, correct?" He gave her his sternest look. He knew he had failed miserably however.

She giggled and opened the door. "Eventually."

Chapter 3

Carrie pulled her Dodge Ram to a stop in front of the chained gate, careful not to get too close. She was still getting use to driving the big brute but Jimmy had insisted and she'd never admit it, but after the accident, she too felt safer driving the big vehicle. She was especially thankful because she was able to haul everything she would need in the box of the truck.

"Can I help you?" A twenty-something guy called through the partially open window.

Carrie jumped. She had been staring into the enclosure, sure that she had seen eyes peering out at her.

"Yes, she pressed the button to lower the window so she could see him clearly. "I'm Carrie Randall. I'll be staying at the cabin. I believe someone notified you I would be arriving." She handed him the paper work she had printed out.

"You're kidding right?" He took the documents and gave it a quick glance. "I mean they said someone would be coming but we didn't expect a woman. Even if this is just a quick fix, without a permanent solution, we are going to destroy all the animals in the enclosure."

"I beg to differ with you. Now that I've arrived...." A sharp yipe interrupted her. "What in the world?"

"Shock him again! The big black bastard is getting too bold!" The young man laughed and ran in front of her truck...

Carrie peered through the windshield to try to see what was happening. "Oh my god. No!" She opened the door and got out slamming it behind her... "Stop It! Stop it right now!" She walked as fast as her limp would allow because standing just inside of the gate stood a big black wolf. He was quivering, surely in pain but not giving an inch as the two men continued to hit the remote that they held in their hand.

"Look at that bastard, he refuses to quit!"

"Stop it!" Carried demanded as she finally reached the two men. "You have no right to treat an animal this way!"

"Look lady, we don't need no animal activist coming in here and telling us what to do." He pointed through the fence. "That big bastard was found right down town. He has no fear of humans. They should have used a bullet instead of a tranquilizer. It would have saved us all a lot of time."

Carrie stared at the wolf. Standing so proud on the dirt trail. "How did he end up here?"

"Game wardens brought him in the night. He was still out of it, but he was mean, snapping and growling. They put the collar on him, shocked him a couple of times to keep him under control and laid him inside the gate. They called the next morning to notify Mr. Cooper about his latest rescue but didn't get an answer."

Carrie was livid. "How did you end up in charge?"

"The game warden continued to try to connect with Cooper. When they didn't receive any reply, they went in. His truck is there and the door was open to his cabin. Blood all over. Near as we can figure, this devil got in sometime during that first night and killed Cooper. The poor son of a bitch worked his whole life to protect these devils and in the end they took his life." He pulled a pistol from the holster on his waist and held it out in front of him, eyeing the monster in the road. "I ought to just put a bullet in him now and get it over with, the murdering bastard."

"I'm in charge now and you are not going to do anything to that wolf!" Carrie stood toe to toe with the man. He may tower over her by at least five inches but she was not going to let him intimidate her. Marcus's life was hanging in the balance and she would not back down.

"Nowhere in those papers does it say you're in charge. You're just some fancy paper pusher from the university sticking their nose in where it doesn't belong. It's a stalling tactic, clear and simple."

"Mr. Cooper left me in charge and I demand that you remove that contraption from that animal right this instant!"

"No way in hell is some hoity toity female coming in here and telling me what I'm going to do! You have no proof that Cooper left you in charge. The man is dead and that's that."

Carrie laughed. "I can assure you that Marcus Cooper was not killed by that wolf or any other."

"Lady, get back in your truck and we'll let you through the gate. If you and that little snack of a dog are stupid enough to go into a den of murders, you are on your own. But there is no way in hell I'm removing that collar from the beast."

"Fine, Mr. ....?"

"It's Nelson. Timothy Nelson."

"Fine, Mr. Nelson, but you are going to feel awfully foolish when I show you the proof that I'm in charge."

"Whatever you say lady." He looked at his friend and whispered. "Stupid bitch! We'll be cleaning up blood from her and her little ankle biter within a day."

Carrie heard his whispers but chose to ignore him. He wouldn't be around for long. "By the way, Mr. Nelson what time does the truck come?"

He looked confused. "What truck would that be?"

"I happen to know that Marcus had a contract with a company to deliver wildlife into the preserve. The wolves have to hunt. It's part of their nature. He would never disrupt their natural habitat."

The man looked sheepish and for the first time glanced down at his feet. "We turned the truck away and cancelled all other shipments."

"Are you crazy? What have they been eating?" She looked in the enclosure, the wolf had moved closer to the wire fence. She took a step to close the distance between them. He looked so forlorn. Slowly she held her hand out towards him.

Tim grabbed her by the arm and pulled her back. "Are you nuts? He'll rip you to shreds!"

The wolf growled and lunged forward. He yiped and jumped through the air as Michael, Tim's companion, again hit the button on the remote control for the collar.

"Stop!" Carrie yelled. "Stop hurting him!"

"He was attacking you! How can you stand there and defend him?"

"No, he was attacking you for touching me! He was fine until you dared to lay your hands on me. I suggest from now on you stay out of my business and leave the wolves to me." She poked him in the chest with her index finger. "And another thing... come tomorrow morning, you can expect the vendors to start making regular deliveries. You never did answer me, what have you been feeding the wolves? The wildlife has got to be depleted by now."

Tim backed away from the wild woman and rubbed the sore spot in the center of his chest. He pointed to the ground inside the gate. "We've been giving them dog food. Even the ones locked in pens behind the cabin. They look pitiful and won't eat, but it's not because we have been neglecting them."

Carrie shook her head and walked away. "You're an idiot! They're wild animals. They need to hunt." She continued on to her truck. "Open the damn gate and let me through." She grabbed the door handle and opened the door. "Scoot over, Sprout, we're going home."

Tim followed her to the truck. "Here" He held out his hand with the pistol in it. "You better take this just to be on the safe side."

Carrie looked at the gun and shook her head. "I don't want it or need it."

"Suit yourself, Miss Randall. But if I were you, I'd keep that little ankle biter mighty close to you or he'll be nothing but a little snack for them."

Carrie nodded and closed the door. "Thanks for your concern. Now open the gate."

Tim lifted his hand and the gate slowly opened as Michael operated the controls from inside the small hut.

Chapter 4

"Well, Sprout... here we go." She reached across and rubbed her companions head. She drove slowly through the gate and watched in her rear view mirror as it slowly closed behind her. Ahead the trees hung over the road, blocking out even the moon much like a tunnel, no light showed through. "I don't know what we're going to do, little man, but first things first. Let's get to the cabin and get a good night's sleep." The trees began to thin and she could now see the silhouette of the cabin. A yard light shone brightly on the utility pole in the front yard. She sighed in relief. "At least the idiots didn't shut the electricity off."

Marcus's black pickup still sat in the driveway. She pulled her truck up close to the steps, the driver's door close to the deck. She wouldn't admit it but she was a little uneasy arriving in the dark. It had taken her longer than she expected to get her things loaded and get on the road. Her limp slowed her down but damned if she would ask for help. She put the truck in park and shut off the engine, pulled the keys out and put them above the visor. It was eerily quiet. She reached over and grabbed her overnight bag from the floorboard on the passenger side. "Okay, little man, we're going to make it in one trip tonight. She pulled the handle on the door and cracked it open. The overhead light came on she squinted at the bright light. "Let's get moving." She put the straps of her bag over her left shoulder and scooped Sprout up in her right. She pushed the door open and slowly lowered herself to the ground. She bumped the door with her hip and shut it. "Here goes nothing." she whispered and looked anxiously around. The grounds were well lit and there was nothing in sight as she walked up the two small steps and onto the deck that extended the entire length of the small cabin. She turned the knob and was relieved that the door was not locked as she'd forgotten the key was on her truck key ring.

She reached through the door and again sighed when her hand connected with a light switch and the house lit up. It was short lived however when she saw the mess. "Wow!" She walked in and set her bag and Sprout down on the floor before quickly shutting the door and sliding the deadbolt home. Somebody or something had torn the place apart. Garbage littered the floor and red stains covered the hardwood.

"Let's get you settled, little man." She unzipped her bag and took out a puppy pad. "I'll get your potty set up tomorrow, I promise, but for tonight this will have to do." Savannah had trained

Sprout to use a litter box, making it easier for her to care for him during her recovery. Next, out came a small can of dog food. She pulled the tab to open it and sat it down on the floor. "I'll find you a dish for water." She limped across the floor, stepping carefully over the garbage. She opened cupboard doors until she found a small Tupperware dish and filled it with water. "Here you go." she said as she walked back and placed it beside the now empty food can.

The sand on the floor was gritty beneath her sneakers. She stepped carefully not wanting to misstep and injure her leg. She had no need to turn behind and look as Sprout followed close behind. "Let's explore our new home, little man." Jimmy teased her often about talking to the small dog as if he were human. But in her eyes, he was her savior, her beloved fur baby. She would have never made it these last terrifying, painful months without him. His constant love and loyalty had seen her through her darkest days.

She eased open the heavy oak door of what she now saw was the master bedroom. The cabin was absolutely beautiful; the walls, floors, ceilings and even doors were all made out of hardwood. She knew immediately that Marcus had built and hand crafted everything in the small dwelling including the massive king size bed made out of logs. She caught her breath at its sheer beauty. The comforter, covered in wildlife prints, lay smoothly over the feather tick mattress. This room lay unblemished, pristine. "Thank goodness we won't have to sleep on the floor." She was tired, her body worn and aching. "We'll clean up this mess tomorrow. Come on, boy. Let's go to bed." She bent down and picked him up and put him on the bed. She pulled back the covers and crawled in. She would leave the lights on tonight in case she needed to get up in the night. She couldn't afford to bump into something and hurt herself. Too much depended on her finding a way to save Marcus.

* * * *

He knew that scent. It was familiar to him. He shook his head. Why could he not think? His thoughts were jumbled. The constant electrical charges pulsing through his body from the collar strapped to his neck kept him on the brink of madness. Too long had he been stuck in his wolf form. The woman had acted as if she had compassion for him; just for seconds he felt the urge to go to her, to allow her to stroke his pelt. To receive comfort where he now only felt pain. The strong electric shock had sent his body into the air and he had to flee away from the men at the gate. The wolf, undeterred, had loped parallel to the big machine as it traveled down the well-worn path to his cabin. He had watched cautiously as the woman limped into his home. Why could he not remember who she was? He needed to release the collar binding him to this form; only then would his mind clear. He tipped his head and used his paws to pull. The tiny prongs only burrowed further into his already sore neck;

the collar would not budge. Defeated, he sat on his haunches and watched the cabin. There was no sign of movement but still the lights remained shining bright. Cautiously he walked across the lit lawn and put first one and then another big paw onto the deck. His sharp claws clicked with every step he took. He peered through the window and saw no sign of the woman; blood still remained on the floor from the young deer, the last in the herd that he had captured and drug into the dwelling. Food was now scarce and only added to his madness. The dried dog food the men threw over the fence was insulting and he refused to eat it. He would starve before he caved into them. He was a wolf, a hunter, but first and foremost, he was a man and he refused to eat from the ground. The rotting, mildewed kernels continued to mound as the men did not even care enough to replenish the rot with fresh. The purebreds were scavenging, eating the tainted food. His heart hurt as he watched the once noble animals gulp the moldy food as instinct for survival kicked in. Eat what was offered or die. It didn't matter; he had heard the men talking. Soon sharp shooters would arrive and destroy all within. What was the woman doing here?

He rounded the end of the house, the deck wrapped around the entire house. He kept to the shadows and peered into the bedroom window. She lay on the bed sound asleep, a small brown and black dog lay curled against her neck. It too looked familiar but he could not remember. Why was it that some things seemed so clear and others a mystery? He shook his head trying to dislodge the prongs that were shooting the small pulses of electrical currents through his body. He was now glad that he had disbanded the pack after the kidnapping of Savannah. Exiling himself, he had saved them all from this pain and humiliation. He hung his head and quietly leaped from the deck and bounded into the woods.

Chapter 5

The floors were finally cleaned of debris. She'd had to get down on her hands and knees to remove the blood stains from the floor, but finally everything was in order. Marcus kept impeccable records and she was able to find the number for the vendors, the trucks would be coming regularly starting today.

"We've got a good bit done this morning, Sprout. What's say I get the truck unloaded and we'll head into town for some groceries?" Breakfast had consisted of black coffee and frozen Eggos. It had eased her hunger, but she needed supplies.

"You stay here." She opened the door a crack and squeezed through, shutting it quickly behind her. Of course the minute she was out of his sight, he began to bark mercilessly. He was loyal and spoiled. She chuckled and shook her head. The sun shone bright in the morning light. She did a thorough look around before stepping away from the door. She was not afraid to be in the enclosure, but it did not hurt to be aware of her surroundings at all times. The truck was parked close enough that she was quickly able to unload everything and set it on the deck; from there it was easy work to move it into the house. She was very aware that the big black wolf sat in the edge of the tree line and watched her. He seemed so lonely. Marcus had chosen to live alone after the pack had been involved, without his knowledge, in the kidnapping of Savannah. But, surely he had kept in touch with at least some of them. He was not the type of person to abandon his friends. He blamed himself and it was not his fault, Jimmy of course did not want to admit that he had finally forgiven Marcus but his helping after the accident had went a long way in softening Jimmy's heart.

Well, Carrie... no time like the present. This is what you came here for. The thoughts whirled through her head as she stepped off the deck and slowly moved around the back of the truck. The wolf got to his feet and she could see the hair rise along his back.

"Easy boy." She held her hand out palm up and continued to walk slowly. "Shit." She swore as her phone began to ring and the wolf darted into the trees. "God damn all the rotten luck!" She grabbed the phone from her pants pocket. "Hello!"

"Ah, Miss Randall?"

"Who is this?"

"It's Tim Nelson from the gate. There's a truck and trailer here filled with elk. The guy said you called him."

"That's right. Open the gate and let them in." Incompetent idiots! How difficult was it to back the trailer to the gate and open the trailer doors?

"You have no right to place such orders, Miss Randall."

This guy was totally pissing her off. "I beg to differ, Mr. Nelson. I'm a representative from the University. We have a vested interest in everything that Mr. Cooper was trying to accomplish here. Don't make me waste my time coming down there just to watch you open the gate and let the damn elk run free!"

"Fine, but I'm not signing for anything! It's not going to be my ass."

"No need. Marcus has a contract with them. Have a good day, Mr. Nelson." She smiled as she hung up on the pompous ass. She was so excited, the first load had already arrived. It had been so simple to go through Marcus's files, find his contacts and those he had signed contracts with first thing this morning. Many would think it was cruel to set the herds free in the fenced enclosure, but in reality this was a preserve, a sanctuary where the animals could roam freely as nature intended. Reintroducing the various herds into their natural environment was what Marcus was trying to do. The wolves as well as the elk, buffalo, deer, rabbits, raccoon, and any other rescues she was able to get a hold of would roam freely and either thrive or perish as nature intended. This is what she went to school to do, what she dreamed of one day doing. It was finally becoming a reality; she only wished that Marcus could share in her joy. She looked toward the woods but saw no sign of him. Someday soon, she prayed, they would work together again to fulfill both their dreams. Of course she'd always had a crush on Marcus aka the bad boy but he simply tolerated her phone calls and emails about the preserve. She'd take care of his dream until he was able to once again take over and then perhaps start her own program to save those in need, maybe she would move up north closer to her family. It would hurt too much to stay near Marcus knowing he didn't feel the same about her.

* * * *

She set Sprout into the seat of the shopping cart.

"You can't bring that dog into the store."

Carrie stopped and turned to look at the short, robust woman that was raising her voice. People stopped what they were doing to turn and watch the exchange.

"Excuse me? He's wearing his service vest. He is a service animal and allowed to go into any public facility." Had these people no idea of laws or did they just not care? She scratched the top of Sprout's head to calm him; his feet were now on the handle of the shopping cart as he pushed his head against her chest. He was so sensitive to her and could tell that these people were somehow upsetting her. "It's alright, little man." she whispered.

"It's not sanitary bringing that filthy animal in here where there's food."

Carrie sighed. Smaller towns just weren't as aware of service dogs as the city. She reached into her purse and pulled out Sprout's certificate and handed it to the woman. "As you can see, I have the paperwork to prove that I am in fact allowed to have him in the store with me and furthermore, he is far from being filthy. He probably has more baths than some people you know." She knew that she was being a bit bitchy but enough was enough.

"Let me see that." A man in blue jeans and a Cabela t-shirt grabbed the certificate from the round little woman. "I know who you are. You're that tree hugger. Come down from the University all high and mighty to protect them killers out there on the refuge."

Carrie took the certificate back and carefully folded it up and replaced it back inside her purse. She counted slowly to ten. "Yes, I'm from the university. Yes, I'm staying at the refuge. No, I'm not a tree hugger. I'm simply carrying out the work that Marcus Cooper has worked for years on until he returns and I'll see that things are handled the same way that he would deal with any problems that arise."

"He won't be returning and you know it. That damned black devil killed him! Government terrorists... that's what those wolves are!"

Carrie laughed. "Government terrorists? What bumper sticker did you read that off of?" She knew that's where he came up with the slick comment… she'd seen it many times on hunter's dog boxes. Many hunters were against wolves because of the damage they could do to hunting dogs. She didn't blame the hunters for being upset.

"The wolves in the refuge can do no harm to you or your livestock. They are confined within the eighty acre enclosure."

"Not for long. I heard tell that they're going to let us go in there and blast anything on four legs."

She'd had enough. She may be small but she also had a very short fuse and this asshat had just stepped over the bounds. "You look here, asshole!" She turned and went toe to toe with the man. Her nose just inches from his. "That's private property and you so much as cross the threshold and I'll pepper your backside with buckshot! You leave me and mine alone and we won't have any problems but you just try to test me and you'll find out just what a hornets' nest you riled. Now, if you all will excuse me, I want to pick up my groceries so I don't have to come back into this lovely establishment or this town any sooner than absolutely necessary."

People stared and whispered as she made her way slowly down each aisle. Normally she would be in and out of the store lickity split as she preferred to eat fresh fruits, vegetables and even meat. But the scene that had just played out changed things. She would need to stock up because no way would she be making frequent trips into town. She'd buy supplies enough to last. Frozen veggies that could be steamed in the microwave and lots of frozen meat. She also stocked up on canned and dry dog food for Sprout.

"Let's get the hell out of here buddy. We're definitely not welcome here." Had Marcus dealt with such animosity or was it because the townspeople thought he had been killed by the wolf and they now felt threatened?

* * * *

She arrived at the gate to find everyone gone. A large Manila envelope was tucked into the wire of the fence. "Now what?" She put the truck in park and got out. Inside the envelope were two remotes, she recognized one as being the controller to the shock collar. The other was the remote for the gate. She opened the letter that was also within the envelope.

Ms.Randall,

It has been decided that now that you have taken over the running of the reserve, our services are no longer needed. We took the liberty of releasing all of the animals that were being housed in the rear kennels. Any and all that had collars, the instruments were removed. All except the big black devil. Enclosed you will find the remote; please use it for your protection.

Timothy Nelson

She was relieved that the men at the front gate were gone. She now had freedom to do what she wanted when she wanted but the thought that they released the animals that were in quarantine caused concern. She had not yet had the time to read through the files and therefore did not know what or why the animals had been confined. The whole situation had been handled poorly and now she needed to get back to the cabin and try to find some answers.

"Slide over, Sprout. We're on our own." She opened the door and stepped on the running boards to slide on to the seat. The gate opened slowly and she drove through before hitting the remote and watching as it closed snuggly behind her. The clip fit easily on the sun visor and she drove down the well-worn path. She had to blow the horn as 3 huge buffalo stood in the path. Alongside the trail about 20 more lounged beneath the trees. How exciting it was to see the majestic animals roaming free. She was happy that apparently more trucks and trailers had made deliveries while she'd been in town.

* * * *

Again Marcus's notes were meticulous. There had only been four animals in the kennels at the back of the house. A small red fox that Marcus had found caught in a trap; he had set its broken leg and was allowing it to heal. A yearling cub, probably chased off by its mom, had been hit by a car. It too was now healed. An owl had also been housed after being shot, its wing damaged. It was the last animal that caused her concern. A cougar.

In his notes he had named the cougar "Justin". Marcus noted that he had found the nuisance cat in a neighborhood heavily populated with families after, of all people, her own brother Jimmy had reported that one had been seen in that area.

Triggering a memory, she remembered that a couple of years ago, Savannah's best friend Cassandra, a cougar shifter, had been on the run from a demented man who wanted to claim her. She had hidden out at the bait shop but he had hunted her down. It had ended quite well as Cassandra's now husband Michael had come also and beat the living hell out of his brother Justin. She remembered that he had run off with his long tail between his legs and hadn't been seen since.

Since Marcus seemed to not be in the habit of naming all the animals he helped in his files, Carrie had to assume that was who he was implying. The woods Marcus had caught him in was part of Sanctuary, the private property where the Cat's all lived in peace. He must have captured him and brought him here to try to talk some sense into him. Looking at the intake date, Marcus had been captured just days later. Holy hell! Justin was going to be one pissed off kitty. Hopefully he had shifted once the collar was removed and was long gone.

* * * *

The sun was bright shining through the leaves making dancing shadows on the grass. Sprout barked and pounced trying to capture them. It was beautiful here; so utterly peaceful. Carrie spread her arms wide and tipped her head back spinning slowly in a circle as she let the warmth from the sun beat down upon her face. This is what she'd been missing. Never had she wanted to be confined in an office. Her entire life she'd run free in the country. The north woods where she grew up had sported lots wild life including bear, deer, wolves, and coyotes. She'd never been afraid of roaming the woods alone. They were all solitary animals so unless they wanted to be seen, you wouldn't see them no matter how hard you looked. For that reason alone she was not afraid now. Eighty acres was a lot of land and there was plenty of room for them all to live peacefully.

Chapter 6

Marcus licked the blood from his lips. The young deer had helped to fill his empty stomach and clear his mind. He now remembered everything as he watched Carrie spinning in the sunshine. She was beautiful; his heart beat faster. The loneliness in his heart began to lift. He eased out of the tree line and sat back on his haunches. The little dog noticed him first and stopped chasing shadows. The hair stood on his back and he started his insistent barking.

Carrie stopped twirling and opened her eyes. She knew immediately that she was no longer alone. "Sprout... quiet, stay." She squatted down, not easy with her bad leg, slowly sank to a knee and then sat on the ground. Sprout crawled into her lap but continued to watch the large wolf.

Marcus rose on all fours and slowly eased forward. He stopped and sat when the small dog began to growl.

"No, Sprout. Hush, it's alright." She continued to stroke the young dog's head until he quieted. Her heart sputtered, she was scared spit-less, hoping and praying that she wasn't making a huge mistake. A mistake that could cost her life. She was not naïve and knew well the damage a lone wolf could do to a person. He could be on her and rip her throat out before she had a chance to scream. But she knew deep within that huge beast's body lurked the tender man that took in wounded animals and healed them, kept them in a safe environment so no more harm could come to them. She was staking her life on Marcus the man to be strong enough to control the animal instincts of the beast he was trapped within.

Marcus belly crawled closer to where she sat. He could see the little dog trembling with excitement but he did not make a sound. Carrie had taught him well. He could also smell the fear in Carrie. She was being very brave and showing him how much she truly trusted him. Of course, she had been around shifters her whole life and even now had one as a sister-in-law. Still, she had to know how dangerous the wolf could be. He wouldn't hurt her for the world but had no way to assure her. He stopped again to gauge her reaction. Tilting his head as he heard her breath hitch and her gasp, he inched closer.

"Oh Marcus," Carrie whispered. Tears rolled down her cheeks, seeing the proud man belly crawling through the dirt so that he didn't scare her or her small dog broke her heart. "What have they done to you?" She brought her hand to her mouth trying to stop the sobs from escaping.

Marcus stopped. He cocked his head. She was crying. Crying for him. No one had ever cried for him. No one had ever cared enough about him to cry. No one until Carrie. She had always showed him kindness, even when everyone else looked at him with disdain. He'd always tried to keep her at arm's length because she was Jimmy's sister and, she was much too young and innocent. But Carrie was stubborn and no amount of deterring kept her away. Even when she went off to college, she'd found ways to keep in contact. She went as far as majoring in zoology and studying wolves. His one great passion was protecting the population. How could he not have strong feelings for the waif sitting before him, crying for him?

She laid her hand in her lap and waited. He was only inches away; she held her breath and didn't move as his muzzle brushed her pant leg. His golden eyes peered up at her as he eased his head on her lap and she swore she could see into his soul. He looked utterly broken. Her hand shook as she placed it on top of his head. He closed his eyes and sighed. Sprout rolled to his back and began licking at the wolf's muzzle. Carrie smiled as the pup knew who was the dominant in this duo.

"It's going to be okay." she whispered. She began rubbing her thumb soothingly across the top of his head. Gently she slid her hand down the back of his neck where she encountered the plastic from the collar. "Let's get rid of this damn contraption." Quickly and with one hand she unbuckled the strap and released it. She flung it away, never wanting to see the torture device again.

Marcus flinched as she tore the collar from his throat but was relieved that the constant pain from the small electrical pulses was now gone. He gazed upon her face. He had not seen her since the accident. Her beautiful face was now marred with a deep scar that ran from just below her eye down her beautifully chiseled cheek to her chin. He rose onto four feet and nuzzled her cheek. Delicately, he licked a path along the scar beginning at the edge and working his way slowly up to the corner of her eye.

Cassandra gasped, surprised by his actions. No one in her family mentioned her scar or her limp. They tried to act like she didn't have either. To be honest, it was probably her fault. During her recovery, Jimmy practically smothered her, carrying her everywhere and waiting on her hand and foot until she eventually snapped. Her one concession was agreeing to get a pickup truck to replace her little compact car which was totaled in the accident. Since then she had become very independent and the family had let her become so. She started to giggle as Marcus continued to nuzzle her cheek and begin a path to her neck, his warm breath tickling her ear.

Cassandra laughed shakily. "Okay, Marcus… as much as I love your wolf, now that the collar is gone, I'd really like to talk to you and find out what in the hell is going on around here. I think we may have a problem with one pissed off kitty. Apparently the powers that be took it upon themselves to, excuse the phrase, release the beasts."

Marcus stepped back. *Released the beasts. Pissed off Kitty. Justin! Oh Hell No!* He took off running.

"Marcus, Wait!" Carrie scrambled to her feet and limped after him. Sprout sprinted after the wolf wanting in on the game. "Sprout! Get back here!" Carrie went as fast as her leg would allow. She rounded the end of the cabin to see Marcus pacing back and forth in front of the empty kennels. Sprout came at her call and now sat at her feet. She walked closer and could hear growls rumbling from Marcus's chest. The wolf, or was it the man, was furious. She felt a tiny bit of fear as she watched the hair rise from his back. He arched and she could hear the bones crunching. She realized than that he was trying to shift.

Fur disappeared to reveal skin, fingers now clear where only seconds before had been paws. Only too soon were they once again fur covered. His muzzle had shortened and she could see his lips forming. He howled in pain and collapsed on his side. Panting, gasping for breath.

Carrie rushed to his prone body and sank to her knees. "What's wrong? Why can't you shift?" She placed her hand on his body checking for injuries. She ran her palms along his side and up to his neck. There was something sticky and wet beneath his neck. She pulled her hands away, they were covered in blood. Blood and puss oozed from the wounds. She could smell the infection. Had she not removed the collar, he would have eventually died from infection.

"Oh my god! What did those bastards do to you?" She lifted his head and bent closer. Pulling the fur away revealed two small holes. The bastards had had the collar so tight that the prongs had started to grow into his neck. "Those slimy bastards! Have they no feelings? And they called you a monster!" She tried to stand but he clamped his teeth tenderly around her wrist to keep her in place. She used her other hand to continue to stroke his big body. "Take your time. You'll be fine. We'll figure this out." *Please God, let this be temporary.* Surely he would be able to shift.

Marcus's body trembled from exhaustion. He'd been in wolf form for too long. He needed to shift. Justin was on the loose and who knew if he was still in the vicinity or if he had fled. Either scenario was bad. If he was still within the refuge, Carrie was in danger. If he had indeed fled, then both Michael and Cassandra were in danger. He needed to regain form and send up a warning. He'd promised Jimmy to protect Michael and Cassandra. He'd failed a friend yet again. Worse... he'd now brought Carrie into the mess. He didn't realize he was growling until he heard her whispers.

"Shh, shh, it'll be okay. Take your time and we'll get inside and get you cleaned up. You just need a little time. Surely within a couple hours you'll be able to shift." She hoped and prayed she was right. *Damn it, she needed him to tell her what was going on.*

He truthfully didn't know when or if he could shift. He'd never stayed in wolf form this long and didn't know anyone that had. Savannah had stayed often in wolf form but he didn't know if she occasionally shifted form when no one was around. He should have asked more questions. Of course, he hadn't been on good terms so couldn't have asked even if he'd thought of it. *Jeez Marcus, you're an incompetent asshat! No wonder your pack fell apart.*

Slowly Marcus rose to his feet. He waited patiently as Carrie awkwardly gained her footing before they made the slow trek back to the small cabin.

"You don't have to wait for me." She wouldn't apologize for having to walk so slowly. Under normal circumstances, she limped at a faster pace, but the uneven ground made it more difficult.

Marcus stopped and looked up at her. *Surely she knew just how beautiful she was.* He nipped her hand in retaliation of her apology and continued the slow pace.

"Ouch! I can't believe you just did that. Watch it, mister, or your fuzzy ass will be sleeping outside again tonight!" She threatened with a grin. She felt lighter at heart just having him near. She prayed that he would soon be able to walk beside her on two legs instead of four.

* * * *

"The evil bastards!" Carrie winced as she used the hot soapy water to dab at the puss and bloody mess seeping from the holes in his neck. "If I could get a hold of those little pricks, I'd wrap that collar around more than their necks!" She rinsed the rag and squeezed out the excess water. The wound looked cleaner so she applied iodine. "I'm so sorry. This probably hurts like a bitch, but I had to clean it out." There was no way to bandage it and being exposed to the air would probably aid in the healing. She rubbed her nose against his, her hands on each side of his muzzle. "I wish I could do more." Her stomach began to growl and she smiled. "I can do something about that. Let's eat." She used the couch to brace herself and rose to her feet.

Fresh steaks were on the menu. Carrie debated briefly on whether to just slap the bloody mess on a plate and set it on the floor for the big black wolf. In the end she just couldn't bring herself to do it and instead cooked it rare. She took her time cutting it into pieces while her steak was cooking. Steamed veggies finished off the meal she put some on her plate and the leftovers into the fridge. "Here you go, Marcus." She set the plate on the floor and sat down at the table with her own. Sprout had his food earlier and was curled up in his bed.

Marcus had watched while she went through the motions of making supper. Her limp was severe and he hurt for her. He remembered watching her years ago as she ran along the country roads. She had such joy in her eyes when she ran. He'd always kept to the shadows so as to not alert her... she'd been off limits to him, a child. But now things had changed. She'd grown into a beautiful woman. Yet still she was untouchable since he was trapped in his wolf's body.

He was accustomed to eating as an animal in his wolf's body yet in front of Carrie, he felt inferior in some way. He so wanted to pull out her chair and sit across from her at his humble table... a wooden table he had painstakingly carved with his own hands. His stomach growled at the smell of the cooked meat and he inched forward and savored each delicious morsel.

Carrie picked at her food. She was suddenly nervous. Not scared but bashful for being enclosed in the house with Marcus. She'd never been alone with the man. She had to smile. He wasn't technically a man at the moment, but she always thought of him that way. She remembered the first moment she'd fallen hopelessly for the bad boy. He'd come striding through the doors of the bait shop that Savannah and Jilly owned. His white t-shirt stretched tight over his muscled chest and abs. His blue jeans molded tight to his butt and thighs, and his cowboy boots had clicked with each stride he had taken across the cement floor. He'd looked aggressive, masculine with his golden eyes sparkling and his long black hair flowing.

Marcus glanced at Carrie and stopped eating, stopped breathing. *What in the hell was she thinking about?* His wolf growled as it caught the scent of arousal.

"What's wrong?" Carrie glanced from Marcus to the few bits of beef still on the plate. "I'm sorry if it's not to your liking. I'm not a mind reader but I just couldn't bring myself to slapping a bloody slab onto your plate." She smiled and continued to eat.

She had a beautiful smile. The scar on her face didn't detour it. It only showed that she was a survivor. He bent back to his plate and finished off the last bites of food. He grabbed the empty plate between his teeth and walked to the counter. Leaping up on his hind legs, he placed both front legs onto the countertop and placed his plate by the sink.

Carrie clapped her hands in appreciation. "Nice trick." She got up from her chair and carried her own plate to the garbage and raked the scraps into it before placing her plate in the sink. Passing the refrigerator, she grabbed a bottle of water and sank onto the couch, her back resting against the arm her legs spread out in front of her. "I don't know about you, big guy, but I'm exhausted." She reached down and picked Sprout up and placed him on the couch beside of her. She grabbed the remote for the DVD player. Marcus didn't have satellite but she'd brought a supply of movies. She clicked it on and soon Last of the Mohicans began to play.

He'd never been one to watch TV he usually spent his evenings running with the wolves or taking care of sick or injured animals. He'd been running for years now and it no longer held the same joy as it had before. He trotted into the living room, his belly now full he lay down on the floor his head on his paws.

"Oh for crying out loud, get off the floor! There's room enough on the couch for all three of us." She shifted her feet to make room.

He leaped onto the couch and sat slightly behind her extended legs. She didn't turn to look at him but seemed absorbed in the half naked man running through the woods while loading a powder gun. Who came up with such movies? She didn't even make it to see the "hero" rescue the damsel before she was sound asleep. He eased closer and placed his head on her hip. He was content to look at her but wanted so badly to run his hands along her body. He tried once again to shift. His bones cracked and moved beneath the fur on his body, his vision blurred but he could not hold out against the pain. *Damn it, how long am I going to be trapped within this body?*

The warmth of her body, the sound of her breathing comforted him. His eyes drooped and he didn't fight the sleep. He didn't need to be on alert... he was safe. Safe within the walls of his home. Safe with a woman he was beginning to care far too much for.

* * * *

The night called to him as it often did. He stared out at the full moon rising above the trees as he stood in the open door of the cabin. His home was set far back from any open area. His choice. He had chosen to live in isolation. The howl of the wolves beckoned him. He shed his clothing and felt the fur ripple across his back. Bones popped and he leapt from the deck and landed smoothly on four feet. He returned the call as he ran towards the woods. He heard their excited yips; they were in hunting mode and had zeroed in on the kill. It wouldn't be long before they brought down their prey. He ran faster, he didn't care to be in on the kill and the feast after but he did love the thrill of the chase. It was all he had, this family he had made with the wild animals. Loneliness ate at him in human form but when he ran with the wolves, he felt as if he belonged.

Suddenly bright lights swept the area from above. Loud, powerful rumbling drowned out the yips of the pack. He weaved to the left and the light chased after him. Whom or what was invading the refuge? He'd have someone's head on a platter as soon as he reached the cabin and his cell phone. This area was off limits to all, including helicopters. The pack ahead scattered as he heard rifle shots. What the hell were these idiots doing? He changed directions and ran toward the last known location of the shooter. He would shift just before making contact. The bastards would know there would be hell to pay, that they had been caught red handed trespassing. Bright lights suddenly blinded him. He heard the shot an instant before pain exploded in his ass. Son of a Bitch! It wasn't a bullet... the assholes had shot him with a tranquilizer. His last thoughts before the sedative overtook him was maybe he should have answered the phone calls that had been endless the last couple weeks.

She was hot. Not fully awake, she pushed at the blankets, trying to get comfortable and came up against fur. Sprout licked her chin... that explained the heat in front but why were her legs so warm? She opened her eyes and looked down her body. The big black wolf's feet and legs jerked as if running. He was dreaming. She smiled, sure that he was having a wonderful time on a hunt. When his breathing became labored, she frowned. His yelps confirmed it was a nightmare.

She was afraid to move, not wishing to wake him but wanting to comfort him, ease him slowly from whatever terror that had its hold on him while he slept unable to protect himself.

"Shhh, you're safe." She placed her hand on his back; his head lay across her stomach and his right leg across her knees. *What hell was he caught in?* "Marcus?" She continued to caress his back, the black fur soft beneath her hand. Awake now, she noticed her blouse was damp; obviously his wound was still draining. Come morning she would search for antibiotics. Meticulous Marcus was sure to have some on hand for treatment of the sick or injured. "What are we going to do?" she whispered.

* * * *

He was awake. He had been since the first moment she laid her hand on his body. He reveled in her touch. It had been too long since someone had touched him; he wanted to savor it for just a moment longer. He didn't know what they were going to do. Was he trapped forever in this form? A prisoner now in the body which he had once felt such sweet joy? Was there a hunter now outside his home, his private refuge, stalking them, just waiting for the opportunity to release vengeance on not just him but the innocent woman laying so trusting beside him? So many unanswered questions. Questions he couldn't answer even if he was able to shift and speak. He absorbed her ministrations for seconds more before raising his head and sitting up behind her legs.

Carrie let her hand fall away and sat up beside him. Sprout whined and so she placed him on the floor. He bounded off and jumped into his litter box.

Marcus watched the antics of the little dog. Unbelievable!

The little dust mop was pissing in kitty litter. He turned his head to look at Carrie.

She giggled. "What? He's not all macho like some dogs I know."

Marcus growled beside her.

"Besides, it was easier while I was recovering, I couldn't take him outside." She leaned her head against Marcus's big body. "Thank you for him." she whispered. "I don't know what I would have done without him this last year."

Marcus put his muzzle on top of her head, enjoying the snuggle even though he yearned to wrap his arms tightly around her petite body.

When Carrie sat up, Marcus leaped to the floor.

"What's wrong?"

He turned to look at her. He liked that she continued to talk to him as if he could answer. He knew that there was no danger outside, his keen sense of smell would have alerted him, but the little fur ball had reminded him that he needed to go out to answer the call of Nature as well. *I'll be damned if I'll cock my leg on the couch. And Hell to the No will I sink to using the litter pan!*

She followed him to the door, a little hurt that he chose going outside for the night rather than staying in with her; then it dawned on her and she felt her cheeks heat with embarrassment.

"Ummm, sorry, I didn't think... are you coming back

tonight? Should I wait?"

He licked her hand in answer before bounding off the steps. It bothered him that Justin was out there somewhere. He hoped that he'd slipped out of the enclosure when the vendors had delivered the herds. Maybe he had sense enough to leave the state and start fresh somewhere else. It didn't take long to take care of business and he leaped up onto the deck. Carrie was waiting in the open door, the soft light from the TV glowing behind her. She looked like an angel. He didn't feel worthy.

As if reading his mind she stepped aside. "Come home, Marcus. Let's go to bed."

He'd been about to cross the threshold when she mentioned "bed". She wasn't seriously considering sleeping together?

She laughed aloud. "Down, big boy. I draw the line at dogs."

He nipped her fingers in retaliation.

"Ouch! Watch it, Bub, or you'll definitely be in a dog house." She shut the door and sashayed to the bedroom

He'd never seen Carrie sashay before. God she was beautiful. He loped behind her enjoying the view.

Chapter 7

Red lights flashed and an alarm blared. Carrie shot straight up in bed reaching for the lamp. "What's going on?" she yelled above the noise placing her hands over her ears to drown out the noise. Sprout twirled around in circles on the bed barking insistently.

Marcus leaped from the most comfortable sleep he had had in months. He stood on his hind legs and pushed a black button that extended from the wall.

Blessed silence. "Thank you." Carrie sighed and lay back down to cover her head with the comforter as the light still shined too brightly.

Marcus moved to the bed, grasped the blanket between his teeth, and backed up.

"Hey! What are you doing?" she complained. It was full dark, not yet 4 am.

He bumped her arm with his muzzle. Turning he headed for

the door. Twice he had to return to nudge her.

"Alright already. I can take a hint. Crazy ass wolf! I hate getting woke up in the middle of the night. No coffee made... this had better be important!" she grumbled as she shoved her feet in her slippers and grabbed a sweater to put on over her Pokémon night shirt.

Marcus waited anxiously at the door, his truck keys in his mouth.

"Looks like we're taking a ride." she sneered and grabbed them as she swung the door open.

He leaped in the truck as she bent down to pick up Sprout and deposit him on the bench seat. The front gate was the obvious destination.

Apparently Marcus had a rather large doorbell. "Who would be visiting at this time of the morning?"

Marcus focused on the path ahead. He was alert to every movement outside of the vehicle. Sweet scents drifted in the open window and his instinct was to run, chase, hunt and kill the prey he knew was replenished and readily available in the land around him. He was fighting to stay in control. He knew Carrie would need him when she opened the gate. He just wasn't sure what would be deposited.

The gate swung wide as she pushed the remote on the sun visor. She quickly drove through shutting the gate behind them.

"Okay Obi-Wan, which way?" She barely had the truck in park before he leaped out the window.

"Oh, for the love of Pete!" She wished she was Dr. Doolittle and could converse with the man/wolf; it'd only been a day but man what a day of not knowing what he was thinking. "Stay put little man." She lifted Sprout from her lap, clicked on the flashlight she'd found on the dash and opened the door. She stepped carefully onto the running board and to the ground, the sun would not be rising for at least another hour and it was pitch black outside, the headlights of the truck did no good when they shined in the opposite direction from where Marcus had disappeared.

She found him to the left of the gate, scratching at a cardboard box. She knelt down beside him a little leery to open the box. "It's safe, right? Nothing's going to leap out at me?" He licked her cheek and returned to staring at the box. She took a deep breath. "Okay, here goes nothing."

The box was not sealed, just the flaps overlapping each other, she could hear rustling and mewling noises coming from inside. Quickly now that she knew it was something live, she opened the lid. "Oh, Marcus!" Inside lay five little bodies. She picked one up, its little eye squinting as the light hit it. "Wolf cubs, someone left wolf cubs. Look at them…so vulnerable, so alone yet someone trusted that you would take care of them." Tears pooled. "You're one remarkable man, you know that?"

He licked the tears away. She was the remarkable one. He had no friends, didn't share this side of his life with anyone until now. Carrie got it; she understood the struggles, the miracle of saving each and every life. He peered in the box and nudged one of the little ones, something was not right. It didn't make a sound, it didn't move. He nudged it again, still nothing. The other little bodies squirmed and cried hungrily, fighting to stay alive but one of the little warriors had lost the battle. He sat on his haunches and hung his head.

"What? Oh no! The poor little guy." She put the squirming pup by its litter mates and picked up the little unmoving body and cradled it gently in her hands. She was much tinier than the other four... obviously the runt of the litter. She'd fought valiantly, but without her mama's milk, or even with, she just was not meant to survive. Survival of the fittest.

Carrie caressed the little head, "I'm so sorry, sweetheart." she whispered placing the little body back in the box and picking it up. "Let's get them home. I assume you have formula and bottles on hand."

He felt so useless. *Why can't I shift?* He needed to help her, the refuge was his responsibility not hers. She would now be getting up every couple of hours to feed the pups. He tried again, arching his back. The muscles rippled and muscular forearms appeared, claws disappeared to be replaced by fingers. His head ached as wolf ears were replaced with long black hair. He cried out in pain and collapsed. *Damn It! I can't hold form!*

"Marcus," she whispered kneeling again beside him, the box again at her feet. She placed her arm on his side as he struggled to catch his breath. "It's too soon; it's only been a day. We'll figure this out. Don't worry about the pups, I've fed hound pups before, I know what I'm doing. We'll get through this. I'm actually excited to be involved and I promise I won't be grouchy with the midnight feedings. Well... as long as there's coffee readily available."

Marcus latched onto her wrist before she could pick up the box. There was one thing he could help her with. He got to his feet and gently plucked the dead puppy out of box. Holding it protectively in his mouth as a mother would do, he waited as Carrie made her way with the rest of the litter to the truck

She knew he was saving her the hurt of disposing of the baby and she was thankful. She turned the truck around and opened the gate. The big black wolf disappeared into the darkness.

She sat in the truck at the front of the cabin and waited for the wolf to appear. He walked slowly with his head down as if mourning. He was a man who had a bad boy reputation but in reality, he was all heart.

"Come on, Sprout." She stepped out and set him on the ground before leaning in to retrieve the box.

Marcus was sitting on the deck waiting when she turned

around. Sand clung to the hair on his paws.

"Thank you for taking care of it. I could have done it and would have, but am so glad that I didn't have to." She smiled as the whining in the box grew louder. "I think we better get these little ones fed."

He followed her into the house and went to the counter. Placing both feet on it. He lifted his snout to point to the cupboard above the stove.

Carrie carried the pups to the couch and came back to get four bottles and the can of powdered puppy formula. "Perfect." She mixed it with warm water from the faucet and tested the warmth on her wrist.

The pups were hungry and took to the nipples easily. Within minutes they were settled in a small basket. It would work for now, but once they became more active, she would have to find a kennel

* * * *

Carrie stared out the window. Marcus had left hours ago and had not returned. She knew it bothered him that he could not shift and was sure that he had gone off alone to experiment. They were both out of their element and didn't have answers but she knew someone who may be able to fill in the blanks. She picked up her phone.

"Hey Carrie, How are things in Madison?"

She didn't want to lie so answered. "I'm doing great, Savannah. How's my niece?"

"She's growing like a weed and has her daddy wrapped around her little finger. When are you coming to visit?

"Ummm... I'm awful busy right now but soon. I promise. Savannah, can I ask you something?"

"Sure, sweetie. What can I do for you?"

"Did you stay in Sable's form all the time or did you shift periodically?"

There was a moment of complete silence. She shouldn't have asked. Savannah had been terribly hurt and hid from the world within the body of the wolf until she fell in love with Jimmy. "Forget I said anything. It's not any of my business."

"No, it's alright. You know I don't keep secrets from you and I hope you know that you can tell me anything."

"I know. You're the best thing that's happened to my big brother and I love you."

"I did shift periodically for short amounts of time. I loved and missed the feel of the sun shining on my face. But I never stayed in human form for long. It was during one of my shifts that your brother happened to see me."

"Was it hard to shift after being in your wolf form for long periods of time?" She knew Savanna was not stupid but damn it, she needed answers.

"Sometimes yes, but the harder I tried the more difficult it seemed to be. I discovered that if I didn't concentrate so hard on shifting it happened more naturally. Eventually my body became adept again and things are now back to normal. Where's this coming from, hon?" Savannah was very worried and very curious.

Just then the pups started whining. It was feeding time.

"What on earth is that noise?"

"I'm feeding some orphaned pups, no big deal." Carrie rushed her reply.

"The University is allowing that?"

"Gotta go, Savannah. Give everyone kisses. Bye!" She ended the call before her sister-in-law could ask any more questions. She hoped and prayed that Savannah was right and Marcus would soon be able to shift back and forth without pain.

She took the puppies out on the deck for their feeding. Sprout followed close behind. She was still sitting on the steps enjoying the peacefulness when Marcus came out of the shadows. "Come sit with me." She patted the plank and when he settled beside her, she leaned into him. "You were gone a long time. I was getting worried. Are you okay?"

As had become habit, he placed his head on top of hers. He'd been out in the woods, trying without success to hold form. His whole body hurt.

Damn it what was wrong with me? Am I forever trapped? I have things to do, vendors to deal with. I need to be walking the fences making sure all is secure. Now pups to care for and possibly a killer on the loose. I need to be the man that she needs me to be.

Savannah reached down and laid her hand on top of his huge paw. They sat there comfortably and watched the sun set. She suddenly felt skin where once there had been fur. She held her breath afraid to look. He wasn't breathing either. Tentatively she looked down and saw his muscled forearm.

"Carrie," he whispered huskily. She looked up and for just a moment saw his handsome face. Then it was gone.

He growled in frustration. She squeezed his paw, not turning loose. "It's okay." She leaned in and kissed him. "I was going over your paperwork today and according to your contract, another shipment should be arriving tomorrow. Does that sound about right?"

She had just kissed him and she expected him to be able to concentrate on contracts? His first kiss from her and he was a Wolf. He couldn't even return it, couldn't pull her in close and hold her, or feel her body rub against his.

* * * *

They'd been sleeping together for a week. Marcus was

always careful to keep distance between them. As if afraid he would harm her during his continued nightmares.

She had an idea that those same nightmares were linked to why he couldn't shift. Even now she could tell by the tempo of his breathing that he was once again caught in the dream. She shifted closer until she felt the heat of him against her back. Carefully, so as to not wake him, she lifted his front leg and placed it around her and waited. "What demons are haunting you?" she whispered.

She barely breathed as she felt a rippling against her back and warm skin beneath her arm. *It's a start*, she thought as tears fell down her cheeks. He was in there, it was just a matter of time.

Later she woke up alone. She could hear the puppies making noise in the living room. They were growing and she no longer had to feed them as often, but by the sounds of them, it was past time for their feeding. "I'm coming, you little monsters. Common courtesy would let me have at least one cup of coffee before making demands." She would miss them when the time came for their release, but was comforted by the fact that they would be safe in the refuge.

"Good morning." she spoke to Marcus as he was jumping back through the living room window. She'd started leaving it open so he could come and go at will. It saved them both the embarrassment and he was a grown man and shouldn't have to ask to go in and out.

"I'll make some breakfast after I feed the minions over there." She quickly made the bottles. They were little gluttons and didn't like to wait their turn to eat. The basket had now been replaced with a kennel. She was so over stepping in puppy poop.

"Here you go, Sprout." She filled his dishes with food and water.

Marcus watched her intently. She was a natural, taking care of everything and everyone. He knew she wasn't a morning person, needed a cup of coffee before she felt human, yet she took care of everyone else before herself.

"How does scrambled eggs sound? She glanced at Marcus. He was watching her every move. "Marcus? Are eggs okay? I'm going to have to make a trip to town. I hate to go back to that nasty little place with those rude people, but we need groceries."

He stood on all fours and growled. He didn't like the idea of anyone being mean to her.

"I'll be fine, they were rude, not dangerous and I won't be gone long.

* * * *

She hurried through the shopping. Thankfully no one paid much attention to her and she was in and out in less than hour. She loaded her items into the truck and noticed a police car driving by slowly. She was surprised such a little burg even had a cop. The cart return was not far from her truck and she was soon on her way. Less than five miles out of town lights and sirens sounded behind her. "Oh great, now what?" She signaled and pulled over.

An officer came to her window. "Hey, you're that lady from the refuge aren't you?"

"Yes sir, is something wrong?" She hadn't been speeding. Had someone at the store accused her of shoplifting?

"I was just on my way out to your place. You've saved me a trip."

"What can I help you with?"

"I had to remove an animal from a home and wondered if you could take it in?"

Carrie shook her head. "I'm sorry for the confusion officer, but we don't take domestic animals, they wouldn't be safe. Isn't there a local shelter you could call?"

He scratched his ear. The tips were red like he was embarrassed. "Well, you see... that's the problem. It's not a domestic. Here, let me get her." He walked back to his squad car and leaned in. She watched in the mirror as he fumbled with a leash.

"What in the world?" She giggled as he came back to the truck holding a 30-pound bobcat with a pink collar and bell attached to a pink leash. "Oh my."

"My thoughts exactly ma'am. Can you help me out? You can

see she was a house cat so she can never be released into the wild."

"I'd love to but, as you can see, I have a little dog and I'm afraid she would have him for a snack."

The officer was already shaking his head. "No ma'am, she was raised with dogs. The lady had about six of the little ankle biters. Problem is she didn't have a permit to have a wild animal. I'm afraid if you don't take her, she'll have to be euthanized."

Marcus was going to kill her. "No, I'll take her. Does she have a name?"

"Yes ma'am. A name and lots of luggage. Her name is Ollie. Here ya go." He practically shoved her through the window. "I'll grab her stuff." It took three trips to transfer all of Ollie's belongings from the squad car to her truck.

"Thank you so much, ma'am. Here's her vet records and ownership papers."

She was speechless. Who knew one cat could have so much stuff? She had obviously been loved. The back of her truck was filled with contraptions. Once the policeman had gotten her okay, he'd radioed another officer who delivered a huge cat tree, food, dishes, a huge litter box and toys galore. She'd been suckered but no way could she allow such a beautiful animal be put down. Her homecoming was definitely going to be interesting.

* * * *

She was late. It shouldn't take this long to buy groceries. Half hour to town, half hour back. She'd been gone for hours. What if she was in another accident? He should have gone with her. He paced back and forth across the hard wood floors. It was too quiet without her here. Once he'd enjoyed the solitude, but now after having Carrie here, he knew he couldn't live in isolation anymore. She was like a ray of sunshine; she made this place a home. He went to the bedroom and leaped upon their bed. That's what it had become, it was no longer his bed, it was theirs. He could smell her. The sweet smell of jasmine. He inhaled her scent drawing it deep into his lungs. Last night he had dreamed he'd been holding her while they slept. It had seemed so real, then the nightmare returned and he was running for his life.

* * * *

Finally home, she was so happy to see the house, but disappointed that Marcus wasn't waiting for her. Maybe that was a good thing. She could get everything in place except of course for the giant kitty condo before he returned. "Ok guys, we're home." Her fears had been for nothing. Sprout and Ollie lay curled together on the passenger seat like they were lifelong pals.

She brought the truck to a stop and eased out placing Sprout on the ground she reached in and grabbed Ollie's pink leash. Ollie bounded to the ground. Startled Sprout began barking feverishly. Ollie hissed and yanked the leash out of her hands.

"Damn! Ollie! Sprout! Stop that! Come back!" Ollie ran through the open door, Sprout hot on her heels.

Marcus heard the vehicle and was coming out of the bedroom when all hell broke loose. 35 pounds of black and tan skidded between his legs and underbelly.

Carrie rushed as fast as she could when she heard the howl. "Oh, hell! Please don't eat my dog or my cat!" She stopped in her tracks for lying on the floor was Marcus in all his naked glory.

Ollie sat on his chest and Sprout was licking his face.

"Hi, honey. I'm home!" She giggled and threw him the afghan off the back of the chair.

Marcus raised his head from the floor in his prone position. "Care to explain?"

She eased herself down on the floor and leaned against the couch. "Do you want to get dressed first?" she smiled.

He pushed the large cat off his chest and rolled to his side. Propping his head on his hand, he adjusted the blanket over his waist. "I'm comfortable in my skin, darlin'." he winked.

"It all started with a cop…"

Chapter 8

Carrie put the steaks in the fridge. The last of the food was put away. She heard the shower shut off, Marcus had heard cop and decided he needed a shower and clothes to hear the rest of the story. Ollie and Sprout had calmed down and were now lying peacefully together on the couch.

"Hey, Marcus." She started to call out then she heard him stomp into his cowboy boots. She shook her head; the man did love his boots. She turned. "Holy cow!"

"What?"

She had to lean against the counter top to keep her balance. "I'd forgotten just how good you look in jeans." His long black hair, freshly shampooed was combed and slicked back, falling way below his shoulders. His white t-shirt was damp and clung lovingly to his body, stretching tight across his chest and shoulders. As he moved, you could see his muscles ripple. And in tight faded blue jeans and cowboy boots, the man was lethal.

"I really missed my boots. Can't wear them without the

jeans." he winked.

There was the man she remembered. He had such confidence. His boot heels clicked with each stride he took. "What did you want to ask me?" He stood gazing out the front door.

"What?" Man he had a nice butt. The denim fit the mold perfectly.

He turned grinning; the devil knew exactly what she'd been staring at. "You wanted something."

"Oh, yeah. I wondered if you'd unload Ollie's things out of the truck?"

"Ollie?" He arched his brow.

She nodded. "You met earlier, the she cat that was sitting on your chest?" she teased.

"You still haven't explained how you went for food and came home with a bobcat. You know she needs to be set free, right?"

"I'll explain while you unload."

He shook his head but went to the back of the pickup and lowered the tailgate. "Senseless to set this all up when she won't be using it." he grumbled. Wild animals were not meant to be pets and he didn't want to hurt Carrie's feelings but the sooner she came to terms with that the better. She studied zoology and should know that all animals were cute but there was a difference between a 10-pound tabby and a 30-pound bobcat.

Carrie watched from the doorway, propped against the jam as she took the weight off of her bad leg. She listened while he grumbled and thought her an idiot for wanting a pet bobcat. She wasn't stupid or naïve... someone else had taken the choice of freedom from Ollie. "She's declawed."

He stopped pulling on the cat tree. "Why would someone do that? She can't defend herself."

"That's why she's here. You'll defend her." And that was that.

Marcus nodded and unloaded the truck. A wolf with a bobcat... who would have thought?

Supper was finished and as had become ritual, they sat on the steps watching the sun set.

"Why are you here, Spr... er Carrie? I can't call you Sprout anymore."

She watched the little dog, all 5 pounds of him wrestling with the cat three times his size. "Fitting name for him, isn't it? Considering where he came from."

She moved to rise, not wishing to answer his questions yet. It was so peaceful, so comforting enjoying the night with him. She wasn't ready to leave and spend her life in a lab for she knew Doc would take her back in a heartbeat and she didn't know if she was confident enough to run a sanctuary on her own.

He grabbed her hand. "You haven't answered my question.

What are you doing here and does your family know that you left the University? You did leave right? You gave up a wonderful job to come here. Why?"

She shook her head. "It wasn't a wonderful job."

"Explain."

"I never wanted to work in the lab."

"Then darlin', why did you?"

"After the accident, no one would hire me to work in the field. My credentials were excellent but as soon as they saw me walk, all the certificates in the world didn't matter."

"That's bullshit!"

"Maybe, but I finally just settled." She sighed, pushing her hair behind her ear. "Don't get me wrong, I learned a lot at the lab and am grateful, but my dream was always, always to be hands on with the animals. I overheard talk about if someone didn't take over the running of the refuge, that snipers were coming in and killing everything, especially the big black devil that had murdered Marcus Cooper, the founder of the refuge. Without anyone to run the refuge, they were going to disband it." She turned and stared into his golden eyes. "I couldn't... wouldn't let that happen."

"It was foolish of you to come here. I could have hurt or even killed you. The wolf had almost taken complete control. I couldn't even shift."

"Well, I've got thoughts on that." she mumbled.

"Wha...?"

She held up her hand, now wasn't the time. "But you didn't... you were stronger than the wolf. I knew you would never hurt me." She placed her hand on his chest. "You have a good heart, Marcus. The proof is all around us."

"I just wanted a place to escape." he denied. She gave him way too much credit.

"You forget, I've had weeks of running this place. Weeks to read all those meticulous records you keep."

He shrugged his shoulders and looked toward the horizon.

"How'd you find me that night?" She rubbed her leg, not that it hurt, but out of a nervous habit.

Big change of topic. He turned to look at her.

She pulled her hair forward to cover the scar.

"Don't." He grasped her hand and placed it on his denim clad thigh holding it in place.

"It's ugly."

"No, it proves that you're a survivor. You should have died in that accident. I'm surprised you can even walk."

"They didn't think I would. I'll always have a limp and when I over tax it, it's much worse."

He squeezed her hand. "I was there."

"Where?" She looked at him, "The accident? I already know that. You told Jimmy how to find me; he didn't realize it was you of course until my gift arrived."

"No, I mean yes, but before that… at the University. I was never as proud as when I watched you walk across that stage and receive your diploma."

She was shocked. She thought she had been all alone that day. Savannah had gone into labor so they had missed her graduation. "I didn't see you. Why didn't you say something?"

"With all those people there I'm not surprised. I didn't want to intrude. It was your special day. A day for family. I didn't see your brother but I'm sure he was there."

She shook her head. "They couldn't make it"

He was outraged. "What could be so god damned important that he'd miss such an important day?" The selfish bastard - he'd like to put his fist through the man's face.

Carrie smiled. "The birth of his daughter."

"What?"

She nodded. "Her name is Samantha and she's absolutely beautiful."

"I'm sorry, darlin'…I didn't know." If he could reach his own ass, he'd kick it. She'd been alone on one of the most important days of her life. "I should have taken you to dinner to celebrate. Maybe if I had this never…"

She placed her finger over his lips. "It's not your fault. It was a deer. You found me. You saved my life. How?"

"It was by accident really. I followed you from the ceremony."

She arched a brow.

He looked sheepish. "I wasn't stalking you. I wanted to give you your graduation present. No one's ever invited me to something like that. I was honored that you'd included me. I figured you and your family would go somewhere to celebrate I was going to slip the box into your car and disappear."

"You didn't want to see me? Talk to me in person?" She was hurt. "Why bother to show up?"

"I've explained all that. I'm not exactly your brother's favorite person."

She gripped his hand tighter. "But you're one of mine."

He swallowed the huge lump in his throat. "Anyway I was surprised when you left town and even more surprised when you headed down Hwy 73. I knew then you must be going home to Jimmy's. It was dumb luck that I was behind you when that damn deer jumped out."

She leaned her head on his shoulder. They'd sat this way often in the past weeks except this time, instead of feeling the soft fur of the wolf's coat, she felt the bulging muscle of man. "You saved my life, you know? The doctors said I would have bled out if you hadn't helped me."

"It was the hardest thing I've ever done leaving you in that wreckage. I followed the ambulance to the hospital."

"I know." she said quietly. "Jimmy saw you outside the window."

"He told you that?" he was shocked.

"Of course not," she waited a breath. "Savannah did."

* * * *

It was late, well after midnight, the house was quiet. Mosquitoes had finally forced them to leave their spot on the porch.

"I'm calling it a day. How about you?" Carrie asked as she came out of the bathroom dressed again in her Pokémon night shirt.

"Sure, I'll grab a blanket and pillow out of the closet." Marcus pushed the big cat off his lap and rose from the couch.

"Oh, for crying out loud, Marcus! You can't sleep on the couch. We've been sleeping together for weeks." She walked into the bedroom and pulled back the animal print comforter.

"Carrie, things have changed. I've changed. Your brother would castrate me if he found us in bed together."

She crawled between the sheets. "I believe in your case the term would be neuter and, lucky for you, my big brother has no idea I'm here. Besides, I'm an adult and it's none of his business."

"You've got to let them know where you are." he argued. "I can't just go to bed with you. I'm all wrong for you."

"Get over yourself. I'm talking about sleeping, nothing else and I talked to Savannah yesterday. She knows I'm fine.

"It's still not right. As a wolf, I knew I couldn't touch you. Now, I don't."

She reached out and turned out the lights. "Come to bed, Marcus, and hold me like you did last night."

She heard his breath catch.

"That wasn't a dream?" She felt the bed dip and heard his boots hit the floor. He stood and she knew his pants were next. "It seemed so real, yet when I woke up this morning I was still in wolf form. I'm almost afraid to sleep. What if I change again?"

"I won't let you." she whispered and scooted closer. She laid her head on his chest listening to his heart stutter and then race.

He wrapped his arms around her and savored the feel. It had been so long since he'd held a woman, been this close to another human. "Earlier you said you had an idea about my shifting, what did you mean?"

"I asked Savannah."

"You what? I'm surprised they're not already pounding on the door." He reared up to jump out of bed.

She pushed gently on his chest. "I asked about her shifting and about staying in form too long. She told me that the harder she tried, the harder it became to shift."

"I've never had the problem before, it was just natural." he argued.

"Exactly, but you weren't kept in wolf form naturally. The electric pulses were keeping you there."

"So what happened to change that?"

"All it took was two little fuzz balls to knock you on your ass." she laughed. "You didn't have time to think, you automatically reacted, trying to catch yourself, unsuccessfully I might add."

"Brought down by an ankle biter and a she-cat." he chuckled. "No one, and I mean No One, can ever know… my reputation would be ruined."

"Your secret's safe with me." she patted his chest then smoothed the hair with her palm.

He stilled her actions, feeling himself begin to harden. "Do you really think it's that simple? That I needed to stop thinking about being trapped and I'd be free?"

"No, I think there's more." she said quietly. She hoped it would be easier for him to talk here in the dark, that's why she'd waited all day to bring it up.

"More like what? Did Savannah say something else?"

She shook her head. "Not intentionally, but something she said nagged at me. I think you unconsciously trapped yourself, almost like Savannah." she held on tight knowing he'd want to run.

He sighed; there was no way to leave the bed without hurting her. He wanted to pace, to reason out and think about what she had said. "Explain. Why would I choose to hide in wolf form?"

"Tell me about your nightmares."

"Jesus H Christ, Carrie! Do you see into my soul? How do you know about the dreams?"

She kissed the skin above his nipple and felt him shudder. "I've been by your side in your bed for weeks. You cry out in your sleep. Yes, you were a wolf, but pain and being terrified are the same whether man or beast. How did they get the collar on you?" she asked because she believed that was the sole reason behind his nightmares.

"I asked for it." he put his arm over his eyes.

She sat up. "What are you talking about?"

"Please, darlin'," he pleaded. "Lay back down." A sliver of moonlight shown through the curtains and he worried that she would see the tears, the fear, and the hatred on his face. And he didn't want to see the pity in her eyes.

"Tell me." she whispered and settled back against his warm body. She felt him tremble and waited patiently for him to continue. She hurt for him.

"I didn't mean that I literally asked to be collared. But I might as well have. I brought it all on myself. For weeks, maybe even a month, I'd been receiving calls. Some were pranks, threatening me and the refuge. You saw how they were in town. I figured it was just some dumb ass shooting his mouth so I quit answering. Hell, I didn't even bother turning my phone on. Apparently some red tape man somewhere got concerned when I didn't return his calls."

She interrupted. "And when they couldn't reach you they thought the worst."

He nodded. "I'd gone running. I shifted in the house so my clothes lay on the floor just inside the door. I'd fed the animals outside a road kill deer earlier in the day so my clothes were covered in blood. I'm sure that's where the story of my death came from."

"But they didn't know any of this until after they had collared you." She was confused by all the events. "Why would they suddenly send in sharp shooters?'

"I'm afraid that's my fault too. I often ran outside the gates."

"Why would you take such a risk?"

"To protect the wild packs and of course the farmers' livestock, domestic animals and even hunters. Whenever I caught wind of an altercation, I tried to run interference. It came with a price, of course, because I was often spotted. It gave me a reputation as a leader or killer."

"So they sent in snipers?"

"No, I'm sure initially they were looking for any sign of Marcus Cooper. When the lights shined on the wolf, they figured I had taken the demon in and it had killed me and that was why no one could reach me. Honest to God, I tried to get away. They had tranquilizer guns. When I came to, I was collared."

"How long?" she whispered.

"Six months. At first they use to come in every month or so, tranq me, loosen the collar and check the batteries but that stopped about six weeks ago. That's why it was growing into my neck. Guess since they planned on shooting everything in here, why bother with the collar."

"It wasn't your fault and you certainly didn't ask for it. There were no laws broken. You have certificates, permits and records galore. Just because some bureaucratic asshat got it in his head to stir up shit gives them no right to trespass. This is your home. If they really needed to talk to you, they could have rung your big ass doorbell!"

He started to laugh. He couldn't help it. She was something else. No one could ever call Carrie meek. "Bureaucratic asshat? And what about my big ass doorbell?"

"You have to agree, Marcus, your doorbell is a little overkill. It scared the bajeezus out of me!"

"It's functional and with eighty acres I needed something loud enough to be able to hear."

"Well, that'll definitely do it." she yawned. "Go to sleep, Marcus. You're safe. I'll keep you grounded.

She was asleep before he even had a chance to answer. Could she be right? Had it been his own demons keeping him trapped? He was exhausted physically and mentally. His body still ached from the change. He closed his eyes and kissed the top of her head. She'd brought him back; he prayed he stayed that way.

* * * *

The sun was shining through the curtains when she woke up. What time was it? She bolted out of bed.

"Good morning, darlin'." She skidded to a halt. Marcus stood in the bedroom doorway.

"Is that coffee?"

Marcus nodded and handed her the cup. "French vanilla with splenda just the way you like it." He took a sip of his own. God how he'd missed the taste of the black liquid.

"How did you know? She asked having already gulped half the cup.

"I might not have been able to talk, but I noticed you're ah… a little touchy in the morning before your java."

She laughed. "A little? Not true. Jimmy wouldn't even attempt to speak to me until I'd had at least two cups." She gulped the rest down. "That was good. Thanks, but I've got to feed Sprout and the puppies."

"Done and done." He pointed behind him to the rug in front of the stone fire place, all four of the wolf pups lay sleeping. Sprout was curled up on the couch.

"How'd you do that? She took a step out into the living room. "When I let them out, the little monsters are running full bore and eating everything in front of them and peeing and pooping on everything behind them."

He winced. "Not on my watch. Go and enjoy another cup. You deserve it."

She padded barefoot to the kitchen, picked up the pot and poured hot coffee, adding liquid French vanilla creamer and one packet of splenda. "Where's Ollie?"

"I don't know. We left the window open last night. She must have gone out sometime during the night."

"Stupid, stupid, stupid!" She set her cup down and headed to get dressed. It was irresponsible of her to leave the window open. "I've got to go find her."

"Carrie, she'll be fine. There's nothing out there to hurt her so enjoy your coffee. If she's not back by the time you're finished we'll go find her."

Carrie tilted her head. "Do you hear that? What is that god awful noise?" It sounded like a wailing mournful cry.

"I would hazard to guess that your kitty has returned."

Just then Ollie jumped through the open window, thumping loudly as she landed. The puppies woke up and yipped excitedly while giving chase. Ollie hissed and took off running.

"Oh my god, Marcus, she just let something loose in the house!" Carrie ran to the kitchen chair and up on to the table. "Is it a mouse? Oh my god, oh my god, kill it, kill it, kill it!"

The rodent ran up onto an unopened window ledge. Marcus laughed uncontrollably. "It's not a mouse. It's a chipmunk."

Sprout had now joined the puppies in the chase. Ollie, avoiding all the commotion, was as the top of her kitty condo seemingly unconcerned with the chaos she had caused.

"I'll get it." Marcus picked up the wooden baseball bat that stood in the corner.

"Don't hurt it!" Carrie came off the table. Where did it go?" She grabbed a large towel off the oven door.

"What are you doing? I thought you wanted me to kill it?"

She waved him away. "That's when I thought it was a mouse. Sprout, no! Marcus help me get the puppies back, I'm going to catch it."

Marcus crossed his arms over his chest. She was magnificent. Not a minute ago she was screaming bloody murder and now she was championing the underdog. "There he is." He pointed as the little guy ran up on top of a bag of kitty litter.

"Ah ha!" She swooped in with the towel. "Got him!" She wrapped the cloth around the little body. "Oh my! You are a quick little bugger." His little head peaked out of the towel. She held on a little tighter. "Can you get the door?"

Marcus shook his head still grinning as he opened the door. He'd never laughed so hard in his life.

Carrie squeezed the towel tightly as she walked down the steps trying desperately to make it to the edge of the woods to release the little guy. "Hold still, you ungrateful little bugger! I just saved your life." Quick as lightening, the rodent slipped free and in no time at all, four little fur balls who had followed her out of the house gave chase. Sprout barked excitedly behind them. She tried to hurry after them.

Marcus caught her arm. "They'll never catch him. Look." The little chipmunk had scampered up a big oak tree. The pups were sniffing around eagerly trying to find the scent. "It's good practice for them, they need to learn how to hunt. Come on, let's go have that coffee."

She leaned into him. "I'll never have an uninterrupted cup while I'm here, will I?

"I don't know, darlin'. My life was pretty quiet and boring until you. Want to stay a while?"

She stumbled. "Don't play with me, Marcus."

"I'm not; I could really use your help. I'm so far behind on paperwork, not to mention all the maintenance work. And wouldn't you like to see the pups have their freedom?"

"You know I would. Shouldn't we bring them in?"

"No, they'll be fine. We'll start letting them run loose during the day and at night put them in the kennels out back." It was past time they moved out of the house.

"I've been coddling them, haven't I? I should have known better." In her heart she knew that they were wild but she'd started becoming too attached. That's how people ended up with pets like Ollie.

"You've done great. You kept them alive and they'll soon be roaming free. That's a win, not a failure. Be proud of what you've achieved. That's why I started this place."

Chapter 9

"Want to take a ride?"

"Sure where to?" Carrie asked and tossed the towel aside that she'd been drying her hair with. The shower had felt wonderful.

"I thought I'd show you around the property and I really need to check the fencing."

"You can do all that by truck?" No way would she be able to walk for miles; her leg, unfortunately, would never hold up.

"Absolutely, I cleared a lot of brush and trees. It was a lot of work, but I have a passable road that goes around the whole perimeter. It's necessary to keep the animals safe."

"That's amazing!" He truly had thought of everything when he started the refuge.

"We'll have to stop at the front gate first. That shipment you mentioned should be arriving soon. And I hope you don't mind, but I used your phone to get mine reconnected."

"Of course not, but why the change of heart?" She grabbed a

bottle of water out of the fridge.

He shrugged his shoulders. "You reminded me with Ollie how important being reachable is to my mission. Under normal circumstances, that cop could have called me and I'd have met him. How many animals in the last several months have those men at the front gate turned away because I was unreachable?"

"That wasn't your fault." she argued.

"Don't defend me darlin', not even from myself."

She sniffed and stalked out the door to the truck. "Let's go, Sprout. The man's an idiot and doesn't know his own worth."

Marcus chuckled and followed her to the truck.

* * * *

"It's beautiful here, Marcus. You really should be proud of what you've accomplished."

Huge pines bordered the property well back from the fencing so that neither animals nor people could gain access over the fence. He had once caught a couple guys with rifles trying to sneak in and so had decided to make the necessary changes to keep the animals safe.

"I did it as much for myself as them. I wanted to be left alone to lick my wounds." He'd grown fond of Jimmy and their friendship had meant a lot but after Savannah's kidnapping, it had all gone to hell. He'd had to cut himself off; it hurt too much to live so close and not have that friendship.

"Look." He stopped the truck; a newborn fawn struggled to gain its balance on spindly legs.

"Oh, isn't it the cutest thing? I'm surprised they're having babies here. They just arrived weeks ago." Her face was practically pressed to the window in her excitement.

"You did that, Carrie. You made sure to call the vendors. They bring in rehabilitated animals. That doe was apparently already carrying when she was injured."

She shook her head. "I can't take credit. You keep such great records; I just followed your direction."

He didn't keep such records by choice. Truth be known, he hated all the paperwork. "It's required to keep this place operational."

He accelerated the truck and crept on. A tree leaned over the roadway and he made a mental note to bring the chain saw out. Its huge branches heavy with leaves could fall and block the roadway. Brush piles littered the forest floor through this section; a testament to the amount of trees he'd had to clear to make the roadway. "This looks like a good spot." He put the truck in park and got out. He waited patiently for Carrie to make it to the open tailgate. Grab hold." He instructed. He was able to do the task on his own but knew how much she would love being involved.

"What about her?" Carrie pointed to the blue dog kennel tucked close to the cab of the truck.

"We'll take her back and put her in the kennel. It will be a couple weeks before the cast can come off." Duncan had brought the small fox along with fifty rabbits to the refuge. The little red fox had been caught in a trap. A vet had set the broken leg and casted it. Now she just needed time to heal.

"It's kind of ironic, they'll all be set free here and yet months from now, some of these guys will fall prey to her." She wasn't sad over that fact, it was the way nature worked. Survival of the fittest.

"Do you want to do the honors?"

"Absolutely, do I just open the door?"

"Yep, let her rip. We'll just sit back and let them come out on their own."

She unlatched all three cages and was surprised when the cottontails didn't immediately bolt for freedom. "Why don't they run?"

"Give them time. Here." He lifted her up to sit on the tailgate of the truck. "They've been in captivity for months. They're being cautious."

"Look at their little noses twitching and those ears." The first brown rabbit took a tentative first step toward freedom. Cautiously one by one they hopped out of the cages to freedom.

"Oh Marcus, look what you made happen." Tears streamed

down her face. "You made this safe haven." The brown rabbits had now spread out, some nibbling on the tender sprigs of grass and others were hopping further away. She would be content to watch them for hours.

Marcus was not paying any attention to the rabbits. He watched the look of pure joy on Carrie's face. Gently he took his thumb to brush the tears from her cheek. He tipped her face up to meet his and before he thought better of it, bent and captured her sweet lips. Her lips were soft and warm beneath his. He kept the kiss gentle, not wishing to frighten her when what he really wanted to do was lay her down in the back of the pickup truck and spend all afternoon loving her.

Carrie returned the kiss. At last she finally knew what he tasted like. His lips were warm, his tongue gently caressed her but he went no further; all too soon he pulled away.

He leaned his forehead against hers. "Are you ready to go home?" His voice was husky. He was very close to crossing the line with this woman. Never had he met anyone that felt the same gratification and awe by the simple act of releasing an animal back into the wild. So often, too often, they were euthanized because most people just didn't want to take the time out of their busy lifestyle.

"Whenever you're ready." She touched her lips with her fingers. They still tingled from his touch. "But we didn't get all the way around the property." She waited because she couldn't leap from the tailgate.

"One thing being here, darlin', there's always tomorrow." He kissed her quickly because he couldn't stop himself and lifted her to the ground. "Besides, we have to get the pups kenneled and this little girl settled."

His phone rang on the trip back.

"We've got to stop at the gate."

"What's happened?

He grimaced. "Well, darlin', don't get excited, but part of being a refuge, I don't discriminate against animals."

"Well of course you don't." She was a little curious by his words. "It can't be that bad."

"Apparently some young tyke brought home a box of kittens…"

"But Marcus we can't have kittens here they'd never survive. This is a wild life refuge. Why didn't you tell them to take them to a local shelter?"

He smiled. "Darlin', they're not house cats."

"Explain." The man was enjoying this entirely too much.

"It's a box of kits as in baby skunks." He waited for her reaction."

"Oh, God! You've got to be kidding! We're going to have skunks?"

"Yep. Apparently the parents had the same reaction when they opened the box."

He jumped out at the gate and placed the box in her lap.

She peeked in. "They are the cutest things I've ever seen." They were black with little white stripes down their backs and those bushy little tails. "But when we release these little buggers, it's going to be seventy nine acres away."

"That's my girl." He winked. He was never releasing her. She had a home here forever as far as he was concerned.

* * * *

The kits were fed and snuggled inside the dog crate in the living room. Marcus had kenneled the wolves and was now starting the grill. "Here's the steaks." she called as she started for the door.

Mrooow!

"Oh God! Here she comes with something else." She now recognized Ollie's call when she was bringing home a gift.

Carrie set the plate of steaks on the counter and turned to look. "Eeeeek! Marcus!!!! It's a mouse! It's a mouse!" She jumped up on the kitchen chair. "No, Ollie, don't drop it! Get outside!"

Ollie tossed her head and threw the gray rodent into the air. She then lay on her side batting at it playfully.

"Sprout, no! Bad dog!" He sat obediently at Carrie's call.

"Marcus, hurry! It's alive!" She screamed from her perch on the chair. "Hurry it's getting away! Ollie, kill that damn thing….Oh yuck, it's climbing the curtain!"

Marcus stood at the entrance. Carrie was practically jumping up and down in the chair. "Darlin', it's just a mouse." he chuckled.

"Just a mouse my ass! I hate mice. Kill it!" Her whole body trembled.

"I've seen you face wolves and bear, how is it you're terrified of mice?"

"If Ollie wants to bring me a wolf or a bear, fine. No problem. But I wish to hell she would quit bringing me mice, and I really don't want her bringing me home anymore live rodents." In the last week alone she'd been forced to rescue three chipmunks that the cat had proudly brought home and released inside the house.

Marcus stepped over the cat who still lay on the floor. He shook the curtain knocking the mouse into a trash can and took it outside.

Carrie climbed down from the chair. "Ollie, you don't need to pay rent or bring me gifts. You're welcome here." She grabbed the steaks and headed out on the deck.

Chapter 10

"You should have told me." He kissed her gently and rolled off of her body. He couldn't believe what they had just done. He'd never felt that way about another woman in his life. He pulled her close.

"If I would have told you I was a virgin, you never would have touched me." she defended. No way would she regret the sweet way he had just made love to her.

"I'm no good for you, Carrie, but I'll be damned if I can stop." He lay spooned behind her. Their bodies fit perfectly. He nibbled the side of her neck.

She arched her neck to give him more access. "I don't understand why you feel that way." Their loving had come so naturally. They'd been sleeping together for months, so absolutely comfortable with one another.

"How can you even ask?" He came up on his elbow and looked over her shoulder. "You know what happened with

Savannah. You know I raped her."

"No." She rolled over and pinned him beneath her upper body.

He put his arm over his eyes. "Yes, I did." He was so ashamed of himself.

She pulled his arm away. "You were living by pack law. You believed in what you were doing. You apologized and she forgave you. Now, damn it, you have got to forgive yourself."

"How can you even stand to have me touch you?"

"You forget, Marcus, that I've known about Jilly, Savannah and even you for years. I've always known what happened. The girls never kept secrets from me. I understood even back then the hurt and confusion you were going through. I never blamed you. You were as much a victim in the whole mess as she was."

"Don't make me out to be a martyr, Carrie. I don't deserve it. I deserved her contempt. I'm glad that she finally forgave me, but I'll forever be ashamed of what I did to her." he told her, looking into her eyes.

"You can be sorry, Marcus, but you need to move on. She has; now it's your turn. You deserve to be happy." She kissed his chin and followed a path to his lips.

He treasured her caresses and opened his mouth as she settled her mouth upon his and when she moved her body over his, he savored the feel of her body welcoming him. They moved together in unison; a slow, gentle loving, his hands roaming over her bare back and holding her hips in place as they both groaned in sweet delight as they reached their peak. "Thank you, darlin'," he whispered and wrapped his arms tight around her.

"You don't have to thank me, I only speak the truth. You're a good man, Marcus Cooper." She lay in the circle of his arms with her head on his chest, slowly drifting to sleep.

Two hours later the damn doorbell rang and the lights flashed. "Sleep darlin', I'll go." he whispered and kissed her lightly before he slipped out of bed. By now Carrie had become accustomed to the noise and barely moved as he turned off the alarm and stepped into his jeans, barefoot he went to see what awaited him at the gate.

* * * *

Mreoow!

"Oh no, not again!" Carrie groaned and pulled the pillow over her head. She could only imagine what kind of gift Ollie was bringing through the window. She knew it would be easier just to shut the window but wanted the big cat to have as much freedom as possible.

"Ollie, damn it. This is getting ridiculous." Marcus scolded. The cat dropped the mouse on the floor and lay down ignoring it.

"You're just lucky Carrie's not out here or we'd be deaf from her screams." He picked the rodent up by the tail and tossed it out the window.

"Good morning." She stood in the doorway.

"Good morning, darlin'. Sorry we woke you. Coffee's hot." He walked over and washed his hands. He smiled as she stumbled across the floor heading toward the coffee pot, her hair was tousled and she'd slipped into his denim shirt before coming out of the bedroom.

She gulped half the cup of coffee before turning around. She leaned against the counter and continued to sip out of the cup.

He waited patiently until she refilled her cup and turned back around. "You really don't do mornings well, do you?"

"I actually love mornings but not until after I've had my coffee. It's so peaceful. I love to just sit and enjoy the quiet before the day starts. Speaking of which, what did Ollie bring this morning?"

"Don't worry about it, I got rid of it. Hey did you see what we got?" He inclined his head.

"Oh my." She carried her coffee cup into the living room and sat it on the coffee table. "They're so tiny." She gripped the dog kennel and sank down on the floor. "What happened to their mama?"

"She was hit by a car. A motorist found the fawns standing

by the body."

"Oh, poor little guys." Car versus deer was never a good outcome. So many animals were killed on the roads. The little guys would have been next as they wouldn't have left their mother.

"Want to feed them?"

"Oh yes." she smiled. "What about the little stinkers?

"Actually they ate pretty well out of a dish this morning." He handed her two baby bottles filled with milk.

She opened the crate and scooped one of the fawns up in her arms. It latched onto the nipple right away. She set it on its feet and laughed as its little tail wagged excitedly. "Look at him go."

"You're a natural at this." He was in awe of her. She didn't back down from anything and jumped in with both feet. What other woman would nurse baby skunks, let a bobcat bring endless supplies of live animals into the house, get woken up at any time day or night to rescue animals and never complain?

"I absolutely love doing this. I hated being stuck in the lab." She put the fawn back in the kennel and grabbed the second. "Do you need help out in the kennels?"

"Nope, all done. The pups are turned out and the fox is doing okay. She even ate a little."

"I'll start some breakfast." The little guy had finished the bottle so she put him back with his sibling.

"Don't worry about it. Drink your coffee." He held out his

hand and helped her to her feet.

"Good morning." He pulled her close and kissed her. "Where's your sidekick this morning?"

She returned the kiss. "He's not an early riser. He's definitely feeling at home here. I'll show you." She held his hand and led him to the bedroom. Sprout lay under the covers with only his tail peeking out.

"He's one spoiled pooch. I envy him."

"Why?" She asked.

"He's been curled up beside you for the last year." He knew he was wearing his heart on his sleeve but didn't give a damn.

"I named him Sprout so I would always have a piece of you with me. He was my lifeline after the accident." she whispered and leaned into him.

"Drink your coffee. We'll drive into town and pick up supplies we can grab something to eat while we're out. We have a bear cub arriving later today."

"Is it injured?" She sipped her coffee at the table.

"No, nuisance bear. It's just a yearling but keeps getting into some elderly lady's bird feeder. I'll release him a distance from the cabin. That way he won't be bothersome."

"It's that time of year when the sows are chasing the yearlings off. I always feel bad for them. The moms want to get rid of them because they want to dally around with some stud." Bears only have cubs every two years so they only keep the cubs with them for one year. During the second year when they breed, they kick their babies out because they will deliver new ones come January while in hibernation.

"Nothing as loyal as a wolf." he winked.

* * * *

"Hey, darlin', your phone is ringing." Marcus called through the bathroom door.

"Go ahead and answer it."

"It's Jimmy."

"Don't answer it!" *Shit.* "Let it go to voicemail." She rinsed the shampoo out of her hair and shut off the water.

"It's ringing again." He opened the bathroom door. "You better answer; maybe something's wrong."

She took the phone. "Hello." She placed it under her ear and held it in place with her head. She wrapped a towel around her body.

"Hey, sis. I was getting worried."

"Hey, Jimmy. Sorry I was in the shower." Her voice hitched as Marcus took the towel from around her body and began to dry her. He stood behind and gently kissed her bare shoulder.

"I thought you'd be home to visit. We miss you."

"I know, I've been so busy." She shivered as Marcus licked a path from the dip in her back up to her neck. He nibbled his way around to the side and suckled until he left a mark. She arched into him giving him complete access.

"Maybe we'll drive down and see you." Jimmy replied.

"Ah…" she moaned as Marcus's hands had now glided around to her front, one on her breast and one moving lower. He spread her legs wide with his feet against her bare feet. He inserted his finger inside, the rhythm of his sucking on her neck matching his finger.

"Now is really not a good time, Jimmy. I'll talk to you later. Love ya. Bye." She ended the call.

"You are so bad…." she moaned and turned in his arms.

He released the button on his jeans and unzipped them.

Carrie pulled down the waist band and he sprung free.

He picked her up in his arms, kissing her hungrily. Last night had been slow and sweet. Today, he couldn't control the tempo; he needed her now.

She straddled his hips. He sank deeply within her. Her warmth surrounded him; she was so wet and ready. He groaned in ecstasy, moved to the counter top and perched her bare ass on the edge where he began plunging into her fiercely.

Her nails raked his back. Never had she felt such pleasure, did not even know such feelings existed. She could feel the pressure mounting and cried out as the climax over took them.

"Oh my gosh," she panted, clutching his body close. There was no way on earth she would be able to stand.

"My feelings exactly, darlin'." He kissed her and set her on the floor before removing his jeans. "Let's get cleaned up and maybe we'll make it to town by lunch." He turned the shower back on and carried her inside.

Chapter 11

Carrie walked through the meadow picking wildflowers. The wind blew gently and she had to keep pushing her hair out of her eyes. "Stop that." She pulled her skirt away from the young fawn.

Marcus leaned back on his hands watching her, a stalk of rye grass hanging out of his mouth. The fawns followed her around like loyal dogs. It was going to be hard on her when they were released. The wolves had been gone for about a month. They still saw them and they were thriving.

"Promise me that when we release the fawns, we do it far from the house. I don't want to know if something happens to them. I'd rather not know." She slipped into his lap.

He sat up straighter, spread his legs and pulled her back against him. He laid his chin on her head. "We can do that. It'll be a while yet. They still need that bottle every once in a while."

"They're growing so fast." She watched as they bedded down nearby. They didn't let the fawn roam freely like they did the wolves for fear that Ollie would take advantage and have them for dinner.

"Do you miss the wolves?" he nuzzled her neck.

"No, I'm happy for them. It's so great that we can drive about and see them running free. That's the way they were meant to be and I'll be happy for the fawns as well, it's just that I'd rather not know if something were to happen to them. Do you understand?"

"I do." he nodded. Life was harsh and she understood that some of the animals in the refuge would not live out their lives here. The refuge was created to let them live naturally even after an injury or being orphaned would not allow them to be released out into the world. "And the kits?" he started to chuckle.

"If I ever see those little stinkers again, it'll be too soon." she laughed. "I didn't think I'd ever get that smell out." She petted Sprout where he now lay sleeping in her lap. The poor little guy had gotten too close and had been sprayed. They released the little buggers the very next day.

"Did I tell you that I saw the red fox the other day?" He loved just sitting in their meadow talking. The refuge was like their own little world. They ventured out to get supplies and to rescue animals but always came home to their happy place.

"No." she shook her head. "How was she?"

"She's dug a den. She's smart. It's not far from where we released all those rabbits. She'll do well there, the creek is close by.

She doesn't even have a limp.

"That's good news. Someday maybe we'll get a male, not that I wish for an injured animal, but it would be nice if she had another of her species here."

"No one wants to be alone, darlin'." he kissed her neck.

"I'm going to have to go home to see my family soon. I can't keep putting Jimmy off." Her brother was becoming more demanding in wanting her to visit; sooner or later he was going to show up at the apartment which she no longer lived in.

"I know, he's calling more regularly." He was afraid to let her go. They were so happy. What if when she went home, she found out that she really didn't want a life here?

"I've decided I'm going to go at the end of the month and visit for a couple of days. It'll give you some time to yourself." she joked.

"I don't need time to myself." He'd miss her like hell.

"I don't want to go, but I really do want to see Samantha and as big as a pain in the ass my brother is, I love him and Savannah." Her family had been her whole world for so long, but now her priorities had shifted. She loved this place and loved being with Marcus. She wasn't ready to share it with anyone yet.

"Are you going to tell him that you quit your job?" He played with her hair, twirling it between her fingers.

She shook her head. "Not this time. I just want to go have a nice visit without any arguments. It's been so long since I've seen them and I really don't want the drama."

"He's not going to be happy when he finds out you've been lying to him," he warned.

"I'm not lying; I'm just not going into detail about what I've been doing and with whom. I love it here and I don't want anyone or anything destroying what we're doing here." She loved her family but they had a way of sticking their nose in things that were none of their business.

"It's your choice, darlin'. I just don't want you getting hurt." If he only had a couple weeks left with her, he was going to do his damnedest to make sure that she came back to him. "I'll miss you." he whispered and rolled with her in his arms. He'd give her plenty to think about and memories to carry with her when she went north.

Chapter 12

Marcus stopped the truck where the road ended. He opened the door and walked around to help Carrie out. He grasped her waist and lifted her to the ground. Sprout lay sleeping on the seat. "Leave the window cracked, he'll be fine."

"Where are we going?"

"You haven't seen this entire place. I want to share everything with you." Marcus linked his fingers with hers.

She leaned into his body as they strolled slowly along the path to the creek.

"I'll never be able to run with you." He knew what she was referring to and it didn't matter.

"I'm tired of running, darlin' and I'm not sure I ever want to shift again. I was a lone wolf for too long and, to be completely honest, I'm afraid to shift. I won't risk it." He nuzzled her cheek.

"Are you sure? I know things would be different if you found someone more like you."

He stopped and turned to face her placing his hands on her shoulders. "You're the one I want to spend the rest of my days with. We share the same hopes and dreams. If, and that's a really big if, I get the itch to run, I'll do it alone or we'll invite that crazy family of yours down and I'll run with Savannah and Jilly. Maybe take a nip or two at your brother just for fun." he joked. Inside he was tormented. Never did he want to feel trapped as he had those awful months he'd been stuck in wolf form; the thrill of the run was not worth the risk of never returning.

She placed her head on his chest. "I don't even want to think about Jimmy right now."

"He's got to be told at some point, darlin'. You're a grown woman free to make your own choices."

"In his eyes I'll always be his baby sister."

"True enough, but he's got to come to terms with the fact that someday another man will take his spot. You don't need a protector, Carrie. You are one of the bravest people I know. You're a survivor. I lost my heart to you a long time ago."

"I love you, too"

The kiss was gentle; he stepped in as close as possible to bring his hard body up tight against hers. A hand clasped on both sides of her face. "Thank you for loving me," he whispered and lowered his head, brushing his lips tenderly across hers.

The attack came from above with no warning. Carrie was

melting into Marcus's warmth and with the next breath, was lying on the ground beneath his body and that of a large cat.

"Don't move." Marcus breathed even as a terrible pain ripped through his shoulder and back. The cat's claws shredded the skin of his back as its teeth sank deep into his shoulder. He'd missed the artery. Marcus prayed that in the cat's frenzy he would forget about the human which lay beneath the pile.

The claws dug into his side and chest. He winced in pain. "Please, darlin'… be still." he pleaded.

Blood was seeping into her jeans. She could feel the warmth. If she didn't do something soon, Marcus would bleed out. "Like hell I will!" She reached into her back pocket and pulled out the little pink canister. "Here kitty, kitty." she sneered and pressed the button. The huge cat snarled and jumped from Marcus's bloody, torn body.

The big cat hissed and cried out in pain. Carrie crawled out from beneath Marcus's prone body. "Come on, shift. I don't know how long he'll be blinded." She got clumsily to her feet.

"I can't." He got to all fours. "I've lost too much blood and the pain won't allow me to shift."

"What the hell good is the power if you can't use it when you need it?"

"Not going to happen, darlin'. I won't leave you."

"You are the most stubborn man… get your ass moving!" Oh God, his back was torn but that wasn't the worst. Blood gushed from the wound between shoulder and neck. His denim shirt was soaked in blood from the wound on his side. "Come on." She grabbed his other arm and leaned down to offer support. "We've got to get to the truck."

"Shit, alright give me a minute to catch my breath."

"Damn it, Marcus! We don't have a minute. Get your fuzzy ass up!"

Even through the pain he chuckled. "I love you, darlin'." He stumbled but made it to his feet. He hated how weak he was and had to rely on her to guide him. "What the hell was that?"

Carrie glance behind them, the cat was rolling in the grass pawing at his eyes. "Over protective brother, remember? He gave me pepper spray when I left for college. He insisted I always carry it. Its second nature now; I always have it in my pocket. I've never had to use it."

His head lolled… too much effort to hold it up. "Remind me to never piss you off."

She could hear Sprout barking insistently. "The truck is just ahead. We're almost there. Hold on, love. I've got ya." She adjusted her arm around his waist, careful to avoid the ripped flesh. She couldn't tell how badly he was injured through his torn shirt but from the amount of blood, she knew it was bad.

Sprout bounced excitedly as they at last reached the truck. "Get over buddy," she opened the door and picked up Marcus's legs to guide him in. He was so pale and barely conscious. "Don't pass out on me!" She slammed the door shut and hurried to the driver's side as fast as her leg would allow. "Where's the closest hospital?"

"No." he mumbled. "Home."

He had to be joking. "We have to get you help!"

He reached across the seat. "No hospital... too dangerous. Take me home."

She nodded. "Okay, hold on." She turned the key and shifted into reverse. The day had gone from heaven to hell in minutes. *But I'll be damned if I break down now.*

She cranked the truck off in a clearing to turn around. The tires gripped and sand flew out behind them as she stepped on the accelerator. Mentally, she planned what she would do once they reached the cabin, ticking off each item she would need.

He grasped her leg. "I'll be all right." His words were starting to slur. *Please don't let him pass out before I get him inside. There is no way in hell I'll be able to carry him.*

She sighed with relief when the cabin came in sight. She made a huge loop bringing his door up as close as possible to the deck. She put the truck in park and shut off the engine. It was eerily quiet as she opened the door glancing about to be sure it was safe.

His head and body were leaning heavily against the door as she eased it open carefully so that he wouldn't tumble out "Marcus, are you still with me? We have to get you into the house." She swung his legs slowly to the open doorway and looping his uninjured arm around her neck. "Stay, Sprout." She ordered the little dog. "I'll come back for you."

"No, grab him now. I don't want you coming back out. Not safe."

"Good, you're awake. Stay with me a bit longer." She scooped the small dog under her arm. He was well trained and would not have run off, but she was afraid of him tripping them up as they struggled across the deck. She bumped the door with her ass to close it and took the first step to safety.

They were both exhausted by the time they made it to the bed. "Just a few more minutes and you can rest. I'll get you cleaned up." She helped him lay down on the bed.

"Not yet." He grabbed her hand before she could take off. "Lock the door, but first under the bed... grab the box and pull it out."

She knelt on the floor and peered under the bed. She gripped the twine handle and pulled the box clear. The craftsmanship was beautiful; another of Marcus's works. Lovingly she caressed the top, awed by his workmanship. Another time she would admire his detailed sculpture. She lifted the lid; a gun and ammunition lay inside. Shocked, she looked at Marcus. He was no longer conscious; he'd fought off the fatigue as long as he was able. She lifted the gun and checked to see that it was indeed loaded. Gently, she shut the lid and gained her feet.

"I'll be right back." She leaned down and kissed his forehead. He was sweating, it had taken all he had to reach safety and now it was her turn to care for him. She was comfortable with the gun as she entered the living room to lock the door. Growing up in the north woods, shooting had been a way of life. She checked out the windows for any movement before pulling the curtains closed.

She grabbed the fully supplied first aid kit from under the sink and carried it to the bedroom. She made three more trips before sitting cautiously on the side of the bed satisfied that she had everything she needed. She gripped his hand and kissed his knuckles. No time to fall apart yet. She had to see how bad he was injured. She stood and started unbuttoning his denim shirt. No way could she ease it from his torn body without causing horrific pain. She grasped the scissors and cut away the blood soaked material. She gasped when she saw the damage. Ragged pieces of flesh were torn and hanging from his neck and torso. Painstakingly she began washing the blood away with warm water and antibiotic soap. The bleeding was easing, but that may be because he had lost too much.

"You may not want a hospital, but we need help." she whispered. She didn't realize she was crying until tears began to fall onto his ravaged body. She'd done all she knew to do and applied gauze and tape to the worst of the wounds.

She went to the kitchen where the reception was best and

called the one person she hoped could help. "Savannah, I need you. she said as the phone stopped ringing."

"Carrie, what's wrong?" her brother demanded.

Crap. "Why are you answering Savannah's phone?" *Of all the damned luck.* She pushed the hair back from her forehead. She was exhausted. Exhausted and scared.

"She's giving the baby a bath. What's wrong? You've been crying."

"I need he..." her voice hitched and she began to ramble. "Marcus, hurt bad... cat attacked. I need Sav..."

"Marcus?! Marcus Cooper? What the hell does he have to do with anything? Where are you? What cat? There aren't any cats in Madison."

"Damn it, Jimmy! Shut up! I don't have time for your bullshit! I need Savannah and Jilly now. I don't give a rat's ass if you come or not, but the man that I love is lying... possibly dying in the bed not fifty feet from me and I need my family!"

"Give me the phone." Savannah's gentle voice could be heard in the background. "Take your daughter and get her dressed."

"But..."

"Carrie, honey what's happened?" Savannah's soothing voice calmed her.

"Put it on speaker!" Jimmy hollered.

"I'm at the refuge with Marcus. He's been attacked by a

cougar." Her voice cracked. "It's bad, Savannah. Before he passed out, he told me no hospitals. I don't know what to do."

"We'll be there in four hours." she promised without hesitation.

"Savannah, don't bring the baby… it's not safe."

"Pffft." Savannah scoffed. "We can handle one cat."

"It's Justin." she replied, hanging up to the sound of Jimmy swearing in the background. Marcus had not said anything but she didn't need his confirmation. He kept records on all the animals in the refuge. There had only been one cougar and that devil was now trying to destroy all that she held dear.

The fever started an hour later. She sponged his body with cool cloths, replaced his bandages while keeping a vigil by his bedside. Sprout lay sleeping by Marcus's legs. She got up to pace trying to stay awake. The family should have been here by now.

"Darlin', you need to rest. Come lay with me." His voice was hoarse and he looked like death.

She went to his side, feeling his head, the heat no longer scared her but he was still too warm. "I need to keep watch."

"Just for a bit, it'll make me feel better…" he pleaded.

She gave in just for a minute until he drifted back to sleep. "I was so scared." she whispered.

"You were… are wonderful. I would have died if you hadn't fought for me."

* * * *

Jimmy stared at his baby sister as she lay curled in the arms of the man he had hated with a passion for years. "Son of a Bitch!"

"Look at it this way… bad as he looks, he could be dead in hours."

"Dylan, really!" Jilly scolded.

He hunched his shoulders then winked at his wife. "What the hell is that?" he pointed at the mound of blankets moving on the other side of Marcus.

"Christ, she's living in a zoo! It looks like a fucking cat."

Carrie yawned and sat up in bed. "It's a bobcat, to be exact." She felt Marcus's head and kissed his cheek before swinging her legs off the side of the bed. "How'd you get in? I forgot about the locked gate."

"I had a key." Savannah held up the tiny remote control. "Hey, sweetie. How are you?" She hugged Carrie and gave her a kiss on the cheek.

"We're not done discussing that." Jimmy promised his wife.

"I don't understand." Carrie didn't think Marcus had kept in contact with Savannah.

"I didn't either, it came in the mail a couple weeks ago with only a note that said "in case of emergency" and he signed his name.

After I got your call, I threw it in my purse."

"Thank you for coming." Carrie felt such relief.

"Honey, you don't need to thank us. That's what family is for. We would have been here earlier but we took the babies to Cassie and Michael's. We figured that would be the safest place for them. Now let's have a look and see what we're dealing with. Is that cat going to let us close to him?" Savannah eyed the cat warily.

"I'll put her in the other room. Come on, Ollie." she called as she tapped her leg. The cat got up and arched her back, her little pink bell ringing as she leaped from the bed and followed Carrie out of the room.

"It's infected." Jilly said looking up from the jagged wound in his side. "So is his neck. He needs to shift."

"He can't or won't." Carrie came back and sponged his forehead with a cool cloth.

"Why ever not? Shifting will rejuvenate him, when he transfers back he'll be good as new."

"He's afraid he won't be able to come back."

"That's ridiculous! Of course he'll…"

"Jill." Savannah interrupted and shook her head.

"Sweetie," Savannah took the rag from Carrie's hand. "That phone call a while back wasn't about me was it? Something happened that has you both running scared."

Carrie nodded. "You all don't understand what he's been

through. He was trapped for months, bolts of electricity connected to a shock collar running through his body." her voice shook as she struggled not to cry. "When I got here, the prongs were growing into his neck. I removed it but it was weeks before he was finally able to shift back into a man. Now he refuses to shift, not knowing if he'll come back."

"You were all alone. Why didn't you call us? We would have come." Savannah hugged her.

Carrie stared over Savannah's shoulder into the tortured eyes of her brother.

"You didn't call because of me."

She broke free from her sister-in-law's embrace and began to pace. "No... well yes, but not for the reasons you think. I know you guys love me and I love you guys so much. You are all my family." She swung her arm to include everyone in the room. "You've all always been there and you can believe if I needed you, I would have called."

"But Carrie, you couldn't have known that the big black bastard wasn't going to hurt you." Jimmy argued.

"He's the whole reason I came here, big brother. I've known who and what Marcus was for years. When I found out he needed me, I dropped everything and came here." She brushed the back of her hand along his cheek. The stubble was abrasive against her skin. "I knew he'd never hurt me and as soon as I needed help, I picked up the phone and called. I knew you would all come running."

"How did Justin get in here?" Dylan had been standing in the background taking it all in. He was married to a wolf and sometimes still didn't understand half the shit that went on.

"He's always been here, well at least since the Michael-Cassie situation."

"Shit!" Jimmy swore and began to pace. He'd been the one to ask for Marcus's help.

"Marcus was trying to talk some sense into him. He was one of the animals the gate people released after I arrived."

"I'm surprised he just attacked and didn't outright kill both of you. He's a ruthless son of a bitch." Dylan eyed Jimmy sympathetically. He knew his best friend blamed himself.

"Marcus covered me with his body. He told me to stay as still as possible. I know his plan was for me to run while he was drawing Justin's wrath, he had a death grip on Marcus's neck. I refused."

"God damn it, Carrie!" Jimmy wanted to shake the shit out of her. "You're too stubborn for your own good."

"She's a survivor." Marcus mumbled from the bed. He reached out his hand and gripped Carrie's.

His grasp was so weak. "You need to rest." she scolded.

"I still don't understand why he let you go? It's against his nature. He's a killer!"

Carrie glanced at her brother and raised her chin defiantly. "Pepper spray."

"Say what?" Jimmy choked.

"Pepper spray. You might think I'm your stupid baby sister, but I'm happy... happier than I've ever been in my life. Finally, I'm doing the work I've always longed to do and I've found someone that has the same dreams as me to share that life. I'll be damned if I was going to let anyone or anything take that from me."

Jimmy grinned. "You still carry it."

She nodded. "I may be stubborn, Jimmy, but I'm not stupid." her voice cracked. "I've had to be stubborn. I had to learn to stand on my own."

"Oh, Carrie." he whispered and took a step toward her, tears filling his eyes. "You've never been alone. Anytime, anywhere... I'd have been there."

She held up her hand to stop his advance. "I know that and I love you, but you have to understand... I *needed* to stand on my own. I needed to prove to myself that I'm strong enough to achieve the goals in the career I chose."

He nodded. "What happened next?"

"We left him rolling in the weeds and beat ass to the truck is what happened."

"She was magnificent. She practically carried me to the truck."

"Marcus, rest or better yet shift so you can get well!" she demanded.

"No darlin', I won't risk not coming back to you."

"Damn it, if you die I'll lose you anyway, you stubborn jack ass!"

He shook his head. "Not going to happen." his voice faded as he drifted into unconsciousness again.

* * * *

"You know as much of a douche as Cooper was, you have to admire how much the man has accomplished here." Dylan watched a fawn nursing on its mama, the little tail going one hundred miles per hour in sheer joy. Too soon it would be weaned as already its white spots were beginning to fade.

"I know and I also know it's my fault that he's lying in that bed fighting for his life." He took his eyes off the dirt road they were driving on. "Damn it, Dylan! Carrie could have been killed!"

"But she wasn't." They'd been driving around the property for hours with no sign of the big cat.

"Maybe the bastard took off. Shit!" He slammed on his brakes as a black bear ran across in front of the truck. The yearling, barely eighty pounds, scampered up a tree.

Dylan smiled as he watched the young bear. Living up North

they saw many, but you never get over the thrill of seeing one. "Maybe, but doubtful. He could have left before and didn't. He's staying for a reason."

Jimmy nodded. "We might as well head back. It was too much to hope we'd find the bastard on our first turn out and I don't like the girls being there alone too long."

"Our girls are pretty tough." Dylan argued. "They'd give him one hell of an ass whooping."

"Normally, I'd agree." Jimmy argued. "But he's one evil son of a bitch." He was disappointed that they hadn't had any luck but was anxious to get back and check on the girls.

"Well, will you look at that!" Dylan pointed across the clearing. They weren't too far from the house now, maybe a mile or so. "Those must be the pups Carrie was talking about." One of the lanky wolves was carrying a rabbit in its mouth. The others were eagerly trying to get it away from him.

"She really loves it here. Did you see how she lights up when she talks about this place?" He was happy that Carrie was so excited, but sad that he was losing his baby sister.

"She's found herself, she's thriving. You should be proud of her. This place is a dream come true for her." Dylan knew Jimmy had mixed feelings. Marcus definitely was not his favorite person.

"I know and regardless of what I think, the two of them seem perfect for each other. But this life can be dangerous and damn it, I want her safe!"

Chapter 13

Jimmy watched curiously as Carrie came out of the bedroom dressed in shorts and a tank top. She pulled on her knee-high mud boots.

"What are you doing?"

"Gathering supplies." she whispered as not to wake anyone. She swung the loaded duffle bag over her shoulder and headed back to the bedroom.

More alarmed than curious, Jimmy followed her. "What in the Sam hell do you think you're doing with a gun?" he was shocked.

"I have orphaned and hurt animals to feed and bandage."

"Leave them. You're not risking your life for some fur balls!"

She ignored him and bent to feel Marcus's head. His fever had raged all night. "I'll be back." she whispered.

"Carrie, be reasonable. You can't go out there. We haven't

had a chance to check every place yet. He could still be out there."

"These animals are my responsibility. Besides, now that Justin's been discovered, he's probably long gone."

Jimmy grabbed her arm. "You are not going out there! I don't care if I have to tie you to a chair."

"Damn it, Jimmy! Let go of me!"

"What's going on?" Dylan, Jilly and Savannah stood in the doorway.

"She thinks she's going out to take care of those damned animals."

She tried again to jerk free. "You're hurting me."

"Let go of her now, Randall!" Marcus growled from the bed.

"Calm down, you big bastard! You know I'd never hurt her." He released Carrie's arm. "It's not safe for her to leave the house and you know it."

"He's right darlin', I'll go with ya." He pushed the covers back and attempted to sit up.

"Jesus H Christ! Keep your fuzzy ass in the bed! You're certainly not in any shape to protect her. If she insists on going out there, I'll go with her."

"Fine." she agreed.

"Let me get dressed. Christ, I haven't even had any coffee yet!"

She snuck out while Jimmy was in the shower and the rest of

the family were tending to Marcus.

He was waiting for her in the kennels. "I thought for sure you'd bring your body guards." he sneered from behind her.

"I wouldn't risk them." Jimmy, Dylan, Savannah and Jilly all had families depending on them. No way would she leave either of the children orphans. Without Marcus, her dreams die. Jimmy would mourn her, of course, but he and his family would move on. They would survive.

"Do your worst." She leaned the gun against the chain length fence. She'd hoped to have the chance to surprise him. She would not have hesitated pulling the trigger.

He laughed. "Oh, I'm not going to kill you... not yet anyway. That would be too easy on the bastard!"

"He won't come for me, he can't. His injuries are too severe."

"Oh, he'll come. I'm not even going to make it hard on him. We'll wait right here." He gave a blood curdling scream that sounded like a woman screaming for help. It was the notorious sound of a big cat. "That should get their attention."

Carrie whipped around, shocked that the man could make such a sound. She gasped and stumbled back, her hand over her mouth; he was grotesquely disfigured.

"Yes, look what you did to me, you bitch!"

His face was blistered, his eyes watery. He brushed at them

with his fur covered arm. Half man/half cat. He shook her, his human hands digging painfully into her upper arms.

She gasped for breath. "Why did you stay? You had every chance to leave, to start over."

"Cooper tricked me! All the way here he preached, promising to help me. Offering to set me up on land in Colorado. Acres and acres where a cat could run with no detection. A fresh start, he said. He lied!" Spittle dripped from the cat-like mouth.

Carrie shook her head. "He didn't, he meant every word."

"As soon as we arrived, he tranqued me and threw me into a cage to rot. When I woke up, I was collared.

* * * *

"What the hell was that?" Jimmy came running out of the bathroom dressed only in his boxers.

"It was a cat." Savannah pulled back the curtain from the bedroom window. "He's got Carrie!"

"Where's the gun?" Jimmy rushed through the living room.

"Jimmy, open the door now and get out of the way!" she warned just before a streak of black raced through the now open door.

Rage and fear burned through him. The sound of the cat's blood curdling victory cry had alerted him and instantly he knew that Justin had captured the love of his life. He could hear them arguing as he rounded the corner of the house.

"No, he didn't collar you. He was imprisoned too."

"You lie!" He slapped her with his beefy hands. He had the strength of the beast inside him.

Carrie cried out and hit the ground from the force of his blow. She heard the howl of rage as the big black wolf leaped on Justin. They landed on top of her.

The wolf had taken over; his mate was threatened, in danger. He heard her cry out in pain. Only one thing on his mind, kill the beast that had dared to touch his love.

"Holy shit!" Dylan exclaimed as they came upon the snarling beasts. "What the fuck is it? I expected to see a big ass cougar or even Justin but he's a mixed up version of both. How does that even happen?" He looked to his wife for answers.

Jilly shook her head. "I've never seen or heard of anything like it." She felt sick to her stomach. The once handsome man was absolutely repulsive.

"We've got to stop them. They're going to kill Carrie with their claws and teeth. Where's the damned gun?" Jimmy yelled. Carrie was lying completely still under the weight of the bodies.

"There!" Dylan pointed to the gun leaning against the kennel.

Jimmy ran the short distance and raised the gun to his

shoulder.

"Jimmy, don't!" Savannah touched his shoulder. "You could hit Marcus or even Carrie." she warned.

"I mean to hit Marcus, he's gone. The wolf has taken over. You heard him. He knew he would lose himself and what if he only comes back so far. God help us if he turns like Justin, the poor bastard."

"Honey, if you shoot Marcus, she'll never forgive you."

Jimmy looked at the love of his life. "If it saves her life, I'll risk it."

Carrie could barely hear them talking above the growls of the two animal. Marcus had a death grip on Justin's neck and she knew his intention was to kill the man. "Marcus, stop." She put her hand on the side of his fur covered head. She pushed her body against Justin, trying desperately to remove his body from hers. The wolf growled and held on tight. "Marcus, I love you." She pushed her other arm between Justin's head and Marcus's so that she now held his head in her grasp. "Look at me, love. Stop. You can't do this." She caressed his face with her thumbs. "Jimmy, Dylan get ready to pull Justin clear!" She stared deeply into Marcus's golden eyes. He was in there somewhere and she had promised him that she would keep him grounded. "You can't kill him. I'm fine. Come back to me." she begged.

He recognized the voice calling to him. The rage in the wolf was strong, he wanted revenge.

"Carrie, he's gone, I won't risk you. He wouldn't want me to." Jimmy argued. He sighted down the barrel of the gun.

"Damn it, Jimmy, be ready!" she kept her voice steady knowing that she held onto Marcus by a tenuous thread. "Come back to me."

"Jimmy, do what she asks and give me the gun, if it has to be done, I'll do it." Savannah promised.

"Please, love, come back to me." Carrie begged.

The wolf released his prey and focused on the voice.

"That's it, love. Come back to me." She raised her head and placed her nose at the end of the wolf's. "I love you. Come back."

That sweet voice soothed him.

"Now, Jimmy. Pull him out now but keep an eye on him because I have a few choice words for that kitty."

Dylan and Jimmy slowly approached the pile. Dylan grabbed a leg and Jimmy an arm. The pulled Justin out.

The wolf growled.

"No, look at me. Come back to me, love. We have such plans for this beautiful place." she locked onto his eyes.

He tried to pull away from her. He had regained control, but what if he turned into the same deranged beast as Justin? He couldn't bear it.

"No, I won't let you run. I need you. Come back to me.

Come back to us." She released his head and placed her hands on her stomach.

He licked her face. His big body arched. Effortlessly and smoothly, dark tan skin and muscle replaced fur. Muscled forearms replaced legs. Where once a four legged wolf stood over the body of a prone woman, now Marcus's naked form sank into her body. "A baby?" his hoarse voice whispered. "We're having a baby?"

She nodded.

He kissed her passionately.

"Oh, good God, Cooper! Get your naked ass off of my sister. You're blinding me, man!"

"It isn't like he can get her pregnant, he's already done that." Dylan chimed in.

"They're beautiful." Jilly sniffed.

Savannah wiped tears from her eyes. "Ummm… guys? I hate to break this up, but we have to do something about Justin."

"Somebody should call Michael." Dylan advised.

"He's already here; he's at the front gate."

"I'll go let him in." Jimmy headed for the truck.

"Uh, hon?" Savannah called.

"Yeah?" he turned.

"You might want to put on some pants first."

He looked down and grinned. "Oh yeah! Shit. I'll grab something for him too." He tilted his head where the couple still lay entwined on the ground. "For the love of Christ, you two, knock it off!"

Marcus grinned against Carrie's lips and flipped Jimmy the bird. He swiftly sat up and pulled Carrie across his lap. "Darlin', don't you ever scare me like that again! I swear my heart stopped when I heard that blood curdling scream." He caressed the deep purple bruise already forming on her cheek. "I should have killed the bastard."

"I'm fine love, and you're a better man than he is."

"Are you hurt anywhere else? We could have killed you. I'm so sorry darlin'; the rage was so strong that the wolf took over."

"Shh," she kissed the corner of his mouth. "I'm fine. We both are."

He laid his big hand on her stomach. "I can't believe we're going to have a baby. You shouldn't have taken such a chance with your lives. Don't deny it, darlin'. You knew exactly what you were doing when you slipped outside alone." he scolded. The thought of what could have happened to her still had him shaken.

"I knew you would come for me. You would have died from infection if you didn't turn and you were too damn stubborn to do it to save yourself but I knew you'd do it to save me. I won't apologize for that." she defended.

"I love you, darlin'. Thank you for fighting for me… us." He kissed her again, melting into the warmth of her.

"Here ya go, Marcus." Savannah handed him a pair of blue jeans Jimmy had thrown from the porch. "Better cover up. We've got company"

He looked to where she pointed and saw Jimmy's blue Dodge pickup coming up the lane followed by another vehicle he didn't recognize. "Help Carrie up, will ya?" He put his hand around Carrie's waist to support her and grinned as Savannah turned her head away while holding out her hand.

Jimmy leaped out of his truck and enfolded Carrie in his arms. "Are you okay?" He'd never been so scared in his life as when he'd seen his baby sister under the pile of snarling beasts but damn had he been proud of how calm she'd remained. "Don't you ever do that again!" he scolded.

Marcus smiled. He and Jimmy were more alike than either wanted to admit. But his focus now was on the five men getting out of the other truck.

"Michael." Savannah greeted the tallest of them and hugged him, kissing his cheek. "What are you doing here? We were going to call you and fill you in"

Michael returned the hug. "I shouldn't have been kept in the dark." he stated. He nodded at Marcus as he walked to where his brother lay on the ground.

"Dylan." He held out his hand.

Dylan shook it. "We wanted to keep you out of it. No one

should have to take out their own family members."

Michael rolled the body over with his foot. He grimaced at what remained of his brother. He was no longer a man yet not a cat either. "We wondered where he went. It's been so peaceful at Sanctuary; everyone is thriving. Was that due to you?" He looked at Marcus.

"Yes, but never did I expect that." He pointed at the beast now beginning to regain consciousness.

"I've only heard of it once, many years ago. It's some kind of virus in the brain. It was mentioned in a journal I have at Sanctuary. Unfortunately, there isn't a cure. It causes a madness that may well explain all of Justin's horrible deeds throughout the years."

"I never intentionally kept him locked up. I hope you know that." Marcus apologized.

Michael nodded and held out his hand. "He was never your responsibility. He was mine."

He pinpointed Jimmy and Dylan. "This was your doing, wasn't it? To protect me and Cassie?"

They nodded. "How did you find out?" Dylan asked.

Michael smiled. "You should never tell secrets in front of your toddlers. I probably know more about what goes on in your homes than you want me to."

Dylan, Jimmy, Savannah and Jilly looked horrified.

"Thank you all for what you've done for my family, but now it's my turn. He'll never be a threat to anyone again. From what little information I've read, once the disease hits this stage, they don't have much time."

"I'm sorry, Michael." Savannah hugged him. Justin was a monster, but he was Michael's brother.

"Thanks, hon. It's actually a relief. I finally understand his hatred for all those years. I'd like to think that had things been different, my children would have had a loving uncle to share secrets with."

"Ugh" Jilly buried her head in Dylan's chest. "I can't believe our daughter is a little blabber mouth. We're going to have to watch what we say from now on."

"Amen." Savannah echoed.

Marcus laughed and Carrie giggled.

"It's not funny! You guys will be in the same boat a couple years from now." Savannah nodded towards Carrie's belly.

"Our baby will be a complete angel, happy and healthy." She vowed resting her hand on her flat stomach.

Marcus agreed. "And he or she would never think of disobeying."

The other two couples plus Michael laughed uproariously. The young couple were in for an eye opener when they welcomed their little one into the world.

Marcus shook his head. "Come on, darlin'." He wrapped his arm around her waist. "Let's check on the kennels and then I think we have some phone calls to make. I've been without a family long enough; yours is dysfunctional to say the least. Our life will never be boring."

They were married a week later, in the open space in front of their home.

The End!

www.ingramcontent.com/pod-product-compliance
Lightning Source LLC
Chambersburg PA
CBHW020630020726
47494CB00001B/130